Advance Comments on

SHADOW
OF A TIGER

"*Shadow of a Tiger* seems to me to get back to the main line of development of English novels.... Its great virtue is simple credibility.... The historian of the future can turn to *Shadow of a Tiger* with entire confidence in it as a transcript of the kind of lower middle-class American life that seldom gets honestly reported. I think the report is something of an achievement."
—HOWARD MUMFORD JONES

"This sensitive chronicle of Midwestern American life at the beginning of the twentieth century evokes a vivid picture of an important phase of our culture and has striking implications for all those who wish to understand American character."
—OSCAR HANDLIN

"I have read *Shadow of a Tiger* with great pleasure, though I seldom read contemporary novels with pleasure.... His ear, his eye, his nose are wonderful, in his dealing with that lost time.... A delightful experience."
—MORRIS BISHOP

"Mr. Davis has written a novel which I have read with unflagging interest. As always, when well handled, the story of a boy and his developing identity as he becomes a man presents the universal human career. And, as an American, I enjoy reading of how it happened, fictionally interpreted, with an individual of my own country and generation."
—GEORGE R. STEWART

Jacket design by Carl Smith

THE JOHN DAY COMPANY
New York

SHADOW OF A TIGER

Books by Clyde Brion Davis

SHADOW OF A TIGER

THE BIG PINK KITE

UNHOLY UPROAR

THE NEWCOMER

THUDBURY: A Modern Comedy

PLAYTIME IS OVER

TEMPER THE WIND

JEREMY BELL

THE STARS INCLINE

THE REBELLION OF LEO McGUIRE

SULLIVAN

FOLLOW THE LEADER

NEBRASKA COAST

"THE GREAT AMERICAN NOVEL—"

THE ANOINTED

SOMETHING FOR NOTHING

THE AGE OF INDISCRETION

THE ARKANSAS

NORTHEND WILDCATS

NORTH WOODS WHAMMY

THE EYES OF BOYHOOD (Editor)

Clyde Brion Davis

SHADOW
OF A TIGER

The John Day Company
New York

PS
3507
.A7137
S52
1963

© 1963 BY DAVID B. DAVIS

All rights reserved. This book, or parts thereof, must not be reproduced in any form without permission. Published by The John Day Company, 62 West 45th Street, New York 36, N.Y., and simultaneously in Canada by Longmans Canada Limited, Toronto.

Library of Congress Catalogue Card Number: 63-15907

MANUFACTURED IN THE UNITED STATES OF AMERICA

Gift of Gerald a. Elliott

SHADOW OF A TIGER

Chapter 1

I FIRST discovered solipsism on a winter night just before Christmas, and it nearly scared me to death. Before that I had been a reasonably happy small boy, taking the world, school, my family and my relation to it all pretty much for granted. Then reality crashed. I remember every detail of that awful night because it had such a profound influence on the rest of my childhood and adolescence and left deep psychological scars.

Oh, I had known fear before. Because of one Paul Gustave Doré, I was dreadfully afraid of hell and of the end of the world. His horribly graphic drawings illustrated our huge, tooled-leather copy of Dante's *Inferno* and also the blue and silver-backed book called *Bible Readings*, both sold to my father by a door-to-door agent, as a necessary accessory to every Christian household. I was afraid of ghosts. I had been in a panic of terror the time old Dolly, noting the absence of my father's firm hands on the reins, took fright at a small boy trying to fly a kite in the street and ran away with my mother and me, wrecking the buggy against a tree, fracturing my mother's left arm and giving me a scalp wound and minor concussion. I was afraid of the rowdy boys from across the tracks, frowzy-headed, ragged boys who chewed tobacco and took the name of our Lord in vain.

But these were ordinary fears, and nothing at all to the horror of realization that night.

I believe I was about nine years old. Even though I was a credulous youngster and had been fed a diet of unquestioning faith by my mother and big sister Laura, I couldn't have been older. After all, I know I was stretching my faith to the utmost and still *trying* to believe in Santa Claus in spite of all contrary evidence.

Downstairs our Christmas tree was up and decorated already, its tinsel and ornaments reflecting the blue glow from the ornate baseburner across the room, and I, snuggled down in my featherbed in my cold room, was too happy and excited over the approach of Christmas to sleep. The arc light on the corner swung in the wind and threw a fascinating dance of shadows on the wall from the swaying bare branches of elms and box elders.

My heart was filled with love for the wonderful drama of life, for my family, for the snug haven of my own room with its old black-walnut bed and marble-topped bureau and commode and chair with haircloth upholstery and one of my two framed pictures. The picture across the room I had reframed myself, taking out a colored print of a blooming apple tree and cottage and country lane with a poem about someone building a house beside the road, and replacing it with a Frederic Remington print from *Collier's Weekly* of a proud Indian scout on a sorrel cayuse leading a rugged group of white men and Indians across a snowy landscape. Laura was disgusted with this substitution, but she was a big girl and incapable of understanding some of the finer, more vigorous things of life.

The picture above my bed was much larger. It was a lithograph in several colors and gold—the Lord's Prayer in illuminated Old English type, surrounded by the Protestant Ten Commandments, interestingly but sometimes confusingly illustrated.

For example, the Seventh Commandment lately had caused me embarrassment, and I still didn't understand the thing. The illustration showed a black-bearded man in a long nightshirt standing above a prostrate lady who held up her hands

[8]

pleading for mercy. The man obviously was in a rage and held his right hand up ready to sock the lady again if she dared get to her feet. Well, I had been told emphatically that it was very wrong, brutal, vulgar and ungentlemanly for a man to strike a lady or, for that matter, for a boy to strike a girl. Therefore, to my mind, the Seventh Commandment translated into everyday English, meant Thou Shalt Not Slug a Female.

In the neighborhood there was an agile, energetic, red-haired hellion of my size named Maisie McConnell whose first object in life was to make a nuisance of herself. She called me Georgie-Porgie, and for that and numerous other reasons I did not like her. When other children were around she usually ignored me, but if I was alone she'd make a great show of friendliness and when I relaxed enough under her blandishments to be off my guard she'd grab my cap and run. If I cornered her, she'd try to throw the cap into a tree or to the roof of an outhouse. Things like that. Often I was sorely tempted to punish her, but always there was the Commandment given to Moses on Mount Sinai, "Thou Shalt Not Slug a Female."

One golden Indian-summer afternoon I was at the workbench in our barn, trying to string white thread for the rigging of a ship model I had made. It probably was a misshapen thing, but to me it was beautiful and very real, and my clumsy young fingers were struggling to get the rigging just right when a shadow fell across the doorway. There was red-headed Maisie McConnell, and I tried to ignore her.

"What you making that fool boat for?" she asked.

"What fur?" I said. "Cat fur to make kitten britches of."

With that she reached out a quick hand and swept the ship model from the bench. It crashed against the wall and fell to the rough floor in a welter of broken masts and white thread. The illusion was destroyed. No longer was my model a beautiful, real ship with a significance and living personality, but an absurd, pitiful thing made by an unskillful kid.

Maisie's ruining my work was bad enough, but her revealing the truth about that work was too much. In a fury, I lashed out with my fist and struck her on her button nose.

Her mouth opened, but no sound came forth. Her green eyes stared at me, and as blood trickled down her upper lip one hand came up and swabbed her nose. It was only after she saw the red smear on her hand that she let out a screech like

[9]

a switch engine, turned and left the barn in a stumbling run on her long, black-stockinged legs, whooping at the top of her voice all the way home.

I picked up my ruined ship and thumped it down on the bench, now overwhelmed by the awful act I had committed. Once a boy had fractured God's Decalogue, it would be difficult to keep from going from sin to sin—stealing, bearing false witness against his neighbor, making graven images and at last dying in the awful electric chair for murder. I decided to go into the house for contemplation and prayer. Also, there was a possibility that Maisie's big brother Patrick might come over to exact reprisals.

My mother was in the kitchen ironing my blue polka-dot shirtwaist. She turned and looked at me.

"Georgie," she said, "what was all that screeching about?"

"Please don't call me Georgie," I said. "My name's George."

"All right, George. Do you know what the screaming was about?"

I stood looking at the linoleum floor, steeped in remorse, and perhaps pale.

"Well?"

I took a deep breath, glanced at her serious face, and turned my eyes back to the floor. "Mama—" I had to clear my throat. "I just don't like to say."

She thumped her flatiron back on the range. "Tell me this instant."

"Well, Mama," I said faintly, "I just committed adultery on Maisie McConnell."

"W-h-a-t?"

I nodded my head miserably.

She took me by the arm. "George," she said severely, "come with me into the living room and tell me what you're talking about." She led me to the leather couch, and we sat down together with the sunlit autumn leaves outside casting a shifting pattern of gold on the green carpet at our feet.

"Now," she said evenly, "where did this happen?"

"In the barn."

She had turned on the couch and was looking at me steadily with an expression in her eyes I never had seen before, an expression I did not like.

"George—do you know what you're talking about?"

"Yes. It's the Seventh Commandment. I'm sorry, but I couldn't help it. Mama, I was in the barn minding my own business, working on my ship, and Maisie came in bothering and asking silly questions, and when I wouldn't pay any attention to her, all of a sudden she knocked my ship off the bench and broke it all to smithereens and it made me so mad I hit her on the nose before I thought."

My mother shook her head. "And then what?"

"Well, she just ran home bawling with a bloody nose."

"Is that all?"

"Why, sure."

My mother made a curious sound, almost a gurgle. Then she recovered and asked, "Well, honey, why did you say you committed adultery?"

I looked at her and she was gazing strangely at the ceiling as if in prayer.

"Well," I said, "the Seventh Commandment shows a man that's knocked a woman down and it says 'Thou shalt not commit adultery.' "

My mother began to laugh. She put her arm around me and she laughed and laughed with tears running down her cheeks. I was glad she wasn't horrified at my sin, but still I didn't like to be laughed at that way.

Finally I said, "Well, I don't see what's so darn funny, but do you mean it was all right for me to sock Maisie McConnell on the nose?"

She drew a handkerchief from her apron pocket and wiped her eyes, swallowed and choked, and at last said, "No, honey, it wasn't at all nice . . . for you . . . to hit Maisie on the nose, even though you had some provocation if she deliberately broke your ship. But, oh dear . . . hitting a girl is not *adultery*."

By this time I was growing indignant. Again she wiped her eyes and stretched her feet out in front of her. "Oh dear . . . Hitting a girl is, well, just hitting a girl. Girls and women usually are not as big and strong as boys and men, and civilized men just don't strike women. Adultery is—well, if a married man left his family and ran away with another woman, that would be adultery."

"But the man in the Seventh Commandment wasn't running away with the lady. He had just socked her and knocked her down and was ready to sock her again."

My mother shook her head. "I don't believe that's a very good picture," she said, "but don't worry about it any more. You didn't commit adultery. Perhaps I should make you go over to McConnells and apologize to Maisie for striking her, but . . ."

Just then I caught sight of tight-lipped, blond Mrs. McConnell stomping determinedly up our brick front walk and I retreated upstairs to my room. The Seventh Commandment was exactly as I remembered it, as were all the other Commandments, including the one of the bearded man sitting on a rock, looking longingly across a fence at a green field which contained a cow, mule, a man and two women.

My mother and Mrs. McConnell moved into the living room where I could not understand anything that was said. Presently, however, Mrs. McConnell began to scream with laughter and she finally departed, still chortling, obviously mollified about her darling pest of a daughter getting punched on the nose.

But it wasn't over yet. That night after I had gone to bed I heard my father guffawing and took it for granted it was at my expense and was disgruntled that my mother couldn't keep our little joke (whatever it was) to herself.

The next day I consulted the dictionary and didn't get very much satisfaction from it either. Judging from words before and after, adultery was a sin committed only by adults, and apparently the joke consisted of my not being an adult yet. Some joke. If I had had my way I'd have taken the big picture off my wall, Lord's Prayer and all, and carried it to the attic.

So as I lay snug and happy in my featherbed with Christmas Eve only about forty-eight hours away, there was only one unloved thing among my surroundings, and actually only a small segment of that. I could ignore that unfriendly canker on the wall above my bed, but it still was there, working its malign spell.

How could a fat old man like Santa Claus get down a narrow chimney with a bag of toys and then back up again? I had put that question to my sister and she answered it with another question— How could a big peach tree grow from a little peach pit? There were many, many things in the world that one could never understand, but had to take on faith.

Well, what about people like the Monroes? They had no fireplace at all. Was I to understand that Santa Claus came down their stovepipe and landed in the fire of their hard-coal stove? Laura, who was a sentimentalist about the joys and illusions of childhood all her life, wouldn't go that far. Probably the Monroes had an understanding with Santa Claus and left their front door unlocked for him.

Of course I had heard other children assert that nobody but babies believed in Santa Claus, that mothers and fathers really bought the Christmas presents and just made up the story about Santa Claus. But why would parents do a thing like that? I could understand lying for an advantage or to avoid punishment but not to escape gratitude for giving presents. However, the Easter-rabbit myth had been exploded years ago, because it obviously was impossible for a rabbit either to lay or to carry all the colored eggs for one household, let alone a neighborhood, and both my mother and sister had encouraged my belief in that nonsense as long as possible.

So if they perpetrated the Easter-rabbit fraud, why should I have unreasoning faith in other things?

From off in the quiet, cold night came the squeak of a faraway pump as some householder drew a bucket of water for the morning, and a nervous dog barked his protest.

If you didn't believe in Santa Claus, Santa Claus wouldn't come and you'd get no Christmas presents. If you didn't believe that Jesus was the Son of God and died on the Cross to save the souls of believers and was resurrected on Easter, you wouldn't go to heaven when you died.

But the Levine children, whose father owned the Bon Marché department store (that meant good bargains), didn't believe in either Santa Claus or Jesus and they got more Christmas presents and more elaborate presents than anyone. Laura explained that by saying Mr. and Mrs. Levine felt sorry for their children because Santa Claus would not visit their house, and gave them bicycles, tricycles, Little Giant steam engines, immense dolls and doll buggies which they could buy at wholesale themselves.

All right, but what about the sallow, ragged, towheaded swamp children from across the tracks? Did Santa Claus fail to visit them because they didn't believe in him, or were they disbelievers because they received little or nothing on Christmas except perhaps a beating from a father who felt bad after getting drunk on Christmas Eve?

The whole idea of Santa Claus didn't seem reasonable when you stopped to analyze the physical difficulties of the situation, but then it didn't seem reasonable for adults to perpetrate such a complicated, nonprofit fraud on children. Perhaps Santa Claus and his reindeer might be constructed of a vaporous, intangible material, like a ghost. But then how could a vaporous Santa Claus tote such solid, tangible articles as the Flexible Flyer sled and the King air rifle I had requisitioned?

Of course I must not forget the possibility of magic, such as King Arthur's Excalibur or the genies in the *Arabian Nights* or the big peach tree being in the little peach pit or the bigger oak tree being in the littler acorn. Yet when adults, who were supposed to know everything, acted the way they did about the Easter rabbit and the Seventh Commandment, how could anyone tell what was real and what wasn't?

That required some meditation, so I meditated. And as I lay there in my featherbed staring wide-eyed at the dance of the intertwined shadows on the wall, considering the possible reality of Santa Claus, a devastating, suffocating thought enveloped me: *There was no reality to anything!*

My supposedly solid, familiar, tangible room was not real. My family was not real. There was no reality to the arc light swinging outside in the wind. The town, the people, the United States, the world, the Milky Way emblazoned across the winter sky existed only as they funneled down to my own small consciousness. And who was I to hold this awful burden? I was a little boy called George Chalmers, quivering with horror, alone and lost in the interstellar void, overwhelmed by what seemed to be sudden truth, and unwilling and afraid to accept the evaporation of the universe. The world was swaying sickeningly, and I clutched desperately at the crazy quilt at my chin, trying vainly to bring a little sanity back to this awful, whirling chaos. I prayed to God. I prayed to Jesus, whimpering for release from the realization I could not endure.

Of course I did not know it, but I had discovered solipsism, or something perhaps more properly called Philosophical

Idealism. All I knew was that I had been seized by the Horror of Horrors. How long I lay there, hollow and trembling and praying, I do not know. It may have been minutes. It may have been hours. It seemed aeons. It seemed eternity—longer than the time since Moses was found in the bulrushes, longer than the time since the ape man climbed down from the trees.

This was the ultimate knowledge, and this, also, was obviously death. I had seen the Truth and Truth meant extinction. I was dying a horrible death and I was alone, alone, alone. I was a dying child and I wanted my mother, real or unreal.

Somehow I got out of bed and stumbled on rubbery legs through the dark hall to my parents' room and cried out, "Mama! Mama!"

She woke up at once and said, "Yes, George, what's the matter?"

In a choked voice I declared, "I'm terrible sick, Mama. I'm dying."

"Oh, Georgie! Where are you sick?"

A match scratched and my father lit the kerosene lamp on the stand next to him.

"I'm sick all over," I said. "I know I'm dying."

"Have you got a pain?"

"Well, kind of. I guess it's my heart and my head too."

"Did you wake up with it?"

"No. I haven't been to sleep. It just came over me all of a sudden."

My father was sitting up in bed, his coarse, gray hair tousled over the bald spot. He rubbed his eyes and said, "He's a little young for it, but he's got the hypos. Most boys get it sooner or later, but I've got some pills that'll cure it."

They were almost strangers, but not quite, and when my mother put out her arms in the long-sleeved flannel nightgown with the pink lace at neck and cuffs, I went to them sobbing. She drew my trembling body close, smoothed back my hair and kissed me on the cheek. "Now," she said, softly and soothingly, "tell Mama what's wrong."

Of course I couldn't tell her. With her substantial, comforting arm around me, how could I explain that I had discovered she did not exist except in my own feverish mind?

My father was out of bed, the flannel nightshirt reaching to the knees of his knobby, hairy legs, and he said sympathetically, "I'll get something that'll straighten him out in just a minute." He picked up the lamp and thumped from the room on his bare feet.

"Now," said my mother, "get under the covers here before you take cold."

The room was comparatively warm from a sizzling chunk of water oak in the oval hot-tamale stove, but I scrambled into the bed and snuggled, quivering, up to my mother, who stroked my forehead in the dark and murmured, "Now, now, honey, everything's going to be all right. *Every*thing's going to be all right."

Presently my father was back with the kerosene lamp in one hand and a glass of water in the other. He carried the glass on the palm of his left hand while the big thumb and forefinger held a small pill. After putting the lamp back on the stand he handed me the pill. It was a cylindrical little pill, flat on each end and slightly yellowish in the lamplight.

"You take that, Sonny," he said, "and drink some water and you'll forget all about it."

I sat up, swallowed the pill and drank some water, looked at him and wondered at his phrasing. *Forget about it!* Was it possible that my unreal father—as unreal as Santa Claus and fairy queens and Easter rabbits, and as unreal as the moon and the world and the furniture in our unreal house—understood his own unreality, understood that he existed only in my terror-stricken mind?

"Now," he said, "you go back to your bed, George, and you'll go to sleep and have happy dreams."

My mother said, "Oh, let him stay here a little while."

My father raised his heavy eyebrows but nodded and climbed back in bed. I asked him to please leave the light on and he chuckled and said, "All right, Son, for a little while."

For a moment I pondered how this gentle but hairy figment of my imagination could understand his own vaporous status, but pushed that from my mind in the comfortable security of lying between my loving parents, and as my mother held my hand my trembling ceased and a sweet drowsiness crept over me.

I have wondered since what my father gave me, whether he believed a sugar tablet and psychology were sufficient or whether he decided my state of hysteria required something more potent than plain psychology. I suspect the latter.

Anyhow it was broad daylight when I awoke and I was in my own bed. Because it was Christmas vacation from school I had been allowed to sleep, and I lay there oddly apathetic, blinking at the brightness reflected from the snowy roof of the McConnell house next door, feeling somewhat as if I was just recovering from a long siege of influenza, or what they then called la grippe.

For an instant a wave of the old night horror descended upon me, but I quickly pushed it away before it could take hold. In desperation I thought, This is the day before the day before Christmas and that really is very close to Christmas. Hurriedly, I got out of bed and into my long woolly union suit, because it was still quite chilly in my unheated room. The underwear had to be folded carefully at the ankles as I pulled on my black "Ironclad" stockings, to prevent a bulge above the shoe tops, and I was shivering before I got into my knickers and dashed into the bathroom where it was warmer. A grating in the floor allowed heat to come up to the bathroom from the big, old kitchen range. There also was warm water—almost enough for a deep bath—in the winter, heated in the water-back of the range.

I brushed my teeth with "Sanatol" from the green bottle with the shiny metal snout, washed my face and hands in warm water and Pear's soap, remembering at the last moment about the back of my neck and ears, and then, in my room, gave my unruly hair a perfunctory whack or two with comb and brush after pulling on my red-and-white-striped turtleneck sweater.

In my chastened state there was no temptation to slide down the banister. I *walked* slowly down the stairs and found my mother in the kitchen.

She greeted me cheerily. "Well, hello, lazybones, how are you this morning?"

"All right," I said. "How are you?"

"Oh, fine. What would you like for breakfast?"

"Anything. You had breakfast?"

She laughed. "Oh, hours ago. Papa's gone to the office and Laura's over to Enid's house. We had pancakes and sausage, and there's plenty of batter left and the griddle's still hot."

"That would be fine, Mama." I was very grateful for her

not mentioning the night before, and, as a matter of fact, neither she nor my father *ever* mentioned it to me, although they must have discussed it.

For days the dark specter stood always by my side and each night for years I prayed God and Jesus to "keep me from having the hypos." On numerous occasions I fought my way out of the black vortex before being swept down into the unknown where, for all I know now, insanity or death may have crouched, waiting for me.

Because I stood in terror of the situation, I was humbled rather than exalted by the feeling that nothing existed except through my own consciousness. It was natural, I suppose, that I assumed I was here for some special and mighty purpose. But I didn't want the job. I'd have been more than happy to trade my responsibility for the apparently carefree existence of a ragged swamp boy, and thrown in my silver dollar and a sack of marbles to boot.

Had I been reared a Roman Catholic I'm sure I should have felt it ordained that I become a priest. There was a quiet boy of my acquaintance named Orville O'Neill who went to the parochial school and who once listened to other boys boasting they were going to be railroad engineers when they grew up or baseball players or President of the United States or generals or circus ringmasters or some other great personages, and then calmly announced he had a vocation to become a priest. It never occurred to me that Orville might have gone through the same harrowing experience which had sobered me and that his ambition for the priesthood might be considered the first step toward what they called the Vicariate of Christ at the Vatican. How could Orville have undergone *my* experience when he only existed through my acquaintance with him?

As it was, I was dreadfully afraid I should be compelled to become a preacher, attain martyrdom for telling the truth to Philistines, and die the most horrible death yet devised by the ingenuity of man. I knew about this death from Leo Siddens, who spoke with the authority of thirteen years and the fact that his father was a policeman. According to Leo, the electric chair had been invented to make the punishment for capital crimes so severe that no one would dare commit murder or be a wartime spy like Major André. Graphically, he described the death of Leon Czolgosz, slayer of President McKinley, in the electric chair.

"Look," he said, "they strap this gink in the big chair and put the thing with the wires on his head and more things with wires on his feet and they turn on the electricity and it shakes him harder and harder and pretty soon the little blood veins begin to break here and there and nothing hurts worse than blood veins breaking, and then they turn on a little more electricity and it shakes his teeth loose and by and by his teeth begin to fly around the room and he moans and yells and they turn on a little more electricity and it shakes his eyeballs out and he hollers to please stop but they just turn on more electricity and his toes and fingers shake off and things are shaking loose inside him hurting just terrible and after a couple hours his heart is shaken to pieces and then he dies."

Leo Siddens reckoned assassins would be slow about shooting any more Presidents when they knew the electric chair awaited them. So did I. And I had a more intense personal interest in the thing. Inasmuch as I was the center of the universe that revolved about me, I obviously had been placed here for some tremendous purpose and it seemed to be a matter of history that the more tremendous a man's purpose the greater the likelihood of his being a martyr. Hanging or crucifixion surely would be bad enough, but I wanted no part of that electric chair as described by Leo Siddens. I didn't feel strong enough nor brave enough to face the future, and I wanted to resign as the preordained leader of the unreal people who inhabited this unreal earth. Apparently it never occurred to me that Leo's electric chair was even more unreal than Leo.

I entered a long period of sadness—not that there weren't moments of joy and even ecstasy. There was such a moment one evening on Hanser's Hill with several other boys and girls when I stood poised with my Christmas sled, ready to go bellybuster down the long snowy slope. I glanced to the west and there was a cold pink streak across the sky—just such a streak as lay in the sky of Frederic Remington's picture of the Indian scout on the pony, hanging on my bedroom wall, and standing there in my rubbered feet and reefer jacket and stocking cap and red-mittened hands, I was transported blissfully to the very real land of romance in the old Wild West where I rode a cayuse across the snow-covered hills of Wyoming or Montana. Then the two-toned bells of the Catholic Church began to ring sadly for vespers and the sadness of the bells swept away my joy. There was no meaning nor romance nor reality in the pink-feathered sky and blue-tinted snowy hills. The Indian scout did not exist.

I clutched my new sled desperately, then ran and threw myself upon it to tear head-on down the hill with powdered snow stinging my face.

Chapter 2

THE more one learns, the greater the number of items for him to fail to understand.

For the illiterate savage approximately everything can be lumped together in a one-package deal as the Mystery of Life. On the periphery of the Big Mystery are several subordinate mysteries of cause and effect under control of various spirits, taboos and totems.

For the American child early in the twentieth century the catalogue of unknowable or at least recondite or esoteric matters also contained but few pages. God made the world in six days. He made Adam of dust. He made Eve from Adam's rib and therefore men had one rib less than women. He created the animals and birds and bugs and the creeping and crawling varments, raw material not stated. He hung the moon and the stars and the sun in the sky. The earth turned on its axis, making a day and night. The earth traveled around the sun, making summer and winter. There was a strange, invisible power called electricity that Benjamin Franklin discovered by flying a kite in a thunderstorm (and, by golly, he might have been killed) and electricity was harnessed by Thomas A. Edison to operate the sputtering arc lights on the streets, run the streetcars in cities, and bring life to wires so one could talk over telephones. It was especially difficult to understand why the all-powerful God, who loved the world so much that He allowed

His only begotten son Jesus to be crucified that whosoever believed in Him might not perish but have everlasting life, didn't love the world enough to have omitted the creation of mosquitoes, flies, fleas, chiggers and poison ivy, to say nothing of Satan and hell. You shouldn't trouble your curly little head over that sort of thing, but have complete faith in the infinite wisdom of the Almighty.

I suppose that astronomers realized then that our sun was a minor star in a minor galaxy called the Milky Way, and probably some of them suspected the unplumbed universe contained uncounted other galaxies with hundreds of billions of stars as great or infinitely greater than our sun—many of them possibly owning satellites such as our Earth and Mars and Venus and Jupiter—but that was far from common knowledge.

Surely most Christian Americans went along with our own Reverend Mr. Reynolds in holding unwavering faith in a heavy-thewed, omnipotent, anthropomorphic God who not only observed every action of every man on earth but also marked the sparrow's fall. This, it was said, was a job of such infinite magnitude that it could not be comprehended by the finite mind of man.

If our tall, slim, black-garbed Reverend Mr. Reynolds had been asked whether our omnipotent, anthropomorphic God had jurisdiction over possible life on any of the planets in the hundreds of billions of solar systems scattered billions of light-years from the earth or whether he reckoned each solar system had its own anthropomorphic, omnipotent God, he probably would have answered that no mention was made in the Holy Writ from Genesis to Revelation of other solar systems or, for that matter, of life anywhere except on earth, in heaven and in hell. God and Satan shared the responsibility for these three regions. In certain areas, such as heathen Asia, Satan temporarily held the upper hand, but our missionaries were doing a noble work to overthrow his reign. Let us contribute generously to advance their cause.

For me, a frightened child called George Vincent Chalmers, the unknown complexities of astronomy, philosophy, biology, psychology, physics and metaphysics, including theology and ontology, worried me no more than nuclear fission or fusion worried George Washington. Well, if I had ever heard of these problems I could have dismissed them as easily as I dismissed Theodore Roosevelt and the King of England: I, George Chalmers, had never seen them; therefore they existed only in legend as did Sir Lancelot and Alice's Red Queen.

But there were some things I could not dismiss. Compound fractions, for example. During this period I was not doing well at school, or anywhere else. Perhaps I had even slipped over the border into precocious dementia praecox—to use redundancy for emphasis. But I had enough wit left to wonder why God couldn't have made me a little brighter and a little braver before saddling me with such grave responsibilities.

I was a dope. I remember standing in right field, spitting into the palm of my glove, and a clump of daisies before me nodded in the sunshine and I said to myself, This is planetary light. Then I wondered why I said that, because I wasn't sure that the sun was really a planet, and I was overwhelmed by unreality. The very real thump of a very real baseball not six feet to my left wakened me, and I chased it to real howls of derision because I had made no effort to catch an easy fly ball.

When the inning was over I was almost afraid to walk in and face the taunts, even though I assured myself that it didn't matter anyhow, because it wasn't real. There seemed to be a certain element of reality to the epithet, "Sleepy Chalmers" or "Sleepy George," which Miss Ruth Anderson, the fifth-grade teacher, had attached to me because I had failed to answer a couple of times when addressed. And there was a happy sense of regained reality when I swung wildly at the first ball grinning Fred Snider pitched to me, and hit it way up the railroad bank for a home run, partially redeeming myself for the unthinkable error of inattention to a baseball game which, by all canons, should be the most important thing in the world for a red-blooded American boy.

After several years I did manage to work up a fairly strong interest in baseball and also some proficiency in the game. But I could lose myself better by reading, and I read omnivorously, borrowing books from the public library and from other boys, devouring trash and classics alike with little discrimination. Orville O'Neill, the boy with the vocation who actually did grow up to become a priest, had a whole shelf of the Horatio Alger, Jr. books. I borrowed and read them all, only slightly annoyed if a secondary character named Frank became Fred toward the end of the book.

Undersized Julian Newton, the brightest boy in my class, lent me half a dozen of his score or more of the swashbuckling "Jack Harkaway" series, but cut me off when I expressed doubt that some of the hero's adventures really happened. The heat of Julian's indignation at my incredulity surprised me, and I wondered briefly whether he found greater reality in the Jack Harkaway books than in his own life. Of course Julian existed only in my own mind, although he didn't act like it, and because he always knew all the answers in school he probably had been placed in my mind only to make me more humble before God. Something like that.

From Max Levine I borrowed all *The Rover Boys* books and was fascinated by their adventures with the ubiquitous villain Dan Baxter. Max said when he was ready for high school he would go to military school like the Rover boys, and he did, too, coming home for vacations in a gorgeous light-blue uniform with gleaming brass buttons, a forage cap and a cape with scarlet lining.

The public library had a collection of the G. A. Henty historical novels for boys—*With Wolfe in Canada, With Clive in India, With Lee in Virginia*, etc., which I devoured, and I myself owned several of the Jacob Abbott biographies such as Julius Caesar and William of Normandy, as well as *Rip Van Winkle, Robinson Crusoe, Aesop's Fables, Swiss Family Robinson, Treasure Island, Kidnapped, Tom Brown's School Days* and *Through the Looking-Glass*.

One sunny afternoon I was on a side street in the western end of town alone. I can't remember what I was doing there, and it was an unusual thing to be over there unless I was with a group going swimming in shallow Oxbow Lake near the river. Perhaps I had been on an errand for my mother or sister to the cottage of Mrs. Harte, the dressmaker. Anyhow I was there and barefoot and for company I carried a club made from a broomstick with the wooden spindle from the end of a roll of wrapping paper pounded on the end. I traveled by hitting a battered tin can ahead of me with the club.

Once, after giving the can a whack, I looked up and saw a boy I knew slightly in the side yard of a big gray house. He was a robust, red-cheeked boy named Calvin Campbell who was a class ahead of me in school. Calvin was pleasant enough, but something of a "loner." You saw him and knew who he was, but didn't know anything about him. Now he was in this side yard under the trees and there was a row of wooden packing boxes with chicken wire nailed over the front. These boxes seemed to be cages with live things inside, so I stopped and called, "Howdy, Cal—you live here?"

Calvin turned and nodded. "Sure," he said. "Want to see my menagerie?"

I looked ahead to note where my tin can had landed, then walked into the unfenced yard. In the biggest box was a raccoon that stood up, grasping the wire screen with its tiny black hands, to peer at me. In the adjoining box was a prairie dog with a crude round turntable to run on. A crow was swinging on a perch in the next cage, and he cocked a bright eye at me and squawked, "Hello, Jim Crow."

"For goodness sake," I said, "did that crow talk?"

"Sure," said Calvin, "but that's all he can say, just 'Hello, Jim Crow.' That's his name, Jim Crow."

"Did you split his tongue to make him talk?"

"No. That's a lot of cruel nonsense, splitting a crow's tongue. Some crows will learn to talk a little and some won't. But they never talk as much as a good parrot, and the best talkers in the world—I mean among birds—are the Asiatic myna birds. I never did see one, but I've read that myna birds learn to talk whole sentences and to sing songs clear through."

"For goodness sake," I said, leaning on my broomstick.

Calvin looked at me with clear gray eyes. "I know they call you Sleepy," he said, "but what's your real name?"

I was appalled that my notoriety had spread clear to the West End. "George," I said, looking at the sky. "George Chalmers."

"Well," said Calvin, "I'll call you George. I don't like calling people by nicknames because sometimes they hate their nicknames. When we lived in York before Dad got the Capitol here I was kind of fat and kids called me Butterbeans. I didn't like that a bit."

"Gosh, no," I said, surveying him. I thought he was still a rather plump boy, but didn't mention it.

"Do you like animals?" he asked.

"Sure," I said. "Well, some of them. Of course I don't like rats and skunks and things like that."

Calvin shook his head. "Oh, rats and skunks are all right.

Rats are very smart animals and I've read that skunks make wonderful pets if you get 'em young."

"I'd think you'd have to have a cold in the head all the time to stand a skunk around."

"Oh, no. Skunks are very clean animals and don't smell a bit unless they get mad and let ding. But if you get 'em young and are kind to them they love you and wouldn't think of spraying you."

"Well, I don't know."

Calvin was growing very animated. "You know, George, almost every living thing except some people respond to kindness. When you let any wild animal understand that you mean him no harm he'll become your friend and not hurt you."

"Tigers?" I asked.

Calvin pondered. Then he nodded. "Well, yes. But there's some trouble with big carnivorous animals like tigers and lions and grizzly bears. Unless they've had some experience with men and are afraid of guns, they'd think a man was a game animal and might eat him up before he could make friends."

"That would be kind of discouraging to the man that wanted to be friends," I said, "and about all he could do to get even would be give the tiger a bellyache."

Calvin looked at me suspiciously. "Well . . ." he said, "I guess about the only way with big carnivora is to catch them young and treat 'em very kind and gentle."

I found myself warming toward this strange big boy with the intense eyes. While I doubt that I knew the word *naive* at the time, that's how I thought of him—in a nice way.

"It's the same, I guess, with rattlesnakes," Calvin continued, "I suppose that even if you went up to a coiled rattlesnake slow and talking kind and soothing he'd probably strike your hand when you put it out, because that's his instinct. I never had any real experience with rattlesnakes, but I got a hunch if you caught one young and talked soothing to him and fed him what he wanted and was careful not to get him excited, that pretty soon he'd learn you were his friend."

"By golly," I said, "I wouldn't want to try it."

Calvin nodded. "You'd have to be mighty careful. But now you take garter snakes, and I've caught 'em with a forked stick and at first they're scared to death of you, but you treat 'em

[25]

kind and pretty soon they're friendly and will crawl all over you."

"Boy, I don't want *any* slimy snake crawling over me."

"They're not a bit slimy," Calvin asserted. "They're smooth and cool and beautiful."

"Not for me. I like animals but I draw the line at snakes—any snakes."

"That's because you don't know snakes," Calvin said warmly. "Some people hate cats because they don't know what interesting animals they are."

"I like cats all right," I said, "at least *some* cats."

"I like all animals, especially wild animals." Calvin looked at me narrowly. "What you going to be?" he asked.

"How do you mean?" I asked, knowing quite well what he meant, but trying to evade the question because I was afraid it was ordained for me to be a minister of the Gospel or some other sort of martyr.

"Well, for instance," he said, "I'm going to be a naturalist like Ernest Thompson Seton."

"Who is he?"

Calvin frowned. "Oh," he said, "I guess you're not a reader."

"Sure, I'm a reader. I read everything. Well, practically everything."

"Well, I don't understand how you never heard of Ernest Thompson Seton, then. I reckon he's the greatest living naturalist, and he's written and illustrated a lot of books—*Wild Animals I Have Known, Lives of the Hunted,* and if you haven't read *Two Little Savages,* well, you sure have got something coming, if you really like to read."

"What's it about?"

"Well, my goodness—it's about everything! It's about a boy named Yan who loves nature and wants to be a naturalist and he builds a shanty out in the woods and—well, finally he goes out on a farm where there's a boy named Sam Rafton and they learn to make an Indian tepee—well, if I loaned you the book would you promise to be very careful of it and wash your hands every time before reading it?"

"Sure," I said, "I'm very careful with books. I've got books of my own."

He looked at me closely and bit his lip. "Well," he said finally, "I don't know you at all, but I just got a feeling you're the kind of a guy who'd get a whole lot out of that book and it might even just change your whole life. I can tell you that there are mighty few boys I know that I'd take a risk loaning that book to them, but if you want it really and promise, I'm going to loan it to you."

"Gee," I said, "that's wonderful and I'll be very careful."

He jerked his head toward the house and said, "Come on."

As we started for the back porch a slim sprite in gingham dress and with rich brown curls hanging down her back came out the door. She was eating a piece of bread and butter and syrup and she had the same level, black-lashed gray eyes as Calvin.

"Hello, Little Egypt," said Calvin.

"Hello, Butterbeans," said she, indignantly.

"George," said Calvin, "that's my kid sister Little Egypt. There's Egypt in her dreamy eyes and Karo in her smile. Karo syrup, I mean."

"My name's Margaret," said the sprite as we passed her.

Calvin's room was wonderful. Spread on one wall was the skin of a spotted calf, on another wall that of a coyote only moderately mangy. Even more exciting, in a weathered black leather holster hung a huge, wooden-handled revolver. I pointed at it and said, "Gosh!"

Calvin grinned and drew the big gun from its holster. "Regular old frontier-model Colt forty-five," he said. The blued finish was pretty well worn from the long barrel, but it was well oiled and shiny. "My Uncle Will used to be a cowboy," he said, "and he gave it to me. Well, it won't shoot on account the firing pin is broken off, but it's fine to have and to practice with and it sure enough would scare the pants off a burglar." Hooking his thumb over the hammer, Calvin flipped the gun down, and it cocked with an impressive double click. Then he brought the barrel down at the coyote skin on the wall and said "Bang!" as he pulled the trigger.

I put out my hand. "Can I see it?" I asked.

"Well—but be very careful."

"I thought you said it wouldn't shoot."

"Doesn't matter. The first thing you got to learn about a firearm is to be careful with it even if you think it won't shoot. An awful lot of people have been shot with guns they didn't think was loaded or they didn't think would shoot."

"But this *won't* shoot, will it?"

"No. But you don't *know* it. So just don't point it at me or yourself or anything."

He handed me the revolver and it was surprisingly heavy, so heavy that when I pointed it at the coyote skin, it wobbled alarmingly. I tried to cock the hammer but my thumb couldn't budge it.

"You got to make the weight of the gun work for you," said Calvin. "Hook your thumb over the hammer and then jerk the gun down."

I tried to do as he had done and the big Colt flew out of my hand to thump dreadfully on the floor.

"Oh dear," I exclaimed. "I'm sorry."

Calvin seized his treasure up from the rug and examined it. "Well, I guess it didn't hurt it any. But, like I said, you've got to be mighty careful with firearms and that's a pretty big gun for a boy your size."

Of course he *was* a little larger than I and quite justified in mentioning it if he wanted to.

"But"—he grinned at me—"no harm done. Forget it." He sighted along the barrel and then carefully slid the revolver back into its holster.

"Can't you get the what-you-call-it fixed?" I asked.

"Oh, sure. I guess I could get a new firing pin all right, but I don't think my dad would let me keep it if it'd shoot."

Calvin looked at his hands and then wiped the palms on his knickers before stepping over to the scroll-sawed bookcase and opening the glass door. He took out a book and held it up. "Here," he said, "is what I think is the greatest book ever written for a certain kind of boys, and I mean the kind of boys who're interested in nature and wild things and Indians and not just baseball and football and cutting up jack, if you know what I mean."

"I know," I said. "I'm interested in Indians and things."

He nodded. "I just thought you were by the looks of you, kind of. I'm going to loan you this book *Two Little Savages*, and if you like it the way I think you're going to, I've got a hunch we're going to be pardners and have some real fun out in the woods."

"That's swell," I said, and I was way ahead of him.

Just then a piano downstairs burst loose with a torrent of music and I knew it was "The Poet and Peasant Overture" because the town band played it.

"Gosh," I said, "you got a player piano?"

He shook his head, "That's Mother," he said, handing me the book.

I whistled softly and said, "My goodness, I didn't know *anybody* could play a regular piano like that."

"Mother's pretty good, I guess. Just look at some of the pictures in *Two Little Savages.*"

We sat down together on his bed, which was covered with a brown blanket instead of a bedspread, but I was so enthralled by the rippling, roaring piano downstairs that it was difficult to show proper interest as Calvin animatedly displayed the illustrations drawn by Ernest Thompson Seton himself of the boy Yan and his shanty, of Yan and Sam, of diagrams showing how to make a genuine Indian tepee, how to stuff an owl, how to make bows and arrows, and scores of marginal sketches of various plants, leaves and animal tracks.

Finally we went downstairs, Calvin clattering ahead of me, and when we reached the downstairs hall the music ceased and Calvin's mother turned on the swivel stool from the grand piano. I gasped, because there went another of the aphorisms I had worked out from my experience with the world, i.e. good guys always have homely mothers. Calvin Campbell obviously was an extremely good and interesting guy. His mother looked like a Gibson Girl, slim waisted, neat, with a gleaming light-brown pompadour, dark brows and the same magnetic but kindly gray eyes as Calvin and Little Egypt. And, speaking of Little Egypt, she was lying on the floor, propped up by her elbows, with an open book before her. She gave me a friendly grin.

"Mother," said Calvin, "this is my friend George Chalmers. He's interested in nature and things too."

The beautiful woman smiled at me. "How nice," she said in a creamy contralto. "I hope you'll come again soon, George."

"Thank you, ma'am," I said.

"And, Mother," Calvin went on, "George likes to read and is careful with books. I'm going to loan him *Two Little Savages.*"

"Lend, darling," said Mrs. Campbell. "Loan is a noun."

[29]

"All right, lend."

"I think that will be very nice, especially if George remembers where he borrowed it."

"Oh I'll remember. My goodness." I said.

"My name's in it." Calvin reassured her.

I wanted very much to ask if she'd mind if I sat down quietly and listened to her play the piano some more, but didn't dare. So I just said good-bye and Calvin said he was sure I'd be crazy about the book and Little Egypt grinned at me again from the floor and I went out the front door. By the time I reached the front sidewalk the piano was going again, but I could not recognize what she was playing.

I was in a curious glow and the world about me seemed very real. There by the sidewalk was my battered tin can, but I had left my broomstick club up in Calvin's room. Well, he probably would save it for me.

I wanted to look through the treasured book as I walked, but decided I had better wait until I could wash my hands.

When I got home I put the book carefully away in my room. Then I found my mother and asked if I could have a piece of bread and butter and Karo syrup.

"Why Karo syrup?" she asked. "We don't have any."

I shrugged my shoulders. "Just thought it would be good," I said.

She laughed. "You've been reading advertisements," she said. "We've got molasses and that's a good deal better."

"Well," I said, "I guess that'll do."

Chapter 3

WHEN my father came home from the office I was lying on my back in the living room with my feet in a chair, thoroughly engrossed in the rather self-pitying beginning chapters of Mr. Seton Thompson's or Thompson Seton's autobiographical book.

"Hey, Buster," he said, "you'll ruin your eyes reading in that

position. Why don't you sit in a chair like a human being instead of hanging upside down like a ringtailed monkey or
possum?"

That question was hard to answer, but I straightened around
and leaned against the couch.

"What are you reading?"

"Wonderful book, Papa. I have to be very careful of it because I borrowed it from a boy named Calvin Campbell who's
going to be a naturalist when he grows up and is very careful
with books."

"Calvin Campbell? Is he Frank Campbell's boy?"

"I don't know what his father's name is. They live in a big
house on the West Side. But they're very nice people. Mrs.
Campbell is a very beautiful lady who plays the piano wonderful."

"Hmm. That's Frank Campbell, all right. Saloonkeeper and
ward heeler. I don't care much for your associating with a son
of his, and I certainly don't want you visiting their home."

"But, Papa! Cal Campbell is just the nicest kid I know. He's
very polite and doesn't use swear words and he loves animals
and knows practically everything and his mother is just the
nicest lady you ever saw."

"I've seen *your* mother."

"Well, sure. Of course I mean outside of her."

"What's that book this Campbell boy lent you?"

"It's called *Two Little Savages*, and—"

"I think you're enough of a savage now without reading
about it."

"Well, gee, Papa, it's just about a boy, or I guess two boys,
who play Indian and learn how to make a tepee and how to
stuff an owl and things."

"Have you got an owl you want to stuff?"

"Well, no. But I might have sometime."

My father grunted. "Nonsense," he said. "I think you might
get better grades next fall if you read something worth while."

"You mean like *The Crucifixion of Philip Strong*?"

"Well—that's a good, Christian book."

"All right, Papa," I said, "I didn't read it, of course, but
Reverend Reynolds preached a sermon about it and their
wanting to stop Sunday newspapers so printers and other people on newspapers wouldn't have to work on the Lord's day and

[31]

Chet Wilson's father is a printer on *The Record* and Chet says his father says that's nutty because they put out the Sunday morning papers on Saturday night and only work Sundays putting out the *Monday* morning paper."

"That's not important. It was a good moral book, and I don't like the sound of a book about little savages. Let me see it."

He drew his spectacles from his vest pocket and put them on.

I said, "Oh, Papa, I'm sure there's nothing wrong with this book or they wouldn't let Calvin have it."

He peered over the tops of his glasses. "A saloonkeeper? Let me see it."

I noted the page I was on and handed the volume to him, very apprehensive as he sat down by a window and began to turn the pages. It would be terrible if he should forbid me to read this bible of Calvin Campbell's. Would I be able to hide it and read it secretly as I had read the stack of borrowed dime novels about Old Cap Collier, Nick Carter, the Liberty Boys of '76 and Buffalo Bill ("Bang, bang, bang, spoke Buffalo Bill's trusty rifle. Three redskins bit the dust") or would he give me a specific order to return *Two Little Savages* at once, an order that could not be disobeyed?

Just then my sister, who was attending normal school, came in the front door and my father took off his glasses.

"Laura," he called, "did you ever hear of a writer named— let's see—Ernest Thompson Seton?"

"Oh yes, Papa," she answered, "he's a very well-known writer about wild animals and things."

"Is he respectable?"

"I don't really know, Papa. Oh, but he *must* be. The *Ladies' Home Journal* ran a continued story of his about some boys in an Indian tepee. Of course, I didn't read it, but it must have been decent or the *Journal* wouldn't have printed it."

My father nodded. "That's what this book seems to be, by the pictures. All right, George, you can read it and take it back to that Campbell boy. But I don't want you to see very much of any son of Frank Campbell or to be hanging around their house. Most especially—and this is important—don't you ever accept anything at all to drink over there. I don't care whether they call it lemonade or soda pop or buttermilk. The liquor interests have a trick of building up a taste for intoxicating liquor in children by putting a little whisky or rum in a so-called soft drink and giving it to boys and girls. And the first thing the youngster knows, he's got a craving for something that will ruin his life. Do you understand that perfectly?"

"Yes, sir," I said.

"All right, and see that you remember it. Here's your book."

So I read *Two Little Savages* and, as Calvin had predicted, I was captivated by it. And in spite of my father's admonition, I saw more than a little of Calvin Campbell from then on.

We had no material for a tepee, but we built a snug shanty in the deep woods down by the river. The sense of partnership in the project was a wonderful thing I never had experienced before. We pledged eternal friendship.

Where did we get the material for the shanty? In a way, the *Ladies' Home Journal* provided it. Until my sister revealed that this female publication had unaccountably printed a continued story by the revered Ernest Thompson Seton, quite possibly *Two Little Savages* itself, I never had even glanced at the magazine. Now I thumbed through each issue on the chance that another aberration might occur, and noted it was conducting an ardent campaign against billboards desecrating the American landscape. In gratitude to the *Journal* for honoring our hero, we enlisted in its campaign. There were plenty of landscape-desecrating billboards on the river road and we dismantled enough of them to build our cabin, although some of them were stubbornly constructed and it was quite hard work.

Though one of the billboards advertised "The Beer that Made Milwaukee Famous," which was quite possibly one of his father's leading lines, I was proud of Calvin's showing no compunction about taking it down. While I wished my father could know how Calvin had thus struck two blows for righteousness on one billboard—one for the *Ladies' Home Journal*'s campaign and one against the "liquor interests"—the whole matter was so complicated that I scarcely knew how to tell him.

Calvin was skillful and strong in the demolition work. And although our material, including second-hand nails, was difficult to handle and our tools consisted of a wobbly claw hammer, an old hand ax and rusty saw, the shanty was a thing of beauty to our eyes. It was about eight feet square with a slightly sloping roof and a doorway. The roof, which was nearly six feet high, didn't leak much except in a severe rainstorm.

We dreamed of the time when we might spend a night in our

castle, but Calvin's plan for him to get permission to spend the night at my house while I got permisison to spend the night with him was embarrassing. I couldn't tell him that my father never in the world would allow me to sleep in a saloonkeeper's house.

Nevertheless, we were able to spend a good deal of time at our sanctuary. I discovered a talent for forgery and could turn out acceptable excuses in the handwriting of Mrs. Campbell and my mother to explain our absence from school. We couldn't have played hooky as often as it seems now or it surely would have been noticed at home on our report cards. But our teachers apparently never noticed that we were ill only on beautiful days.

We acquired a tin skillet from the Bon Marché basement for a dime. Bread, eggs, bacon and the like could be lifted from family kitchens in reasonable amounts without notice. But of course these tame foods were only supplementary to the catfish we caught in the river and fried over our campfire.

When I wished we had a twenty-two rifle so we could shoot rabbits and squirrels for the frying pan, Calvin said soberly, "No, I'm glad we haven't. Unless I really needed them for food I'd hate to kill any wild animal, and what we eat out here is just in addition to our two meals at home and school lunch. We don't need them."

His conscience apparently didn't bother him about the fish we caught and ate.

In spite of *Two Little Savages*, we did not play Indian. I don't know why, unless it was because I was a little light complexioned to make a credible Indian. Instead, we were pioneers, explorers living far from the trammeling forces of civilization, until Calvin's Ingersoll watch told us we must return to our homes.

The days we played hooky were better even than the Saturdays when our excursions were more legitimate. I remember one such spring day when the spongy, alluvial soil near the river was covered with violets, spring beauties and Mayflowers, and the willows and water oaks and black walnuts were in tender leaf, and the woods were in an actual uproar of bird song, far and near, with cardinal calling cardinal, phoebe calling phoebe, thrush calling thrush, finch calling finch and mockingbird calling everyone to be happy. Every breath was a joy, redolent with the spices of spring, and I, old Trapper George Chalmers, sat on a dead log with hickory fish pole in my hands, watching my cork bobber in the yellow eddy of the river. My tried and true pardner, Calvin Campbell, was just in sight downstream, similarly engaged.

Presently we would clean our fish and fry them with bacon and eat them with our fingers and jackknives, together with our school-lunch sandwiches and apples and cookies, and we had no thoughts about our parents worrying over our waning appetites at supper nor about our contemporaries chewing their pencils at school over square root or over "that mood of a verb representing the denoted action or state not as fact but as contingent, possible, doubtful, desirable, etc."

And our play here on the enchanted wooded riverside as old pards Campbell and Chalmers was so real that I wriggled my bare toes in the dark sand and made up what I thought was an aphorism—"There's nothing really real in the world but the happy unreal." I believe other philosophers such as Mary Baker Eddy have made similar observations.

And I was in love. I was in love with that fey child whom I thought of as Little Egypt because her brother called her Little Egypt. Also, in a different way, I was in love with their beautiful mother, who several times had allowed me to sit in quiet worship while she played music I had never heard before with a brilliance I never had heard before.

Sometimes I would talk with Little Egypt on the front or back steps of the Campbell house while waiting for Calvin. I don't know what we talked about, but she was perfectly at ease with me and her beautifully shaped child's lips were almost as red as if they were rouged. There were a few freckles on her pert little nose and, to me, her black-lashed gray eyes seemed to carry the mystic wisdom of the ages. Her dark hair carried a perfume, maybe natural, maybe from soap, that sent warm tingles to the tips of my fingers and toes.

Of course I never spoke of it to anyone, but there was no doubt in my mind that Little Egypt and I should marry when we grew up. That would have the added advantage of making Calvin my brother and their mother my mother-in-law. I didn't think one way or the other about bald-headed, bluff Frank Campbell, the saloonkeeper.

A boy approaching puberty is usually, for all practical purposes, a pretty primitive form of Homo sapiens, and like most primitives, I attached great importance to signs, portents and dreams.

And I had an extremely real dream in color. There was a treeless, windy hill reaching to the horizon where a large stone house with many chimneys stood against the cloud-scudding sky. To the right, dark blue water stretched to blend far away with the stormy blue-gray sky. I was walking slowly up the hill toward the stone house and there were undulations in the gray-green grass-covered slope with here and there a low shrub spangled with faint lavender, dimmer in color than the mignonette in my sister Laura's flower garden. With me was a girl wearing a red woolen cap and a checkered dress of coarse wool. Her dark hair hung down her back in a thick braid. This girl seemed somewhat larger than Little Egypt, but she was Little Egypt all right. There was no mistaking that when she turned with the familiar enigmatic expression in her black-lashed gray eyes and said something that didn't seem to make sense. Then she put out her hand and I took it and hand in hand we went running up the hill toward the stone house.

This dream impressed me mightily. I had heard of reincarnation, and like so many primitives, was inclined to believe in it. Whether I believed this little scene was something that had happened in another life or was ordained to happen in this life or both, I don't know. But the dream seemed more real than life itself and I was sure it was profoundly significant. I pondered over it at length. There was, for example, the great blue ocean, which seemed most familiar, yet in my present life I never had looked upon water wider than our river at floodtime. And, surely, the very least the dream could mean was that the enchanting Little Egypt and I were inexorably mated in the Great Book of Life, whatever that was.

Some days later this idea seemed to be completely confirmed when I was sitting on the Campbell back steps, waiting for Calvin, and Little Egypt came out eating an apple.

"Want an apple, George?" she asked.

"Well, thank you," I said, "if you've got one to spare handy."

"Just a second."

She let the screen door slam and reappeared a moment later

[36]

with another red Jonathan, handed it to me, and sat down beside me on the steps.

I thought immediately of the dream and I said, "Look, Little Egypt, did you ever see a big stone house on top of a hill with a lot of chimneys and the ocean stretching off from the bottom of the hill?"

She turned at me with an odd grin. Then she took a bite of apple and nodded her head. "Bermouth," she said.

"Bermouth," I asked, "what's that?"

She nodded her head again with a peculiar grin and squinted her eyes at me. "Sure, we used to live there."

"You did! Where is it?"

"Scotland, of course. Why?"

"Well," I said, with prickles running up my spine, "I just wondered."

Just then Calvin appeared and I went off with him. By and by, after several futile attempts, I managed to say, "Look, Cal, I didn't know you ever lived in Scotland."

He frowned at me. "Scotland?" he said. "I never lived in Scotland. We used to live over in York before we moved here, but that's all. Whatever gave you the idea—well, I reckon Campbell's a Scottish name, but even Grandpa Campbell was born in the United States." He laughed and then said, "I bet Little Egypt told you we used to live in Scotland, didn't she?"

"Well," I said, "as a matter of fact—"

"Listen, pard," said Cal, "if you believe everything that kid says you'll sure go nuts. She's liable to say anything at any time."

Chapter 4

MY FATHER, Jerome Vincent Chalmers, was nearly fifty years old when I was born. He was a big man and, as I know now, considerably overweight.

Before my time he had been connected with several enterprises, from mining to real-estate development, each expected by him to make millions. But each time "circumstances beyond the control of mortal man" intervened. I suspect he was inclined to play long shots and counted too much on the power of prayer to lessen the odds.

When I was a small boy he was in a period between great enterprises and operating a modest real-estate and insurance business. But he was constantly holding a wet finger to the wind for signs of something really big.

My mother, the former Millicent Mosby, said she first fell in love with my father's high-stepping team of Morgans and his glistening, rubber-tired carriage, then with his curly brown beard. By the time I came along the Morgans were gone and the beard was reduced to a large, graying mustache.

Four children were born of their union—first my sister Laura and then, three years apart, a boy named Jerome Mosby and a girl named Frances Mosby. Jerome and Frances both died of diphtheria within hours of each other before I was born. So my surviving sister was nearly ten years older than I, and was practically a second mother to me.

I was tutored, pampered, petted and spoiled. In some matters, such as reading, I was advanced. In other matters I was retarded.

When my father decided it was time to inform me about sex, he succeeded both in revolting and frightening me. He was a dignified man and perhaps also pompous. I never heard anyone but my mother address him by his first name, and she never reduced the Jerome to Jerry.

Of course I had heard about sex before. After all, there were animals around, uninhibited in their sexual affairs, and there was talk among boys, especially among the riffraff from across the tracks. But Calvin Campbell had come to a sensible conclusion and had convinced me of its truth.

One day when we were alone upstairs in his house, he showed me a small black syringe he had discovered in a drawer. Naturally, he explained, decent people would not resort to the crude and actually horrifying practices of animals, Negroes and dirty white trash for the purpose of reproduction. So when a respectable man and wife decided they wanted a child, the husband would discreetly load such a syringe with the male seed and leave it for his wife, perhaps in the medicine cabinet, and she would apply it in a private and decent manner.

So it was shocking indeed to hear my own father talk about the conception of babies just as if he didn't know about the modern and decent method with a small black syringe. I was tempted to inform him that he really was horribly behind the times, but his manner was so serious and even severe that I couldn't interrupt him. Then he got to the matter of what he called "self-abuse" with its penalty of physical disintegration, blindness and insanity, and because I had not yet been driven to such practices, I didn't know what he was talking about. But his warnings were so terrifically graphic that I began to regard this salient portion of my anatomy as if it were a hand grenade with the pin pulled and, to be on the safe side, I took to sitting down when I went to the bathroom.

Despite my innate conviction that I must be destined for great things, Fate seemed determined for some singular reason to cast me only in what seemed to be ridiculous roles. My few boyhood triumphs failed miserably to put me on the pedestal of even a bush-league Frank Merriwell.

For example, there was the high-school interclass track meet when I was in the seventh grade. Because of my success, perhaps, in escaping numerous tough boys from across the tracks, I considered myself the fastest runner in the world, and I was interested in running. So I went to the Fair Grounds race track that afternoon to see the big high-school boys run, jump and throw weights. I was wearing only a light shirt, overalls and a broad-brimmed straw hat and was carrying my newspaper sack. I also had a cigar, because there was a shooting gallery on my paper route and the shooting-gallery man would give me three shots twice a week in payment for the paper. Frequently I was able to win a cigar.

The running of the big farm boys did not impress me particularly, so when the half-mile run was announced I approached the high-school coach and asked permission to participate.

He looked me up and down and said, "What makes you think you'd have a chance with the big boys?"

I said, "Well, Mr. Lloyd, I think I can run faster than they can."

"Modest squirt, aren't you?"

"I guess not, sir," I said, "but I sure enough can run."

He laughed and asked my name and my grade. Then he looked at my bare feet and said, "You know these boys have long, sharp spikes on their shoes and it wouldn't be very good to have them step on your bare feet."

"I'll keep out of their way," I said.

Then he laughed again and said, "All right, squirt, line up with them if you want to."

So I put my straw hat and paper sack and cigar down in the grass of the half-mile track's infield and lined up on the outside of the half-dozen athletes. The youth next to me was nearly a foot taller than I. When Mr. Lloyd called "On your marks" and the runners squatted, I, not being trained in the conventional start, merely crouched slightly. But when the little pistol barked I leaped away, keeping far outside of those menacing spikes, and sprinted as hard as I could go, giving no thought to the eight hundred and eighty yards that lay ahead. Let them take care of themselves. At the far side of the track I took a quick glance back and found myself an unbelievable distance ahead of the nearest big-track suit. I also found myself exhausted.

Then I was being driven by forces beyond myself. My pursuers represented the terrors of the unknown and I was fleeing to the haven of sane reality that lay in front of the grandstand far, far away. Extreme fatigue was nothing. I must keep going without lessening speed. Much better, I thought in desperation, to die in full stride than to falter.

My bare feet were numb but they kept pounding the dirt and there I was, making the turn into the home stretch with my lungs burning and the trees and the gray old grandstand quivering like heat waves down a country road and I took another glance backward and the giants in the white suits and murderous spikes were gaining, but still a long way back, and I stumbled but recovered, and I said to my wobbling legs, "It doesn't matter. Just keep going," and there was a lot of noise, partly from my pounding pulse and partly from the grandstand, and the white string at the finish line was at my chest with the nearest pursuer nearly fifty yards behind.

I fell through the fence to the infield and sprawled out to die beside my paper sack and straw hat. Then, although nearly blind from exhaustion, I saw a figure standing over me and finally recognized it as Mr. Lloyd, who was laughing with tears running down his seamed cheeks, and it suddenly seemed to me that the noise from the grandstand was not cheers for my triumph but howling laughter.

I picked up my dead cigar, struck a match on the seat of my overalls and relit the cigar.

"Hey, there," Mr. Lloyd said, chortling again, "give me that thing."

I blinked to clear my vision.

"You're too young to be smoking," he said sternly, and then exclaimed, "Oh my God," chortled and demanded again that I give him my cigar.

I gave it to him and he threw it far out to the infield. Then he said, "You take care of yourself and quit smoking and you'll be a pretty good runner in a couple of years when you're in high school."

I thought I recognized a compliment veiled by that "couple of years," but I didn't see the necessity of veiling it when I had just demonstrated my running ability by beating all those great big high-school boys, and I certainly couldn't see what was so funny about it. I put on my straw hat, picked up my paper sack and got to my feet, still a little dizzy. Mr. Lloyd slapped me on the back, but he was still laughing, as were some of the people around the side of the grandstand when I passed them on stiffening legs and sore feet on my way back to town to get my papers at the *Evening Journal* office.

For some days after the interclass track meet mere acquaintances hailed me with "Hi, there, half-miler!" and it seemed in the nature of a taunt and made me unhappy. I thought, Well, that just goes to show. If Fred Snider, for instance, had run away from the big high-school boys like I did, he'd be a big hero, and when Sleepy Chalmers does it they think it's a big joke. It was all very puzzling. In the first place, why had I extended myself so desperately? That was ridiculous, but why was it funny to others?

Although my pard Calvin Campbell must have heard of my exploit on the Fair Grounds track, he had the good taste never to mention it. Never in the world would Calvin have made a public spectacle of himself.

That spring my uncle George Mosby visited us and he had

a sort of proprietary interest in me because I had been named for him. He was a big, hearty farmer from Kansas, and he came up with the exciting proposal that I spend at least part of my summer vacation on his ranch. I had been growing tall and skinny, and he suggested that ranch life would put some meat on my bones, that I could help out with chores and have fun with his youngest son Fred, riding horseback, hunting prairie chickens, and all sorts of romantic things.

While Uncle George did not actually specify that I should be wearing leather chaps and a forty-five in a low-slung holster, my imagination readily filled in those entrancing Wild West details, and I pictured myself lassoing and branding calves in the roundup, even if it was improbable that I should shoot it out with Trampas on the main street of the cowtown.

Girls naturally did not enter the picture. My own true love, Little Egypt, would be waiting patiently on the West Side for her hero's return.

Her brother Calvin nodded seriously when I announced that I should go to the Wild West when vacation came. "Of course you've got to go," he said, "even if it means the end of The Project."

"Well," I replied, "we can save The Project until I get back or until next spring."

"Well, I don't know," said Calvin gloomily.

The Project actually was only in its tentative stages. By then we both had read *Tom Sawyer* and *Huckleberry Finn*, and we had talked about continuing our assistance to the *Ladies' Home Journal* campaign to make America beautiful by dismantling enough billboards to construct a raft and then, with or without parental permission, float down our little river at high-water stage, finally making the great Mississippi and continuing perhaps even to New Orleans. We would live on fish, provender from riverside farms (as Huck and Jim did) and game we would shoot with an old twenty-two rifle Max Levine would sell me for three dollars. Calvin had saved about ten dollars from his allowance and I had fifteen or sixteen dollars put away from my paper-route money. But did either of us seriously believe we actually would run away from home once we had such a raft built? I don't know.

Anyhow, here was my opportunity to go to what I assumed was the old Wild West, plus the wonderful, long train ride, and while I did wish very much that my old pard Calvin was going along, there was no question about my going.

So I went, traveling most of the way with my head well out the open window, breathing the entrancing reek of soft-coal smoke, collecting cinders in my eyes and soot in my ears, munching crackerjack bought from the train butcher, sandwiches, bananas, and doughnuts from my lunch box—packed with loving care by my mother—drinking ice water from the chained graniteware cup at the water cooler, going to the "bathroom" and seeing the blur of railroad ties tearing beneath the seat, and writing down the name of every station for future reference in a small red-covered notebook.

My Uncle George and Aunt Jenny met me with their two-horse rig and I was somewhat surprised that Uncle George wasn't wearing chaps and a holstered revolver. Aunt Jenny, who was plump, pleasant and apple cheeked, exclaimed, "My goodness, where have you been riding—in the engine? I never saw so much soot on one face."

So Uncle George got my small, round-topped trunk from the baggage car, carrying it easily on his broad shoulder, and deposited it in the rear of the surrey, and Aunt Jenny asked how I left my family and I said fine, and wondered what they were doing at the moment, and Uncle George helped Aunt Jenny up to the front seat and I got into the back seat, and some boys about my age down to the depot to see the train come in looked at me in unfriendly fashion and spat on the platform and Uncle George stood at the horses' heads, saying, "It's all right, Bonnie, it's all right, Bert," as the train began to pull out with the red-plush seat I had lately occupied completely empty except perhaps for a few crumbs of crackerjack, and the horses acted as if they weren't quite convinced that it was "all right."

Then Uncle George untied the team, got nimbly into the front seat, lifted the buggy whip from its socket and said "Giddap."

He looked over his left shoulder at me and grinned. "Well, boy," he said, "mighty glad to have you with us. You'll have a great time."

When Uncle George said that I felt better. I had been looking at the little town's business district with its false-fronted, wooden buildings and didn't think much of it, although I surely would have been disappointed had the main street been filled with brick structures two and three stories high. This was supposed to be the Wild West.

We trotted briskly out of town and, for goodness sake, the country didn't look much different from back home, except that perhaps the road was a little yellower with sand and there were fewer trees. Fence posts carried blue tin signs advertising Pearline. Billboards advertised Bull Durham tobacco and Clabber Girl baking powder. Red barns were painted black on the road side as a background for Union Leader chewing tobacco signs.

Aunt Genevieve turned in the seat and in an effort to make conversation asked what grade I was in.

"The eighth," I said.

"Well," she said, "then you'll be in high school next fall."

"No, ma'am," I replied faintly. "I mean I'll be in the eighth grade next fall."

"Do you get good grades?"

"Well—pretty good in some things. I'm good in history and drawing, but not very good in arithmetic."

"Arithmetic is the most important thing for a businessman or a farmer. Have you decided what you're going to do when you grow up?"

"Well, Aunt Jenny, I'm afraid not."

Uncle George said gruffly, "Nobody decides what he's going to do when he's a young kid unless he's a genius and going to be a long-haired fiddler or poet or something. You're not a genius, are you, boy?"

"No, sir," I said, although of course I knew I *must* be some sort of genius or I shouldn't be the center of the universe; and I didn't like this sort of cross-examination and I felt unhappy and tired and homesick and I wished to goodness that I had never come.

After a couple of miles of travel through farming country, Uncle George turned in a lane toward a drab two-story farmhouse with a windmill and bigger barns and outbuildings to the rear and said, "Well, there's the shack."

My heart fell. "Yes," I said, knowing instantly that was the wrong thing to say. But this was a complete fraud. This was no cattle ranch with broad, unfenced range and cowboys. This was just an old farm like those back home, only less attractive than most. A few scraggy cottonwoods grew near the house and

[44]

in the rear was a vegetable garden, a chicken yard and back of that a pigpen. And, yes, there was a structure which I, living in a house with a bathroom, had come to call an "awful-awful" in early childhood. Had I expected a ranch house to have indoor plumbing? That was something I hadn't even considered. Although I surely had never pondered the problem, I supposed cowboys relieved themselves in any convenient spot, as boys did in the woods.

Even worse than all these things was a cornfield—a *cornfield,* of all things—stretching away on the other side of the road. The Wild West—what a fraud!

Uncle George drove around a stand of giant sunflowers, called "Whoa!" to the team and said, "You can go in, Jenny, and George will help me unhitch."

Aunt Genevieve, in her purple hat and veil and billowing black dress, twisted and backed down from the surrey with some effort, and then gathered up a number of packages she apparently had purchased before my train arrived. Then Uncle George drove into the barn. I wasn't much help in unhitching because some of the buckles on a harness should never, never be touched, and I didn't know which was which.

But after Bonnie and Bert were in their stalls and given measures of grain, we went to the house, Uncle George carrying my trunk again, and I my small satchel. On the back porch a black-and-white shepherd dog and two tiger cats were savoring the odor of frying meat and Uncle George said, "Hello, there, Maje, old boy," and the dog wagged his tail. He didn't speak to the cats.

In the kitchen a big red-haired girl was standing by the range frying what appeared to be pork steak in an enormous skillet. She was apparently about eighteen, three or four inches taller than I, and she had what the boys back home called prominent lungs.

"Hello, Nardelle," said Uncle George. "Miss Duffy, this is our nephew George."

The sturdy girl grinned broadly. "Howdy, kid," she greeted. "Behave yourself and you'll have no trouble with me." She was wearing a full-length apron and her muscular arms were bare to the elbow. With a pancake turner she flipped several slices of the frying meat.

Uncle George, with my trunk still on his shoulder, said to

me, "Nardelle lives down the road a piece, but she does a little work for Mrs. Mosby."

"Haw!" Nardelle scoffed. "A little, huh? Well, Miz Mosby's satisfied I earn my dough. You menfolks just keep out of our kitchen and we get along all right. I'd had supper ready by now only how'd I know the train wasn't late?"

"It was twenty minutes late," said Uncle George, starting off with my trunk.

"Well, see?"

I followed him up a flight of creaking stairs and down a hall to a small room where he deposited my trunk against the wall. It was growing dark and I couldn't see very well, but the place smelled musty, as if it had been closed off for a long time. There was one window that looked into a mass of cottonwood leaves. The walls were of unpapered white plaster and there was a narrow iron bed covered with a bright crazy quilt, a bureau with mirror and a splint-bottom chair.

"Well, boy, this will be your own private room," Uncle George said. "Thought some of putting you in with Fred, but I reckon you're used to sleeping alone and you won't be lonesome here, will you?"

"Oh no, sir," I said, feeling that I should be utterly miserable here.

"Oh, Fred!" Uncle George called.

"Yeah, Paw, I'll be right there," a bass voice boomed, and into the hall came a towering figure, well over six feet tall. He was slim, but his shoulder muscles filled out his red-jersey sleeves. He was wearing clean, blue, bibless overalls and stitched cowboy boots with spurs and his dark hair was roached and smelled like a barbershop. This was the cousin I was to "play" with.

"Howdy, Cousin George," he boomed, enveloping my hand with a giant paw. "Glad to see you."

"Glad to see you, Cousin Winfred," I squeaked.

"Forget the first part. It's Fred."

"You smell like Winnie," said his father. "You're not going fussing again tonight?"

"Naw. Just thought I'd ride in and shoot a little pool with the boys."

"Well, don't stay out until all hours. You got to get up in the morning."

[46]

We all went downstairs and Aunt Jenny ordered me to wash my hands and face at the kitchen sink where there was an iron pump and a washbasin. I followed her orders with tar soap, found a comparatively dry spot on the brown roller towel and then gave my hair a few licks with a red comb that lay on the draining board.

On the dining table with its red-and-white-checked cloth was a platter heaped with fried pork steak, a tureen of brown gravy, another platter with a mountain of fried potatoes, a bowl of string beans with bacon, another bowl of sliced tomatoes and onion drenched with vinegar, salt and pepper, a jar of cucumber pickles, a bottle of homemade chili sauce, a large glass dish of gooseberry sauce, a platter of hot baking-powder biscuits covered with a napkin, a form of home-churned butter perhaps two pounds in weight, a giant pie, about half a chocolate cake, a gallon pitcher of buttermilk and a huge coffee pot. I gathered that no matter what other disappointments might befall me here in Kansas, I'd not leave the Mosby table hungry. This was just supper, not dinner.

Nardelle, flushed of face and with a tendril of red hair hanging down her forehead, sat down with the family and bowed her head while Uncle George said the blessing, although, as I learned later, she considered Protestant prayers a presumptuous mockery. She was sitting opposite Cousin Fred, and as we were heaping our plates with provender she remarked, "Well, I see our little Winnie is going to give the town gals another treat."

"Look, Fat, Red and Ugly," said Cousin Fred, "you lay off that Winnie or one of these days I'll give you the what-for."

"You and what troop of calvary?" scoffed Nardelle.

"It's not calvary, stupid," said Fred. "It's cavalry. Calvary is where they crucified Christ."

"Ha!" Nardelle sneered. "Just look what's calling me stupid. Now, you listen to me, Mr. Wisenheimer, my pop was in the calvary and he calls it calvary and my brother Jim's in the calvary and he calls it calvary and who knows more about the calvary, a calvaryman or some half-baked farm kid that thinks he's a cowboy?"

"Now, children," said Aunt Jenny.

"Well, your paw must have been a great soldier against the

Spaniards," Cousin Fred said. "Nothing he couldn't lick except a pint of blind tiger juice."

Nardelle turned serious and perhaps even wistful. "Don't think a pint ever licked Pop," she said. "It was the quarts that give him trouble."

"Well, Nardelle," said Uncle George soothingly, "I think he may have that whipped now. He's a good man when he's sober, and he hasn't had a drink now in six weeks. He'll be out of jail in a couple more weeks and he swears he'll never touch another drop."

"Well . . ." The girl shook her head sadly. "Of course he's swore that before. If they'd just enforce a little law around here and close up those blind tigers . . ."

My uncle frowned. "Pretty hard to do that when Kansas is surrounded by wet states. Someday we'll have national prohibition to stop the manufacture of the stuff and then people like your father will be protected."

"Just looks like," said Nardelle, "that the sheriff and marshal and all them could close up the blind pigs if they wasn't getting paid off to keep 'em open. That's the way it looks like to Mom and me and if you voters would vote in some Democrats or Populists for a change maybe they'd clean up the town."

Cousin Fred laughed and said, "Just how silly can a gal get?"

Uncle George said gently, "The trouble with that is, Nardelle, that all the bootleggers and blind-tiger operators are Democrats themselves."

"And Irish to boot," said Cousin Fred.

"You ought to know, I reckon," the girl snapped. "You probably been in all of 'em."

"Now, now, Nardelle," said Aunt Jenny.

Nardelle's face was flushed. "Well, look, what's worse—selling a bottle of booze when you know you can get away with it, or being an officer that's paid to enforce the law and taking bribes not to enforce the law? That's what I want to know."

Uncle George was smiling. "I take it, Nardelle, that you think a Democratic politician would be less likely to take a bribe from a Democratic blind-tiger operator than a Republican politician?"

"Well, the Republicans sure enough ain't doing so good, and I think it wouldn't hurt to try a change, maybe with a Populist."

"No, girl, it's more than a local problem. It's got to be national prohibition and that will come eventually. But maybe that'll have to wait until they have national woman suffrage. I think we can count on women to vote out the saloons and distilleries."

"You can count on me when I get old enough to vote," said Nardelle.

I felt sorry for the girl, who obviously had suffered much, with her father in jail through what was called the demon rum, and I resolved that I surely would cast a ballot for national prohibition when I had the vote.

After supper Cousin Fred went galloping off toward town on his Texas pony Carlos, the women did the dishes, Uncle George repaired to the living room, lit a big kerosene lamp and lay on the couch with his pipe and *Farm and Fireside*. I wandered around away from the house in the twilight, threw crab apples at a fence post and cried a little from homesickness.

There was a stench from the hog pen and barnyard and I didn't know whether I could force myself to go to the outside privy. I didn't have to search for reality. Reality was there. I was enveloped by it and I hated it.

When bedtime came I knelt and said my prayers, begging God and Jesus to let me get away from this awful place as soon as possible. The bed was alien. That strange, musty odor was in my nostrils. I was tired, but I never would be able to sleep a wink in this unfriendly room. But I *did* go to sleep in a few minutes and I never even heard Cousin Fred come home.

Chapter 5

UNCLE GEORGE and Aunt Jenny found plenty of entertainment for me, such as weeding the garden, hoeing the corn, whitewashing the chicken house, feeding the chickens, slopping the hogs, currying the horses, bringing the milk cows in from the pasture and driving them back again and helping milk, although Cousin Fred was astonished that any boy my age didn't know intuitively how to strip a cow.

I was permitted to ride an ancient mustard-colored cayuse named Pete and was given a weather-beaten small saddle with the wooden tree showing through where the leather had worn completely away. Also Cousin Fred bequeathed me a pair of outgrown cowboy boots and rusty iron spurs which I wore almost constantly although the boots were too large for me and walking on the high heels was not very comfortable.

One Sunday afternoon, possibly at the suggestion of Uncle George, Cousin Fred took me prairie-chicken hunting. Of course I had no gun, but Fred had his Winchester pump, of which he was very proud.

It was one of those Kansas summer days with heaped-up turrets of cumulus clouds that might or might not presage a thunderstorm. We rode our fiery steeds up the dirt road past Duffy's place, technically together, although I sometimes had trouble keeping Cousin Fred in sight. A jab of the spur would put old Pete into an arthritic gallop for fifty yards or so and then he would subside with dreary sighs into a lope or even a walk. But Cousin Fred pulled up at a dry wash and waited for me. Then we turned left up the gully for a hundred yards or so and Fred dismounted, tied Carlos to a willow, and I followed suit with old Pete.

"If Carlos wasn't so damn gun shy we could hunt chickens from horseback, but I think they're using not far from here."

He drew his pump gun from the saddle boot and pushed five shells into the magazine.

"Maybe we should ought to brought old Major along," I said.

"Oh no. That old dog can't smell his own breakfast. A good trained bird dog might be a help, but we'll get all we need without a dog."

He pumped a shell into the barrel and stuck another into the magazine. As we climbed up the bank to a broad area of eroded land full of brush and tall, coarse grass, I noted that Cousin Fred hadn't lowered the hammer of his shotgun and, although I had read in *Outdoor Life* that no good hunter ever walked around with a cocked gun, I didn't feel like giving Cousin Fred a lecture. Instead, I tried to keep a little to the rear and away from the muzzle of the Winchester.

Walking in high heels and spurs in the brush and grass was difficult and I wished I had worn my regular shoes. But Fred didn't seem to be having any trouble, moving cautiously forward and lifting his feet high. Then there was a startling whirr and half-a-dozen big brown birds exploded into the air no more than fifteen feet ahead of us. The shotgun blasted *Wham!—click-clack—Wham!* And through the white cirrus cloud of black-powder smoke two of the birds plummeted down.

"Pretty good double," observed Fred. I ran forward, forgetting the menace of that cocked shotgun, and picked up one of the beautifully mottled prairie chickens, now sadly specked with bright blood. Fred retrieved the other and, hooking their legs together with a leather thong, gave them to me to carry.

Within fifty yards he got another, and then another. The field seemed to be fairly alive with these prairie grouse.

"Could I please try it?" I asked.

Cousin Fred squinted doubtfully at me. "Ever shoot a scattergun?"

"No, but I've shot a twenty-two rifle a lot and I guess there's not much diff."

"You'd be surprised. A twelve bore'd buck a kid your size pretty hard, and there's a lot of difference in shooting a twenty-two at a tin can and knocking down a flying bird. Those hens are traveling, and you got to remember to lead 'em."

I didn't know what he meant by that, but I said I'd sure like to try and Fred pumped a new shell into the barrel and handed the cocked shotgun to me.

"Well," I said, "I reckon I'd better let that hammer down."

"No, no. Those chickens go up fast and you got to be ready to let 'em have it. But be careful how you point that gun at me or your own foot. She's got a hair trigger."

So I hobbled through the weeds on my high heels, crouching slightly and glancing intently to left and right like an alert scout. Fred was now slightly behind me, carrying the slain prairie chickens, and I was alone for all practical purposes, a romantic plainsman right out of Owen Wister or Frederic Remington. The prairie wind was sweet and the beautiful shotgun was at ready in my hands, very real, as was the untilled field and the prospect of more grouse flying up, and I had a thought that perhaps the lure of hunting was the sense of acute reality it gave the hunter.

With the roar of a sudden windstorm through cottonwood trees, a flock of birds took flight only a few feet ahead of me. I threw up the gun, pointed and pulled the trigger. The blast was terrifying. I had failed to get the stock firmly against my shoulder and it smote me brutally, not only bruising my chest and shoulder, but also striking my cheek and nose. Through tears I saw one brown bird falling while the flock winged away.

"Gosh!" I exclaimed, and Cousin Fred was doubled over, howling with laughter. I felt blood trickling down from my nose, and mopped it with my red bandanna while I held the shotgun by its warm barrel.

"Well," Cousin Fred chortled, "you got one, but I'll bet a dime to a penny it wasn't the one you shot at."

There was nothing to say to that, because I hadn't shot at any particular bird, but in my excitement had just pointed in the general direction of the flock.

"Guess I should ought to warned you to hold the butt tight against your shoulder," Fred said, "but I took it for granted you knew that much."

We retrieved my bird and it was beautiful—but terribly dead despite its warmth, and I thought this was the first thing I ever killed except flies and mosquitoes and other bugs and maybe fish, if you could call it killing to take a catfish out of water so it died. Suddenly I felt like weeping as I looked at my pitiful victim, but staved it off and thought I was one whale of a frontiersman if I was going to be a crybaby over shooting a game bird, and I mopped my nose again with the bandanna and thought that the prairie chicken might be glad that its murderer got a bloody nose.

"Okay," said Cousin Fred, "we'd better get a couple more for good measure."

"Here," I said, handing him his gun, "I got one and that's enough for me the first time."

"Sure," he said, giving me the leather carrier with the dead birds. "You did all right for the first time, but of course a hunter could have got a double out of that flock and maybe three."

Cousin Fred did get a double out of the next flock, and we

went back to the horses and rode home with the birds bleeding against my overall leg.

Fried by Nardelle that evening, they were delicious with cream gravy for supper. And later I wrote a letter to old pard Calvin Campbell, giving a romanticized account of my life on the Great Plains, telling of my cayuse Pete, my cowboy boots and spurs, and about going prairie-chicken hunting with my cousin that afternoon. While I failed to report that there was only one shotgun and that I had fired it only once, I did inform him that a "twelve-bore kicks like a Missouri mule" and that my shoulder was so sore it was difficult to write. And that part was strictly true. Because I knew how he felt about killing wild things unnecessarily, I did admit some pangs at committing murder, but reconciled it by stating that on the "frontier" one had to do things for himself that the butcher did for him in the city. I closed by sending my best wishes to his mother and, most casually, to "Little Egypt," my preordained beloved.

While I told no actual lies in the letter, the essence of what I wrote was glamorized and untrue, and I knew it. But the writing of it made my life in Kansas seem much more interesting to me, and the underlying fiction endowed the truth with added reality. It was about this time when I discovered that writing down an account of even a dream (yes, even a garbled account) gave the dream a substance surpassing an *unrecorded* actual event. Perhaps that is the reason for the existence of so many keepers of diaries and other writers, professional and amateur.

But there are some events in everyone's life of such pronounced importance that every detail is clearly engraved in memory without being written down.

Such was the case of Nardelle Duffy. Mostly she treated me with the bantering contempt due a younger and inferior male by a superior female. Superficially, her attitude toward me was quite like that toward Cousin Fred, but with a subtle difference. Toward me there was an underlying kindliness absent in the epithets hurled at the big boy. If she called me a "lazy, stupid, awkward nincompoop without enough brains to pour pee out of a boot if the directions was on the heel," she spoke the words automatically, with no real emphasis. But with Fred, although she might be smiling, she spoke with a conviction that indicated no joke was intended.

[53]

One balmy summer evening after supper, when Cousin Fred had galloped away on Carlos to "give the town girls a treat" or to play pool or to forgather with his contemporaries, I was sitting on the back steps reading *The Black Cat*, one of the fiction magazines Cousin Fred favored. Inside the screen door was the murmur of conversation between Aunt Jenny and Nardelle and the clatter of dishes. Then Nardelle was saying, "Well, good night, Miz Mosby," and she was on the back porch, with her sunbonnet over her red hair.

I moved to one side of the steps with my magazine to let her by and she said, "You keep filling your head with that story-book nonsense of Winfred's and like as not you grow up like him."

"Oh, he's not so bad," I said.

"Bad enough. If you want to read, why don't you read true things instead of made-up stories?"

"Well," I said, "I generally read what I can get hold of."

"All right," she said, "you come on with me up to the house and I'll loan you a true book that'll make your hair stand on end. It's *Cole Younger and the James Boys* and it's the true story of Jesse and Frank James and Cole Younger and not just made up."

So I took *The Black Cat* back into the house and went up the road with Nardelle Duffy. A robin was chirruping his evening song in a cottonwood tree and farther away a meadow lark was calling plaintively, "Weep no more my la-dy," while a flock of blackbirds, mostly bronze grackles, but with a sprinkling of red-winged blackbirds, took off from the brush-grown fence to pump their way through the soft glow toward a night roost. The air was redolent from the newly cut hayfield that sloped down to the left.

Nardelle pushed her sunbonnet to the back of her head and took a deep breath.

"My," she said, "this is the nicest part of the day."

"Sure," I said, "now you don't have to do any more work."

Her sturdy elbow caught me in the ribs. "Look, small fry," she said with mock fierceness, "you trying to make out I'm lazy or something?"

Her elbow hurt, so I folded my arms and gave her a bump, "rooster-fighting" fashion.

"Well, you want to rooster fight, do you?" she exclaimed and, folding her arms, she gave me a bump that sent me a couple of feet sideways. I charged her with a more violent bump and she retaliated with one that put me into the ditch on the left side of the road and followed up with a bump that drove me into the brush that practically formed a hedge at the end of the meadow. I grabbed her in self-defense and my right hand accidentally caught a firm breast that obviously was covered by nothing except her blue gingham dress. Even in the throes of combat, that was curiously exciting.

"Oh, so you think you can wrestle, do you?" she breathed, and we stumbled clear through the brush into the mowed meadow beyond. Her sunbonnet now was hanging at the back of her neck, held by the strings under her chin, a strand of red hair was over her forehead, and the strange expression in her green eyes indicated that she wasn't playing any more, that I had a real fight on my hands to escape a drubbing; but still deep in my consciousness was my childhood misinterpretation of the Seventh Commandment, "Thou Shalt Not Slug a Female." I struggled with Nardelle, but was badly handicapped by my high-heeled boots and spurs. She was tremendously strong. Also, she outweighed me by many pounds. And presently we went down in the sweet-smelling stubble with Nardelle on top. She sat astride me and held my arms with steel fingers. Her teeth were white back of her parted red lips and she was breathing heavily from her exertions.

"He's such a cute little boy," she said, "and he thinks he's a big strong man. Ha!"

"Okay," I puffed, "you win."

"Ha, ha, ha," said Nardelle, bouncing on me.

Then she brought my hands to my chest, grasped both wrists with her capable right hand and started to tickle me with her left. I gurgled and wriggled and begged her to stop. "Big strong boy, eh?" she whispered, and the meadow scent mingled with that of Nardelle. I was strangely excited and for a moment ceased resisting when her tickling became more of a caress. Then her left hand took undue liberties and I cried in some alarm, "Hey, there, that's not fair, Nardelle, listen. Hey, that's playing dirty."

But Nardelle was astonishingly deft, and before I scarcely realized the situation, I was cooperating with a frenzy that almost matched hers, smothered by her but clasping her tightly, unimaginable ecstasy whipping through my body and exploding in blue sparks from the tips of my fingers and toes, with the pink clouds of eventide rolling across the clean Kansas Sky, and I all unaware of the hay stubble raking my bare bottom. Then there was panting exhaustion and emptiness and Nardelle's sulfurous breath, and, above all, astonishment.

And, while more blackbirds winged naturally across the evening sky, the whole world had changed. First among the puzzling things, and seemingly of paramount importance, was the fact that I was barefoot. I looked past Nardelle's gingham shoulder and sunbonnet and wriggled my toes to make sure. Up the slope, far up the slope, with the twin cannon mouths of their leather legs aligned nicely toward us, were my boots with the cast-iron spurs jammed firmly into the good Kansas soil. Nardelle had pumped me out of my boots and on down the hill.

Chapter 6

NARDELLE laughed until she cried as I recovered my boots and pulled them on. But little was said until we were approaching her house on the road, walking with a good space between us. Then she cleared her throat and said, "Listen to me, George, don't you ever dare tell that Fred Mosby about *that.*"

"My goodness," I said, "I'm not likely to be telling *anybody*. What do you think?"

"Just see that you don't." Her voice was grim. "I think I'd just kill you if you did."

I looked at her flushed face and believed her.

When we had gone up the three crooked steps to the sagging porch she didn't invite me into the house. "Wait here," she ordered, "and I'll get you the book."

The screen door was patched with two pieces of cheesecloth, and the smell of cooked cabbage came from the kitchen. An old yellow dog waddled up to me wagging his thick tail, and I patted his head. He grinned and panted in appreciation and his breath was fetid. I turned and looked at the sad, dying sunset above the skimpy row of mock-orange trees on the horizon.

Then Nardelle was pushing the door open with her foot. "Here's that book," she said, with curious formality. "Hope you like it."

"Thank you," I said, taking the battered volume. "Well, good night."

"Good night," she said, letting the screen door close.

I turned to go and one of my spurs caught on the top step, sending me in an awkward plunge down to the cinder path where I barely retained my footing. Nardelle, at the door, laughed. "Those spurs will be the death of you yet," she remarked.

I giggled in embarrassment, said good night again and went on my way toward home. I thought about John Wilkes Booth's spur catching on the flag draping the presidential box when the assassin leaped to the stage of Ford's theater. Spurs could be dangerous to people, no matter what their mission. I thought that someone should invent a spur that folded back out of the way when the wearer was not on horseback. I tried to think of any manner of things unrelated to that inner aching void which once held my more or less innocent soul. But how could I help thinking of my grievous sin when it enveloped me like a leaden shroud?

My booted feet dragged in the dusty road. How could I ever face my decent uncle and aunt? The sin of sins must be written on my face in letters of scarlet. It was growing dark and perhaps they might not notice tonight in the lamplight. But what of tomorrow? And the next day and the next? Once smirched by the tar of immorality, the mark could not be erased. When I went home it would be there for my mother and father to see. And Laura. And Calvin Campbell. And even Little Egypt no doubt would sense that something essentially and deeply evil in my nature had been brought to the surface.

For a moment I tried to place all blame on Nardelle. I spoke aloud, "Well, darn Nardelle, anyway. Yes, *damn* her." But I knew I was being dishonest with myself when I said it. Without my enthusiastic cooperation the real sin never could have been committed. Had I been a really decent boy, nothing would have occurred except the humiliation of having a big strong girl take shocking liberties with my person.

Stumbling along the road with *Cole Younger and the James Boys* in my hand, I could see that no doubt Nardelle had been only an agent of the Lord to test me, and that I had been found sadly wanting. I had failed the test and miserably. I was a gross creature at heart, as bad, surely, as the worst of the profane tobacco-chewing tough boys from across the tracks. Whatever great purpose had been my preordained goal, it could be forgotten now, for I had been tested and rejected. Venus glowed white in the western sky and the yellow lamplight in the downstairs windows of the Mosby house was unfriendly. The darkening Kansas world about me was sharply real and the reality was overwhelmingly sad. There was a new and accusing note to the song of the katydids in the tall grass and suddenly they were not calling *"Katee-did"* but "goin'-to-hell, *goin'-to-hell*" and a tree toad in the cottonwoods took up the refrain, "Hell, hell, hell," and of course I *was* going to hell because I had committed the unforgivable sin.

In the living room Uncle George was taking a nap on the couch and Aunt Genevieve was in the base rocker by the big lamp on the marble-topped center table darning a basketful of stockings and socks. As I entered the room fearfully, she placed a finger to her lips and nodded toward Uncle George. I sat in the nearest chair and took off my boots. It was dark enough there so she couldn't see my sin-ravished face, but yet light enough for me to see there still was dirt in the rowels of my spurs and to suffer one more reminder. I sat there silently with *Cole Younger and the James Boys* on my lap, not daring to move into the circle of lamplight where I could read until Uncle George sat up, yawned, stretched and said, "Well, I guess it's time to wake up and go to bed. Come on, Jenny."

"No," she said, "I've got to finish these socks. Beats all how you men wear so many holes, and it does seem you'd have a little consideration and cut your toenails."

I spoke up faintly from my corner. "I haven't been wearing any holes because I've been beating the government."

"What do you mean?"

"Well, I haven't got any socks and there's a tax on stockings and when you wear your boots or shoes without stockings they call it beating the government."

"Never heard of such a thing."

"Well, that's what the boys call it back home."

"Ridiculous. Never heard of such a thing, and I know there's no tax on stockings or socks in Kansas or I'd have heard of it. If you don't wear socks or stockings you get the bed sheets dirty."

I said, "I just thought I would save dirtying and wearing holes in my stockings."

Aunt Genevieve sniffed. "It's a heap easier for Nardelle to wash a pair of stockings than a couple bed sheets."

I winced at mention of Nardelle and then said faintly, "All right, Aunt Jenny, I'll put on some stockings tomorrow."

After we went to bed I lay wide-eyed and worrying long after I heard Carlos' hoofs in the barnyard and Cousin Fred's bootless feet coming softly up the stairs.

Suddenly the simmering horror of my sin bubbled sharply with a new thought.

Suppose Nardelle had a baby!

It was my understanding that a boy was not mature enough for procreation until after he was fourteen, but just suppose I was a trifle precocious? There were a few signs which indicated to me that this might be possible, but I didn't know. I just didn't know. Between adults, I assumed that conception was almost inevitable with sexual intercourse, because owners of stallions and bulls advertised, guaranteeing a foal or calf with a breeding.

Nardelle must be an idiot to take such a risk even with a thirteen-year-old boy. But then I had heard of shotgun weddings that came sometimes from a young woman luring a weak-willed youth into this sort of intimacy, and then the girl's father, shotgun in hand, forced a marriage. Suppose Mr. Duffy, now out of jail and sober, appeared with a shotgun and a Catholic priest, demanding that I marry Nardelle to give her child a name and I should be a married man and a father by the time I was fourteen years old—married to big, homely, red-haired and red-faced Nardelle and separated from my true love and preordained bride Little Egypt for life. And, oh, the disgrace of it! How could my mother and father and Laura stand it? I cried a little into my hard pillow in shame and self-pity. I couldn't stand it. I simply couldn't stand it.

Perhaps I had better make some excuse and go back home immediately. But if it became necessary for me to pay for my sin in the worst possible material way, it would be better to be confronted by Mr. Duffy and his shotgun at the Mosbys' than at home.

I wondered how long it took for a woman to determine she was with child. From *The Old Farmer's Almanac* I knew that the period of gestation for a mare was about eleven months, for a cow about ten months, for a dog about two months and for a human woman about nine months. But it said nothing about how long a period must pass before the owner of a mare or cow could call on the advertiser of a stallion or bull to make good his guarantee, let alone how long it took for a woman exposed to conception to determine whether the seed had taken root. Perhaps it would take several months, but perhaps her woman's instinct told her within a few days. I hoped for the latter, feeling sure I should die of anxiety otherwise.

But suppose I did die? No doubt my life was ruined anyhow, so perhaps it would be better if I did die soon. Perhaps it would be better if I borrowed Cousin Fred's pump gun and had an accident.

It seemed quite obvious to me, inasmuch as nothing seemed to exist except through my own consciousness, that I had been created for some great mission on earth. And now I had been tested and found to be too weak and corrupt for God's great purpose; I was culled and discarded like an apple with a rotten core.

Finally I fell into a troubled sleep, waking shortly after dawn with aching legs and a lump of alum in my stomach. At chores before breakfast Cousin Fred said, "Hey, kid, you look kind of dragged out and peaked. You been playing with yourself or has old Nardy got to you?"

"I'm all right," I said, "but I wouldn't be if I stayed out all night like you."

"I ain't got circles under my eyes," said Fred.

I suppose I flushed, for Cousin Fred guffawed and said, "Take my advice and don't fool around that big redhead. She could kill you."

Back in the kitchen, Nardelle didn't even look at me, and for several days I tried my best to avoid her, although she threw me a sly wink a couple of times.

Then one day I was cornered and she spoke very casually, "Hi, kiddo, you read that book?"

I cleared my throat. "Well, I'm reading it. I don't think it's hardly an excuse for the James boys to turn train robbers at all, but you can see how they'd be pretty mad about the Pinkertons throwing that bomb in the window and blowing off their mother's hand."

"You got to consider one thing," Nardelle said emphatically. "They just robbed the rich and they give it to the poor. Jesse didn't have no dough left when that stinking Bob Ford murdered him, and Frank went to the penitentiary. You don't see them sending any of the rich folks to the pen for robbing the poor and keeping it. You got to consider that."

"You in favor of bank robbers?" I asked.

"No, but you just got to consider. It takes a brave man to hold up a train or a bank. Any rich coward can foreclose a mortgage on poor folks."

"Foreclosing a mortgage isn't against the law when the people don't pay when the time comes."

"Sure, sure. That's just it. There's one law for the poor and another law for the rich."

"I think you're a Socialist," I said.

"Well, maybe I am and what of it?"

She reached out a quick hand and tickled my ribs.

"Hey," I said, moving back. "Don't."

But in spite of myself I grinned when I said it.

It was only a few days later when I got the awful letter from old pard Calvin Campbell. It read:

DEAR OLD PARD: I surely wish you were here to talk to, and the best substitute is to write you a letter because a terrible tradgedy has come to us and I can't understand how God could possibly let such a thing happen.

I know you will be very sad also to hear that my dear little sister Margaret is dead. It don't seem possible, but it is true.

Just night before last Margaret woke up in the middle of the night with a bad stomache ache and woke up Mother who gave her some oil of peppermint but it got worse and finally Father called Dr. Davenport who said Margaret had acute appendiseedus (I hope that is spelled right) and must have an immediate operation.

So Mother woke me up at about 5 A.M. in the morning to tell me they were taking her to the hospital and I just had a glimpse while Father was carrying her bundled in a quilt and maybe not even conscience but moaning a little to the carriage.

Dr. Davenport operated right away but it was too late because the appendis had ruptered and she died a couple hours afterwards.

I think Father is taking it even worse than Mother who is practically in a nervous breakdown and I never felt so bad and lost in my life. I don't know how we are going to stand the funeral in the church and graveyard tomorrow.

She was a wonderful little sister and I keep thinking about how I used to tease her and call her "Little Egypt" and all that and it makes me sorrier than ever.

Please write me soon.

Your Old Pard,
CAL.

I read Calvin's letter sitting on the back porch right after the R.F.D. man had put it in the Mosbys' box. I had been hoeing the kitchen garden, but now I left the abandoned hoe and went to my room, closed the door, threw myself on my bed and wept.

I never, never could tell old pard Cal, but I knew why Little Egypt had died. Her death was simply part of the general picture of my rejection. My sin had proved me unworthy of my mysterious great mission and especially unworthy of my beloved preordained bride, so the jealous God of the Holy Writ had taken her to Heaven. In effect I was guilty of Little Egypt's murder.

Shaken with sobs, I prayed God for the forgiveness I knew never could be granted and begged to be relieved from my wretched life.

But God saw fit neither to lift my sorrowing soul from Kansas nor to comfort me in my culpability, and after a while I rose, poured water from the pitcher into the rose-garlanded washbasin and washed my tear-streaked face. Then I put on my broadbrimmed straw hat and went back out into the sunshine to pick up the very tangible hoe with its tangible weathered gray handle, dark and smooth toward the end from the perspiration and pressure of my own palms and those of various Mosbys, and continued my slaughter of God's tangible and thrifty weeds that menaced the existence of the Mosbys' less thrifty string beans. My shadow was short and very black, as black as my conscience, as black as my bitter soul.

Nothing in the world mattered any more. A couple of days later Nardelle found occasion to lure me into the haymow and taught me the orthodox method of sex relationship. She laughed scornfully at my apprehensions.

"Don't flatter yourself, kid," she said. "You ain't man enough yet to be dangerous."

This experience settled it. Being a confirmed sinner was somehow more comfortable than carrying the burden of unknown responsibilities over the stony road of rectitude. Having lost everything, I had no more to lose. Therefore I became almost happy before I returned home.

Chapter 7

THAT fall old pard Cal Campbell was in high school and inevitably somewhat patronizing to a mere eighth grader, giving me the impression that he felt we now were living in separate generations. This was annoying to me when I considered how he little realized in his innocence that I not only had become an adult, but an adult with a heart blackened by sin.

We didn't talk about the death of Little Egypt. He did not seem disposed to mention her and my conscience was far too sore to bring up the subject. His interest in my descriptions of Kansas was perfunctory and seemed merely polite. On the other hand I was bored by his perhaps unconscious air of superiority as he related the esoteric routine of secondary-school education, appraising the teachers of elementary algebra, Latin, English and zoology. He obviously had fallen in love immediately with tall, rangy Miss Wills, who taught zoology and botany and who had recognized a kindred spirit in old pard Cal.

I was moody and moony and wasn't doing too well, even in the simple world of the eighth grade. At home a curious female alliance seemed to have deepened between Laura and our mother that closed a door on me. I could even imagine they were aware of my vileness, so I accepted the role of pariah and retreated further into my shell, brooding hopelessly over the sad, unreal world. I am not sure that I seriously contemplated actual suicide, but I was so far gone in not caring what happened that several times I recklessly put on my right stocking and shoe first in the morning and was surprised and perhaps disappointed when no real catastrophe followed such a rash challenge to fate.

Coming home from school one afternoon, however, I thought my morning's indiscretion had caught up with me. I was walking alone carrying my books when a boy from across the tracks called Buck Christopher came up from behind on a battered old bicycle. He called gruffly, "Get the hell out of the way, you sleepy bastard."

Buck Christopher was a short, burly, black-shocked lad with a jutting chin and a wide, slit mouth usually stained at the corners with chewing tobacco. He was reputed to be fifteen or sixteen years old and to have whipped several grown men in fist fights. He had chased me on a number of occasions and I was terribly afraid of him. But I heard myself yelling the current witticism of contempt, "Aw, go way back and sit down!"

Buck braked his bicycle to a stop, dropped it sprawling on the sidewalk and stalked menacingly toward me. His voice was harsh and husky. "What did you say?" he demanded.

"Well," I said, mildly, "it's against the law to ride bikes on the sidewalk. You think you own the sidewalk?"

His thin mouth spread into a grin. "Ha—you want to fight, do you?"

"No, I don't want to fight. But you got no right to call me a bastard."

"I'll call you anything I want, and what you going to do about it?"

By then several other boys had come up and stood wide eyed, well out of range of the impending massacre. A thought flashed that if they would only join me we might destroy this perennial peril, but I knew they wouldn't. I also thought that now was the time to turn swiftly and run for all I was worth because I knew from experience that Buck couldn't catch me. But I didn't.

Buck took off his cap and threw it down, stalking stiff-legged toward me. "You skinny bastard," he drawled, "I can lick you with one hand tied behind me."

"Probably," I said, "but what good will it do you?"

He struck me on the chest, not too hard, and I stepped backward, spilling my books on the ground. Not a word came from the other boys.

"Now, look, Buck," I exclaimed, raising my hands. With that he slapped me sharply in the face with his open hand and my reaction was automatic. All my pent-up fears, anger, resentment and disgust exploded in one swift right-hand punch that caught Buck Christopher on his jutting jaw. His head snapped back, his mouth opened, his black eyes stared and he collapsed face down on the brick sidewalk. He twitched convulsively for two or three seconds, then rolled over, and his face was smeared with dirt from the sidewalk. Through my astonishment came the thought that he now would get up and really murder me, and I had better start running. But I didn't.

One of the other boys spoke huskily, "Well, my gosh!"

Buck twisted and brought himself to his knees, staring at me with unbelieving eyes. Then, whether he was fifteen or sixteen years old or not, whether he had whipped grown men or not, he began bawling like a very little boy. He scrambled to his feet and I squared off desperately with my fists raised. But the formidable, fearsome Buck Christopher grabbed up his cap, stumbled to his streakily blue-painted old bicycle and went off toward the railroad tracks, pushing the bike and sobbing loudly.

"Well, my gosh," a boy said again. I looked at them and they were Orville O'Neill, Max Levine and Fred Snider. Fred Snider, the best all-round athlete in our class, said, "Golly, George, that beats anything I ever saw in my whole life. Ever'body in town scared to death of old Buck and you knock him out like a prizefighter, and just one punch."

However astonished Fred and the other boys may have been, they weren't as astonished as I. I knew I had been very lucky and there was a definite possibility that Buck wasn't as tough as his reputation. Also, could it be that God had relented just a little in his rejection of an unregenerate sinner and endowed my fist with Almighty power? The fist itself hurt where it had come in contact with Buck's jaw, and I rubbed the knuckles.

"Well," I said, "I hope it teaches that roughneck a lesson not to go round calling people dirty names."

"What gets me," Fred Snider said, "is how you could do it. You don't look like you had so much muscle. You been getting boxing lessons someplace?"

"No." I shrugged my shoulders. "But after all I put in the summer working on a ranch out West."

"Well, gosh," said Orville O'Neill. He stepped up and took hold of my arm and I tensed the biceps. He shook his head. "It's not so awful big," he said, "but it's sure hard."

I allowed Max and Fred to feel my suddenly famous right arm then, and Fred said, "Even so, I never heard of a kid our age knocking anybody down and out with one punch. Look, George, if you ever get mad at me let's kind of settle it, you know, without fighting?"

By then I was feeling pretty heroic so I chuckled and said, "Don't worry, Freddie, I never fight anybody unless he forces me to."

So I picked up my books and went on home and up to my room and instead of doing my homework started reading a most fascinating novel called *The Little Shepherd of Kingdom Come* which I had drawn from the library. My right hand hurt and was beginning to swell across the knuckles.

Presently I heard steps on the stairs and my mother stood in the door. "George," she said, "I want to speak to you."

"Yes, ma'am." I sat up and closed the book on a finger.

"Mrs. McConnell just told me something disturbing, George."

"Oh?"

"She was out in her yard and a poor boy from across the tracks came along crying bitterly and Mrs. McConnell asked him what was wrong and the little boy said George Chalmers had hit him in the face as hard as he could."

"Oh, that Mrs. McConnell!" I blurted. "That *little* boy is a very tough kid about fifteen or sixteen years old who goes around picking fights and he hit me twice before I hit him just once and knocked him down."

"There must have been some reason for him to hit you."

"Well, there you go. I'm always in the wrong and everybody else is always in the right."

[66]

"George, that's no tone of voice to use to your mother."

"Well, I can't help it. It just looks like everybody's against me whatever I do even if it's just defending myself against a tough bully that everybody is afraid of, when he calls me a dirty name and hits me first."

She drew her lips tight and placed her hands on her hips with elbows forward.

"George," she said, "I think your father should have a talk with you."

"Fine," I said, "I'm always glad to have a talk with Jerome V. Chalmers at any time."

"None of your impertinence, young man."

"Well, for goodness sake, Mama. Just anything I say. Look, here I say I'll be glad to talk with my father and I'm being impertinent."

"It wasn't so much what you said but the way you said it."

So my father talked with me that evening, and after I had told him the truth about the affair with Buck Christopher, he said quietly, "Well, George, I don't feel very happy about my son engaging in street brawls like a common hoodlum."

"But, Papa, he called me a dirty name and hit me first."

"If you'd have ignored him, he wouldn't have hit you. If you show you're too proud to notice what such ruffians say, he and other people would respect you."

I shook my head. "Papa, I just don't think so. I think the other kids respect me more because I socked him good and hard and sent him off bawling. Everybody has been scared of Buck Christopher, and I have too, but now they see he's just a big bully. Before this I've run from Buck Christopher, but I just got tired of running and being a coward and this time I stood up to him and licked him easy."

"It's not being a coward to be a gentleman and to refuse to engage in fist fights on the street. What would you think of me if I had a fist fight on the street?"

"Well, what would you do if some man slapped your face?"

"I hope," my father said, solemnly, "that I'm a good enough Christian to turn the other cheek, and I hope that I shan't be shamed and humiliated in the future by hearing of my son engaging in any more street brawls."

"Well—I hope so."

[67]

"Now," he went on, "there's one more thing I don't understand. Why did this boy call you a name in the first place?"

"Why, I told you, Papa. He was riding that old bicycle on the sidewalk, which is strictly against the law and—"

"I know. But why did he call you a name when he asked you to give him room?"

"That's just the kind of a kid he is—mean. And I guess he just doesn't like me."

My father nodded. "That's what I'm getting at, George. I've noticed, myself, and your mother spoke to me about it— for some time, and I think it's been ever since you got home from Kansas, you've been going around pretty much with a surly expression on your face. What's wrong, Son? Tell me, aren't you happy here in your home?"

"Yes, sir, I guess I'm happy enough. I didn't know I looked surly. For goodness' sake."

"Well, here's something you should think about. Surly people just aren't liked. If you look pleasant, you'll be surprised at how different the world looks. Look sour and other people are sour at you. Look pleasant and people are pleasant with you. A nice smile wins friends but a scowl makes enemies. Don't you know that?"

"Maybe. But you don't see any pictures of Jesus or Abraham Lincoln with big grins on their faces."

My father frowned himself, and very effectively. "By the lord Harry," he said, "that's practically a sacrilege and I'm shocked at you. Jesus and Lincoln had the sins and the sorrows of the world on their shoulders. Do you think you're Jesus or Lincoln?"

"No, sir. I'm George Chalmers."

"Don't be impertinent."

"Papa, for goodness sake, every time I say anything to Mama she says I'm impertinent. Now you say I'm impertinent because I say I'm George Chalmers. I am George Chalmers, ain't I? Or am I some orphan you just picked up?"

"You're my son, all right, and that's why I want you to act like a gentleman and not like a surly street urchin with a chip on your shoulder. Now I want you to promise me that you'll try to be more pleasant with everyone, including your family, and once you get into the habit, you'll be surprised at how much brighter the world will look."

[68]

So, with some misgivings, I promised to try to be more pleasant. And for the rest of the evening, when I caught my father's eye I gave him a grin. And he grinned back.

Chapter 8

THERE was a girl in my eighth grade who reminded me of Nardelle Duffy. Of course she was not nearly as large as Nardelle and her hair was brown instead of red. But Annette Shaw had the same country-girl walk, her cheeks were ruddy, her blue eyes were bold and challenging like Nardelle's and she exuded femaleness to a remarkable degree for a thirteen-year-old child.

I wondered about Annette, especially after a vivid erotic dream in which she was strangely combined with Nardelle. Braver boys than I tried to kid Annette in crude, small-boy fashion and she met their poor witticisms with cold contempt. So her manner as well as her appearance gave me the impression that Annette, like myself, was an earthy sophisticate with no time for children.

She lived, I knew, on a small farm south of town and usually walked to and from school. It seemed that the obvious thing would be to ask if I could walk home with her, but that was impossible because I had to go for my papers when school let out. I had lent my paper route for the summer to a boy named Harley Richards and got it back only after an argument not only with Harley but his mother, who insisted I had *given* him the route. Paper routes were valuable and were sold instead of given away, I told Mrs. Richards, and it was only through my great generosity that I had lent my property for nothing, and I suggested that she go speak to the publisher if she didn't believe me, and at last she surrendered reluctantly, calling me an Indian giver who would come to no good.

I employed what I considered a subtle approach to my campaign of seduction, looking at Annette whenever I got a chance, with a faint understanding smile. Her reaction to this varied. Sometimes she'd lift her head and glare at me in return. Well,

Nardelle would have done that. Other times she'd merely curl her full upper lip and look away. But, I told myself, this showed that she was aware of my interest, and possibly why.

Then one warm Saturday morning, when I was out collecting for my paper route, I met Annette right in front of Hill's Pharmacy on Main Street.

"Hello, Annie," I said cheerfully.

"My name's Annette," she snapped. "And Miss Shaw to you."

I nodded my head at the cool twilight inside the drugstore, where overhead fans turned lazily. "Okay, Miss Shaw," I said, "I'd be happy if you'd join me in a delicious ice-cream soda." I was standing in front of her and I said this with an air of *noblesse oblige*. After all, my social standing as a town boy was infinitely higher than that of any chubby farm girl with cow manure under her heels. It surely never occurred to me that she would consider our positions exactly opposite because she stood near the head of our class and I close to the foot.

"No, thank you," she said, and started to move around me.

"Oh, come on," I said, and took her arm.

She wrenched it away and stamped her foot. "Wake up, Sleepy, and hear the birdies sing," she said. "You're a stupid fool, and if you don't quit staring at me in school you'll be sorry." Then she was gone, loping down Main Street in her loose, farm-girl stride, and I looked at myself in Hadley's Emporium window and saw a gangling lout with oversize mouth, ears and nose, and I felt crushed and humiliated and very ashamed of my project. And I quit staring at Annette Shaw in school. She really wasn't a bit attractive, and what was there about the ability to do square root quickly and to diagram sentences to make her so proud of herself? She was, after all, just a smaller, younger Nardelle with just one purpose in the world and some country jake could have it for all of me.

Well, to a considerable extent I still associated sex only with the lower classes and with depraved wretches like myself even though I had abandoned the quasi-immaculate theory of reproduction old pard Calvin had convinced me the better-class decent humans employed. So it came as a definite shock when the cause of all that mumbo jumbo between my mother and sister was finally revealed. Laura was to be married in October. Ralph Sterling was coming from Colorado and they were to live in Denver.

Thought of sex in connection with Laura was so foreign that it was almost a shuddering horror. Slim, cool, quiet Laura, with her practically boyish figure, couldn't have been much different from Nardelle and still remain a member of the same species. Would she and Ralph Sterling or wouldn't they? Well, if they wanted children they probably would. But I didn't like to think about it and I resolutely pushed the thought from my mind.

At that time I didn't have a very clear picture of Ralph although he had called on Laura and had taken her places many times while they were going to high school and later to the normal, where he studied bookkeeping. There were other young men, and to me he was one of the least impressive. I had called him Four-Eyes because few young men wore glasses in those days. I remembered that he was painfully polite and always rose to his feet when my mother or any other woman entered the room. My mother thought that was wonderful, and not only squelched my scoffing at the practice but demanded that I follow Ralph's example.

Ralph had moved to Denver to take a job in a bank where his uncle was president, and now that he had risen to the important post of cashier, he had bought a house and was coming back to marry Laura. Apparently they had been corresponding all the time since he had left, and apparently a lot of things could be going on around me without my knowledge. I was somewhat indignant about it.

So there was a golden Saturday afternoon when I had finished collecting on my paper route and had planned to go to the high-school football game, but under firm orders from my mother I was moodily raking leaves from the back lawn, even though there were still plenty of leaves on the trees that came down in eccentric scarlet and chrome showers with every breeze. The house was spotless inside and out for the home-coming of the great Ralph and now the lawn must be the same way. I was muttering to myself that the whole thing was a big fraud, trying to make out that Laura was such a hot housekeeper, but he'd soon find out that it was Mama who was the neat house-keeper and that Mama even had to nag Laura about her own room. Then some dry leaves crunched under footsteps and there was Ralph Sterling himself.

"Look, old man," he said jovially, "talking to yourself is a bad sign. Next you'll be asking questions out loud and answering them."

"Well," I said, "howdy." He shook hands vigorously and his small, white hand was surprisingly strong. I said I had no clear picture of Ralph, but I would have recognized him even if I hadn't known he was coming although he had grown a small black mustache and was shorter than I remembered. As a matter of fact, he was no taller than I except for the tall-crowned derby hat and that meant Laura would be at least as tall as he with ordinarily high heels. His rimless nose glasses sparkled before his round brown eyes and were attached to a gold loop hooked around his left ear by a fine gold chain. His lips were rather full and red, and when he smiled the black mustache and a small gold filling accentuated the whiteness of his teeth. He wore a tall wing collar and a figured four-in-hand tie with an opal tiepin. I learned later that the opal was his birthstone and that he scorned the belief that they were unlucky. His blue serge suit was well-fitted with heavily padded shoulders, the vest was piped with white and a Masonic charm was suspended from his watch chain. Completing the ensemble were glittering patent-leather button shoes with very pointed toes.

"Well," I said, "Laura was expecting you. Does she know you're here?"

He laughed. "Oh, my goodness, yes," he said. "She met my train with my mother."

I leaned on my rake and studied him. "Well," I said, "I hear you're going to get married. Congratulations."

He chuckled. "Yes, George, I'm a very lucky man. I've been in love with your sister for many years and she has finally consented to become my bride. And now that we're going to be brothers, I hope you and I will become the best of friends."

"Brothers?" I asked. "Oh, yes, brother-in-laws. Well."

"Yes, George, you're not losing a sister; you're gaining a brother."

"Well, that's fine," I said, "except that my sister is moving away."

He chuckled again. "That's true, of course. But you can come out and visit us. We're going to have a spare room and you'd love Colorado and Denver with the magnificent snow-capped Rampart Range to the west. The air is so clear and dry it's like wine."

"I don't drink wine," I said.

"Neither do I," said Ralph, "but that's just a saying in Colorado—the air is like wine."

"Well," I said, "I've never seen a mountain, but I'd like to climb one. Have you climbed a Rocky Mountain?"

"No—not a high one. But I've been up Pikes Peak on the cog road, and that's fourteen thousand, one hundred and ten feet high, nearly three miles high."

I whistled. "My, wasn't that scary?"

"No, not really. But you feel a little dizzy up there because the air is so thin. It isn't good for old people or people with weak hearts to go up Pikes Peak, but the view from the top is simply magnificent and you can see practically to Kansas."

"Well," I said, "I spent last summer on a ranch in Kansas."

Then Laura came to the back door and called Ralph in and I went back to raking leaves.

I had to get a new suit for Laura's wedding and to pay for it with paper-route money because my father had so many expenses in connection with the wedding and reception. This annoyed me because I didn't believe I needed a new suit and because it would cost enough to buy a beautiful Seroco camera from Sears, Roebuck, complete with red-leather bellows, genuine "rapid rectilinear" lens, varnished maple tripod, three double plateholders, twelve plates, three developing trays, a bottle each of developer and hypo, a kerosene red lantern, a box of photographic print paper and a printing frame.

But they broke down my resistance and I agreed that I would buy the suit provided I could have long pants.

"No," said my mother firmly, "you certainly are not going to have long pants yet. You're still a little boy and you'd look freakish in long pants."

"Oh, rats," I said, "lots of people no bigger than I am wear long pants. Just for instance, Ralph Sterling himself isn't any bigger than I am."

My mother interrupted me. "Of course Ralph is taller than you, and it doesn't matter how tall you are, you still look like a little boy and you'd look very freakish in long pants. That settles it."

So my mother went with me to the Bon Marché and selected a blue serge with two pairs of knickers and a vest with white piping. I objected to that.

[73]

"Why, George," my mother said, "that makes it look very neat."

"Oh, rats," I said, "and besides that white will get dirty right away." I resolved that I'd *see* to it that it got dirty right away.

"George, I wish you wouldn't say 'rats' all the time. It sounds vulgar."

"Oh," put in the clerk, "that white piping is just the thing now, and it's quite easy to take off and wash."

The suit took eight dollars and ninety-five cents of my hoarded money, more than four weeks' return from my paper route, but the Bon Marché threw in a fine pair of red suspenders with FIRE LADDIE stamped on the buckles.

Laura and Ralph were married in our church by the Reverend Mr. Reynolds amid decorations of autumn leaves and cosmos, and Laura looked practically pretty in her yards and yards of white wedding gown and veil.

Our house was oppressively full of shrieking people at the reception, people eating wedding cake and ice cream, and the air was sickeningly heavy with the odors of sachet, cologne, cinnamon and witch hazel. I had cranked out two big freezers of the ice cream, in our freezer and one borrowed from the McConnells, and, certainly for the first time in my life, I grumbled about making ice cream.

"I'll sure enough be glad when this shindig's over," I said to my mother. "But I guess I'm lucky you're not making me be flower girl."

"Hush," she said. "It'd seem that you'd be glad to do a little for a sister who's been as kind to you as Laura has."

I didn't say anything, but tried to hark back to when Laura had been kind to me, and I had no trouble at all in that. Of course she had been kind to me, and if I was honest with myself, I realized I had little against her except deserting her family for Four-Eyes Sterling, in my catalogue a sissy little speenort.

Well, Ralph had old Tod McLain's hack waiting outside during the reception, and presently Laura appeared, no longer in her wedding gown but in her new gray traveling suit and hat with a corsage of violets, and her eyes were bright and her cheeks were flushed as she kissed me good-bye and said, "Now you be a good boy, Georgie, and don't forget to write to me," and I promised I wouldn't.

Then Laura and Ralph, arm in arm, were running down the front steps in a shower of rice and shrieks and Tod McLain drove them to the depot to catch the five-oh-four with an array of tin cans, buckets, old shoes and a cardboard sign JUST MARRIED on the rear of the hack. Laura had asked tensely that we not go to the depot to see them off, so my mother and father stood on the porch watching the hack move down the street with the tin-ware clattering behind, and some of the reception guests still shrieking, and there was a fixed smile on my mother's flushed face while she said good-bye to some of the people who probably were going to hurry down to the depot to embarrass the bride and groom more, and then we all, including several of the guests, went back in the house and my mother still had that strained smile on her face, but my father was looking a little grim. Finally they were all gone and my mother sat down on the leather couch, put her face in her hands and began to sob. My father sat beside her, put his arm around her, cleared his throat and spoke huskily, "There, there, Millie." I went out in the kitchen, found there was a little melting ice cream left in one of the freezers. I washed out a dish and spoon at the sink and scooped up what I could. Then I sat down in a kitchen chair, slowly ate the soft cream and thought about a good many things. I spilled some ice cream on my new white-piped vest. But I wet the corner of a dish towel and cleaned it off pretty well.

Laura and Ralph spent their honeymoon in Colorado Springs and she sent us daily colored postcards showing the wonders of the Garden of the Gods, Pikes Peak, the Seven Falls and Helen Hunt Jackson's grave. She was simply enthralled by the Rocky Mountain country and, obviously, by life in general.

Chapter 9

I BARELY squeaked through the eighth grade. As a matter of fact, I'd have been flunked because of my low marks in arithmetic except that Miss Elliot kept me after school for a conference and I promised to do some work during summer vacation so I shouldn't disgrace her when I entered high school in the fall.

Because of my poor spelling and limping grammar, she also could give me no higher than a "C" in English, although she told me I showed good imagination and originality in my compositions. My only good subjects were art, which really was just drawing, and history, which interested me. She praised me (except for spelling and grammar) for my book reviews of *The Last of the Mohicans* and *Ivanhoe*, but declared it was extremely presumptuous for an ignorant boy to criticize such literary classics as *Silas Marner* and *Little Women*.

I said, "Well, Miss Elliot, you wanted me to be honest, didn't you?"

She said, "Yes, George, I wanted you to be honest, but I hoped you had developed enough literary taste by now to appreciate some of the best books in the English language."

As a matter of fact, I was quite lucky to be graduated from grammar school at all because of an incident early in the spring which placed me on probation.

When the bell rang for the close of the school day, the pupils in each room lined up to march from the building in order. Each teacher stood in the hall to give the signal to the leading youngster by the door, and this left the file of boys and girls without supervision. On this unfortunate day a large, officious boy named Quincy Burwell was standing behind me and I was daydreaming with my books in my newspaper bag slung over my shoulder. I did not notice that the file ahead of me had closed up, leaving a space of six or seven feet between me and the girl ahead. We were standing beside a blackboard and Quincy Burwell picked up a blackboard eraser charged with chalk dust, reached forward and slapped me in the mouth with it. "Wake up you dope!" he said in a gruff whisper. The chalk dust went into my mouth and up my nose. I sneezed. Then I turned and swiftly punched him on the mouth just as I had slugged Buck Christopher. He went down violently, banging his head against the brown wainscoting beneath the blackboard, and lay there a moment staring up at me in astonishment.

"Don't you ever do that again," I said, "or I'll give you worse than that."

Of course there was an uproar and the line disintegrated as a couple of boys helped Quincy to his feet and a girl picked up his books. Miss Elliot was there and you couldn't see her eyes because the westering sun was absorbed by the chalk dust on her glasses.

"What is this! What is this?" she demanded in a shrill voice that almost sounded frightened.

"Well, it's a fight," some boy said.

Annette Shaw said very calmly, "George Chalmers struck Quincy in the face and knocked him down."

I glared at Annette and said, "Well, look, he hit me first in the mouth with a blackboard eraser."

Quincy Burwell was wiping the blood from his mouth with a dirty handkerchief and Miss Elliot said, "All right, both of you take your seats and the rest of you get back in line and start marching out. Forward march!"

My right hand was stinging and Quincy's front teeth had cut my knuckles. I sucked the wounds and Quincy was in the next aisle forward with shoulders hunched.

Then Miss Elliot was standing by her desk looking grim and her voice seemed to echo in the empty room. "You boys know quite well that I will not tolerate this sort of thing in my room. Now we're going to see Mr. Ward."

She led us downstairs to the principal's office and at her knock Mr. Ward's tenor voice sang out, "*Come* in." He was at his desk, tall, thin, balding, spectacled and irrepressibly jolly.

"Well," he said, "to what happy event do I owe this unexpected pleasure?"

"Mr. Ward," said Miss Elliot firmly, "this is George Chalmers and Quincy Burwell. They engaged in a fist fight in dismissal line in my room and I'm going to turn them over to you."

"Well, well," said Mr. Ward, looking at us in turn, "a couple of roughnecks, eh? Are they persistent troublemakers?"

"Oh, I can't really say that, Mr. Ward. You know I simply will not tolerate disturbances in my classroom."

"How is their scholastic standing?"

Miss Elliot shook her head. "Quincy is perhaps average. George is below average, I'm afraid."

"The smaller one is distinguished by being more stupid?"

"Perhaps. Well, I'm not so sure that he's really stupid, but he certainly doesn't apply himself to his lessons as he should. I wouldn't predict that either will ever become a brilliant student, but both could do better if they tried."

"Do you think we should expel the pair of them if they're more interested in being rowdies than getting an education?"

"Well, Mr. Ward, I don't know that I should go that far, but . . ."

Mr. Ward pointed a long, white finger at Quincy. "What does your father do?" he demanded.

"He's—well, Mr. Ward, he's a traveling salesman for Star Brand shoes."

"Do you think he wants you to grow up to be an uneducated thug—maybe a prizefighter?"

"Oh, no, sir. I'm not really a fighter, sir. I . . ."

"Do you want to go to high school?"

"Oh, yes, sir."

"Why?"

"To get an education."

The principal turned swiftly on me. "How about you? What's your father's business?"

"He's in the real-estate and insurance business."

"I see. Are you any relation to Laura Chalmers?"

"Yes, sir. She's my sister. She's in Denver, Colorado, now and married to a man named Ralph Sterling."

He nodded. "I taught them both Latin in high school. Laura was a very good student. Is she brighter than you?"

"Yes, sir, she is."

Mr. Ward's eyes glittered behind their glasses. "Well, you're honest, anyhow. Tell me, what would your father think of your having a fist fight in a classroom?"

"He'd be pretty angry."

"Now, Miss Elliot," Mr. Ward said in a calmer voice, "please tell me just what happened."

"Well, Mr. Ward, the class was lined up for dismissal and I was in the hall so I really didn't see it. I heard a commotion and rushed in the door to see Quincy getting up from the floor with blood on his mouth and I was told that George had knocked him down."

Mr. Ward pointed at Quincy. "Is that what happened?"

"Yes, sir."

"Without provocation?"

"Without what?"

"Why did he strike you?"

"Well—he didn't have no reason to slug me like that."

"Mr. Ward," I said, "look, we were standing in line with Quincy Burwell right behind me and all of a sudden he took a blackboard eraser full of chalk and reached up and smacked me right in the mouth with it. So I just slugged him before I thought."

"I just tapped you," said Quincy. "I just tapped you to wake you up on account you was standing there like a dope when the girl ahead of you had moved up a long way."

"You hit me hard enough to fill my mouth and nose with chalk dust, and who do you think you are, an army general or somebody to take charge of the marching line?"

"Well," said Mr. Ward, "now we seem to be getting to the root of this thing. I noticed something white on the Chalmers boy's mouth and nose but supposed he had just powdered the shine off his nose before going out."

Quincy Burwell giggled and Mr. Ward said to him, "It does seem to me, Master Burwell, that you were pretty officious and also showed rather poor judgment in not being ready to duck after powdering the nose of a boy who obviously can deliver a sockdolager—I believe you would call it."

Quincy looked down at the floor. "And you, Master Chalmers," Mr. Ward went on, "why were you standing there asleep? Don't you get enough sleep at night?"

"Yes, sir. I wasn't asleep. I was just thinking of something else."

"Oh, in spite of your being below average in the class, you *are* capable of thinking?"

"Yes, sir."

"You must have some pretty deep and profound thoughts, to make you completely oblivious to your surroundings."

"Well," I said, "sometimes I do."

Mr. Ward smiled in an infuriating manner and said, "Would you please give me an example of your profound thoughts?"

This was very embarrassing and I felt my cheeks burning, but I had a sudden impulse to blast him out of his shoes. "Well, Mr. Ward," I said, "sometimes I try to figure out—well, I mean I wonder if God is scared of something."

[79]

"W-h-a-t?" Mr. Ward was frowning and smiling at the same time.

Miss Elliot said, "Mr. Ward, if you don't need me any more, I'd like to be excused."

Mr. Ward nodded. "I believe I can handle this all right, Miss Elliot."

Miss Elliot departed and Mr. Ward said to me, "What ever gave you such a weird idea?"

"Well," I said, "there's supposed to be only one God, isn't there?"

"Certainly. But of course there's the Holy Trinity—the Father, Son and Holy Ghost."

"But God never would be scared of His son Jesus or the Holy Ghost, would He?"

"Certainly not."

"Now," I said, "in the very first Commandment God gave to Moses it says, 'Thou shalt have no other gods before me,' and He must have thought that was mighty important for Him to make it the first Commandment, so I have wondered if there weren't some other gods around and God was afraid one of them might move into His territory, you know, like here's a grocery store doing very good business on a street so another grocery man opens across the way from him."

"Saloons do that," said Quincy Burwell.

"So," I went on, "maybe God was just making His customers promise they wouldn't trade at another store in case one opened or else He wouldn't take care of them any more, and maybe even some god had threatened to start competition and that scared God and it makes Him feel more sure of himself when thousands of His customers get down on their knees and worship Him. If God was awfully sure of Himself I don't think He'd want people to do that. You take a boy who owns a dog and—"

Mr. Ward interrupted me. "Master Chalmers," he said, "I find this discourse disturbing and somewhat shocking. It's really a sacrilege. More mature and much greater minds than you'll ever own have pondered the nature of God and found their only answer in faith and the Bible. Do you go to Sunday school and church?"

"Yes, sir."

"Good. Learn your Sunday-school lessons and have faith in

them. For a boy to go much beyond that is to invite a flock of bats into his belfry. Your standing in the class shows that you need to apply whatever brain you have to your designated studies and quit worrying about God. God is quite capable of handling His own affairs without your help. But it looks as if you need God's help in handling *your* affairs. If you want to be promoted out of the eighth grade, you'd better pray for help and then knuckle down and study your lessons."

"Yes, sir," I said, "but I don't worry about God all the time. You asked me for an example and I just gave you an example of what I think about sometimes. I think about other things like why is a rabbit, but—"

"What subject does that come under—arithmetic, English, history? Listen to me, young man, you've got to get control of yourself. What do you want to do when you're a man?"

"I don't know, exactly, Mr. Ward. Maybe a naturalist and artist."

"Hmm. Do you think you could do that without an education? Again I tell you, if you want to get into high school, you'd better show some improvement in your schoolwork.

"Now both of you listen to me carefully. I have been thinking of suspending you two for brawling in a classroom. If I do that both of you will flunk out of the eighth grade. If I don't suspend you, you both have a chance if you behave yourselves and work. So I'll tell you what I'm going to do. I'm going to put you both on probation and I'm going to tell Miss Elliot to report on you. If either of you commits the slightest infraction of the rules between now and the end of the term, out you go."

"Look, Mr. Ward," said Quincy Burwell, "do you mean if this guy does something wrong I get kicked out too?"

"I mean nothing of the kind, and you know it. Now, if I let you go now will you two start fighting again as soon as you get out?"

"No, sir," I said, "not unless he starts it."

"No, sir," said Quincy.

"All right, then," said Mr. Ward. "I want you to apologize to each other and shake hands."

Quincy gave me a limp hand.

"I'm sorry I stuck the eraser in your mouth," said Quincy.

"I'm sorry I hit you so hard," I said.

Mr. Ward asked, "Aren't you sorry you hit him at all?"

"I'm sorry I hit him in the schoolhouse," I said.

Mr. Ward sniffed and said, "All right, get out of here. I have work to do."

Neither of us said anything until we were outdoors, and then Quincy squinted his eyes at me and said, "Why is a rabbit? Jesus, Sleepy, you're even nuttier than I thought."

"How did you like the taste of my knuckles?"

"I've tasted dirt before. Anyhow that was just a lucky punch."

I said, "There's plenty more lucky punches in both my dukes for anybody that starts things."

"Nuts. Who do you think you are, Jim Jeffries?"

"No," I said, "I think I'm George Chalmers and I don't start fights. I just stop 'em."

"Nuts," said Quincy Burwell, and his upper lip was swollen out.

I went after my papers and of course I had lost my place among the carriers and had to wait at the end of the line. While I was waiting I thought that I had grown pretty brave and confident of myself after my quick triumphs over Buck Christopher and Quincy Burwell, but that I probably wouldn't be so brave if someone slugged me first real hard on the nose.

Only a few days after my graduation from grammar school, with a nice little rolled diploma tied with a red ribbon, I was informed that Laura was going to have a baby and was feeling miserable. She wanted her mother there.

So there was a great scurry of packing and excitement and apprehension, and my father and I loaded her, flushed and breathless, onto the train. She would have to ride all night, and my father wanted to get her a Pullman berth, but Mother wouldn't hear to such extravagance.

Then we were keeping bachelors' hall in the empty, sad house, and my father was to do the cooking and I was to do the dishwashing and sweeping and run the carpet sweeper. And there was no doubt now that sex—disgusting, beastly, fascinating sex—had entered the life of my clean, cool, circumspect sister just as if she had been a farm girl or one of the grubby females from across the tracks. Somehow the thought seemed more revolting because her partner in the act was obviously the excessively neat and supposedly immaculate Ralph Sterling. I told myself that, after all, they were married and procreation was one of the purposes of marriage, but except for that technicality, there was still a feeling that Laura now was practically as sunk in degradation as I myself and that she surely would die in childbirth to pay for it and that Ralph Sterling would be her murderer.

But Laura did not die. My father opened the telegram's yellow envelope with thick, trembling fingers and then chortled. Laura had given birth to twins, a boy named Benjamin after Ralph's bank-president uncle, and a girl named Millicent after the attending grandmother. Both mother and babies doing well.

"Well, well, Uncle George!" my father cried. "A double uncle in one fell swoop. I didn't think that little fellow had it in him."

"Well, gosh," I said.

"That calls for a celebration," he said. "I'll go to town and send a telegram of congratulations and get a sirloin steak and broil it Western style. Tell you what you do while I'm gone. Take some of that Gold Dust Twins stuff and scrub off the top of the stove real good and I'll broil you the best steak you ever tasted."

"You mean you'll cook it on top of the stove without a skillet?"

"That's exactly what I mean."

"But—Mama always fries a steak in the big skillet."

"I know she does. But this isn't going to be a fried steak. This is going to be a thick, juicy broiled sirloin to celebrate my becoming grampaw and your becoming uncle."

"But won't it burn just on top of the stove lids? And won't it make an awful mess? And how can you make gravy with it just on top of the stove lids?"

My father laughed. "Never gravy with a broiled steak. Now you go to work with the scrubbing brush on the stove and then go pick some lettuce and pull some radishes and onions and wash them. If I'm not back by then you can peel a few potatoes."

Dubious as I was, I went to scrubbing off the top of the kitchen range, and as I scrubbed I thought of the shocking event in Denver which seemed to please my father so much. Having two babies at once was definitely carrying things too far. It was—well, it was really obscene, and not at all like the conservative Laura. I brooded over it and was quite unhappy as I picked the lettuce, radishes and spring onions from the garden.

When my father returned, he had a huge chunk of beef nearly two inches thick, dark red, rimmed and streaked slightly with white.

"Well, gosh, Pop," I said, "that don't look like a steak to me. It kind of looks like a funny roast."

"Fine sirloin," he said. "Just you leave it to me. Now, suppose you peel some potatoes and slice them thin."

He rubbed a piece of the meat paper over the top of the stove to see whether it was as clean as he wished, and then built up a roaring fire while I obeyed his instructions with the potatoes.

"You going to fry potatoes raw?" I asked.

"Yep."

"Well," I said, "Mama always cuts up boiled potatoes to fry."

"I know."

"You think they'll be all right just to fry 'em raw?"

"I wouldn't do it if I didn't think so."

He spooned some lard into a frying pan, and when it was smoking hot on the stove, dumped my potatoes into the pan. He stirred the sliced potatoes around a couple of times and then held the palm of his hand over the stove to test its heat. "Here goes," he said, spearing the steak up with the big three-tined cooking fork. He slapped it on top of the hot stove and the meat screamed in protest. Blue smoke rose and my father said, "Better shut the dining-room door and open the back door to let the smoke out." Then he stirred the potatoes and shook salt onto them.

I took care of the doors, thinking I was going to be faced with an inedible supper.

"All right, boy," he said, "what about the lettuce? Did you wash it well to get the sand out?"

"Yes, sir."

"All right. Get a couple of small plates and divide the lettuce on it. Then you can set the kitchen table here and put the radishes and scallions on another small plate."

"Scallions?"

"Spring onions. Put the vinegar cruet on the table for the lettuce, and get that bottle of olive oil from the bathroom."

A tablespoon of olive oil was his remedy for any enteric disturbance, and I whistled. "What you want that awful stuff for?" I asked.

"To put on the lettuce with the vinegar and salt and pepper."

"Not for me," I said. "I ain't sick."

Prospects for a decent dinner were growing darker and darker, but the smoke from the scorching steak really smelled appetizing, I had to admit. I got the olive-oil bottle, however, and by the time I returned to the kitchen my father had flipped the steak over and, just as I feared, the upper surface looked burned. He had got the butter dish from the refrigerator and now was spreading butter liberally on the top of the steak. I thought he had better try to scrape it first like a piece of burned toast before buttering, but decided I had said enough.

He grinned at me as I put down the oily bottle with its red-and-green label and said, "You've no idea how much a little olive oil with the vinegar helps a salad."

I said, "Mama never uses it."

"No. She's prejudiced against it. But you try it and you'll see how much better it makes the lettuce." He stirred the frying potatoes again and with the fork lifted a corner of the steak to peek under. "Coming right along. Maybe I should have made some coffee to go with our feast, but I guess Adam's ale will be good enough to drink with this. Or we've got plenty of milk, if you want it."

"What's Adam's ale?"

"Aqua pura. Good, clear, cool water."

"Water's been a little riley lately," I said.

"Roily," he corrected. "R-o-i-l-y."

"Everybody says riley," I objected. "I think that 'o' is silent like the 'o' in the big flower that's pronounced 'piney' and spelled 'p-e-o-n-y.'"

"And the correct pronunciation of the flower is "pee-o-ny,'" he asserted. "Now, get me the big platter for the steak and the small platter for the spuds."

"Well," I said, "if I ever heard anybody call a piney a pee-oh-nie I didn't know what they were talking about, and after supper I'm going to look in the dictionary."

"That's an excellent idea. Now, get me the platters."

The potatoes were browning in the frying pan as he stirred them again, and, while I kept a suspicious eye on his operations, I got the bread knife, took a homemade loaf from the bread box and whittled off several slices. With the ice pick I spiked off three pieces of ice from the chunk in the top of the refrigerator, washed the sawdust from them at the sink, and clunked them into the water pitcher and filled the pitcher with water.

By the time I got the pitcher and water goblets and bread in place on the oilcloth-covered table, my father was lifting the steak from the stove to the big platter where it lay, still angry and hissing with hot juice exuding over the ironstone china and actually smelling quite savory. I glanced over at the stove and, as I feared, the top was an awful mess.

"Well," he said, spooning the fried potatoes to the small platter, "get me the carving knife from the dining room and let's get at this chore while it's hot."

So I got the big knife and we sat down to the kitchen table and my father thanked God for bringing Laura safely through her ordeal and for the blessing of twin grandchildren as well as for our sumptuous meal. Then he cut into the steak with the carving knife, grinned and said, "Boy, it's as tender as a saint's heart."

He served me a large piece with fried potatoes and I sat and looked at it while he served himself. He seemed very happy and I was embarrassed. Then he looked at me and said, "Well, George, what's the matter?"

I said, "Gosh, Pop, it's not done. Well, I guess it's done on the outside, but you didn't cook it long enough. It's completely raw inside."

"Nonsense, boy. It's just exactly right." An expression of rapture was on his heavy face as he chewed a piece of steak. "Well, maybe it needs just a wee bit more salt. Try it, boy, try it."

I was trying a small, brown piece of fried potato and it was all right, but I shook my head. "Pop," I said, "that meat is so raw it's red, and Mama says never to eat beef that's not thoroughly cooked or you'll get tapeworm."

He shook his head. "That's an old wives' tale," he said. "Well, perhaps if it was from a grandma cow that was kept in a filthy barnyard and fed slops there might be something to it. But this is clean Western steer beef broiled Western style and there's nothing better in this world. When I was a young man I ate hundreds of rare steaks and knew hundreds of other peo-

ple who ate hundreds of rare steaks and I never heard of anybody getting anything from them except good health and
strong muscles. This is just kind of medium rare, George, and
simply delicious. I certainly wouldn't urge you to do anything
that wasn't good for you. I've really got a treat for you here and
I'll feel very badly if you let a prejudice cheat you out of it."

"Well . . ."

I ate a radish in an effort to hide the nasty taste of raw meat,
sawed off a piece of steak and put it in my mouth. My father
watched as I chewed. "How about it?" he asked.

"I guess I can eat a little of it."

I ate some potato and it was good. Then I took another piece
of steak and it was good too. Then I took another with a tiny
bit of crisp fat attached, and there was a flavor I never had
experienced before—hearty, delectable, revitalizing, soul-sat-
isfying. I looked at my father and said, "My goodness."

My father was a fast eater and he really was tearing into his
steak and potatoes. He peered up at me with a grin, and I said,
"Well, Pop, it's really wonderful. I never ate anything like it."

"This is man food," he said. "Women are fine cooks when it
comes to pies and cake and frying chicken, but they just overcook most meat and vegetables. Well, you've got to cook pork
very well done or you'll get sick. Moses knew that and that's
why the children of Israel were forbidden to eat pork at all."

He had picked a teacup from the kitchen shelf and was pour-
ing vinegar and a little olive oil into it as he talked. Then he
put in a little sugar, salted it, peppered it and stirred it vigorously with a teaspoon.

"Why," I asked, "didn't Moses just tell them to cook their
pork thoroughly?"

"I don't know. Maybe they didn't have the facilities.
Maybe he didn't really know about the trichina worm but
had noticed that people got very sick from eating underdone
pork and so prohibited it altogether. Now, you spoon some of
this dressing on your lettuce and see how good it makes it."

After the experience with the steak, I needed no more convincing that he knew about food and I dipped the vinegar and
oil over my lettuce. Again I found he was right.

"Gee," I said, "I think I'll elect you the family cook and
maybe Mama could run your office."

He laughed. "She's really a very good cook, George, and you

know it. But all the women I've ever known want to overcook things. The best vegetable cook is a Chinaman. I knew several out West and they didn't cook the life out of a vegetable. They cooked 'em just enough so there was still some character in them. And rice—I've never cared much for rice except a China-man's rice, and that is good."

"Why haven't you told Mama about these things?"

"Tell her? Boy, you've got things to learn. No man can tell a woman anything about housekeeping. A few times when she's been under the weather before Laura had grown up or when Laura was away I had bad luck getting your mother some-thing to eat. Well, she'd want something like poached eggs and they'd come out a mess. So how could I tell her anything about cooking a healthy man's meal? But don't misunderstand me, I'm quite satisfied to let her do the cooking. She keeps us well fed and healthy, doesn't she?"

"Yes, sir. She sure does."

"Well, that's all that matters."

"But," I said, "I'm sure enough enjoying this man's steak and fried potatoes and lettuce for a change."

He nodded his head happily. "Yes. But I keep thinking of Laura and those little devils out in Denver. I wonder who they're going to look like, if anybody?"

I said, "Well, I guess it might be a good thing if the boy looked like Laura and the girl like Ralph. He's prettier than she is."

"What a thing to say! Laura's certainly pretty enough."

"Well, sure. Of course she was never Queen of the May or anything like that, and Ralph is awful pretty for a man with his black, curly hair and pink cheeks."

My father looked at me and chuckled and I felt warmly in rapport although I realized he would avoid criticizing his son-in-law in any way.

We demolished the dinner, down to the last radish and on-ion and, although my father consumed almost twice as much steak as I, I was full to bursting. If waistlines were any standard of judging, he easily had twice the cargo space in his huge torso as existed in my slim midsection.

He sighed loudly and stretched his big arms. "Well, God bless the little Sterlings," he said, "and now for forty winks."

So he took a nap on the living-room couch while I did the

dishes. I had to wait a while for the kitchen range to cool off before scrubbing it again. But I felt extremely well fed and happy. Never before had I been so close to my father, and it was a wonderful feeling.

Chapter 10

AT BREAKFAST on the following Saturday my father told me to mow the lawn so it would look neat for Sunday. I told him I'd do it in the afternoon after I'd finished collecting on my paper route in the morning.

Before school closed I had thought about getting a regular job for summer and had done some scouting. The box factory, I found, would hire me as an offbearer inasmuch as I had reached the legal age of fourteen. But the pay was only three dollars for a sixty-hour week, and that would compel me to relinquish my paper route which, on the average, brought me two dollars a week and left practically the whole day free for odd jobs and for doing the studying I had promised Miss Elliot to do. So I found three lawns to mow (in addition to our own) at twenty-five cents a lawn, and this gave me a total income not far under what the arduous box-factory job would pay.

It was an unseasonably hot day for early June and when I got home from my collecting I took a cool bath although I knew that wasn't at all practical because I would get sweaty all over again from mowing. Then I got a cold lunch from the refrigerator—some cold beans, a glass of buttermilk and some of that delicious, new-fangled butter made from ground-up peanuts which I spread with grape jelly on baker's bread. Of course we had run out of homemade bread, but the indifferent store loaves were edible when spread with peanut butter and jelly.

I had just put things away and cleaned up after lunch when I heard some kids yelling for me out front and Fred Snider and Orville O'Neill and Max Levine and Chet Wilson were there with their baseball equipment.

"Look, Sleepy," Fred Snider said, "we're getting up a regular baseball team, a bunch of us, and why don't you come along to the town diamond and practice? Maybe we'll have a regular game next week with the Southsiders. They got a team already."

"Well," I said, "I don't know. I'm supposed to mow the yard this afternoon."

Orville O'Neill said, "Aw, it's too hot to mow the yard now. Why don't you do it this evening?"

That sounded sensible to me so I got my glove and straw hat and went with them. Because I had been in Kansas most of the previous summer and had scarcely touched a baseball, I was somewhat apprehensive, but after a few minutes of practice I was most pleasantly surprised to discover that my skills had improved. In batting practice I was meeting the ball squarely. Once, in the outfield, I surprised myself as much as anyone else by running at top speed for a hard-hit ball, leaping and spearing it with my glove hand, and at pitching I found I could throw a faster ball than even Fred Snider's and control it fairly well although my little curve was uncertain and wild.

I went home in a happy frame of mind although sweatier than before I took my bath. But as I approached the house, slapping my thigh with the glove, I whistled to myself and said, Oh-oh, now I'm in for it.

My father was mowing the front lawn. He was wearing a battered old straw hat, his face was a fiery red, his collar was off and his striped white shirt was black with sweat bordering his suspenders in back.

I called out, "Hey, Pop, I'll do that. I was going to do it this evening when it got a little cooler."

He leaned on the mower, panting, and looked at me without a smile. He said, "You said you'd do it this afternoon, and I didn't know where you were. Now the afternoon is nearly gone." He took out a handkerchief and mopped his glowing face and then his balding head. He had slumped as he stood there, and it seemed that his belly bulged enormously and that he looked very old. While he was sixty-three, I hadn't thought of him as an old man, really.

I said, "Well, some boys came by and wanted me to play ball and I thought I'd have plenty of time when I got back and maybe it would be cooler."

He shook his head and said mildly, "I suppose it was cooler playing baseball than here in the yard."

"It wasn't so cool down there. But let me take that mower. Well, I want a drink of water first."

We went into the house together and he was breathing heavily when we went slowly up the front steps. I looked at him and asked if he was all right.

He sighed. "Oh, yes, I'm all right. Just warm, and I get tired quicker now than I did forty years ago. Wonder if there's any buttermilk in the icebox?"

"Yes," I said. "I had some for lunch, but there's plenty left."

He got a glass from the kitchen shelf. "Nothing like buttermilk when you're hot and tired," he said. His hand shook slightly when he poured from the two-quart buttermilk jug.

"Well," I said, "I like buttermilk all right, but when I'm thirsty I'd rather have lemonade or strawberry pop. Buttermilk is kind of sticky just to drink when you're thirsty."

He sat down on a kitchen chair while I drank tap water from the kitchen tin cup. "Sorry I didn't think to get some lemons when I marketed this afternoon," he said. "Lemonade is very good, but I don't think much of soda pop."

To tease him I said, "Well, I've heard men say there's nothing like good cold beer in hot weather."

"That's sheer nonsense. Beer makes you sweat and feel even hotter."

"Did you ever drink any beer?"

"I certainly have. And whisky too—when I was young and foolish."

This was interesting. I had taken it for granted that he was a lifelong prohibitionist. "Was this," I asked, "when you were out West in the mines and all?"

"Yes."

"You never did tell me much about your adventures out there."

"Not much to tell. It was a rough life among rough people. I'm not ashamed of it, but I'm not proud of it either."

"Did you ever see any gun fights?"

"I saw a couple of shootings—and one hanging."

"Gee," I said, leaning against the sink. "I wish you'd tell me about those things sometime."

[91]

"Well—sometime, perhaps. Now I'm going to go lie down on the couch for a while."

I put the buttermilk away and rinsed out his glass. Then I looked at the kitchen clock and it was nearly four. I went into the living room and he was sitting on the edge of the leather couch taking off his shoes.

"Look, Pop," I said, "I didn't know it was so late and I've got to go for my papers now. I'll do the rest of the yard right away when I get home. Now, you won't go out there mowing again while I'm away, will you?"

"No," he said, "I won't." His shirt sleeves were rolled up and his big hairy forearms were limp on his thighs as he sat hunched forward on the couch. One shoe was off and there was a hole in the toe of the black sock.

He looked up at me and asked, "What do you want for supper?"

"Oh, anything."

He smiled and there was the white mark of buttermilk on his gray mustache. "I'm afraid we're just out of that," he said.

I laughed at his joke. "Why don't you take a nap while I'm gone?" I asked.

"That's just what I plan to do," he said.

So I got my sack from the hall seat and went after my papers. A good many people were sitting on their front porches when they were on the shady side of the street and that cost me considerable time. It wouldn't be at all polite to throw the paper on the porch and possibly hit someone in the face, so I'd have to walk up and hand it to them, and that frequently resulted in some conversation.

I was in a hurry because I wanted to get the rest of that lawn mowed before dinnertime.

There still was plenty of daylight left when I finally got home and my father was lying peacefully on his back, apparently asleep. Both shoes were off now and I was amused to see that there was a hole in each sock. I put our paper on the couch beside him and went quietly upstairs to the bathroom so as not to disturb him. Then I finished mowing the front and side lawn, noted that my father had taken care of the big back yard first, and I put the lawn mower away in the barn.

I sat down on the back steps and cleaned the grass off my feet before going inside. When I peeked into the living room my father was still lying there so I went up to my hot room, lay on my bed and read a story in *The Youth's Companion* by C. A. Stephens about a big family up in Maine. I thought Maine must be a wonderful place and that I should like to live there among such interesting people.

Then I began to get hungry and went back downstairs. My father hadn't moved, and, with a catch in my throat, I noticed his usually ruddy face was pale.

I called out, "Oh, Pop." Then louder, "Hey, Pop!" When he didn't move I dashed over to the couch and took hold of his hand. It was limp and lifeless.

"My gosh," I whispered, dizzy with an awful thought, and dropped his hand. It fell against the newspaper and knocked it off the couch to the floor. I stepped backward and breathed, "No, Pop, no. You can't be *dead*. Not *now!*"

I collapsed into a chair and sat looking at my inert father while my heart pounded violently in terror. At last my whirling brain resolved itself into a coherent thought—perhaps my father wasn't really dead but only very sick and unconscious. I must get a doctor immediately.

Gasping for breath, I stumbled to the wall telephone in the dining room and turned the crank violently. The operator's voice answered, "Numbah, please."

"Oh," I said, "I want a doctor right away and didn't have time to look up the number. Please, this is a real emergency."

"What doctor do you want?" the calm voice asked.

"Oh, Dr. Davenport, I guess. Please hurry, miss. Please."

"Just a moment, please."

Then I heard the buzz of a phone ringing and at last a woman's voice replied.

"Can I speak to Dr. Davenport?" I asked and my changing voice broke and squeaked annoyingly on the name.

"Well, the doctor is just eating his supper. Can I take a message?"

"Tell him," I said, "this is a real emergency. My father is very sick and unconscious and I'm afraid he's dying maybe. Please."

"Who is this?"

"This is George Chalmers and—" My voice broke terribly again.

"Who?"

"My father's Jerome Chalmers. The doctor knows him, and tell him he's terribly sick and I don't know what to do and—"

"Just hold the phone."

The receiver slipped a bit in my sweating, trembling hand as I waited and the telephone's electric insect hummed steadily in my ear. Finally a man cleared his throat and asked, "What seems to be the trouble?"

"Well, Doctor," I squeaked, "I don't know. My father's unconscious on the couch."

"Isn't there an adult there with you?"

"Just my father and he's—"

"All right, I'll be right over." The phone clicked, so I hung up the receiver and rang off.

I went back into the living room and I thought for a moment he'd moved his right arm which now hung off the couch with his hand resting on the *Evening Journal* on the floor. I wanted to lift the hand and arm back on the couch, but didn't dare.

Again I sat down in the chair and breathed a prayer, "Please, God, don't let Pop be dead. Please don't."

I wished fervently that my mother were home. But if she were home she'd be very embarrassed by both of Pop's big toes showing through holes in his socks with the doctor coming. But, of course, the holes wouldn't be there if she were home.

The clock on the mantel was ticking away and it was twenty to seven. It was still light enough in the room, but it would be growing dusk soon so I went into the kitchen, got a match and lit the big lamp in the living room. Then I discovered I was crying and felt ashamed of myself and went back to the kitchen and washed my face in cool water.

Oh, I wished the doctor would hurry. Minute by minute I grew more certain there was no hope. What was I going to do? I'd have to send a telegram to my mother in Denver and she'd just have to come home no matter how badly Laura needed her. And sending a telegram meant going to the railroad depot. Even if Pop was still alive but just very sick I'd have to send a telegram and I wondered how much it would cost. I'd have to get some money out of the savings jar in my room. It was growing dark on the stairway and I ran up two steps at a time as if I were pursued. In my familiar room with the picture of the Indian scout on one wall and the Ten Commandments on the other it was lighter than the stairway, and I took my earthenware jar from the commode. Would a couple of dollars be enough to send a telegram to Denver? I took three to make sure and started hesitantly downstairs. Oh, if Dr. Davenport would only hurry.

I glanced into the living room and didn't believe my father had moved a bit. Then I went out on the porch and sat down on the front steps to wait for the doctor. A robin was singing in a nearby tree and a late-working hummingbird hovered around the porch trumpet vine, flashing red and gold as he attacked the orange-hued blossoms.

A gasoline automobile came chugging along and I recognized it as the Rambler owned by a lawyer named Norris. Long after it had passed I could smell the stink of it even above the clean smell of the newly mowed lawn. My father didn't like Mr. Norris and I remembered his saying Norris would be happy to defend the lowest crook on earth in court if he was paid for it. My eyes filled with tears again and I wiped them away with the back of my hand. Why didn't Dr. Davenport hurry? Old Mr. Yancey came walking slowly toward town, his derbied head bowed in thought. He didn't look at me sitting on the porch steps and little did he know about my father inside the house, motionless on the leather couch, although Mr. Yancey had sat in that living room on several occasions talking politics or civic affairs with my father. Where the paint had worn away on the steps the old wood looked like silver, but perhaps that was only because I saw it through tears.

At last Dr. Davenport's buggy pulled up in front of the house and he got out with his black bag and then lifted out the hitching weight which he dropped on the grass to hold his bay mare. I went down to meet him.

The doctor smiled slightly at me and asked, "Well, son, how does he seem now?"

I swallowed and said, "I'm scared, Doctor."

We were walking toward the house. "Where's your mother?" he asked.

"She's in Denver, Colorado. She went out because my sister Laura was having twin babies."

"I see. And you're here alone with your father?"

"Yes, sir."

I held the screen door for him and the doctor, not pausing in stride, deftly hooked his derby on the hall hatrack as he moved into the living room.

The big table lamp threw his shadow black and gigantic against the wall as the doctor bent over my father. The stethoscope was out of the bag and in Dr. Davenport's ears. My father's shirt and undershirt were open over his hairy chest while the doctor listened intently, and the robin outside still sang in the growing darkness, and I thought, curiously, that it would have been better if my father's chest had grown bald instead of his head.

The doctor straightened with the stethoscope dangling and ran a hand over his own grizzly, bearded jaw before turning to me and shaking his head. "I'm sorry, son," he said.

"You mean . . ."

He nodded. "He's gone."

I began to cry and the doctor put his arm around me. "There, there," he said, "I know this is awful, but try to tell me what happened."

"Nothing happened," I said. "He was just hot and tired and drank some buttermilk and said he was going to take a nap. So I went out and mowed the yard and when I came back he was—well, this way."

He shook his head. "It could have been apoplexy," he said, "but more likely a heart attack. Did he complain of a headache?"

"No, sir. He just said he was hot and tired and was going to lay down on the couch for a while."

"Well, he obviously went in his sleep and without pain. That should be some comfort. Now we've things to do. First, we must inform your mother and get her back here right away."

"Yes, sir. I'll have to go to the depot and send her a telegram."

"No, boy, I'll take care of that. Tell me where she is in Denver."

I gave him Laura's address and he wrote it down on a pad of prescription blanks. Then he went to the telephone, called a number and said, "Hello, Mike. This is Dr. Davenport. I want to send a telegram to Denver, Colorado, for immediate transmission. Ready?" He gave my mother's name and Laura's address, then, "Mr. Chalmers died suddenly of heart attack this evening. Please return at once. Dr. Davenport. Look, Mike, charge that to the Chalmers' number, four-oh-two. Got it? Good-bye."

Even in my grogginess I was surprised that one could charge a telegram to a telephone number and I didn't think my father knew it or he wouldn't have gone to the depot to send congratulations about the twins. After ringing off, the doctor turned and rubbed his beard. "Now, son," he said slowly, "I don't suppose you have any idea what undertaker your mother would prefer, but we've got to get someone to come and get father."

"My goodness," I said, "there can't be a funeral until my mother gets home."

"Oh, no. But your father has to be taken care of right away."

"Well, I never did think about anything like that, of course, but Mr. Lister is a member of our church."

The doctor nodded. "John Lister is very good." He cranked the phone and gave a number and I wondered if he knew all the numbers by heart. In a moment he spoke into the transmitter, "Hello, John. Dr. Davenport. John, I'm out at Jerome Chalmers' house and Mr. Chalmers just passed away from a heart attack. Yes, very sudden. Mrs. Chalmers is in Colorado and I have wired her, but there's no one here but a young boy and I'll wait until you arrive . . . Naturally, we'll have to wait until Mrs. Chalmers gets home for that . . . I'd think by Monday evening, but I don't know about the trains . . . I haven't the slightest idea about that, John, but I expect it's all right. You know as much about that as I do. Make it as soon as possible, will you? I've got a couple of house calls to make. So long."

Dr. Davenport came slowly back into the living room, pushed the protruding stethoscope back into the satchel, and closed the bag. He looked at me and shook his head sadly. "I know it's mighty rough, boy, but you've just got to keep a stiff upper lip and be a man before your time."

My cheeks were wet again. I felt for a handkerchief but didn't have one and I wiped the tears away with the back of my hand. I was sitting stiffly on a straight chair across the room and the doctor sat down in my father's favorite armchair. He seemed a little embarrassed and he said, "Let's see, your name is . . ."

"George," I said, "George Vincent Chalmers."

"Of course. Well, George, you naturally haven't had time to think about what you're going to do."

"No, sir." And I thought, What in the world can we *ever* do without Pop? I couldn't earn a living for my mother and myself and maybe she'd have to take in washing or something awful like that.

"Well," said the doctor, "you can't stay here alone until your mother gets home."

I nodded my head. "Oh, sure I can. I can stay here all right."

"Have you had supper?"

"No, sir, but I don't want any. I'm kind of sick to my stomach."

"Haven't you some friends around here you could stay with?"

"I don't want to. I'll stay here all right."

"Hmm. I don't believe that's a very good idea. We'll see what can be done."

"I'll be fine."

Dr. Davenport mused a moment and then said, "I trust your sister is all right after plural birth."

"I guess so. Anyhow the telegram said she and the twins were doing well."

"What are they, boys or girls?"

"Both."

"Well, well, I wouldn't have thought that little Sterling had it in him."

It hurt my face but I grinned. "That's exactly what my father—said." At the "said" my voice broke and tears gushed again. I rubbed them away and said, "I'm sorry to be such a darn baby."

"You're no baby, George. You're being very brave in the face of a terrible tragedy, but it's a tragedy we all have to face sooner or later."

I looked at my father on the couch. I had never seen a dead person before, but he looked awfully dead with his hands now folded where the doctor had put them and no color in his face. Now I should never, never hear any stories about his life in the mining country of the Wild West. Why hadn't he told me before? Why hadn't I asked him?

Dr. Davenport shifted uneasily in his chair, then took out a brier pipe, stoked it from a pouch and lit it with a kitchen match. Then he looked around him but my father didn't use tobacco so we had no ashtrays or cuspidors. I took the burned match, carried it to the kitchen and then returned to my straight chair.

At last the windowless black hearse drew up in front of the house and Mr. Lister and another man came in with a stretcher and a sheet and brown blanket.

Mr. Lister spoke softly to Dr. Davenport and me and looked at my father. "Oh, this is sad, very sad indeed," he said. "Mr. Chalmers was a fine Christian man. I saw him only a few days ago and he seemed in perfect health."

"Yes," said Dr. Davenport, "his son can be grateful at least that his father went quickly and painlessly instead of after a lingering illness."

I didn't say anything, but I thought, Well, if he'd been sick at least we could have kind of expected it and Mama would have been home.

The man with Mr. Lister put the stretcher down beside the couch and there was a knock at the front door. Dr. Davenport went into the hall and I heard a woman's voice, hushed but yet shrill, "Oh, Doctor, what *is* it?"

"Mr. Chalmers," said the doctor. "Heart attack. Very sudden."

"Oh, my God! Don't say so."

Mrs. McConnell from next door was in the room, her blue eyes wide, her lips parted. She was wearing a blue-and-pink flowered long apron. "My heavens," she said, "I was in the kitchen and my son Pat called out, 'Hey, Mom, there's a hearse pulled up at the Chalmers,' and I couldn't think what in the world and dashed right over."

She continued talking, but Mr. Lister and his man were about to lift my father to the stretcher and I put my hand on my father's forehead. It was shockingly cool. Then they lifted him down to the stretcher and the assistant covered my father completely first with the white sheet and then with the brown blanket.

"I'll talk with you later, John," said the doctor.

"All right, Doc," Mr. Lister said. Then he and his man lifted the stretcher and the assistant said, "Big, heavy man," and they carried the stretcher out and slid it through the back door of the black, windowless hearse, slammed the door, climbed up to the front seat, clucked to the horses and maneuvered the big vehicle around in the middle of the street and moved slowly back toward town. Several children, including Patrick and Maisie McConnell, were on the sidewalk watching and old Mr. and Mrs. Mallon were standing on their front porch across the street.

Mrs. McConnell put her arm around me and kissed me wetly on the cheek. "Oh, Georgie," she said, "I just can't tell you how terribly sorry I am, and you all alone here when it happened. Why didn't you call me?"

"I've been worrying about this boy," said Dr. Davenport. "His mother's in Colorado and I have wired her, but—"

"Don't you worry another instant," Mrs. McConnell said. "He's coming home with me until his mother gets back. He can sleep with my boy Patrick."

"I'll be all right here," I said.

"Here alone? I wouldn't hear of such a thing. You just go get your nightie and toothbrush. And I'll just bet you haven't had any supper, have you?"

"I'm not a bit hungry."

"Well, honey, you've got to eat something anyhow. We've already had our supper, but I'll fix you something you'll like."

"No, Mrs. McConnell, I'll be perfectly all right here at home."

"Now, George," said Dr. Davenport, "I can't leave you here alone and I must make some house calls now. You've got to be a big fellow and not a stubborn child, so you go along with Mrs. McConnell without any more argument."

Mrs. McConnell put her arm around me and squeezed my shoulder. I blinked away some tears and said, "All right."

Chapter 11

FOR all practical purposes I was suspended in space until my mother got home from Denver Monday night, exhausted from grief and a sleepless night on the train.

I lived in a daze with my sorrow compounded by a suffocating sense of guilt which I dared not mention. If I had obeyed my father and mowed the lawn instead of going to practice baseball with the boys, he would not have undertaken my chore in the unseasonable afternoon heat and would still be alive. My disobedience had killed my father. In effect I had murdered him.

All the McConnells went out of the way to be kind to me. Even Maisie and Pat called me George instead of Sleepy and coaxed me into games of parcheesi and flinch to take my mind off my bereavement.

Ralph Sterling telegraphed the time of my mother's arrival and Mr. and Mrs. McConnell went with me to meet the train. She stumbled slightly when she stepped from the porter's stool on the station platform, and Mr. McConnell caught her arm and took her suitcase. She was pale and red-eyed as she clutched me desperately and kissed me. "Oh, Georgie," she said, "you're the only man I've got now. You'll just have to be strong for both of us."

We were blocking passage from the car, and Mr. McConnell gently led us to one side. Mrs. McConnell kissed her then and my mother said, "How kind of you to come and meet me."

Mrs. McConnell said, "George has been staying with us since, since . . ."

"Oh, how kind of you," said my mother. "I'd wondered and worried about what the poor boy could do."

"He was just like one of the family," Mrs. McConnell said.

We walked slowly home with Mr. McConnell carrying the suitcase and Mrs. McConnell trying to divert my mother's thoughts with countless questions about Laura and the twins.

Our house was dark and unbearably gloomy-looking and I wished that I had been bright enough to go in and light some lamps before going to the station. But Mrs. McConnell insisted that we go in her house first where she whipped up some scrambled eggs and bacon and made a pot of coffee for my mother, and that gave me a chance to slip out the back door and light a couple of lamps and leave the front door open to get rid of the musty smell. Although I had been home once since they took my father away, just to get his Sunday suit and a white shirt, collar and tie for the undertaker, that was in the daylight and quite different from entering this pitch-dark house of death. With the big living-room lamp lit, I could almost see the shadow of my father still on the leather couch. With a shock, I saw that his shoes were still where he dropped them and I picked them up and put them in the hall seat. I wondered why I hadn't given Mr. Lister my father's Sunday shoes, but, acting like an automaton, I had taken precisely what he had asked for. Why, I hadn't even taken a clean pair of socks from the bureau and, if unaccountably, my father was going to his own funeral shoeless, my mother surely would be horrified to see him with those holes in his socks. I carried the small lamp upstairs, found a neatly rolled pair of black socks in the bureau drawer and put them into my pocket. Tomorrow I would slip them surreptitiously to the undertaker.

Mr. McConnell carried the suitcase into our hall, bade us a sad but awkward good night and fled.

In the night I heard my mother sobbing in her room and that was an awful thing. I thought it was my duty to go and try to comfort her, but before I could resolve myself to move I was crying myself and couldn't do it.

The church was nearly half full for my father's funeral and the organ moaned and my father lay on cream-colored satin in his black coffin, and I need not have worried about shoes or socks either because the coffin lid was a sort of Dutch door with only the upper part open, revealing him from the waist up. His eyes were closed and he looked peaceful but very strange with his cheeks pink and white like a young girl or a wax doll, and the bridge of his nose was bony and thin. I had the thought that this was not my father at all but something like the dry shell of a cicada one saw on fences and tree trunks after the adult had escaped.

The words of the Reverend Mr. Reynolds in praising my father as a wonderful Christian gentleman who now was assuredly in Paradise strengthened that thought, but his lugubrious voice and manner were not consistent with that assurance, nor were the tears of my mother beside me. Sitting stiffly in the church, I tried to tell myself that we who loved my father should not mourn because he had broken free from his earthly chrysalis and gone to his greater glory. But I couldn't get rid of the bitter lump in my throat nor the paralyzing worry about what in the world my mother and I could do now.

We rode to the cemetery in one of Mr. Lister's carriages behind the hearse with its bobbing black plumes—to the shocking mound of raw, yellow clay beside the modest headstones of Jerome and Frances Chalmers, the brother and sister I never saw—followed by a dozen or so other carriages. My mother and I were ushered to the graveside while the people who followed grouped around and the men took off their hats. Unconcerned by the sorrows of humans, a mockingbird sang brilliantly nearby while the Reverend Mr. Reynolds, his thinning hair ruffled by the June breeze, spoke again and gave a prayer. Then, by means of heavy straps, the pallbearers lowered my father's coffin into the yellow hole, the minister dropped a clod of clay after it, murmuring about ashes and dust, and we were driven on our sad way home.

So it was all over. Apologizing for not attending Protestant services, Mrs. McConnell invited us to supper and we went and I discovered I had an appetite for the first time in days, although my mother ate sparingly of the creamed new peas and potatoes, roast pork, spiced crab apples and canned peaches.

In settling my father's estate, it was found that he had one hundred and eighty-three dollars in his checking account, a two-thousand-dollar life-insurance policy against which he had borrowed two hundred dollars the year before when Laura was married, the equity in our mortgaged home, our furniture and his office furniture, and a few unpaid commissions on insurance policies he had sold. However, the latter and the money in the bank would be consumed largely by outstanding debts, including the shocking expense of the funeral.

What were we to do? Well, the sensible solution seemed to lie in letters from Laura and Ralph, urging my mother to sell the house and furniture and move to Denver. Laura was not at all well and she needed her mother. She also needed someone to help her with the housework and caring for the twins. There was the nice spare room for grandma and the fine sleeping porch for me. Sleeping porches were very popular in Denver's salubrious climate and I would love it. I could go to a wonderful city high school which had so many advantages over that of our small town, and I could care for the lawn and garden and shovel snow in the winter.

With the frown wrinkles cutting deeper into her forehead, my mother kept asking, "Now, what do you really think, George—should we or shouldn't we?"

I didn't know what to say. Leaving the only home I ever had known, and leaving it permanently for the unknown, would be a painful wrench and even frightening. But then, going to the romantic Rocky Mountains and the big city of Denver would be an exciting adventure and, after all, it appeared that we had to do something until I was old enough and big enough to hold down a man's job at a man's pay so I could support my mother.

So in the end my mother sold our equity in the house at a sacrifice for a quick sale, debated over whether to hold an auction or to call in second-hand-furniture dealers, and decided on the latter because she didn't believe she could stand the melodrama of her possessions going under the auctioneer's hammer. We retained only her favorite wicker rocking chair, two old trunks filled with clothing and linen and a few cherished books and pictures.

In my room she pointed to my Remington print of the Indian scout and asked, "You don't want to keep that old thing do you?"

I said, "Well, Mama, I suppose not, but it's pretty familiar and would make any place seem like home. It doesn't take up much room."

"All right," she said, "and I suppose you'll want the Lord's Prayer, naturally."

I shook my head. "I can get along all right without that," I said. "I know the Lord's Prayer and Ten Commandments by heart anyhow."

It was a confused, hectic, hot, weary, disconsolate period before we finally got away, but I found time to walk over to the West Side to see old pard Cal Campbell once more. He still had his menagerie and still was planning on a career as a naturalist, but he seemed more restrained and perhaps more mature than when we were so closely associated in building our cabin out on the river. I told him I wished I had time for us to hike out to our once beloved retreat.

"No, George," he said, "it's just as well that you can't. I've been out and had a hard time finding where our cabin used to be. It's gone. Don't know whatever happened to it, but there's just a few sticks and scraps of tin left in the weeds. Maybe somebody just knocked it down and maybe the river got high enough in the last floodtime to wash it away."

It was a sad thing to me that the prime relic of our fine friendship was eradicated, but I was pleased that he had been moved to walk out to the scene of our mutual enterprise. This was somewhat puzzling also. Our drifting apart had been largely his doing, not mine.

We shook hands solemnly on parting. "Drop me a line, will you?" he asked.

"Of course," I said. And after we had been in Denver a couple of weeks, I wrote him a long, descriptive letter. He replied more briefly, complimenting me on my "fine writing." I wrote again, thinking that this cherished friendship was being revived, but he did not answer that one and I never heard from him again. To this day I have no idea what ever happened to old pard Calvin Campbell.

On the day before we took the train, my mother and I walked out to my father's grave, carrying pink and yellow roses. We knelt and prayed by the new tombstone and my mother said chokingly, "It just doesn't seem that I can go away and leave him here. But we've got to go, and we can't take him with us."

Chapter 12

SO WE moved to Denver. Although the trip was full of interest, it still was a long, tiresome journey, putting in nearly three hours in the sooty, echoing waiting room of the old Kansas City, Missouri, Union Station to change to the Santa Fe Railroad's Denver train. Then, dozing now and then in a chair-car seat through the endless night, with crossing bells ringing clang, *clang*, CLANG, *Clang*, swelling to crescendo and fading quickly diminuendo as we ripped through little light-spangled Kansas towns, with the whistle up ahead booming its contempt for sleeping villagers.

My mother sat with me and when she moved she woke me

and when I moved she moaned as if life were too hopeless to bear. But at last gray light began to show beneath the window shade and I pinched the center clasp and pushed up the shade a trifle so I could look out on the most astonishingly flat country I had ever imagined, stretching south for miles and miles with only the faintest of undulations to a lavender horizon that blended with the cloudless sky in no really sharp dividing line. Once in a long while a tiny ranch house and outbuildings squatted in the vastness, with its inevitable windmill and perhaps a clump of weary trees and long, lonely shadows stretching westward, steeped in the melancholy of a dog's howl at midnight.

So this was part of the romantic cattle country where the romantic cowboys roamed. I decided that New Mexico or Colorado or Wyoming would be more wholesome.

Presently a trainman announced from the front of the car that we would stop at Dodge City for breakfast in about twenty minutes and the name Dodge City rang a responsive note as the scene of Wild West gun battles. I pictured bechapped and begunned badmen riding across these very plains, but now no living thing was in sight except a scrawny, long-horned cow and suckling calf next to the railroad's barbed-wire fence.

I went to the men's room and two tousled middle-aged men were sitting gloomily on the bench, waiting for the washbasin, while a younger man, obviously a dude, stood spread-legged and galluses suspended before the small mirror, carefully shaving with a straight razor. I went back out, drank two cups of ice water from the tank, ran my fingers through my hair and returned to my seat.

We were traveling very fast. By my Ingersoll watch, the mileposts were ripping past every fifty-six seconds. My mother staggered to the ladies' end of the car and when she returned, the whistle was blowing and we were slowing for Dodge City and there was a scramble for the exits.

On the platform a white-jacketed Negro was pounding rapidly on a three-foot gong, the reverberations of one *bong* interrupted by the next before they were half spent. As my mother and I followed the rush into the Harvey House a man said to us, "My, breathe that air! Better than two-thousand-feet elevation here. Don't get air like that down in the Mississippi Valley."

I took a lungful as recommended and it was good fresh air all right. I remembered Ralph Sterling's saying the air in Colorado was like wine, and I wondered if the air at Denver's five thousand feet would be substantially more exhilarating than this. Another lungful of western Kansas air failed to give me the joyous sense which I assumed drinkers sought from alcohol. I just felt tired, leg-achy, melancholy and homeless.

We found seats together at one of the crowded counters and had bowls of oatmeal with milk and coffee while most of the people around us seemed to be wolfing down ham and eggs, pancakes with bacon or sausage or even small steaks with potatoes. I did not envy them. As a matter of fact, the oatmeal felt like a solid lump in my stomach when we went back to our sad, red-plush seat in the train.

So Westward, Ho! And a trainman announced that we should have dinner at "La Hoonta, Colorado" shortly after noon—a station which, because it was spelled La Junta, seemed strangely missing from our timetable. I did not tell my mother because she might worry. While I stared out the window at a winding band of cottonwoods and brush that now seemed to be following the course of a stream, she was turning the pages of a *Woman's Home Companion* Mrs. McConnell had given her at the depot. The next time I looked at her she was taking a nap, and while she was asleep we stopped at a town called Garden City. I thought they probably had named the place as a joke, like calling a fat boy Skinny. Still, I saw a rank of tall sunflowers growing by a cottage and another of hollyhocks by a blacksmith shop. Perhaps they could constitute a garden in this otherwise dreary land.

My mother slept a long time and when she finally awoke I crawled past her to the men's room and washed my hands and face and combed my hair. As I was finishing, a portly, gray-haired man came in and announced that we were now in Colorado. "That was Holly we just passed through," he said gayly.

"Well," I said, "can you see the Rocky Mountains now?"

He shook his head. "Not for a long time yet. Not until after dinner and maybe not until we've come to Pueblo and turned north. Then we run right alongside 'em, and at Colorado Springs, Pikes Peak is right there. This your first trip out?"

"Yes, sir," I said, "but I'm going to live in Denver."

"You'll love it. Health-seeker?"

"I beg your pardon?"

"Well, excuse me," he said, steadying himself against the door of the toilet, "but you look a little skinny and tired and an awful lot of people go to Colorado on account of lungs."

"Gosh," I said, "my lungs are fine. Of course I hope to be healthy in Colorado, but I was healthy at home too. Well, my father died so my mother and I are going out, well to be with relatives—well, for a while anyhow."

"Oh, I'm sorry." He looked sorry and rubbed one hand over his broad mouth as if to wipe out the words he'd spoken. "Going to school in Denver?"

"Yes, sir. For a while anyhow."

"Very good schools in Denver. How far along are you?"

"I'll be in first year high school."

"Good. You want to finish high school. These days you got to have an education to get any place. Take a commercial traveler like me and you might say all he needs is the gift of gab. Well, I've got that all right, but I always regretted never finishing high school. What you want to make of yourself?"

I had no wish to confess to this man that I'd like to be an artist or a naturalist or some kind of author so I said, "Well, I don't know exactly, but I reckon it will depend on what kind of an opportunity comes along. I reckon the thing to do is to get a job with a good company and work hard and learn the business and get promoted."

He grinned and slapped me on the shoulder. "That's the stuff, boy," he said. "Too many modern kids have nothing but highfalutin ideas. They want to be nothing but doctors or lawyers or orators and run for governor or President or something. So they wind up being teamsters or pushing a pen in somebody's office. The best motto I know for a young fellow is a poem that goes, 'Early to bed, early to rise, work like hell and advertise.' That don't just mean putting an ad in the paper. That means when you do a good job just seeing to it, one way or another, that the boss finds out about it. I don't mean you got to go around blowing your own horn all the time, but I don't care what you may read in your Ralph Waldo Emersons and Elbert Hubbards, being too modest has hurt more men than a little polite bragging."

"Well," I said, "I suppose so, but right now I haven't got much to brag about."

"You're proud, aren't you?"

"Gosh, mister," I said, "I don't know what in the world I've got to be proud of."

"What's your name?"

"George Chalmers."

"Very good name. Shows good ancestors. Be proud of your name. Be proud that you're an American with a good old American name and not something like Ignatz Mussijowski, for heaven's sake. You be proud of your name and proud of yourself and you'll find that carries you over the rough spots. Everybody has rough spots now and then and gets feeling low. George Washington had it so rough at Valley Forge that most everybody else would have given up. But, by golly, he knew he was George Washington and he was proud of it and there was no give up to him."

"I guess you're right," I said.

"Your darn tootin I'm right. Take me. My name's Claude McCarthy and I'm proud of it. My name and being proud of it has carried me over manys the bad bump. Suppose business is bad, but I think I've got one big deal nailed down. I'm counting on that big deal to carry me on, and then it falls through. That's really bad and I'm feeling mighty low, maybe as low as George Washington at Valley Forge. I go back to my hotel room and hang up my coat and vest and am about to lay down on the bed and maybe feel sorry for myself when I see myself in the looking glass, kind of slump-shouldered, and I say, 'Hey, what is *this!* Is that Claude McCarthy feeling licked just because he's been knocked down?' I straighten up my shoulders and look myself in the eye and I say, 'Of course that wasn't Claude McCarthy. This is the Claude McCarthy, the old champ, and nobody on earth can put him down for keeps.' Then I have to laugh at the very idea of Claude McCarthy ever feeling low because one stinking deal fell through, and I wash my face and comb my hair and put my hat on straight and I walk out of there banging my heels down hard and I say, 'Look out, world, here comes Claude McCarthy on the warpath. He's dangerous any time, but he's most dangerous when he's been clipped.' And, believe me, it never fails that business begins to pick up right away."

"Well, Mr. McCarthy," I said, "it's sure good to know that."

"You remember that, boy. Be proud of yourself and be proud

of your name. Then when the going gets tough you just say, I'm George Chandler and there's nothing on earth can put George Chandler down for keeps."

"Chalmers," I said.

"Well, Chalmers," he said.

I thanked him for his encouragement and went back to my mother, and said to myself, I'm George Chalmers, *the* George Chalmers, and nothing on earth can put me down for keeps. But I couldn't make it sound very convincing and I decided it probably took a good deal of practice to make the magic phrase work and that perhaps one had to be a successful salesman or politician to persuade oneself of complete invincibility.

The train was more than two hours late getting to La Junta for dinner because several cars of a freight train were derailed ahead of us. We sat on the eastern Colorado prairie in the bright sunshine while a wrecker crew ahead finished repairing the track, lifting the recalcitrant boxcars back on the rails and sending the freight on its way. A good many passengers walked up to watch this operation, but I wandered south where I could stand alone on the buffalo-grass desert and absorb a sense of being where no human had ever stood before. This was slightly difficult with the very human clanking and banging racket of the wrecking crew in my ears, but I did it. There was yucca growing and prickly pear, and the sun was brighter than I had ever seen it before, on the coarse, reddish sand. Curiously, I remembered the day years before when I was playing baseball and looked at the sunshine and said, This is planetary light, and I thought I was pretty ridiculous in those days. Then I thought that no doubt I was just as ridiculous now as then, if I could only see it. I knew now for certain that the sun was no planet, but I knew precious little else. Then I laughed to myself, stuck out my chest and said, I'm proud to be the real George Chalmers and nobody on earth can lick me, and that includes Jim Jeffries and the Czar of Russia. Then I spoke aloud and said, "Nuts." My voice sounded odd because the prairie wind carried it away.

I discovered a huge ant hill, well over a foot high, swarming with giant red ants, and was examining it when I became conscious of a voice faintly calling, "George! George!" Turning, I saw my mother out on the railroad embankment, beckoning me to return. I trotted back and she caught me by the arm. "My land," she said, "haven't I got enough troubles without you worrying me to death?"

"Gosh, Mama," I said, "I don't know what you mean. I was just out there looking at the biggest ant hill you ever saw in your life."

"Suppose the train had started up and left you out there alone?"

"The train can't start while the track ahead is still blocked, and besides there's a lot of other passengers up there watching and they'd never start without blowing the whistle first and you'd be surprised at how fast I'd get back here if they blew the whistle."

"I suppose you could run faster than the train."

"Trains start out slow, and anyhow they wouldn't start for a while after they blew the whistle."

"How can you know any such thing? Besides, I don't see why ever you'd want to go wandering off in this awful country. There's certainly nothing to see."

"Why, sure there is, Mama," I said. "There was that great big ant hill I told you about and cactus and . . ."

We were back to the car step and it was so high above the cindered embankment that it presented a real problem to my mother. She looked at it and said, "My land."

"How'd you ever get down it?" I asked.

"I was so worried about you that I jumped down."

"Well," I said, "haven't I got enough troubles without you worrying me to death by jumping down something without thinking how you're going to get back?"

"Enough of that, young man," she said severely. She raised one foot tentatively and couldn't get it more than halfway to the level of the lower step.

"There must be some way out of this," I said. "If it was just possible to get that wrecker-car derrick back here, they could lift you up."

"You hush. I'm not that heavy. Do you think you could boost me?"

"Well, I'll try." I stooped, clasped my arms about her waist and although she weighed perhaps twenty pounds more than I did, I lifted her about a foot off the embankment. She clutched desperately for the second step with her hands and as I pushed her forward she doubled up and banged one knee on the lower step. When I relaxed my grip she almost toppled backward, but I gave her a hard shove that sent her forward, and she scrambled up to the vestibule on hands and knees. I swung up and helped her to her feet. There was a smudge on one cheek where she either had struck the vestibule floor or had left a mark from a dirty hand.

She grimaced and rubbed her right knee. "I whacked my knee terribly," she said.

"I'm sorry, Mom."

"You should be. And I don't think you had to be so rough with your mother, either."

"Well, gosh, Mom, it was all I could do to get you up there any way at all. I didn't mean to get rough. I guess we should have waited for some man to come along and help, but if I had just thought, I could have got down on my hands and knees and you could have taken off your shoes and stood on my back and then it would have been an easy step up for you."

"It's a little late to think of that now."

"Of course," I said, "we could go down and do it over."

"No, thank you."

"Then maybe you'd better go to the ladies' room and wash your face."

"Is my face dirty?"

"Yes, ma'am."

She frowned and limped to the far end of the car, and I returned to our seat and looked out the window at the now familiar landscape. About fifty yards away a jack rabbit stood up surprisingly tall, inspected the train, and then hopped off on his business. It wasn't long after my mother came back with cheeks scrubbed pink that the engineer gave a long blast on his whistle, and two men passengers entered the car, arguing loudly. One was castigating the Santa Fe Railroad and saying that sort of thing didn't happen on the Rock Island where the trains were modern enough to carry dining cars. The other was even more scornful of the Rock Island, declaring its roadbed was so rough that he'd rather go hungry than to try to eat in one of its dining cars. Then the whistle blew again and again and presently we began to move slowly. We moved and we stopped. We moved and slowed to a walk. We stopped. We blew our whistle. We moved and increased our speed to perhaps thirty miles an hour, to a small town where we stopped long enough for the freight train and the wrecker to take to a side track. And, at last, we came to La Junta where another white-jacketed Negro beat on a gong and, at a counter similar to the one in Dodge City, my mother and I devoured bowls of beef stew that seemed delicious to me, bread and butter, soggy apple pie and coffee. I could have consumed another bowl of stew easily, but even before we had finished our pie a trainman was shouting, " 'Board! All aboard!" obviously trying to make up some time by cutting the meal period short.

My mother was still limping as we made our way toward our car, and Claude McCarthy, toothpick in mouth, came beside us. "Well, Mr. McCarthy," I said, "we finally made it."

He glanced at me, said, "Oh, hullo," and hurried on. He seemed embarrassed and I thought I understood why. I thought he was a compulsive talker and now was uncomfortable because he had confided so much of his own struggle with life to a strange, half-grown boy when he had only set out to impress me with some sage advice. Now he blamed me for his embarrassment and hated me and never wanted to see me again. I felt rather sorry for Mr. McCarthy.

So on westward to the smoky city of Pueblo and the exciting flare of steel plants, then north and here were the Rocky Mountains just outside our window, tree-clad but disappointingly low to me who had expected them to plunge into the sky. At Colorado Springs, however, the mountains came closer to my picture of them. Braving my mother's displeasure, I slipped off the car to the station platform and stared at the terrestrial upheaval before me. It was actually chilly out there and a very thin young man on the platform was wearing a heavy, roll-neck, gray sweater. I asked him if the highest mountain in sight was Pikes Peak.

"Oh, no," he said. "That's just Cheyenne Mountain, scarcely half as high as Pikes. The bald, snowy crown of Pikes is lost in the clouds back there."

He pointed and I made out the cog railroad winding up the flanks of the giant. This was a thrill and I forgot my homelessness and melancholy. "My goodness," I said, "have you been up there?"

The young man shook his head. "I'd love to go," he said, "but I'm a lunger and I'm not allowed to. Next year when I'm well I'll go, though."

I looked at him and his face was tanned and ruddy. Except for his thinness, he looked remarkably healthy to me. I wondered if sometimes people who had been very ill got into the habit of thinking of themselves as sick and couldn't get over the habit even after they were completely cured.

My mother was struggling with the car window when I returned and she said, "It's downright cold in this place, summer or not."

I got the window down and said, "Well, after all, Pikes Peak is right out there and a man told me there's snow on top of it even if you can't see it because of the clouds."

She craned her neck to look and said mildly, "Just imagine." Then she looked at me seriously and said, "George, I didn't tell you this because I thought you knew. You're not supposed to go to the toilet when the train's standing at a station."

"Sure, Mama, I know," I said. I didn't say that I had been down on the station platform instead of in the toilet and she didn't ask for an explanation.

At Palmer Lake, which seemed to be right in a mountain valley, they turned the car lights on and my mother took a nap while we roared downgrade through the gathering darkness toward Denver, the whistle whooping gleefully as we neared the end of our long journey. I was hungry and wished a train butcher would come along selling crackerjack or bananas or something.

Then clusters of lights were flitting by and the whistle grew even more excited and passengers began to stand up and take articles down from the baggage rack and I knew we were entering the great city of Denver, Colorado. There was the clang of crossing bells and arc lights raced past and rows of brick-red boxcars and switch engines and factory smokestacks in the distance and a maze of railroad tracks and the sigh of airbrakes and a trainman calling, "Denver, Denver, Colorado. Everyone out at Denver," and we were stopping amidst the weird, sharp shadows under train sheds and with thumping heart I was getting my mother's suitcase and coat down from the baggage rack and my own suitcase from under the seat and I was helping her on with her coat because she still thought it was cold, and people were filing down the aisle with their baggage while she fixed her hat firmly on her head and I put on my cap and she gathered up her handbag and magazine and started to take her suitcase.

"No, Mama," I said, "I can handle both suitcases fine."

"You sure?"

"Sure, I'm sure."

I followed her into the aisle and bumped the suitcases a little against the seats, but not much, out into the vestibule and down the steps to the porter's stool and up a cement ramp toward a broad, iron gate where a crowd of people waited. I swept my eyes across the gate, trying to find Laura and Ralph. They didn't seem to be there and I wondered how in the world we'd ever find our way to their house unless my mother remembered the way, which didn't seem likely.

Then the gate opened and the people swarmed forward and suddenly there was Ralph Sterling wearing a straw boater, the arc lights glittering on his eyeglasses, immaculate and grinning as he rushed up. He kissed my mother on the cheek, saying, "My, my, I'm so glad to see you. Your train was so late we were beginning to worry."

"Hope you didn't have to wait long," my mother said.

"No, we phoned and knew the train was very late, but we were afraid there might have been a wreck or something."

"There *was* a freight-train wreck ahead of us," I said. I put down a suitcase and shook hands with him.

"Well, George," he said, "I'm glad to see you, too. My, you've really been growing."

There was no doubt about my being taller than Ralph now, by several inches. Passengers were flowing around us like a stream around a snag, and I bent to pick up the suitcases.

"No, George," said Ralph, "let me have one of them and let's get started home."

I asked, "Didn't Laura come?"

"Hardly," he said. "She had to stay at home with two handfuls of twins."

As we passed through the wide doors of the Union Station, Ralph said, "Why, Mother Chalmers, you're limping."

"Oh," she said, "I just whacked my knee on the train."

Ralph gasped and paused in midstride. "You did! Well, I do hope it's nothing serious, but—"

"No, I looked at it in the ladies' room and the skin isn't broken. Just a bruise, but it kind of hurts to walk."

"Well," said Ralph, "we'll just have a doctor look into that and the railroad will be held strictly to account."

"Oh no, no," she exclaimed. "It wasn't the railroad's fault at all, at all. If it was anybody's fault, it was George's."

"Well, we'll talk about that later." He nudged me with his elbow. "Maybe we'll have to sue George."

An arch spanned the street in front of the station carrying the word WELCOME outlined in electric light.

"Now, isn't that nice?" my mother said. "A welcome to everybody who comes to Denver. I never noticed that when I was here before."

"That was in the daytime," said Ralph, "and you don't notice it so much when it isn't lighted up. On the other side it says 'Mizpah.' That's Hebrew for 'May God be with thee until we meet again.' "

We had passed under the arch and I looked back to see that it did indeed read MIZPAH, and said, "Hebrew is certainly a fine language to say a lot in a little space. In Hebrew you could send the whole Declaration of Independence in a ten-word telegram."

But as I dallied, my mother and Ralph had pulled ahead of me and paid no attention. They were heading for a red-and-yellow streetcar and I thought that this electric trolley car was the first I had ever seen in my life and it was going to be a new experience to ride on it and that no doubt new experiences were going to crowd one upon another for a long time now that I was going to live in this big city. Ralph politely helped my mother aboard the car and I followed. The rear of the car was open with slatted board seats and had a sort of carnival air, but Ralph directed my mother inside where they sat together on a rattan seat and I squatted opposite them with my suitcase.

Presently a bell went *ding-ding* and the car started forward with a tenor whine, and a blue-jacketed and capped conductor came forward and began taking fares, making change from a nickel-plated, clever apparatus he wore on his belt. As he approached us Ralph held up his hand and said, "Three," jerking his head toward me.

"Thank you, sir," I said.

"Quite all right," Ralph said, seriously, turning back to my mother. I couldn't hear what they were talking about over the clatter and growl of the streetcar, but I was happy to see my mother laugh several times and I thought she seemed more cheerful than at any time since my father died.

We were going through a well-lighted business district, stopping at every corner where more people got on. I hoped no one would want to share my seat because I didn't know what to do with the suitcase, and it so happened that by the time our section of the car was half filled we were out of the business district and growling up a hill through a darker residential district with trees and big brick houses set further back from the street than stores. We rode for a long time and it was much like riding on a train, only jerkier. Sometimes a gong in front went *clang-clang*, but I couldn't see why. At other times the small bell made a single *ding* and the car stopped at the next intersection to let passengers off. The car started again after the bell clinked twice. That was interesting to know—one ding to stop, two to go. Perhaps three dings would mean to back up, if it were possible to back a trolley car.

We screeched around several turns and finally Ralph stood up and pulled a cord that draped along above the windows, causing the bell to ding. He smiled at me and said, "Here we are, George." So the car stopped and we descended to a street of coarse gravel, and when the car went on its way we crossed the streetcar tracks and walked up the dimly lit intersecting street half a block, past brick houses, and turned up four cement steps of a terrace to a brick house with a white wooden porch much like the other brick houses in the block. Ralph turned a key in the front door, pushed the door open and stood aside to allow my mother and me to enter the hall.

My sister Laura dashed into the hall and threw her arms around our mother. "Oh, Mama, Mama," she cried, "I'm *so* glad you're here." Then she hugged and kissed me and exclaimed, "Why Georgie, you've grown practically into a man."

"Well," I said, "I'm still in short pants." I felt warm and happy to see Laura. She seemed thinner in the face but otherwise just the same. Ralph took my cap and hung it with his straw hat on a hall tree and we went into the living room, lighted by an electric chandelier in the center of the ceiling. The living room was smaller than ours at home, and furnished with a flowered davenport, a big leather rocking chair, a wicker rocker, a golden-oak armchair with leather seat and back, a straight chair, an oak table, and a phonograph with petunia horn on a stand that had a record cabinet beneath. There was a small fireplace with grate on the far side of the room and above the mantel, in a gilt frame, hung a large oil painting of a Rocky Mountain scene with a stream cascading down the center. On the table were copies of the *Saturday Evening Post,* the *Ladies' Home Journal,* and the *Literary Digest* and a book. The book was *The Trail of the Lonesome Pine* by John Fox, Jr.

My mother had dropped heavily into the big leather rocker and her feet were off the floor as it swayed back. "Now," she said, "how are the little darlings?"

"Oh fine, Mama, just fine," Laura said. "Of course they're asleep now. You'll want to take a peek at them before you go to bed, but I think George can wait until morning. I don't want to risk waking them up."

"Gosh," I said, "you think I'd yell at them or something?"

"Of course," said Ralph. "You couldn't help giving three cheers when you see how wonderful they are."

"Oh, Mama," said Laura, "I'm taking it for granted that you ate on the train. Of course we had dinner when the train was so late, but I can get you something in a jiffy."

"No, thank you," my mother said, "I couldn't eat a bite. We didn't eat on the train, but we stopped at places for something to eat."

"Yes," said Ralph, "that's the way the Santa Fe does it. They don't carry dining cars."

Everyone seemed to take it for granted that if my mother couldn't eat a bite I couldn't either. This was a mistake, but I couldn't bring myself to speak up and say I was starved.

"I hate to say this when we just got here," my mother said, "but I've had a hard time and am really tuckered out. All I want is to get to bed as soon as possible."

"Of course, darling," said Laura. "Ralph, will you please carry Mama's suitcase upstairs?"

The three of them went upstairs, and I felt uncomfortable sitting stiffly alone in this strange place. I picked up the *Saturday Evening Post* from the table and was looking at the illustrations when Ralph returned.

"Well, old boy," he said, "I understand you're ready for high school."

I put the magazine back on the table. "Yes, sir, I reckon I am."

"That's fine, George. But you shouldn't use 'reckon' in that sense. Using 'reckon' that way sounds like an ignorant hillbilly." He laughed. "I'm telling you because I used to say 'I reckon' until I learned better myself. 'Reckon' really means to come to a conclusion after taking into account all facets of a situation, good and bad."

I said, "Yes, sir," but I thought he had described exactly what I had done—considered my good chances and my bad chances and decided that *perhaps* I was ready for high school.

"I suppose," he said, "that you'll probably go to Central. That's not the newest high school in the city, but it's the closest and certainly one of the best. I know Tom Sparks, the principal, and he's a very fine man and an able administrator. They have an exceptional faculty at Central."

"Good," I said.

"Have you reached any sort of decision on what you want to try to make of yourself?"

"Not exactly, sir." Then I remembered how Mr. Claude McCarthy had responded to my spur-of-the-moment inspiration on the train and said, "I reckon—I mean I suppose—it'll depend on what opportunities I have. What I've thought of is to try to get a job with a real good company and work very hard and learn everything about the business I can learn every chance I get and be polite and try to get promoted to better and better jobs."

Ralph nodded. "A sound idea," he said. "A very sound idea for a boy your age, and I hope you stick to it. And a boy can't start working too early. You'll be able to find a job where you can work after school and earn enough to pay your carfare and for your books and lunches and clothing. Most boys these days are lazy and loaf on the job, so a trustworthy, energetic, honest boy never has any trouble getting and keeping a job."

"Is the high school too far away to walk?" I asked. "I'm a pretty good walker."

Ralph pursed his mouth. "I wouldn't say it was *too* far to walk, but considering the amount of shoe leather you'd wear out, I'd think you could put your time to better advantage by spending a nickel and riding the tramway—that's what they call the streetcars here."

Laura came downstairs then and patted my shoulder. "You come along now, George," she said, "and I'll show you your sleeping porch. Of course you don't have to go to bed until you want to."

I picked up my suitcase and followed her through the dining room into the kitchen where she flipped on an electric light. It was a much neater kitchen than I would have expected Laura to have and I decided she had learned to be a good housekeeper out of necessity. There was a clean gas range, a Hoover kitchen cabinet, a big oak refrigerator, a kitchen table and chairs, and the floor was covered with bright linoleum. I thought that if I were at home I'd just see what there might be in the refrigerator for a snack, but I naturally put that thought aside here.

She led me out the kitchen door to the back porch which stretched the width of the house. The far half was curtained off with green-and-white-striped canvas that slid on metal rings. Laura pushed the curtain to the right and pulled a cord which turned on a naked electric bulb that hung from the ceiling.

Other green-and-white-striped curtains covered the two open sides of the porch, which converted this end of the porch into a sort of tent, except for the brick wall of the house and one window with drawn shade on the inside.

"I think you'll find this pretty snug," she said. "Before you go to bed you can slide one of the outside curtains open a little so you get plenty of this wonderful Colorado air. The sanitary couch there is just right for a boy, not too soft and not too hard."

The cot in question was covered by a crazy quilt which I recognized as my Grandmother Mosby's handiwork and which obviously had been given to Laura by my mother. Besides the cot there was a small pine dresser and a kitchen chair. On the wall a stained board had been fixed, apparently by nailing it into the mortar between bricks, and half-a-dozen hooks had been screwed into the board. On one of the hooks was a clean towel. On two others were wire coat hangers.

"You can keep your towel here, George," said Laura, "and hang your clothing on the hooks, what you don't put neatly away in the drawers."

"I haven't got much clothing with me," I said. "The rest is coming in our trunks."

"I know. Now, George, the bathroom is right at the head of

the stairs and the light switch is beside the door inside the bathroom."

"Yes, ma'am." As I said this I thought that probably was the first time in my life I ever had said "yes, ma'am" to my sister.

She was looking at me seriously. "George," she said, "I want you to know you're just as welcome here as the flowers in May. But there are a few things you'd better understand right in the beginning. This is Ralph's home and Ralph is a very sensitive man. A lot of things irritate him that some men—say, Papa— would never notice. I want you to try very hard not to annoy him. I want you to be polite and neat and to act like a gentleman."

"Well, gosh, Laura," I said, "I always try—"

"I know, I know. But sometimes you can be pretty sloppy and loud. I want you the leave the bathroom just as you found it after using it for any purpose. I want you to make your bed here."

"I've been making my own bed at home for years. You were the one who used to go away in the morning without making your bed."

"Nonsense. Look, George, don't get your dander up and think I'm being too critical. Ralph and I are both very happy to have you here, but when two families are moving in together it's just wise to have an understanding about certain things to begin with. You will try to be agreeable, won't you?"

"Of course."

"Well, that's fine." She kissed me on the cheek. "Now if you want to go to the bathroom and clean up, I think the coast is clear."

She left and I opened my suitcase on the cot, found my toothbrush, took my towel and went upstairs where someone had thoughtfully left the light on in the bathroom. It was a much nicer, brighter one than ours at home. Before leaving, I wiped the washbowl out neatly with the tail of my towel.

Downstairs Laura was lying on the divan reading *The Trail of the Lonesome Pine*. Ralph was in the big leather rocker reading the *Literary Digest*. I asked, "Does anyone mind if I take that *Saturday Evening Post* out to the porch?"

Laura looked up from her book. "Why, honey," she said, "you don't have to go out to the porch to read. You can sit right here and read it."

"Well," I said, "I didn't get much sleep last night and I'm kind of tired. Just thought I might read a little in bed before going to sleep."

"Reading in bed is a very bad habit," said Ralph.

"I don't know," I said. "I've been reading in bed for a long time and neither Pop nor Mom ever said anything against it."

"It's hard on your eyes and bad for you generally to read in bed," Ralph declared.

"Nothing wrong with my eyes," I said.

Ralph looked at me sharply through his rimless glasses. "There will be," he said, "if you keep abusing them."

"George," said Laura, "if you want to read the *Saturday Evening Post*, why don't you just sit down there quietly and read it? Otherwise—"

"No," I said, "I'm tired and want to go to bed. Good night."

"Good night," said Ralph.

"Happy dreams, honey," said Laura.

On the porch I took my shirts, underwear, stockings, hand-kerchiefs and nightshirts from the suitcase and put them in the shallow drawers of the dresser. I hung my spare pair of knickers and sweater on a hook, took off my suit coat and put it on a hanger. I put my brush and comb on the dresser. I left my old shoes, my arithmetic and grammar-school books which I was supposed to study, together with a tablet, pencils, envelopes and such oddments as a rubber slingshot, a harmonica, my fielder's glove and a stained and scuffed baseball in the suitcase, snapped it shut and put it at the far end of the couch.

I felt strange and a little dizzy as I undressed and put on a clean nightshirt. Then I turned down the bed, wound my Ingersoll watch and tucked it under the pillow. This was it. I pulled the light cord, plunging the porch into blackness, and fumbled with the outside canvas curtain until I managed to slide it open a couple of feet.

A faint moon revealed the smooth back yard with a walk, apparently of cement, running down to a board fence in the rear. At the fence stood a curious white object resembling pictures of an Eskimo's igloo, nearly five feet high. Later I was to discover that this was a Denver institution, an ashpit in which trash was burned and furnace ashes dumped. On the lawn was one small tree and along the bordering fences there seemed to be flower beds. There was no vegetable garden nor room for one.

I groped my way to the couch, crawled in and pulled up the covers. The bed was definitely not too soft. Under the pillow my dollar watch ticked comfortingly. Down on the streetcar line a car wow-wow-wowed through the night and clanged its bell, and a small dog yapped and yapped. A long way off someone was playing a piano, but not very well, and I didn't know the piece. The Ingersoll under my pillow was saying, "Everything's going to be all right, boy, everything's going to be all right, boy," and I said to myself, Nuts, nothing matters. None of it's real anyhow, so what the heck? The whole thing's just a silly dream and why take it seriously?

This was dangerous ground, and I knew it well. For several years I had played with that line of thought guardedly and checked it quickly before it went too far. Now, suddenly, I was over the brink and into the vortex of my childhood horrors. The black nothingness around me rocked and I sat up gasping for breath, staring at the pale rectangle between the curtains— the gateway between my awful cell and the equally awful, unreal world beyond.

I struggled out of bed and to my feet, reaching up desperately with both hands for the cord which would bring light and perhaps life and sanity. I couldn't find it . . . I couldn't find it. But the search itself for something tangible brought me out slightly from the very center of the vortex. My leg banged into the kitchen chair, making a harsh, scraping noise, and something fell on one bare foot. My pants, which I had folded carefully, had slipped off the chair and had touched my foot to remind me that they were real, with real things in the pockets— my wallet might be imitation leather, but it was real, real, real, with real hard-earned money in it. My jackknife was real and I could hold it in my hand and open the sharp blades and cut with it.

Now I believed I remembered the position of the light cord in relation to the chair, groped for it, found it and flooded my cubicle with light. That was better, but I was still dizzy and gasping for breath. My mouth was parched and my throat constricted. Perhaps I could go to the kitchen and get a drink of water. While I debated that project, I picked up my knickers, folded them again and put them back on the chair. Then I pushed aside the far curtain, which allowed enough light to fall on the back porch for me to open the back door and enter the kitchen. In the darkness I could make out the sink but could locate no tin cup, which I supposed was standard equipment for all kitchen sinks. So I leaned forward, turned on the faucet and drank greedily of delicious, cold water.

While drinking from the faucet I was blinded by the ceiling light coming on, and there stood Ralph.

"I just wanted a drink," I said, "but couldn't find the tin cup."

He chuckled and I was embarrassed, standing there in my nightshirt. "The family tin cup is a thing of the past," he said. "They were insanitary. So is drinking from the faucet. When you want a drink take a glass from the cupboard here, and it's a good thing for you to have a drink before you go to bed because I have to lock the back door before I go upstairs."

"Well," I said, "if I'm locked out of the house, suppose I have to go to the bathroom in the middle of the night?"

"A boy your age should be able to wait until morning."

"I don't know. Once in a while I do have to go, but I guess I could go in the back yard."

"Don't you ever think of such a thing here. This is a city and that's strictly against the law, for any number of reasons."

"Well," I said, "gosh, I don't know, but maybe you could leave the window in my tent unlocked and I could go in there."

"Window in your tent?"

"Well, the window that opens on the sleeping porch."

Ralph shook his head. "I don't like that idea, and besides, the goldfish aquarium is in front of that window."

"Suppose then I just take the key to the back door and lock it from the outside and keep the key and unlock the door early next morning?"

Ralph looked doubtful. "Do you think I could trust you to be responsible and not forget to lock the door and not to lose the key and to remember to unlock the door early enough in the morning and to put the key back on the inside?"

"Of course," I said. "After all, I'm not any baby." As I said this I wondered if I was telling the truth in view of the night horrors that still lingered as a metallic taste in my mouth.

He was looking at me closely. "All right, George," he said at last. "The responsibility for the back door is yours—at least until you make one slip. Burglars have an exaggerated idea of the money and valuables in a banker's house, and I simply cannot afford any carelessness."

"I won't be careless," I promised and we said good night again, and he watched while I took the key from the back door, shut the door and locked it from the outside. I held up the key so he could see it through the door window. He nodded and turned out the kitchen light.

Back on my sleeping porch I looked for a good place to put the key and decided on my pants pocket. I felt much easier now, after the exchange with Ralph and my small victory over the key. With the sense of walking a tight wire, I pulled out the light, crawled back into bed and turned my face to the wall. I thought of the romantic Rocky Mountains right outside the city where my father had lived and adventured in his youth. The friendly watch under my pillow, constant and tireless, ticked its reassuring message, and I awoke to the plaint of mourning doves outside the once pallid rectangle between the curtains which now was bright with sunshine.

Chapter 13

I LOOKED at my watch and it was half past six. Not knowing how early Laura and Ralph ordinarily got up in the morning, I hurriedly dressed, putting on my extra pants and old shoes and deciding that my traveling shirt could stand another day's wear. While dressing, I was impressed by the extraordinary greenness of that back yard, a characteristic of Denver lawns, I was to learn later.

Through the back-door window I saw there was no one in the kitchen so at least I was not late in opening the door. I turned the key, entered the kitchen and put the key on the inside. There were no sounds of anyone stirring so I peeked in the refrigerator, but there was nothing I dared disturb. Then

I looked into the kitchen cabinet to see if any crackers or cookies were readily available. There weren't.

In the dining room the oblong aquarium Ralph had mentioned stood by the shaded back window and four goldfish and two silverfish stirred as languidly as carp, around a stone castle.

I returned to the kitchen and out the back door. On the north side a profusion of electric-blue morning-glories bloomed on a trellis clear to the porch eaves where a finch twittered happily. Then I remembered the Rocky Mountains and looked west, and through the trees and between houses the front range loomed blue and mighty with, yes, spots of white around the summits. I grinned and said to myself, Well! Then I walked around the house and on the front porch a wooden swing was suspended from the ceiling by chains. Also on the porch was a newspaper and I picked it up and sat in the swing. The newspaper was *The Rocky Mountain News*. I liked that name. A banner line ran across the top of the first page reading, DENVER MAN SHOOTS WIFE, KILLS SELF. It seemed that this woman had left her husband and he felt he couldn't live without her so he went to her sister's house where she was staying and shot her in the abdomen with a thirty-two-caliber revolver, but, fortunately, a corset stay had deflected the bullet sufficiently so her condition was only serious but not critical. He, however, died instantly from a bullet in the temple. There were pictures of all concerned, including some policemen. There wasn't much else of interest on the first page—just some financier predicting an upswing in business, and President Roosevelt calling William Howard Taft a great statesman who would make a great President.

Being careful not to disarrange the paper, I turned back to the sports section to see loudly proclaimed the fact that the Denver Bears had larruped the Pueblo Chiefs. I had never heard of either. More important to me was a terse account of the Cardinals shutting out the Cubs. There also was a local interview with Battling Nelson who said he was willing to fight Packey McFarland anyplace at any time if McFarland would make a hundred and thirty-three pounds, but that McFarland was a welterweight and knew it and couldn't make the lightweight limit without cutting off a leg.

The front door opened and there was Ralph, astonishingly dishabille, coatless, vestless and without his usual high linen collar and tie. His shoulders were narrower than I had thought and the beginnings of a paunch showed above his suspendered trousers.

"Good morning, Ralph," I said. "I was just looking at your newspaper."

"Good morning," he said, "you're up early."

"Well," I said, "a man told me the secret of success is early to bed, early to rise, work like hell and advertise."

He pursed his red lips. "I don't approve of profanity," he said, "but the sentiment is good. Any news?"

I handed him *The Rocky Mountain News*, neatly folded. "It seems that a man shot his wife and himself."

"Hmm."

I became conscious of a strange noise that had been going on for some time and I said, "Say, I think there's a baby around here somewhere."

Ralph didn't smile. "You're minimizing the situation," he said. I followed him into the house and Laura was in the kitchen, in a blue wrapper, heating two baby bottles in a pan of water.

"Good morning, honey," she said. "Did you sleep well?"

"Sure. Did you?"

"Yes. Of course there was the two-o'clock feeding. Hope the babies or I didn't wake you up."

"I didn't hear a thing. Do you reckon the bathroom is clear?"

"I think so. Mama is trying to keep her grandchildren under control until they get their bottles."

It was plain now that at least two babies were squalling at once, and I said, "It doesn't sound as if she was getting very far with it." And I got my towel, toothbrush, comb and hairbrush from the porch and went upstairs. A door was open off the hall and I saw my mother in her pink robe, sitting in a chair and jouncing a very small, howling infant in each arm. She was murmuring, "There, there, Mummy is bringing your breakfast right away."

I stepped into the doorway and stared. "Can you tell which is which?" I asked.

My mother looked up, smiling. "Of course," she said. "Millicent has the curly hair. But they're both beautiful."

This struck me as one of the most ridiculous statements I ever had heard my mother make. Both babies seemed outrageously ugly to me and both heads were covered with a dark fuzz.

"Now don't you think they're beautiful, George?" she asked.

"Mama," I said, "you've taught me to be polite and you've taught me to be truthful and you just hadn't ought to ask me a question like that."

Laura spoke behind me. "Why, you little stinker," she said. "You were the homeliest baby anybody ever laid eyes on. You didn't even look human."

"Now, Laura," said my mother, "George was a nice-looking baby, but I must admit he never was as pretty as Milly and Benny."

Laura's face was flushed and angry. "If I thought for one minute," she said, "that my babies would grow into such a stupid gawk, I'd go drown them."

"Laura, Laura!" my mother exclaimed. "How can you say such a thing to your brother?"

"Okay," I said, "if I'm so darn repulsive I turn your stomach, I don't have to stay here. I'll go pack my grip right now."

Laura put her free hand on my shoulder and I pulled away. "I'm sorry, George," she said. "I'm very, very sorry I said such a thing and I'll never say it again. I suppose it's just natural for a mother to get mad if anyone doesn't think her babies are the most wonderful in the world."

"Okay," I said. "Your babies are purely wonderful and I reckon even a female wart hog will fight for her children."

"I don't know that I like that," she said and shoved a bottle nipple into each squalling mouth. My mother skillfully shifted to hold both a baby and a bottle on each side, and in the unearthly quietude I went to the bathroom.

Downstairs Laura was getting breakfast while Ralph was reading the paper in the living room. She said to me, "Mama and I are going to have oatmeal and toast and coffee, but Ralph likes bacon and eggs for breakfast. You wouldn't want bacon and eggs, would you?"

"No, thank you," I said and took my toilet articles to my sleeping porch and made up my sanitary couch. I stayed there until Laura called me to breakfast.

We ate in the dining room, and as I passed through the kitchen the aroma of frying bacon made my mouth water. My mother was late getting down, having dressed after feeding, burping and bedding down the babies. Little was said at the table and when I was on my second bowl of oatmeal I tried to make a little conversation by remarking, "I saw by the paper that Teddy Roosevelt says Mr. Taft would make a good President."

Ralph didn't look up from his plate. "Mr. Taft certainly has all the qualifications to make a *great* President," he said.

Well, I thought, I guess Ralph's a Republican. I suggested that Mr. Taft was pretty fat.

"All men who are healthy in body and mind get fat in middle age," said Ralph. "When you get old enough to read Shakespeare with understanding, you'll learn that men with a lean and hungry look think too much and are dangerous."

"Aren't Presidents supposed to think a lot?" I asked.

"They're supposed to think wholesome, Christian thoughts, but not to fret and worry. It's worry that makes a person thin and dyspeptic, but it never in the world ever solved a problem."

"I wonder if the Democrats will run Mr. Bryan?" I asked.

"They're crazy if they do."

Ralph drained the last of his coffee, pushed his chair back, slapped his napkin down and said, "Excuse me."

"Certainly," said Laura. We all went on with our breakfasts while Ralph pounded upstairs. When he reappeared, he was dressed in a neat brown suit, high collar, brown four-in-hand with the opal tiepin, and the Masonic charm suspended from his watch chain. He stooped and kissed Laura on the cheek.

"Have a good day, darling," said Laura.

"Thank you," said Ralph, "and the same to you all."

When he was gone, Laura said, "Well, George, if you feel like it, you can mow the lawn this morning. The mower and grass shears are down in the basement."

"Okay," I said, "glad to do it."

"The sun will be too high for you to irrigate by the time you finish mowing, but you can do that this evening."

"Irrigate?"

"Water the lawn with the hose."

"Gee," I said, "it looks wonderfully green now. I don't think it needs any watering."

She shook her head.

"We get very little rain in the summer here and the lawns

have to be watered every day. Denver has beautiful lawns, but they'd be brown and dead if it weren't for irrigating."

"Every day?"

"Every day. Well, once in a long while there'll be a good rain so you can skip one day."

I doubted this but finished my third piece of toast and didn't say anything. The outside entrance to the basement was from the sidewalk, along the north side of the house. I went down the stairs from the kitchen, found the mower and garden shears, and carried them up to the outside door and out to the cement walk. Both the shears and the mower were pretty rusty and the mower even squeaked when I pushed it.

I went into the kitchen and called, "Hey, Laura, where's the oil?"

Laura dashed frowning into the kitchen, holding her wrapper about her. "Heavens to Betsy," she said, "don't scream like that and wake the babies."

"I didn't scream. I just asked you where is the oil."

"Oil?"

"Sure. Oil. That lawn mower is in terrible shape and needs oiling."

"It can't be in terrible shape. Ralph mowed the lawn himself less than a week ago."

"Well, it sure enough needs oil now."

"Please, George, please don't be helpless around here. If there's any oil for the lawn mower, it must be down in the basement somewhere near where you found the mower. Go and look around."

So I went back to the basement and finally found an old can of Three-in-One oil on the ledge and managed to squeeze a few drops into the mower's oil holes. But there was none left for the rusty blades.

It didn't take long to mow the small back lawn, even with the hard-pushing old mower which I guessed Ralph must have got secondhand. The terrace in front presented more of a problem. Pushing down and then hauling back up again was unsatisfactory. So I was trying to cut an even swath as I balanced along laterally on the forty-five-degree slope. At last, although it taxed my strength, I settled on pushing the mower upward from the bottom. It took me longer to trim the edges with the shears than did the actual mowing.

Back in the house I found Laura and my mother in the living room, each cuddling a baby. Both looked quite pleased, and neither infant was crying.

"See here, Uncle George," said Laura, "it's about time you held Benny or Millicent."

"Well," I said.

Laura rose and ordered me to sit down and I sat in the armchair while she placed a baby in my arms. It rolled slate-colored eyes at me and twisted its moist mouth.

"Which one is it?" I asked, uncomfortably.

"*He* is Benny," said Laura.

"That's good," I said. "I reckon the boy would be less apt to break if I dropped it."

"You just drop him and you'll get snatched bald-headed," said Laura, emphatically.

I looked at her and thought, You needn't act so high and mighty toward me, Sis, because I know quite well that these gifts from Heaven are really the result of your sexual depravity. I thought that no doubt a lot of innocent, nice girls became pregnant because their lustful husbands forced them, but that, for goodness sake, Laura certainly was big enough and strong enough so that Ralph Sterling couldn't have had his way with her if she hadn't wanted him to. I held the small bit of protoplasm, gingerly, and wondered how my once revered sister could pretend to be so casual about this proof of her sensuality.

The soft, helpless caricature of a human being in my arms twisted and gasped and I exclaimed, "Gosh, I think something happened right here while I was holding it."

"Oh, you silly goose," said Laura. "Let me have him."

Willingly, I passed the bundle over to her. "Will Ralph hold them?" I asked.

"Will Ralph hold them! Ralph's crazy about his twins. How could any normal man be otherwise?"

Laura started for the stairs, and my mother also rose with her baby, to follow Laura. It was quite a while before they returned without their burdens, announcing that the little darlings were asleep again. I thought that the only good thing you could say about the creatures was that they apparently spent most of their time sleeping.

I said, "Well, I guess I'll go out and take a walk and see what Denver looks like in the daylight."

"That's a good idea," said Laura, "but why don't you wait until after lunch and then you can get back in time to irrigate?"

So I went back to my porch, took out my English grammar and tried to fix in my mind the distinction between "will" and "shall" as well as "would" and "should" and decided the easiest way around such a mess was to use "I'll" for both "will" and "shall" and "I'd" for both "would" and "should."

Then my mother called me to lunch, which was canned tomato soup, bread and butter and Colorado head lettuce with mayonnaise. Laura declared Colorado lettuce was the best in the world, and I certainly never had eaten any so crisp and flavorful. We had no more than finished eating at the kitchen table when a baby began to cry, and then another. I excused myself, got my cap and walked down to the carline.

Here was a good view of the mountains, stretching excitingly from north to south, and I decided that within the next day or so I should take a streetcar as far as it ran west and then walk the rest of the way to this blue, serrated ridge which seemed only a mile or two from where I stood.

I walked dreamily west on the carline street until I came to a drugstore with a soda fountain. I couldn't resist that, so I went in and had a delicious chocolate ice-cream soda, but was annoyed when I found it cost a dime instead of the nickel they charged for similar sodas back home.

Outside on the corner a woman stepped into the street as a trolley car approached, and, on an impulse, I followed her aboard. A wonderful sense of adventure rode with me as we ripped along toward the business district, past rank after rank of brick and stone houses set in those astonishingly green lawns bordered by flower beds and hedges and trees, trees, trees. I wondered if there was another city in the world as beautiful as Denver.

We stopped by one vacant lot adorned by a big billboard with a hand-painted picture of gigantic snow-capped mountains and a train with a cabbage-stack locomotive crossing an awesome, spindly bridge that curved in a horseshoe advertising THE FAR-FAMED GEORGETOWN LOOP—$2.50. That would be a marvelous trip to look forward to. When I got a part-time job I would take it, even if it cost more than a week's pay.

After we had traversed the business district for several blocks, I got off the car and decided to look for a hardware store. It would be a nice gesture for me to contribute a can of oil to the Sterlings and if I blew myself also for a file I could sharpen that old lawn mower—which wouldn't be an altogether unselfish act inasmuch as I'd be using it.

I wandered up a side street and then down another, looking in windows. At one small clothing store a short, plump man spoke to me in friendly fashion: "Well, young man, what can I interest you in today?"

"Oh," I said, "I don't know. I was just looking."

"You're a pretty tall fellow to be wearing knickers," he suggested, and I was astonished at his sagacity.

"Well, I might look at some long pants," I said, "but nothing expensive."

"Come in, come in," he urged with fine hospitality. "You're under no obligation to buy anything."

Once inside the store, which smelled interestingly of new cloth and moth balls, the little man whipped out a tape measure, slipped it around my meager waist, breathed "Hmm," squatted and measured from my crotch to ankle bone. "Well, young man," he said, "you're lucky. I have some new patterns just in that'll fit you, and very cheap too."

Toward the rear of the store he pulled a pair of trousers from a stack and held them for me to admire. They were a bright purple and I shook my head. "Don't like the color," I said.

He pursed his full lips and shrugged his shoulders. "Very latest thing," he declared.

"No," I insisted, "they remind me of Easter eggs."

"Are Easter eggs bad, then?"

"You know what I mean. The color is all right for Easter eggs, but I don't like it for pants."

He threw the purple trousers over on another pile and pulled forth a gray pair checked not too prominently with black and red. "Now here's a real superior article. Just go over there behind that screen and try 'em on so you can see how you look in 'em."

"Well . . ."

"Go ahead. No obligation."

So I went behind the screen, hung my knickers on a hook, drew the long pants over my legs and buttoned them. They felt

[133]

nice but were so ample at the top that I could put both fists inside the waistband. When I stepped out, holding up the trousers with both hands, I was greeted with a warm smile. "Wonderful, wonderful," he said. "Just the right length and they look wonderful on you."

"They're mighty big around the waist," I said.

"That's good," he asserted. "You wear a belt and that'll draw in the slack. You certainly wouldn't want them too tight to begin with because you're going to put on a lot of weight when you've been in Colorado a month or two."

I looked at him in amazement. "How did you know I just came to Denver?" I asked.

He grinned. "Everything told me. The way you talk, for one thing."

"Well, I declare."

"And I can tell you something else, young man. When you've been here in this wonderful dry climate a month or two you're going to be feeling so much better you won't recognize yourself."

"My goodness, I'm not sick. I feel fine."

"I know, I know. But you'll be feeling a lot better and you'll put on ten–fifteen pounds, maybe more, and you'll come here and thank me for not selling you too-tight pants, and such beautiful pants, too, that everybody will admire you in 'em, especially the young ladies."

"Well, how much are they?"

"To you, four dollars."

I whistled. "I had no idea long pants cost so much."

"For this quality that is very, very cheap. Just between you and I, I got pants for swells that sell at ten bucks and look no better and will wear no longer than this wonderful value, and I wouldn't lie to you."

I shook my head. "Maybe when I get a job, but I couldn't spend four bucks for a pair of pants now."

"My friend, these pants would *help* you get a job. I'll tell what I'll do, and only because I'll expect you to be a steady customer now you've come to Denver. I'll let you have 'em for three seventy-five."

"No," I said, firmly, "that's only a quarter less than four dollars."

He frowned and looked very unhappy. "I just hate to see a

fine, tall boy like you going around looking for a job in short pants. As a citizen of Denver, I kind of feel like it's my duty to help you and make you understand what the spirit of Denver is." He tapped me on the chest with a short forefinger as I stood there clutching both sides of the checkered trousers to keep them from tumbling about my knees. "I'm telling you honest," he went on, "those fine trousers cost me more than three dollars, but I'm going to say, 'To hell with profit. Give me three and a quarter, take the pants and God bless you.'"

"Well," I said.

"All I ask is that when folks admire your trousers, just tell where you got 'em, but *not* the price."

"All right," I said. "I think then I'll just wear the long pants and you can wrap up the knickers."

He took out a small penknife and cut tags from the waistband. "You're a smart young man," he said, "and if everybody was as smart I'd have to go out of business. Nobody can make a living selling pants that are a bargain at four dollars for three and a quarter, but I'm counting on you sending me business."

So I transferred my money and other property from my short pants to the stiff, new pockets on my long pants, cinched up my belt and tried to even up the puckers at the waistline. Then, with the brown-paper package under my arm, I walked on down the street, looking at my manly legs in windows and thinking that perhaps I should revert to my boyhood vice in spite of Coach Lloyd's advice and buy a nickel cigar.

I was looking for a hardware store, but apparently I was on the wrong street because I walked many blocks without seeing one. At last, when the clatter of shunting cars and the clang of switch-engine bells told me I was approaching the railroad yards, I turned on another side street. It was a strange street with a few ornate houses where all window shades were drawn, but mostly tiny cottages built very close together.

As I passed one of these tiny cottages someone rapped on a window and a smiling woman pushed back the lace curtain and waved at me. I waved back, thinking she had mistaken me for some Denver boy of her acquaintance and that she, at least, couldn't spot me immediately as a stranger. Then a couple of cottages farther on a very fat woman rapped on the window and smiled lewdly at me and I realized with a catch in my throat that I must be on a street devoted to commercial sin. I had heard of such places in big towns but scarcely believed it although there were rumors of such goings on at the Rock Island House down by the railroad back home. These women, for heaven's sake, were professional *whores,* a word I had learned from the Holy Bible and looked up in the dictionary, and because of my long pants they were soliciting my business. I was both flattered and appalled. Neither woman was attractive in the least.

Another hard-faced woman spoke to me through her open window, "Hello, chicken, want to spend some money?"

"No, thank you," I said, thinking that was a poor way to offer her services, but this was surely a new experience and rather exciting. Then from behind a screened window a young, almost pretty, girl spoke, "Hello, kiddo," she said, "how'd you like to come in and have some fun?"

My heart was thumping and I paused. Her hair was light brown and curly and she smiled. "Come on in, kiddo," she purred. "I'll treat you right."

Before I knew what I was doing, she was opening the door for me and I was in a tiny room heavy with perfume. The room contained two chairs and a small table. On the table was a plate red with tomato sauce and the desiccated remnants of a serving of spaghetti, a knife and fork, and an empty beer bottle and glass. The girl was very small, probably under five feet, and she wore a knee-length dress much like a child's pinafore and red stockings. She was much less attractive and older than she had seemed through the window screen, and she was quite as capable of taking command as was Nardelle Duffy back in Kansas.

She led me into the smaller back room which contained nothing but a narrow bed and a washstand with pitcher and a bowl of green-tinted water. After the brief preliminaries she said, "All right, give me a dollar," and I gave her the silver dollar I'd received in change when I bought my new long pants.

From the time I entered the door until I departed with my brown-paper parcel, not more than five minutes passed. I retraced my steps on the street, slightly dizzy and sick with disgust and remorse.

I asked myself why in the world I ever did such a thing. My mouth was dry and I spat froth on the sidewalk. It seemed that I was just naturally a sex maniac and unable to control my impulses. But this really was a horrible, filthy experience and it had taught me a lesson. I never, never would do such a thing again. It not only was beastly, but it had cost me a silver dollar, almost half enough to take that wonderful Georgetown Loop trip. Not only that—a really appalling thought struck me —but men who consorted with whores contracted dreadful diseases. I stopped short on the sidewalk and took a deep breath of the supposedly wonderful Colorado air, but the air was tainted with the reek of the woman's perfume. There was old man Provo who walked laboriously slap-footed with two canes because he had locomotor ataxia and that came, so the boys said, from his sinful youth when he was reckless enough to go to bed with bad women. Well, no one could be more reckless and sinful than I.

Standing there on the street, I breathed a prayer, "Please, God, give me another chance. I'll never, never do it again."

I went on my way and presently came to a wide street and down the street a couple of blocks was an arch and on the arch was the word MIZPAH. So then I knew where I was and decided to go right home and to buy the lawn-mower oil and file another time. But as I walked toward the arch I couldn't get the sickish scent of the woman out of my nostrils. I lifted the front of my shirt and it was saturated with the perfume.

Now here was a problem. My mother and Laura would smell me the instant I got inside the house. What possible explanation could I give for that? I simply could not go home in this condition. Even my new long pants never would create enough excitement so this damning scent would go unnoticed. If I bought a new shirt, put it on and threw this one away, they'd still know something was very, very wrong. People just didn't throw away perfectly good shirts, and this one was practically new. Suppose I said the man who sold me the long pants tried to sell me some perfume and sprayed some on me so my mother could tell whether she liked it. Would they believe that? I knew I never would believe such a story myself. Hopelessly sunk in remorse, bewildered by what seemed to be an insoluble problem, I was unable to take refuge in the thought that it was all unreal and unimportant anyhow. My whole situation seemed desperately real and I was approaching a state of panic when I sighted a striped barber pole.

God was really forgiving and God had sent the answer to at

least one question. I'd get a haircut and have the barber put on some of that high-smelling tonic. If that didn't actually cover up my present odor, it would at least give a plausible explanation.

So I went in the barbershop and got a haircut and asked for some "nice-smelling" tonic to make my hair lie down, and after the barber had clipped up the sides and back of my head and saturated my scalp with a perfumed concoction from a fancy bottle, he remarked, "Well, boy, that little girl will love you tonight. You smell like a night-blooming cereus." It seemed to me that Denver people were unnecessarily vocal about sex, and at the moment I could think of nothing more abhorrent.

Next to the barbershop was a small lunch counter so, being famished, I went inside and had a bowl of chili con carne with crackers. Then I caught a streetcar. Although I did not know then that several carlines ran on Seventeenth Street, fortunately it was the right one.

When we passed the big billboard advertising the Far-Famed Georgetown Loop, $2.50, I considered the money I had spent on my first trip to town. There was a nickel carfare plus my long pants and that made three-thirty; there was the ice-cream soda, three-forty; there was the haircut, twenty-five, and hair tonic a dime, making thirty-five and—oh, dear, this was getting complicated and I needed a pencil and paper—and the chili, a dime, and the carfare a nickel again, plus the unmentionable silver dollar. Well, I'd have to figure it out later on paper.

I was sitting on a side seat in the open end of the car and most of the other passengers were women, middle-aged women, young women, elderly women, respectable women on their way home with their bundles after shopping or after attending high-minded meetings of the ladies' aid society or something. Little did these decent housewives and mothers realize what a depraved wretch sat among them in the guise of a half-grown boy. If they only knew, some of them probably would get off the car at the next stop to avoid contamination by a moral leper with the reek of a whore upon him, obscured if not obliterated by the more pungent lotion from a barber's bottle.

I didn't recognize my street until we were passing it, so had to walk back a block. I didn't mind that, not being at all anxious to confront my mother and Laura. But confront them I must, and it was Laura who saw me first as I entered the front hall.

"Great day in the morning!" she cried. "Mama, Mama! Come see what's happened to your precious." Then she broke into almost hysterical laughter.

I hung my cap on the hall tree and growled, "Well, what's so darn funny? Ralph wears long pants, doesn't he?"

My mother appeared wide-eyed in the kitchen door and exclaimed, "Oh, George!"

Laura said, "Where in the world have you been? It's not only those awful pants, but you smell like a—well, like a scarlet lady."

I said coldly, "Maybe you know what a scarlet lady smells like, but I went to a Denver barbershop and got a haircut and the barber put some stuff on my hair to keep me from getting bald-headed."

Laura shook her head. "I surely would rather be bald as an egg than to smell like that. Your father was bald and if you ever grow up to be even half the man he was, it'll be a miracle. Anyhow, you haven't answered my question. Where have you been?"

"Well, I just started to take a walk and a trolley car came along and I just went downtown."

"Why, George," said my mother. "Going way downtown by yourself when you just got to Denver. It's a wonder you didn't get lost."

"Maybe," I said, "I'm not quite as stupid as you women seem to think I am."

Laura laughed scornfully. "I'll admit you've never shown any signs of being a genius, but I declare I never thought you'd be stupid enough to buy anything quite as awful as those pants."

"Awful!" I shouted. "Now what the Sam Patch is wrong with my having some long pants when I'm as tall as I am? I'm going to try to get a job for the rest of the summer and a tall guy like me never could get a job looking ridiculous in short pants."

"Now, George," my mother said, "you don't look at all ridiculous in knickers and you're not much taller than the average fourteen-year-old boy."

"I'm five feet nine."

"Ridiculous," said Laura.

"Well, I am. Anyhow, I am with my shoes on."

"And standing on tiptoes. I'm only five feet six and you're not so much taller than I."

"I'm a mile taller than you."

"Anyhow," said my mother, "if you felt you *must* have long pants, I wish you'd waited until I could go with you. That pattern really could be nicer."

"It couldn't be much worse," scoffed Laura.

"That just shows what you know," I blurted. "They even had some bright purple pants they tried to sell me and I wouldn't take them."

"Hmm. What store was this?" asked Laura.

"Heck. I don't know, but a nice, friendly man ran it."

"I'll bet he was friendly," Laura said, "and he certainly saw you coming. It's not only the awful pattern, Mama, but look, they're way too big for him. Look how they're puckered at the top. For goodness sake, look."

"They're a little bit big around the waist," I admitted, "but I'm growing all the time and I certainly wouldn't want 'em too tight."

My mother had sat down in the living room. "Come here, George," she said, "and let me see."

I started in, and Laura said, "They're also plenty droopy in the seat. You'd have to grow a mighty lot to fill that up."

"Here, loosen your belt," my mother ordered.

I loosened my belt and dropped my package to clutch the waistband. "Oh, my," my mother said. "You really should take them back."

"Well, I'm not going to. They're fine pants and I'm going to wear 'em. Everybody gains weight in Colorado and I'll fill up those pants fine."

"I haven't gained any weight here," said Laura.

You're already grown up, and besides you've been sick."

"I haven't been sick. What do you mean?"

"Well, you've been having a lot of babies."

"I haven't had a *lot* of babies. And women usually put on weight after having a baby or two."

"Turn around," said my mother.

I turned around and my mother took hold of my pants and

sighed. "Well," she said, "if you're going to be so stubborn, I suppose I can rip out the rear seam and take out a piece."

Just then one of the babies began to squall upstairs and the other took up the chorus.

As Laura started upstairs I said, "Well, it sure enough sounds like a lot of babies to me."

She turned on the stairs and said, "I wish you'd go to the bathroom and wash some of that stench out of your hair before Ralph gets home. It would make him sick to sit at the same dinner table with you."

So, obediently, I tightened the belt on my new long pants, took my knickers to the sleeping porch and got my towel, brush and comb and a clean shirt. In the bathroom I rubbed the worn shirt briskly over my hair to blend the odors and gave my clipped but still bushy head a scrubbing. Then I put on the clean shirt and went out in the back yard to water the lawn and flower beds.

Chapter 14

IN THE next few days my mother seemed to have adjusted herself as a member of the Sterling household. Her limp was gone and she seemed happy in the division of housework with Laura. She didn't seem to resent the obvious fact that Laura was boss or that her daughter's suggestions sounded more like orders to me.

While I still felt alien and uncomfortable, the tension of my position was gradually lessening. I wanted a job and I studied the "boy-wanted" ads in the newspapers. When I answered two of these ads and found fifteen or twenty boys of various ages, sizes and complexions ahead of me, it was apparent that the supply of youngsters in Denver far exceeded the number of jobs.

Then there was an ad by a large specialty grocer:

WANTED—ENERGETIC, AMBITIOUS BOY FOR HELPER ON DELIVERY WAGON. GOOD PAY.

The next morning, which was Saturday, I got up at five thirty and went to town without breakfast. It was a long wait, but I was first in line and I got the job. When the nervous, white-aproned young man who hired me asked if I could go right to work, I assured him I'd be happy to do so. Had I known, however, that I should have to wait more than half an hour for my boss, Chet Bartell, I'd have asked for time to get some breakfast. I was to need that breakfast. But I was happy while waiting, for my pay was to be seventy-five cents a day.

Chet Bartell was a morose, chunky fellow of indeterminate age, doomed at birth to no higher status than driving a grocery wagon and talented only in means of conserving his own slight physical energy. When we were introduced he remarked with no optimism, "Just hope you'll be better than the last kid they give me."

Chet's wagon, along with two mates, was backed to the rear door of the store and he directed me to help carry wooden boxes of grocery orders and cases of wine into the dusky depths of the black oilcloth-covered wagon. I thought he showed some intelligence by having me stack the boxes according to his route, with the last areas to be visited put in the rear of the truck.

He viewed me skeptically, mouthing his quid of tobacco. "You don't look particular stout," he said. "Lots of ladies now ordering hundred-pound sacks of sugar and a good many all the time buy ninety-eight-pound sacks of flour. If you ain't stout enough to shoulder a hundred-pound sack, you better go see Harold and quit right now."

While I probably weighed no more than one hundred and twenty at that time, I assured him that a hundred pounds was nothing to me. "All right," he said, consulting several slips of paper, "we got orders for three hundred-pound sugars. Sugar is stacked right back there, just this side the warehouse door. Go get 'em."

"Well," I said, "I'll have to carry 'em one at a time."

"Wise kid, eh? Well, go get 'em."

I went back and there were stacks and stacks of big brown sugar sacks, the stacks as high as my head. At the near end, however, the pile was down to two sacks. I attacked the upper sack, and, not knowing the technique of lifting a heavy, clumsy, obstinate object that offered no handles, I had a desperate struggle, with one instant of near defeat, before at last I had the awkward thing on my shoulder. I tried to walk back to the wagon without staggering while Chet stood to one side registering boredom. I thought, All right, he's just testing me and I'll show him. So I loaded the sack into the wagon and went back to the stack.

For a moment I stood there, breathing deeply of that fine Colorado air, spiced delicately with good grocery smells, but not realizing that the fine Colorado air was slightly shy on oxygen for an unacclimated person doing heavy work. I looked at the single, inert brown burden squatting so solidly on the floor and then I looked at the next pile with the top sack less than a foot above my shoulder and I told myself that one could save one's back in this sort of endeavor simply by using one's God-given brain.

I wrangled and wriggled the top sack out for more than half its length and then backed up to the pile and clutched the sack with both hands over my right shoulder. It was stubborn, but I yanked it back and forth until it began to yield to my efforts plus gravitation and came down. Perhaps there is a mathematical formula that shows how much force gravitation imparts to one hundred pounds of mass in a fall of eight or nine inches, but I didn't know it then and I don't know it now. Whatever, it was too much for my legs. I hit the floor and so did the sack of sugar. Perhaps my shoulder and neck broke its fall somewhat. At least it didn't split open although it jammed my chin into the floor and I bruised my knees and elbows.

I pulled myself up quickly and apparently no one had noticed the mishap. People were scurrying around the store about their business, all but Chet Bartell. He was standing by the loading door, talking with another driver. I was mad at myself for my bright idea and mad at the sack of sugar. I also was mad at Chet Bartell. After all, what was wrong with two men carrying a hundred-pound weight instead of one carrying and the other loafing? But he was my boss and maybe I was thinking Socialist thoughts.

Well, there was the sack of sugar on the floor and there was I, standing up with my knees hurting and my elbows hurting and my neck hurting, so I lifted the sack on end, stooped to rest the upper end against my thighs, reached down to grasp the sack below its middle and hoisted. It didn't come up easily, but it came up and I got my shoulder under it and stomped to the wagon. I didn't look at Chet as I passed him, but thumped the sack down solidly on the wagon bed.

"Hey, there, kid," Chet called. "Watch how you bang that thing down. You bust open a sack of sugar and there'll be merry hell to pay."

"Sorry," I said, and went back for the third sack. While my legs were trembling by this time and my knees in particular were stinging, I got it and loaded it and thought, They advertised for a boy, but by golly it seems like you got to be a man to be a boy in Denver.

"All right," said Chet, "we got places to go."

We both swung down to the alley and I climbed into the left-side seat while Chet picked up the hitching weight, dumped it on the floor, and mounted to the driver's seat with practiced ease. He flapped the reins, said "Giddap, Molly, out we go again," and we clopped down the cobbled alley, and, without a pause, turned left into an asphalt-paved street. An automobile honked its horn at us and Chet grumbled, "Goddamn autoists think they own the world."

It was pleasant riding through the bright Denver morning over streets of dark asphalt or gravel, and to the west the Rocky Mountains loomed blue and exciting. I pointed to massive Mount Evans whose austere summit was dappled with white, and asked, "Mr. Bartell, what's the name of that big mountain right over there?"

"We call it Old Baldy."

"You ever climb it?"

"Hell, no. I never lost anything up there."

"You ever take that far-famed Georgetown Loop trip?"

"What's that?"

This was amazing. "Well," I said, "I don't know, but it's a train trip they advertise that goes way up into the mountains and then swings around a very high railroad trestle. There are pictures of it."

"Naw. I got better use for my dough."

"How long you lived in Denver?"

Chet spat over the side. "All my life. Well, I was born in Longmont, but my folks moved to Denver when I was so young I don't remember the trip. Well, here's our first delivery. Name's Morris. Box of groceries, case of wine. Put 'em on kitchen table. Don't bring back wine case. Don't get fresh with cook or she'll give you a black eye."

He had pulled Molly over to the curb so I got out, found the Morris boxes near the tailgate, and carried the case of wine around to the rear of the house and knocked on the back door.

A buxom young woman with a lace cap pinned to her brown hair opened the door. "Oh, you're a new one," she said.

"Yes, ma'am."

"Well, don't bother to knock. Come right in and put the stuff on the table. Hey, where are the groceries?"

"I'll bring 'em right in."

I went back to the wagon and got the box of groceries. Chet called to me, "What's the matter? Couldn't you put the groceries on top of the case and carry 'em in one trip?"

"Well—maybe I could, but all those bottles were fairly heavy and it was easier to make two trips."

He shook his head and spat. "We ain't got all day for one delivery, you know. We got another trip to make this afternoon."

On my third delivery a kind-faced housewife offered me a dime.

"What's that for?" I asked.

"Just a little tip for getting here early and wiping your feet on the door mat."

"No, thank you," I said. "I get paid for delivering your groceries and I don't take tips."

When I delivered the first sack of sugar followed by a box of groceries, I remarked to my boss, "Maybe I'm just puny, but I really couldn't carry the groceries and the sugar in one trip."

Chet grunted and clucked to the horse. One of the grocery deliveries was on the third floor of an apartment, and as I struggled up the back stairs I prayed that no such cliff dweller had ordered a hundredweight of sugar. I knew I never could make it.

On three occasions, and for no apparent reason, Chet said, "Here, you hold the horse and I'll make this one." Each time he was gone longer than seemed necessary to me, and, while it seemed improbable that any woman could be interested in such a character, I suspected he was dallying with some servant.

Once, while I held the reins on docile old Molly, I looked at my watch and was vastly discouraged because it was only ten thirty. My stomach was flat and grumbling and I felt weak from hunger and fatigue. It just didn't seem that I could make it until noon.

But make it I did. Well before twelve o'clock all the boxes in the wagon were empty and we were clopping back toward the store.

Chet watered old Molly and hung a nose bag of oats over her ears. Then he said, "Well, we got about an hour. You better go put on the feed bag yourself."

"Aren't you going to eat?" I asked.

"I ain't on no hunger strike. You can come along with me to Barney's place if you want."

So I accompanied Chet to a lunch counter where we both ordered the day's special—a huge platter of New England boiled dinner, made up of beef, cabbage, potatoes, carrots and onions swimming in juice—for twenty cents. It seemed delicious to me and I wolfed it down, polishing the plate with a piece of bread.

At the counter Chet made his first show of friendliness. "Well," he said, "this is the big night and I'll be ready for it."

"How do you mean?"

"Saturday night."

This puzzled me slightly. Obviously he wasn't looking to a bath with such pleasure.

"The ghost walks this evening, and all day Sunday to recover."

"The ghost walks?"

He looked at me. "You *are* a greenhorn. Payday."

"Oh, I see. But why do they call it that?"

"Hell, I don't know. They always have."

I wondered about needing all day Sunday to recover from payday and decided that perhaps Saturday night meant a dissolute drunken spree for Chet Bartell.

I asked, "Are you married, Mr. Bartell?"

"Naw!" he blurted, forking up more food. "Why keep a cow when milk's so cheap?"

I pondered that a moment, then saw what he meant and made no comment. What right had I to feel revolted? Was he any more degraded than I? Chet had a piece of apple pie and a cup of coffee. I was tempted, but already had brought my day's income down to fifty-five cents and I felt comfortably restored and strengthened by the big boiled dinner. We strolled back to the store, both plying toothpicks, and began loading the wagon again. Boxes and boxes of groceries, cases of wine, another sack of sugar and two forty-eight-pound sacks of flour, and the afternoon load was even larger than the morning one.

By midafternoon I had even lost interest in the magnificently terraced range to the west, let alone the new Denver streets we visited. It was a relief when the hundredweight of sugar was delivered early, with only four or five steps to struggle up, but the hours stretched on interminably and it was well after six o'clock when I made the last delivery and climbed wearily up beside Chet to ride back to the store. When I let out an involuntary sigh, Chet chuckled sympathetically. "Saturday's a long day," he said. "It'll be a lot easier Monday."

His mention of Monday, I thought, meant I had given enough satisfaction to be expected to come back to work. My pleasure in that was only moderate.

At the store one wagon crew already was carrying its empty boxes back and stacking them in the rear. Chet unbent and cheerfully helped in this task, probably, I suspected, because the eyes of the management might be upon him. When the wagon was empty, he remarked, "Well, all we got to do now is to take care of Molly and the wagon and then we can collect what we been working for."

The stable was a block from the store, and, because of my experience on Uncle George Mosby's farm, I was able to assist in unharnessing the horse. This brought forth Chet's only compliment of the day. "Not many city boys know a hame strap from a crupper," he said. It didn't seem worth while to confess that I didn't either, but I did know which harness buckles should be left alone.

The third wagon pulled up to the stable just as we were leaving, and Chet paused long enough to engage the driver in conversation about someone both agreed was a lying bastard, a sodomite and a son of a bitch in spades. Chet was vehement and muttered to himself on our way back to the store where the cashier handed him several folded bills that he examined furtively before stalking off without saying good night either to the cashier or me.

She looked at me suspiciously, this hollow-eyed, harried young woman. "Your name?"

[147]

"George Chalmers."

She consulted a sheet and without another word handed me a half dollar and a quarter. The clock on the wall showed ten after seven. I hobbled out on stiffening knees. My back ached. My neck hurt. The Sterlings and my mother would have finished dinner by now and they wouldn't know what had become of me. By the time I got home everything would be put away. My mother would be worried. Laura might be angry with me. I felt that I should be happy over having a job and carrying off the first day's work successfully, but I was too tired to be happy and was curiously depressed. I went back to Barney's lunch counter and had a hamburger sandwich on a bun and a cup of coffee. The sandwich included a few potato chips and a pickle. I counted on my fingers and this fifteen cents plus my twenty-cent dinner plus carfare morning and night brought my hard day's income down to thirty cents, and that really was discouraging.

It was nearly eight o'clock when I got home and a frowning Laura greeted me at the door. "Where in the world have you been?"

The babies were crying and my mother obviously was upstairs caring for them. Ralph was in the big leather rocking chair, staring at me over the top of the evening paper.

"Heck," I said, "I just got a job and have been working hard all day."

"A job? A job where and doing what?"

"For a big grocery store called McIntyre's, delivering groceries."

"Well, for goodness sake, Mama has been worrying herself sick. Why couldn't you let us know?"

"How could I? I was too busy."

"You know how to use a telephone, don't you?"

"Yes, but I just didn't have time and I just got through work a little bit ago."

"Wait a minute," said Ralph from the living room. "Let's get this thing straight. How could you deliver groceries when you don't know the city?"

"I didn't need to know the city. A man name of Chet Bartell drove the wagon, and I carried the groceries and flour and hundred-pound sacks of sugar into the houses and apartments."

I hung up my cap, went into the living room and slumped

exhausted onto the davenport. The dining-room table had been cleared except for a plate and silver at my place. Maybe I was to get some dinner after all and I could have saved that fifteen cents I spent on the sandwich and coffee.

Ralph's glasses glittered. "Let's not make this thing *too* good, George," he said. "You claim you've been carrying hundred-pound sacks of sugar into houses. If you want us to believe this story at all just say that you *helped* the man carry the sacks of sugar into the houses."

"But, gosh," I said, "do you think I'm lying or something? After all, I'm not puny."

Ralph raised his newspaper as if to close the conversation. The babies had stopped crying and when my mother came down the stairs I repeated my story.

"But, George," she said, "you went off this morning without your breakfast. What have you had to eat?"

"I had a dandy boiled dinner this noon."

"But no breakfast or supper?"

"I had a sandwich tonight."

Ralph grumbled something from behind his paper.

Laura said, "We had a fine pork roast for dinner. It's getting cold by now, but you can have a slice of that if you want it."

"Well, fine," I said, "if it's all right with you."

Ralph lowered his paper. "Look, George," he said, "you say you have been delivering groceries for McIntyre's all day. Did you deliver anything else?"

"Gee," I said, "I don't know what you mean, but like I said there was sugar and—"

"I happen to know," Ralph said firmly, "that McIntyre's sells intoxicating beverages."

"Well," I said, "I don't know whether they were intoxicating or not, but I delivered a lot of wine, cases of wine, but maybe it was unfermented wine like they have in church."

"Nonsense," said Ralph. "McIntyre's advertise intoxicating wine and if you were delivering for them you were delivering intoxicating beverages."

"Oh, George!" exclaimed my mother.

I blurted wearily, "Well, if the people buy it, what difference does it make who delivers it?"

"George, George," my mother said, shaking her head sadly, "what would your father think of his son doing that?"

"Not only that," said Ralph severely, "but I'm certainly not going to have anyone living in my house connected with the liquor interests."

My mother brought in a tray with a plate of sliced pork, bread and butter and a glass of milk to the dining table and called me. I rose painfully from the davenport, and she said, "There's one thing sure, George, you're not going back to that place Monday."

"That is definite," said Laura.

As a matter of form, I remonstrated mildly. Jobs weren't easy to get. Delivering groceries was a healthful, outdoor job that gave me a chance to learn the city, but I knew I had no chance whatever of winning the argument and was glad of it.

Tired as I was, sleep evaded me for hours that night. My knees throbbed, my legs ached, my back was lame and I couldn't get my head in any position so my stiff neck didn't hurt. I tried to suppress a feeling of gratitude toward my mother and Laura and Ralph for relieving me of the stigma of softy and quitter. I tried to tell myself that I would go back to McIntyre's Monday morning if it were not for their orders. But I didn't want to go. I didn't want to be associated any more with Chet Bartell, whom I despised. I hoped I'd never see Chet Bartell again as long as I lived. Of course pulling the sack of sugar down on my shoulder had not been Chet Bartell's idea, but my bruises and wrenched muscles were all tied up with the general picture of that long Saturday and the picture was dominated by Chet Bartell who at that very moment was probably swilling intoxicating liquor and more than likely in company with abominable women down on that street of horror where the whores plied their shameful trade.

Getting up that Sunday morning was a torture, but I got up and I went to church with Laura and Ralph after Laura insisted that I go change my new long pants to the knickers of my gray suit. I sang enthusiastically with the congregation although my voice cracked several times. I listened seriously to the serious young minister, cringing at his reference to the shocking increase in laxity of conduct and actual sin among adolescents encouraged by ragtime music, and young boys and girls being allowed to sit together in darkened moving-picture houses.

Out on the sunny street, I was stiffer than ever. Each step

required a distinct effort, for both knees were swollen and painful. I tried to hide my difficulty, but Laura asked why I was walking so funny and I said I guessed I was just stiff and sore from carrying loads up so many stairs. I didn't want to confess my misadventure with the sack of sugar because they thought I was stupid and clumsy enough without adding that.

Ralph said glumly, "Odd that a boy your age would get crippled from just that."

I could think of no answer I could make reasonably, but I thought, Well, Mister Banker, I'd like to see what shape you'd be in if you went through what I did yesterday. But that thought was followed by one that almost made me collapse on the sidewalk. My knees seemed unnaturally sore from merely going down from a standing position, even with the weight of the sugar sack added to mine. Suppose this bruising fall had hastened the onset of that horrible disease which crippled old man Provo for his sins! Suppose that right now I had the beginnings of locomotor ataxia! Of course I knew nothing of the symptoms or period of incubation of syphilis nor the manifestations of its progress. All I knew was the legend that the slap-footed gait of locomotor ataxia came from sexual sin, and I tried desperately to correct my two-legged limp on the rest of the way home. It couldn't happen to me. I wouldn't let it happen to me. I could feel the cold sweat of terror running down my ribs as I climbed painfully up the front steps.

Both babies were crying when we entered the house. I went right to my sleeping porch and hung up my suit coat. Then I got down on my sore knees by the cot and prayed fervently for God's forgiveness and a rescue from locomotor ataxia.

Chapter 15

GOD apparently answered my prayers and put me on probation, for I did not come down with locomotor ataxia or any other dire malady. In a few days most of the soreness was gone from my knees and I was practically as good as new, and back at the discouraging business of answering "boy-wanted" ads.

At last I was presumptuous enough to appear at the outer office of a large law firm in the E. & C. building in response to an ad, BRIGHT BOY WANTED; SPLENDID OPPORTUNITY FOR THE RIGHT BOY. Six or seven other boys gathered in this anteroom, eyeing one another grimly until a firm-mouthed woman appeared, looked over the group dubiously and finally pointed a yellow pencil at one boy and said, "You stay." The rest of us started glumly toward the door, but the woman spoke sharply, "Keep your shirts on a minute, will you?" and pointed the pencil at another boy. "You stay too," she said. Then, astonishingly, the pencil was directed at me. "You stay," she said, "and the rest of you can go."

She led us through a door into a library with shelves of yellow-backed lawbooks reaching to the ceiling and told us to sit on three sides of a long table. Then she handed each of us a sharpened pencil and two sheets of yellow foolscap. "All right," she said, "each of you write a brief letter to Mr. Herbert Spence, Denver, Colorado, stating just why you would like employment here. Make it short and to the point and sign your full name and address. I'll be back in a few minutes."

I looked at my two competitors and felt confident. My handwriting was good. And while I had got only a "C" in eighth-grade English, Miss Elliot had praised my composition except for grammar and spelling. I wrote that it would be an honor to work for a noted law firm where a boy could learn things of value. I wanted to say *ambitious* boy but wasn't sure whether to spell it with a "t" or a "c." I wrote that I needed a job because my mother was a widow. I wrote that my mother had taught me to be polite and honest, and then, remembering what my father had said about lawyer Norris back home, I wondered if honesty was such an important asset with lawyers. However, they surely would prefer honest employees, in any event. I promised to be prompt and faithful and to work very hard if given the job, and I signed the sheet with the Sterling address and looked up to see both the other boys still writing. The sturdy, dark boy across from me was left-handed and was laboring hard, chewing his tongue with each downstroke of the pencil. I eliminated him immediately. The neat, handsome boy at the end of the table, however, looked too bright and competent for comfort. As I looked at him he finished his task, put his pencil down and caught my eye. He smiled as if to say, "Well, pal, it's in the lap of the gods now." I liked him.

When the woman returned, the southpaw was still writing and I saw that his long, yellow sheet was nearly full of a close, backhand script.

"Time's up," said the woman.

"Well, just a minute," said the southpaw.

"That's enough. You don't need to tell the story of your life. Sign your name."

The boy frowned and signed his name.

Gathering up the papers, the grim woman said, "Wait here. Mr. Spence will want to talk to you separately after he reads what you have written."

When she had gone, the left-handed boy said, "Gosh, she didn't give us much time."

I said, "Well, you got to be on your toes these days in a city like Denver, Colorado."

The handsome boy chuckled. "Seems to me," he said, "that they're making a pretty big thing out of hiring an office boy. You'd think they were after a vice-president or something."

"Maybe they are," I said. "The ad said splendid opportunity, so maybe they want a boy who wants to learn the business and work hard and get promoted."

"Oh, horsefeathers," said the handsome boy, "what have you been reading—Alger books?"

"Not altogether," I said stiffly, and eliminated the neat, handsome boy. So I was not at all surprised when the grim woman appeared and called, "George Chalmers."

Mr. Herbert Spence sat in a mahogany swivel chair before a mahogany roll-top desk. On the desk was a neat pile of papers held down by a silver horseshoe; also a large, businesslike inkwell, a penholder and the yellow foolscap we competitors had written on. Behind him was a glass-doored sectional bookcase filled with solemn books. On two walls were steel-engraving portraits of three solemn, unidentified men. On the wall opposite Mr. Spence a large, white-faced clock clucked off the solemn seconds. Mr. Spence spoke in a solemn bass voice, "You are George V. Chalmers?"

"Yes, sir."

He motioned to an armchair beside the desk. "Well, sit down, George."

I sat down and he looked at me steadily. He was a slim man of great dignity with iron-gray, wavy hair and mustache. He wore a gates-ajar collar and black bow tie, a black cutaway coat with a white carnation on the lapel and gray-striped trousers.

At last he spoke. "Well, George, are you Irish?"

This, I thought, was an odd thing to ask. "No, sir," I said, "I'm an American for a long way back, but I guess I'm Scotch and English descent."

He didn't change expression, but picked up my page of foolscap. "I thought I detected a bit of Irish blarney in your first sentence here."

"I'm sorry, sir."

He shook his head. "It's all right, it's all right. Sometimes a little Irish blarney goes a long way in this business—or in any business. Are you going to school?"

"Well, I had planned to go to Central High School in the fall."

"Would you be willing to work afternoons after school and on Saturdays?"

"Oh, yes, sir. I'd like to do that very much."

"Hmm. Would you like to become an attorney at law?"

"Oh, yes, sir."

"Why?"

"Well, sir, Mr. Taft's a lawyer, Mr. Bryan's a lawyer, Abraham Lincoln was a lawyer, you're a lawyer."

A faint smile showed under his mustache. "And you say you're not Irish? Do you realize that it's a long, hard pull before a boy can become an attorney?"

"I suppose it is. I suppose it's a long, hard pull before a boy can amount to anything in any business, but I want to amount to something and I'm willing to work hard."

"Good. And becoming a lawyer isn't an impossible ambition. You wrote here that your mother is a widow. Have you any means to pay your way through college or law school?"

"No, sir, I'd have to earn my own way."

"That's not impossible, either. Now, if you came to work here as office boy and were energetic and faithful and didn't take all day in running errands, you probably could keep your job until you get out of high school. How much more school have you?"

"Well, I'm just starting high school this fall."

"I see. How old are you?"

"Fourteen, going on fifteen."

"I see. You look a little older."

"Thank you, sir."

Again the faint smile. "At my age, George, we don't consider it a compliment to be told we look older. Well, as I was about to say, if you were alert and kept your eyes open around here you might learn enough to be a clerk by the time you get out of high school. Then you could go to Westminster law school night sessions and be a practicing attorney shortly after you're old enough to vote."

I was glowing to my fingertips over the interest this elegant member of the Denver Bar was showing me. "That would really be wonderful, Mr. Spence," I said. "Can I have the job, then?"

This time he really smiled. "Well," he said, "we shouldn't be precipitant about this. It would scarcely be fair to give you the position right now without talking with the other boys, would it?"

"I suppose not."

"All right, George, you'll hear from us within two or three days if I decide you're the right boy. You can go out the side door there."

He put out his hand and I wiped the sweat from my palm on the thigh of my new long pants before responding to his firm handclasp.

I went home riding the finest wave of elation I had felt since my father died, and I confronted Laura in the kitchen. "Look, Sis," I cried, "I'm going to be a lawyer."

"*Shh,*" she hissed, "don't wake the babies. You're *what?*"

"I'm going to have a job in a big, fine law office and keep my eyes open and learn how to become a clerk and then I'll go to law school at night and become a lawyer and when I'm a lawyer I'll practice law a while and make some money and then run for mayor, and be a good mayor and then maybe run for Governor of Colorado and be a very good governor and so honest in fighting for the common people that I'll be famous all over the country and for all you know the next thing you'll be

[155]

bragging that you're the sister of the President of the United States."

Laura narrowed her eyes and felt my forehead. "Well," she said, "you don't feel feverish, but you do sound batty as all get out. What's this all about? Have you really got a job in a law office?"

"I think so," I said. "Anyhow, I saw a famous lawyer named Mr. Herbert Spence and he practically told me I have the job and explained how I could become an attorney at law, and I'll be getting a letter from him in two or three days."

"Were there any other boys after the job?"

I laughed. "I should say so. A whole crowd of 'em. But they told them all to go except two other boys and me and had us three go into a big room full of lawbooks and write letters to Mr. Spence. I wrote a very good letter which impressed Mr. Spence and I was the first to be called into his office."

"Well," said Laura, "I wish you luck, but the boys they sent away must have been a pretty tacky bunch if they let you stay with those awful pants on."

My mother, of course, was delighted at my report. At dinner Laura asked Ralph if he knew Lawyer Herbert Spence. Ralph nodded. "He's a member of the law firm of Ramsey, Curtis, Spence and Kline. In the E. & C. building. It's one of the better law firms in the city. Why?"

"George seems to have a job with them. Isn't that nice?"

Ralph showed his surprise. "Well, good," he said, "doing what?"

I said, "It's just office boy at first, but Mr. Spence said I could work into being a clerk and then it could be fixed so I could go to law school at night and become a lawyer."

Ralph asked, "What are they going to pay you?"

"Gee," I said, "I don't know."

He wiped his black mustache with his napkin. "You mean you didn't even ask?"

"Well, I was just more interested in this fine opportunity than what they paid me to start, but Mr. Spence is a very fine man and I know he'll pay me what the job's worth."

Ralph shook his head. "I just hope they don't charge you a fee for allowing you to work," he said.

I didn't like that idea and could think of no reply.

Because there would be no chance of hearing from Mr.

Spence the following day, I had decided to take a streetcar to the western part of the city and then walk to the mountains. But it seemed that the mountains were much farther away than they appeared to be. At breakfast Ralph said the nearest foothills were thirteen miles from downtown Denver, but I could take an interurban trolley car from the loop to the town of Golden which was right in the foothills and walk up from there.

So my mother made me a couple of sandwiches and put them in a paper sack with two homemade raisin cookies and I took a streetcar to the Tramway Loop, where, after twenty or thirty minutes, the great interurban car, green-black in color and almost as large as a railroad coach, groaned around a sharp curve and came to a stop before the waiting room. This was adventure. While the big car went no faster than a regular streetcar in crossing a long viaduct over a network of railroad tracks and a narrow river and through the streets of North Denver, we were out of the city quickly and traveling at what seemed to be terrific speed, with the car rocking and the air whistle tooting for crossings, over flat country that was mostly desert but spotted with an occasional bright green field and farmhouses with windmills and outbuildings, and the mountains looming more and more magnificently ahead. A sense of wonderful freedom surged within me. I was on my own, going into the Rocky Mountains. My apprehensions and discontent were swept away. Everything was going to be all right and more than all right. Everything was going to be wonderful. Now I was on a fine adventure by myself. And now, with assistance from no one, my future was practically assured. Perhaps I was not the smartest boy in the country, but perhaps, again, I was a good deal smarter than some people thought and I was willing to work harder than anyone else. Thomas A. Edison had said something like genius being 10 percent inspiration and 90 percent perspiration. When Laura wanted to be nasty-nice she called it transpiration. Well, by golly, I called it *sweat* and I wasn't afraid of sweat by any name. Maybe I couldn't learn things quite as fast as Laura and some other people, but I could learn anything if I sweat over it enough and I was going to learn everything. My grades in high school were going to be all As—well, with maybe a few Bs, but there'd be no more Cs and Ds. My days as Sleepy Chalmers were all over. From now on I'd be Wide-Awake Chalmers, and when I became a famous and rich lawyer I would remember this glorious day on the Golden interurban car as a changing point in my life. Then there was another thing. My knees were nearly well, proving that God had forgiven my sins and that I was spared the horror of locomotor ataxia. Many a promising young man, so I had heard and so I believed, had been destroyed because he had ventured into sin. Well, I had ventured into sin at an early age with two women, but through the mercy of God and Jesus I had escaped destruction. I had learned my lesson and learned it young enough so I never again would be tempted. As the car sped toward the mountains I was in a state of ecstasy practically religious in nature.

The conductor was friendly and I asked if he knew a good route from Golden for a hike into the mountains.

"Well," he said, "there's a trail up Lookout Mountain and a grand view of the plains from the top, but that's a long, hard drag and hot. If I was you, I'll tell you what I'd do: I'd just go to the Colorado & Southern depot and follow the narrow-gauge track up Clear Creek. It's real pretty up the canyon with the creek a-roaring down and the granite cliffs and plenty of slopes to go up if you feel like climbing. The track's wide enough up there to get out of the way if a train comes along."

I thanked him and when we reached the Golden station, he pointed out where I could find the Colorado & Southern narrow-gauge tracks. The village of Golden itself was exciting, set inside a massive flat-topped mountain with a cable railroad running at an acute angle up the top, and I stood wide-eyed, watching one tiny car going slowly up while another descended. I wondered how much it cost for the trip but decided that could wait.

The great, snowy range now was hidden by closer mountains, mostly dun colored instead of blue, with clumps of green trees sparsely scattered along folds of the slope. I walked hurriedly up the strange little railroad track as if the mountains might not wait, and presently I was into the mouth of the canyon with Clear Creek boiling its milky flood into the open. Not knowing that the discoloration came from the smelters above at Idaho Springs, I wondered why they called the stream Clear Creek.

Inside of fifteen minutes I was in the depths of the canyon with the walls rising to the brilliant green-blue sky, sometimes sloping steeply with stubborn shrubbery and small evergreen trees growing in the rubble and sometimes sheer red granite cliffs that held in and amplified the roar of the creek. The air was redolent, surprisingly to me, from pink wild roses that grew in profusion where they could find a foothold along the railroad track. I wondered if my father had known of this place in his youth in the mountains. Very likely he had ridden on a train up and down this very canyon; at least he must have known of it.

The track crossed to the other side of the canyon on a wooden trestle, and as I walked the ties I thought it would be most uncomfortable to be caught there by a speeding train. I had no more than reached the far side when a shriek, far more shrill than any train whistle I had ever heard, was repeated over and over from down-canyon and two little locomotives with great, swelling smokestacks appeared from around the bend, followed by four passenger cars. I got off the track and well up the slope before the train labored over the bridge, with the twin exhausts roaring in a rhythmless staccato. Passengers leaning from the windows waved at me and I waved back joyfully with the elation born on the interurban car still running high. Perhaps I should have been even more thrilled had I known this little train was heading for my far-famed Georgetown Loop.

When the train had disappeared around the upstream bend with more shrill whistling, leaving nothing but the sharp scent of coal smoke to mingle with the aroma of wild roses, I looked up the slope where I stood and decided that here would be a good place to climb. Soon I found myself in a dry watercourse where the ascent was not too difficult but where occasional pockets of loose stones made footing uncertain. I circled these spots, moving into the coarse bunch grass that grew in the thin soil above the sides of the declivity. Once in a while in my climb, I encountered a cluster of cactus or a spread of Spanish bayonet and as I approached one of these spiny clumps I was arrested by a sharp burring sound. Never before had I heard or seen a wild rattlesnake, but I knew what it was immediately, and there he was, small and yellow in a menacing coil with his coffin-shaped head drawn back to strike and his horny tail blipping and blipping above the coil. I didn't know whether he would attack even if I did not advance, but I picked up a stone and threw it, hitting him in the middle. Instantly he uncoiled and started to retreat, but my second stone caught him right back of the head and he writhed helplessly in the coarse, disintegrated granite. Another stone hurled from above crushed his head and I stood looking down at the battered body with a mixture of fascination and revulsion. He was not more than eighteen inches long, but there were four rattles on his tail. Old pard Cal Campbell would be very indignant at my killing the creature even though it was a venomous reptile and probably capable of killing a human being. If I had not heard him and seen him, I had no doubt that he would have struck me, leaving me incapable at least of getting back to Golden. Nevertheless, Calvin would have said, I was supposed to keep my eyes and ears open, and the rattlesnake had as much right to God-given life as I. Well, I was not Calvin. Putting down my sack of lunch, I got out my pocketknife and haggled off the four rattles and wrapped them in a piece of the sack paper and put them in my pocket. Then I wiped off the knife blade on my stocking, wiped my hands on my thighs and turned to look back.

I had come quite a way and at this point Clear Creek no longer was visible. A couple of long-tailed birds flew down the canyon, screaming somewhat like blue jays above the still loud rumble of the stream.

I decided to climb to the top of the ridge where I presumed I could get a good view of everything, including the snowy range. But when I reached what I supposed was the top of the ridge, it turned out to be merely a fold in the upheaval with another crest just beyond. And when I reached the second supposed crest, I found it was yet another fold with another crest just beyond. Stopping to catch my breath, I surveyed the terrain and saw it probably would be more interesting to leave this watercourse and clamber up the steeper slope to the left, where, perhaps a hundred feet above, a sprinkling of small evergreens grew. At least the trees looked cool and the sun now was beating down fiercely.

Once I reached the level of the little trees, there seemed to be a real summit back toward the canyon, and I struggled over broken rock toward it until suddenly I came to the brink.

The abruptness of it made me gasp. One more step and I could have gone over the edge of a practically vertical cliff. In the dizzying depths, hundreds or maybe a thousand feet below, was the tiny, silver trickle of Clear Creek and the tinier glitter of the railroad track. Beyond this awful gash in the only world I knew were mountains, rising in fold after hazy blue fold into infinity against that even more complete blue infinity of the sky. To the left were mountains, to the right were mountains, behind me were mountains, enveloping me in their brooding silence. Otherwise there was only the sun throbbing cruelly in my temples, symbol not of life but of death in these parched and decaying red rocks.

I looked down again and was seized by vertigo. It seemed that some horrible force was pushing me inexorably over the brink and I stepped back, catching my heel against a rock and nearly falling. The unreal blue mountains beyond the canyon vibrated against the dazzling sky, and I heard my paper sack of lunch scrape and rattle against rocks as I dropped face down and clutched my fingers desperately into bunch grass to control the quivering earth beneath me.

The horror of horrors was upon me again and I was alone, alone, alone in the total immensity that was not made up of the Rocky Mountains nor Colorado nor that meager planet called the Earth, reputedly inhabited by such pitiful microcosms as rattlesnakes and the human race, reputedly swinging in an orbit about that scorching, bright eye above. I never had heard of my mother nor my late father nor my sister Laura nor Ralph Sterling nor sin nor God. I was one white, suffering, trembling nerve only half aware of its existence as it drifted or sped through an eternity of nothingness.

There was no question whether I was dying or whether I had been swept to the depths of insanity. There simply was *no* question. There was no life but the half life of lonely horror.

In the aeons that I lay there, every second a year or a decade, while the awful centuries were born and grew and declined, the tension of my fingers in the bunch grass finally relaxed and I fell into the sleep of exhaustion.

When I awoke the sun was nearing the rim of a mountain to the west and the sense of ineffable horror also had sunk into a twilight. On hands and knees I moved farther back from the cliff edge and then rose unsteadily to my feet. I was sick and dizzy, but began a stumbling descent back and down toward the dry watercourse. Twice I fell to my hands and knees because I was hurrying away from terror faster than I could have traveled safely, even had I been well.

It was almost dark by the time I reached the narrow-gauge track at the bottom of the canyon and quite dark when I staggered into the Golden interurban station. The conductor had to waken me at the Denver Loop, and I was burning with thirst. But I was too tired to look or to inquire for drinking water and dragged myself to the streetcar that would take me to Sterlings'.

Dinner was long over, of course, but I escaped a scolding because my illness was so apparent. My explanation that I had been seized with a sudden sickness in the mountains and had to lie down for hours was accepted without question and even with sympathy. Ralph diagnosed my trouble as mountain sickness, common with those not acclimated to high altitudes after climbing, and I was quite willing to let it go at that.

No, I didn't want any dinner. All I wanted was a drink of cold water. Yes, I would like a drink of milk, but please some water first.

My mother felt my forehead and observed that I had considerable fever and maybe they'd better call a doctor. I wanted no doctor and Ralph assured her it was nothing serious, that I'd be all right in a day or so and probably would be recovered tomorrow.

I gulped down the glass of water my mother brought me, in spite of her admonition to take it slowly, and Laura remarked that I could use a little water on my face too. My mother inquired with some embarrassment into the state of my bowels and I replied that I couldn't remember, that I had such a headache I couldn't remember anything.

"In that case," said my mother, "I think you need to take something. Laura, have you got some Epsom salts?"

"No," said Laura, "but there's a box of Rocky Mountain tea in the kitchen cabinet. You just heat some water and the directions are on the box."

"I don't want anything," I declared, "except to go to bed, except maybe that glass of cold milk you talked about."

My mother took the water glass and was followed into the kitchen by Laura.

Ralph asked where I went and I told him I had walked up Clear Creek Canyon from Golden and then climbed into the mountains.

"How high did you climb?"

"Don't know. Pretty high, I guess."

My mother returned with the glass filled with milk, and I said, "Hope I'm not shortchanging the twins."

"No," she said, "I think there's enough and the milkman comes in the morning."

I sipped on the delicious milk, and Laura returned with my towel and toothbrush, patted me on the shoulder and spoke in her oldtime kindly fashion, "Now, Buster, you go get washed up and then you can have your Rocky Mountain tea and go to bed."

I never would have dreamed that any stairway could be so difficult to climb, but I made it, each step a throb to my aching head. From groveling in the dirt so long, my face was a sorry thing to look at in the mirror, even if the image was curiously hazy. Cool water was a blessing to it.

Going down, I held to the banister to keep from stumbling, bade Laura and Ralph good night and started for my sleeping porch. In the kitchen my mother intercepted me and made me sit down and drink a steaming concoction whose basic nasty taste was partly disguised with the flavor of anise. Then I wound my Ingersoll and went to bed to sleep fitfully and dream troubled, confused dreams about people I did not know except that a girl who was supposed to be my lost love Little Egypt was not Little Egypt because Little Egypt was dead.

They allowed me to sleep late in the morning and Ralph was gone before I rose and was given a breakfast of Cream of Wheat and toast. My headache was practically gone, but I felt weak and apathetic and unreasonably sad. After breakfast I made my bed and lay down on it again and went back to sleep.

At noon I revived with a thought and asked if the mailman had brought a letter for me. He hadn't. And when there was nothing in the afternoon delivery, I felt certain I should hear from Mr. Spence the following day. But I didn't. Nor on the succeeding day.

On the fifth day I was desperate enough to telephone Ramsey, Curtis, Spence and Kline. I asked the girl who rattled off the firm's name if I could please speak to Mr. Spence, trying to make my voice sound adult and important.

"Who is speaking, please?"

"Tell him Mr. George V. Chalmers."

"Just what was it you wished to speak to Mr. Spence about, Mr. Chalmers?"

"Well," I said, "as a matter of fact, I was talking to Mr. Spence in his office the other day and he said he would write me a letter in a couple of days and I haven't heard from him."

"Hmm—well, just a moment, Mr. Chalmers."

Presently another woman's voice spoke and I thought I recognized the grim-faced woman. "You are George Chalmers?"

"Yes, ma'am."

"Aren't you one of the boys who applied here for an office-boy's job?"

"Well," I said, "yes, ma'am, and Mr. Spence said he would write me a letter."

"I'm sorry, but Mr. Spence said he would write you *if* you were selected. It happens that he chose another boy and the situation has been satisfactorily filled. Sorry."

"Thank you, ma'am," I said, and hung up the receiver.

Chapter 16

IT was a depressing period with many, many applications before I got a job "making myself useful" in Ben Jowett's Cut-Rate Pharmacy at the end of July. The pay was four dollars a week and "making myself useful" consisted of mopping the tile floor at 7:30 A.M., washing windows, polishing the glass counters, dusting shelves and countless bottles and sundries, running errands and delivering telephoned orders on an old bicycle with a huge wire carrier in front.

I rather liked the job. Mr. Jowett was pleasant and considerate after I proved I was not lazy, and, in addition to my pay, he allowed me a free ice-cream soda or sundae at the soda fountain once a day. When I was not busy, I was permitted to sit in the back room and read unsold magazines before bundling them for return to the distributors.

Each week Laura collected two of my four dollars toward my board, counting on my care of the lawn and other odd jobs around the house to make up the deficit. That left me two dollars a week of my own, which was as much as I averaged on my paper route at home.

When the time came to register at Central High School, I was apprehensive of many things. First, there was a question of this big-city high school's accepting my small-town credentials. Then there was grave doubt in my mind whether I ever could find my way around and do passable work in classes that I pictured as gigantic rooms filled with hundreds of pupils. Then there was the matter of my job. Was it possible that Mr. Jowett would let me work after school?

I settled the latter question quickly. My white-jacketed employer put a kindly hand on my shoulder. "Sure, George," he said. "You arrange your study-hall periods to come at the end of your schedule. Then you can fix it to duck study hall and get to work by one o'clock. You can do your studying in the back room there instead of reading those silly magazines."

Obviously, Mr. Jowett knew things about high schools that I never suspected, and I was delighted at his attitude.

"Of course," he went on, "you wouldn't expect to get the same pay for half-a-day's work."

"Oh, no," I said, "of course not."

"Well, then, George, I'll tell you what I'm going to do. You're a good worker and I was thinking about raising your pay anyhow, so I'm going to give you three dollars a week for working from one o'clock to six."

This was wonderful, a far better situation than I ever could have hoped for. I'd reserve Saturday mornings for the Sterlings' lawnwork, continue paying Laura her two dollars a week and still have a dollar a week of my own.

When it came to registering, I decided to see if I could be accepted just on my diploma of graduation from grammar school without presenting my last miserable report card, and, somewhat to my surprise, the venture was successful. Studying over the first-year curriculum, I was pleased to see that I could take a course called zoology, which seemed to approximate natural history, as well as the mandatory courses of English and algebra. Physical education was required every other day and on alternate days I could study art.

Both Laura and Ralph were disgusted at my signing up for zoology instead of Latin.

"What in the world do you want of bugology?" he asked.

"I don't think it's just bugs," I said. "I know it isn't. It's all about animals and birds, too, and I'm just interested in 'em."

"What good's it going to do you?"

"Maybe a lot of good. Maybe I'll be a naturalist or something."

Ralph shook his head.

"Well, what good's learning an old dead language?" I asked.

"Latin," said Laura, "is the foundation of the English language. You can't know proper English without knowing Latin."

"I don't know," I said, "but it would seem like you could learn English pretty good studying English."

"It would seem *like*," said Laura in her most sarcastic tone, "that you need a good deal of studying before you learn English *pretty good*."

Ralph laughed.

"All right," I said. "I'm pretty dumb and I don't know what's so funny, but I'm going to make up for my dumbness by studying harder than anybody else and you'll just see."

"Good for you, Georgie," said my mother.

"No one could complain about that resolution," said Ralph. "Are you still going to be a lawyer?"

Anger welled up in me. "I don't know," I said. "But if I do, I'm going to be a good one."

In school it was encouraging to find that there were not hundreds in the classes but only thirty or so. But with no study periods, I was to discover that studying "harder than anybody else" was to be a problem for me. On my half-day shift at the drugstore I had little time to myself in the back room. Even in late September it was too cold on my sleeping porch to study and inside the house the distractions of crying babies and family conversation were difficult to cope with. Because of my poor knowledge of arithmetic, algebra was a horror, a hopeless horror. Miss Cohen, the teacher, was not a patient woman and she gave up on me early, although I devoted most of my small study time to that harsh science. Zoology was a joy. The teacher was a round, jolly little man named Mr. Fletcher and I did well with him, though I never opened the textbook except in class and even worked on my illustrated notebook there.

I gloated to Laura: "Look, you yelled that I should ought to be taking Latin. Well let me tell you, I'm learning plenty Latin in zoology. You studied a lot of Latin, but do you know what a *coleopteron* is? Or a *hymenopteron?* Or a *cimex lectularius.* Or a *ursus horribilis?"*

"Well," she said, "I know that *ursus* is a bear, but—"

"Yeah," I said, "but what kind of a bear? Well, I'll tell you it's a grizzly bear, and a *coleopteron* is a beetle, and a *hymenopteron* is a bee, and a *cimex lectularius* is a bedbug."

"That's really wonderful," she said, "and what good will it ever do you? It doesn't teach you any grammar. It doesn't teach you not to say 'should ought.' "

The hour of those alternate classes, art and physical education, was what I looked forward to with pleasure, and in neither were the students separated by classes. Big seniors and little freshmen were together, with no distinction except performance. The art class was presided over by charming Miss Mignon Maloney, petite, young, blue-eyed, laughing, with a freckled snub nose, who, for the sheer joy of life, couldn't restrain a dance step or two when she walked around the room. I fell in love with her not only because she praised my charcoal drawings of plaster casts and held them up as examples to the coterie of scornful big senior and junior girls who made up most of the class, but for the aura of kindness, hope and happiness that enveloped her and spread out to a radius of about twenty-five feet. I even speculated about her at first. She couldn't be more than about twenty-two years old, I thought, and I was nearly fifteen. After all, that was only seven years. Then one morning she seemed more ebullient even than usual, and a large diamond was throwing blue fire from her ring finger. Time and some grown man, probably a millionaire, had disrupted my dream. But I still loved her and she marked an A on my report card each month.

On the alternate days in physical education I also received monthly A's, the only freshman to be so honored. Being light in proportion to my strength, I was adept at such exercises as the parallel bars, "horses" and flying rings, and quick and aggressive at the gymnasium games. Then, as winter waned, we had an indoor track meet in which I did well. There were five entrants for the half-mile handicap run on the twenty-four-lap track suspended halfway to the ceiling of the two-story gymnasium, and Central's star half-miler, a lean senior named Morris, was scratch man. I had the biggest handicap—three-quarters of a lap. Running in sneakers on the rubber-matted track, I made up that quarter lap between Morris and me in a quick spurt. And before the race was over I had lapped the scratch man as well as the other runners.

Bucky Saunders, the coach, hugged me and paid no attention to Senior Morris' excuse that he had a bad cold.

In early spring they held an interclass track meet at the half-mile track in City Park, and when I won the eight-eighty over Morris by approximately twenty-five yards, Mr. Saunders threw a blanket around my sweaty shoulders and cried, "Boy, do you know what you've done?"

I gasped, "Well, I beat a senior."

"Yes," he said, "you beat our best half-miler and you also broke the Rocky Mountain interscholastic record by four full seconds. Boy, are we going to tear this town apart next year when you're eligible for the track team, and if you could just put on about twenty pounds, you might make a halfback."

In this meet, which was held on a Friday afternoon and which I was able to attend because Mr. Jowett was kind enough to give me the day off, I competed also in the high jump, the broad jump and the hundred-yard dash, failing to place in the first but coming third in both of the others.

Mr. Saunders bolstered my ego, as did Miss Maloney—a pleasantness absent from my other classes. Physical education had one more joy to offer me and that was the mandatory hot and cold shower after a workout, and that freed me from the no small problem of finding free time for the Sterling bathtub when there remained hot water in the tank.

Despite my interest in the zoology course, Mr. Fletcher gave me only average grades. Because of my fumbling ineptitude in algebra, poor, harried, hollow-eyed, leather-cheeked, frizzle-haired Miss Cohen could not give me passing marks. And my worst downfall came at the hands of Miss Blanche Zink, in English. Miss Zink was a big young woman with a high, light-brown pompadour, broad nose and pale, plump face. She was bosomy and broad-hipped, shirtwaisted and sarcastic. And she was a stickler for the grammatical fetishes of that day. Ending a sentence with a preposition was a mark of complete illiteracy. She was ready to impeach the Governor of Colorado because he reputedly split an infinitive in an extemporaneous speech. She cringed even at a split verb. And the subjunctive mood was one of the holy of the holies.

Because I had a fairly retentive memory and was able to learn some Wordsworth, Burns, Thomas Campbell and Shelley, assigned us from *Palgrave's Golden Treasury*, in the few moments I could spare from algebra, she had accorded me grudging C's until the explosion.

This came in late winter when an unseasonable warm spell gave me a chance to work on my sleeping porch, wearing my cap and overcoat. The assignment was in addition to our regular lessons and we had two weeks in which to write a short story. This, I thought, was my opportunity to establish myself as a boy genius and to bring my month's grade up at least to a B. I felt sure I could write a thrilling short story. But on what theme? I wished my father had got around to telling me of his adventures as a young man in the West.

I felt that I must come up with something that would really impress Miss Zink, but I racked my brain vainly for an adequate idea. Then I thought of a story I had read the previous summer in the back room of Mr. Jowett's pharmacy. It was, I thought, in a magazine that no woman like Miss Zink ever in the world would read, and it was about three bandits who had held up a train and were trying to escape across a burning desert with their loot. Two of the bandits murdered the third to get his share of the gold and his canteen. Indians stampeded their horses, wounded one of the bandits and punctured a canteen with a bullet. Stumbling across the desert on foot, the sound bandit knew his wounded pal was a liability who consumed precious drinking water, and as a matter of practical business, put him out of his misery. Then he staggered along alone, burdened by the sack of gold and followed by circling vultures overhead. The vultures led the posse to the third bandit's body with the loot beside it and the quaint old deputy spat tobacco juice into the sand and remarked, "Money you get like that just never does you any good."

I thought this was a wonderful story and I wished I had a copy of that magazine. But I remembered the details so well that I didn't really need to copy it. It was a thrilling thing to write it down as I remembered it, even if I had to blow on my numb hand now and then as I worked. I turned it in with pride and confidence.

[169]

It's a curious thing that I felt pride because I knew quite well it was dishonest to pass off the essence of a magazine story as my own, and both my father and mother had stressed nothing more than honesty in lectures on conduct. I never had stolen. And I was not given to telling falsehoods.

My desire for praise and a higher grade led me not only into dishonesty but stupidity in thinking that women read nothing but women's magazines.

It so happened that Miss Zink *had* read my story in *Everybody's* magazine and her reaction was startling.

Standing before the class with her head thrown back, she stared at me with steady, pale eyes while she smoothed her dark skirt at the hips with big, white hands. "George Chalmers," she said, "I am giving you a large red zero on your story and I believe you know why. Don't you?"

This was awful. Being prepared for extravagant praise in spite of a few possible misspellings and grammatical errors, this was devastating.

I heard my faint voice saying, "No, ma'am."

"Do you know what plagiarism is?"

"No, ma'am."

"Well, for your information and for the information of the rest of the class, plagiarism is one of the most despicable forms of theft." She pointed a finger at me and continued, "George Chalmers, I am holding you up to scorn because you are guilty of plagiarism. You stole this story you tried to pass off as your own, and don't try to lie out of it because I read it last summer in *Everybody's* magazine."

Through my haze of misery I was conscious of every eye in the room peering at me. I said huskily, "Well, Miss Zink, I didn't really copy it. I just kind of borrowed the idea because I thought it was a very good story and I didn't know—"

She interrupted. "You mean you didn't believe I would have read the magazine story and you could get away with it. Isn't that it?"

So completely wretched that I would gladly have walked to the gallows, I said, "Maybe. I'm sorry, but I just—"

"Not only that," she went on, "but you showed execrable taste in what you stole. It was a terrible story to begin with, and, considering your solecisms and bad spelling, I never would have given your paper more than a C, even if I thought it was original. You have proved yourself not only dishonest but ignorant and entirely devoid of literary taste. Now I hope this will be a lesson to you and to the rest of the class also in case any of you are ever tempted to foist off another's work as your own."

From then on I was a pariah in English class and my monthly grade dropped from C to a barely passing E. Miss Zink plainly held me in contempt and my morale dropped to match the red zero on the short story. Each month my mother signed my report cards, sighing sometimes because I wasn't doing better. But when Laura asked to see my final card that spring she was appalled.

"Your only two important subjects were algebra and English, and what do you do?" she exclaimed. "A complete, disgraceful failure in one and a practical failure in the other."

She was not at all impressed by my B in zoology and A's in both art and physical education. "It seems quite plain," she said, "that you're wasting your time in school. If you're not interested in getting an education, you should be learning a trade so you can be self-supporting."

We were in the living room after dinner and Ralph was reading the evening paper in the big leather chair, apparently paying no attention to Laura and me.

"Gosh," I said, "I'm interested in getting an education. After all."

"Your awful grades don't show it," she asserted. "If you were interested you would have studied, and if you had studied you wouldn't have failed."

I thought about telling her I didn't really fail in English and that I would have got at least a C except that Miss Zink was mad at me. But then I should have to explain why Miss Zink was mad at me and I decided to leave that matter alone.

Ralph rocked a few times in his chair and spoke over his newspaper, "I'm in favor of everyone getting all the education he can assimilate. Maybe George will do better next year."

This unexpected support from the leather chair was gratifying. "Sure, I will," I said.

"Or worse," Laura snapped. "George certainly knew he was on trial this last year and he was too lazy and indifferent to try."

"My goodness," I cried, "I *tried*. I swear I tried."

[171]

"All right," said Laura stiffly, "if you really tried, then it's quite apparent that you've got all the formal education you can assimilate and I say it's time for you to quit wasting time in school and to begin learning some decent trade."

My mother came in from the kitchen, wearing her apron and looking troubled. Standing in the doorway, she said, "Laura, you're not arguing that George should quit school, are you? Nobody can amount to anything these days unless he has a high-school education."

Laura turned and faced her. "Mama," she said, "I know it's hard for mothers to realize this, but all sons aren't fitted to become bankers or doctors or lawyers or ministers. There's room in the professions for a very limited number of men and it's a mistake for any boy to try to enter the professions except those with special ability in that direction. Can't you see that? And I'm sure an expert mechanic is a more useful citizen than a third-rate professional man, and would lead a happier life."

"Well, gosh," I said, "I've *got* to go back to school in the fall."

Laura asked, "Got to? Who says so?"

"Well, Bucky Saunders, the coach. Didn't I tell you I broke the interscholastic record for the half mile this spring? And there's going to be football this fall and—"

"Competitive athletics are idiotic," Laura asserted.

"Now, Laura," said Ralph mildly, "don't be unreasonable. Athletics in moderation can be character building."

"That's all very well, but schools are for education and not for playing games. George is *my* brother, not yours, and I'm not going to have you paying the expenses of my brother to play games and run races at school when he's either not interested in studying or is incapable of it."

My mother had slumped in a chair, looking very sad. "Well," she asked faintly, "what sort of trade do you think George should learn? Ralph, do you think you could get him into the bank so he could learn that business?"

Ralph shook his head. "I'm afraid not, Mother Chalmers," he said. "In the first place there's no opening, and then I think it would be a mistake for any young fellow to try to get ahead in banking unless he has a special aptitude for mathematics and training in it. That doesn't mean—"

I blurted out, "Oh, quit worrying about me. I'm big enough

to pass for seventeen and if you'll just say I'm seventeen I'll go join the Navy and not bother you any more."

"No, George," said Laura, "we're just trying to help you and nobody is going to lie about your age, especially not to get you in the Navy."

My mother spoke with some spirit, "Well, Laura, George has been contributing toward his support and he looks after the furnace and mows the lawn and I'm doing his laundry."

"Yes, Mama," said Laura, "I know that very well. Ralph has been kind enough to take my brother into his home as a member of the family, and George naturally would want to do his share of the household chores. If my brother were doing reasonably well in school I wouldn't say a word and I'm sure Ralph wouldn't even think of it. But I'm not going to ask Ralph to support my brother's career of playing games and running races while he loafs through high school."

"It seems to me," said our mother, "that George is a very good worker."

"Of course he is," Laura agreed, "at anything within his capacity. That's why I say he should be learning a practical trade or business. There are a great many things George could do well or even excel at, and both Ralph and I would be only too happy to help him all we can while he's learning. I'm just opposed to his wasting any more time at this formative period of his life, failing at things he's supposed to learn and perhaps coming to think of himself as a failure even before he's grown. That could ruin his life. It's George himself I'm thinking of, Mama. Can't you see that?"

My mother sighed. "Well, maybe," she said. "Georgie, have you any idea of a trade you'd like to learn?"

"Yes," I said, "I'm pretty good at drawing. I'd like to go to an art school and learn to be an artist."

Laura covered her eyes. "Oh, Heaven help me," she moaned.

Chapter 17

I SPOKE to kind Mr. Jowett about the process of becoming a pharmacist, and that was hopeless. Not only did one have to finish high school, but one must spend three years in pharmacy school before earning a license. There were about a million drugs, chemicals, poisons, elixirs, tinctures and compounds to learn with their derivations, component parts and effects on the human system in sickness and health by grains, grams and milligrams. And, as a final crusher, all physicians wrote their prescriptions in Latin.

My announcement that I was quitting school disappointed Mr. Jowett. "I wonder," he said, "if you realize what quitting school now means? It probably means you will be mopping floors and doing other menial work all your life."

"I don't think so," I said. "I'm going to learn a good trade."

"George," he said, "as a loyal alumnus of old Central, I was counting on your hitting the high spots athletically next year. If it's a matter of money, I'll stretch it a point and pay you five dollars a week during the summer and four when school starts."

I thanked him and told him it was no use, that family matters made it necessary for me to learn a trade. Continuing to work for Mr. Jowett on the half-day basis, I devoted mornings to hunting for an apprenticeship. Dressed in the neat blue serge suit I had saved up for and wearing an uncomfortably high, stiff linen collar, I made halfhearted inquiries at printing offices, machine shops, photo-engraving plants, automobile-repair shops, construction companies, railroad roundhouses, newspaper offices, flour mills, everything I could think of, and no one was interested in hiring an apprentice—at least not a gangling fifteen-year-old in a blue serge suit and too-tight linen collar. The responses ranged from kindly, "Not right at present, but you might call again in a few months," to a gruff, "Naw, nothing doing."

At the Burlington Railroad offices, when I finally had been

shuttled to the proper department to apply for a chance to learn to be a brakeman or fireman, the square-jawed, steely-eyed official squinted at me.

"How old are you?" he demanded.

"Well, sir," I stammered, "I'm eighteen."

"Nuts," he said. "You haven't even got any fuzz on your face. Go home and grow up and come back in about three years."

It was all most discouraging. And, while she didn't actually say so, Laura indicated doubt that I really was trying very hard.

Then one morning I read in the want-ad section of the *Morning Journal:*

> WANTED: STRONG, ACTIVE BOY OR YOUNG MAN NOT AFRAID OF WORK OR GETTING HANDS DIRTY. GOOD PAY AND OPPORTUNITY FOR RIGHT PARTY. APPLY IN PERSON, DON'T PHONE, JAKE KRUEGER, LAMBERT'S HARDWARE, LARIMER ST. SISSIES, DON'T WASTE MY TIME.

I was dressed already in my blue suit and white shirt, but I rushed to my sleeping porch and hurriedly changed to an old blue shirt and my first long trousers, put on an old cap instead of my brown felt hat, and dashed out to catch the streetcar for Larimer St. Although it must have been eight thirty by the time I reached the store, no line of applicants was waiting. Had I thought, I should have realized that the ad was not designed to attract many vacationing boys.

A clerk directed me to the rear of the store where Jake Krueger had a desk and telephone. "Set down," he ordered, waving a meaty hand at a kitchen chair. He looked at me and I looked at him, and he was a massive, thick-chested, sallow, middle-aged man with a leather cap pushed to the back of his big head. He was chewing a frazzled cigar and his thick lips were stained by it. His pouchy eyes were small, colorless and shrewd.

"You a schoolboy?" he asked in a rumbling bass voice.

"Just finished first year high school," I said, "but I've got to quit."

"You ever work?"

"Yes, sir. I've been working in a drugstore for nearly a year —part time when I was going to school."

"Soda jerk?"

"No, sir. Mopping floors, washing windows and counters, delivering on a bicycle."

"You scared to get on high places?"

I thought of my horrible experience on the cliff above Clear Creek and when I hesitated he said, "I don't mean being a steeplejack and climbing up the Globeville smelter stack. I mean like working on the roof of a dwelling house."

I wasn't entirely sure whether I could work on a house roof comfortably or not, but I said, "I could do that all right, I guess. Doing what on a house roof?"

Jake Krueger talked around his dead cigar. "I got my own business, see? Independent of Lambert's here, but I buy supplies from 'em and pay 'em for this desk space and they answer the phone for me when I'm not here. Mostly from now on until fall my big work will be cleaning chimneys, but I'm a heating expert and I repair old furnaces and put in new furnaces that Lambert's here sell, although I sell a few now and then myself, but, like I say, most of the work from now to fall will be cleaning chimneys."

"You mean," I asked, thinking of the boy Tom in Kingsley's *Water Babies*, "you want me to go down chimneys, sweeping 'em?"

He laughed boomingly. "Naw! Maybe I'm built kind of like Santa Claus now, but I never went down no chimneys. Long time ago, I guess they used to make great big chimneys and chimney sweeps would go down 'em and maybe up 'em again, but not many chimneys in Denver now where even a slim kid like you could get down. No, I got a special instrument I invented that we clean chimneys with from the top. Then we shovel and brush out the soot from the flue in the cellar. How're you working with tools?"

"Pretty good, I think. And I can learn things you do with your hands."

"You don't look especially stout."

"Well, I'm strong for my size, Mr. Krueger, and I'm growing all the time."

"I'm giving it to you straight, see, before we make any kind of a deal." He spat into a tin cuspidor. "I pay good money for the right kid because it's damn hard, dirty work sometimes, like changing the warped old grate bars in an old furnace and you got to crawl in the ashpit and cut 'em loose with a cold chisel and hammer without room to swing the hammer good and the dirt comes down in your eyes and maybe the chisel slips and you bang your thumb and unless you got guts you say to hell with it and get a job being a ribbon-counter clerk. I've got no time for ribbon-counter clerks, but for a kid with guts who'll stay with me and learn the trade, I'll make it worth his while."

"Well," I said, "I think I've got guts and I want to learn a good trade and I'm willing to work hard. How much do you pay?"

He looked at me steadily. "I'm telling you straight," he said. "I make good money in my business and I'm not figuring on getting rich at the expense of my helper. I've told you enough so's you ought to know what you're getting into. If you want the job I'll try you out and I'll pay you nine dollars a week to start and more if you make good. And, if you know anything about what kids usually get in Denver, you know that's big money."

"I know," I said, "and I'll take the job and do my best."

"Good boy." He put out his big, scarred hand to shake on the bargain. "Now, you got rubber-soled tennis shoes? And you got overalls and a jumper?"

"I've got rubber-soled gym shoes," I said, "and I'll get some overalls."

"And a bandanna to tie around your neck and a jumper. You'll need it up on breezy roofs. Be here at eight o'clock tomorrow morning and we'll go to work."

I thanked him, and at a nearby store bought overalls, a blue denim jacket with brass buttons, a couple of red bandanna handkerchiefs, and a denim cap to match the uniform. Nine dollars a week! That was half again as much as I ever hoped for. And a promise of more and perhaps a good deal more if I made good. Well, I *would* make good. What did I care that the work would be hard and dirty? It had become increasingly apparent that hard and dirty work was what I was fitted for at present, and I could save money on this job and perhaps I could go to a night school and fit myself for something better by the time I was twenty-one. I wondered if perhaps there was a school in Denver where one could study art at night.

In my elation over my new job I boasted to Laura about my nine dollars a week to start. She congratulated me warmly and said, "With nine dollars a week, you can afford to pay at least three dollars a week toward your board." This was something that had not occurred to me, but her suggestion seemed reasonable enough and I agreed to it. That still would leave me six dollars a week, minus streetcar fare and lunch money, from which I could save a good deal.

The next morning Jake Krueger and I set out on several chimney-cleaning missions with his spring wagon and sorrel gelding Teddy. His equipment consisted of an extension ladder and two smaller ones; two dark tarpaulins; a battered metal washtub, two galvanized buckets, a collection of steel brushes of various sizes and shapes; several shovels, big and little; a padlocked zink toolbox filled with wrenches, cold chisels and regular chisels, hammers, trowels, cans of asbestos, cement and oddments; and his own chimney-cleaning invention, which consisted of a long, quarter-inch manila rope tied tightly to a gunny sack containing two bricks. Lashed laterally to the middle of the sack was a woman's corset rolled into a tight cylinder, stiff with steel stays and black with soot.

Our first job was simple—a one-story brick cottage with a single chimney. With the dignity of a United States Senator on a foreign junket, Jake inspected the house and basement, and, finding everything in order, he said, "Okay, let's do it."

He helped me place a ladder against the low eaves and told me to take the sack and rope up and let the sack down the chimney until it touched bottom. "Then you pump her up and down easy until I tell you to stop."

Standing with one rubber-soled sneaker on each side of the ridgepole I found the corset a pretty snug fit for the small chimney, but the stays bent and the bricks were heavy enough to take the sack to the bottom.

"Easy now," Jake boomed from the lawn. "Clear to the top and down again slow."

When I had repeated this several times, he told me to pull the sack out and turn the "scraper" to get the other sides of the chimney.

It was nice up there on the roof, in communion with the leafy trees. Across the street a couple of young girls were watching me and I felt worth while and even important. Presently Jake called up, "Okay, that ought to do it. Come on down."

So we went into the basement with the tub, broom, brushes, a fire shovel and a tarp. Jake spread the tarp on the floor next to the furnace flue and put the tub on it. Then he took down the furnace smoke pipe, thumped the sections into the tub and said, "All right, George, shovel the soot out of the flue."

I got a surprising amount of soot from the flue with the fire shovel, and we got a surprising amount of soot from the furnace pipes with the brushes, and a surprising amount of soot got on me during the operations. I carried the tub of soot out to the ashpit by the alley and dumped it. We folded up the tarp and I swept the cement floor where we had been working. Then the housewife paid Jake four dollars and we were on our way to the second job within forty minutes after arrival, and I could see how Jake could afford to pay me nine dollars a week. Of course this four dollars was not clear profit. There was Jake's investment to consider and feed for the horse as well as paying for small ads in the newspapers, rent for his desk space, and wear and tear on the wagon and the corset.

The second assignment was a two-story house with two chimneys, but that took only slightly more than an hour and Jake collected eight dollars. The third house was the same, making a total of twenty dollars for the morning.

Jake looked at his big silver watch. "Well, it ain't quite noon yet," he said, "but we might as well feed our faces now and get it out of the way." He frowned at me. "But I never noticed you carrying any lunch."

"No, sir," I admitted, "I haven't any lunch with me, but—"

"You got any money?"

"Sure," I said, "if there's a lunch counter or something around here—"

Jake's huge chest pumped out a chuckle. "Well, there ain't. But, looking the way you do, a lunch counter probably would chase you away. They'd think you was a nigger. I never see a kid spread so much soot over himself on three little jobs. Well, there's a grocery store a couple blocks down the street, and you can buy something to eat and we'll drive in a quiet alley and scoff."

"Scoff?"

"Yeah, that's hobo for eat. I was a hobo once when I was a kid and rode the rattlers from coast to coast. Yeah, I've known what hard times are until I learned this trade and went into business for myself. That's why I believe in treating people right that works for me. You're doing fine so far and you keep it up and you'll see what I mean."

At the grocery I bought a nickel can of sardines, a nickel's worth of soda crackers, and two bananas for another nickel. Jake drove into an alley in the shade of a tree and asked permission at a back door to draw water from a hose tap for the horse. Then, after watering Teddy and putting on his nose bag, we sat on the seat and ate. Jake's big tin dinner pail was filled with thick meat sandwiches, pickles, a small bowl of beans and a wedge of pie. The upper container was filled with cold black coffee, which he insisted on sharing with me.

"Can't you get somebody to put up a lunch for you?" he asked.

"Maybe," I said, thinking that inasmuch as I should be paying three dollars a week for board now that perhaps my mother would be permitted to put up a lunch for me. "I don't know for sure, but I'll see."

That afternoon we cleaned six more chimneys in three two-story houses, giving Jake Krueger a total gross income of forty-four dollars for the day. I felt happy in being a part of this profitable enterprise, even though my part was only one dollar and a half. It had been pleasant working with this genial, gross, fat man who assured me again at the end of the day that I was doing fine. I warmed to him as we drove through the Denver streets and he entertained me with anecdotes of his varied life, before success and independence came his way, as well as adventures and misadventures in his present business.

"There was this damn fool kid, and I won't mention his name on account you might run into him sometime. A pure dope, see. I tell him and tell him like I told you, 'Don't pump that sack up and down fast. Let it down easy. Pull it up easy. That's all you need.' But, by God, he still drops her down fast and yanks it up fast. So one day we're working on a chimney and I hears the lady let out a war whoop, and I know something's wrong because it's not the kind of war whoop some ladies let out when they hear something funny over the telephone and I calls out to the kid to stop. Well, the dope is thinking about some dolly or something because he just keeps pumping that sack up and down and the lady lets out another war whoop and I really yell this time, 'STOP!' "

At this, the horse cocked his ears and stopped in the middle of the street. "Christ, Teddy," said Jake, "I didn't mean you. Giddap. Well, the fool kid stopped then and called down,

'You mean you want me to stop this?' And I says, 'Stop don't mean go ahead does it?' and I beat it into the house. Well, my God, the flue stopper had come out of the flue with all that pumping and every time the sack went up or down soot just blew all over that parlor. The carpet, the chairs, the davenport, the piano, the lace curtains, ever goddamn thing in that room was black with soot. Even the lady's face and hair was sooty. You never saw such a god-awful mess in your life. We did what we could, which wasn't very much, and maybe you won't believe this, but it cost me twenty-six dollars to get that place cleaned up right and the cleaners made me a wholesale price. And at that I didn't even pay for having the lady's hair washed and I expect she did that herself. Well, I told that kid he'd better find another job where muscle is more important than brains."

I didn't say so, but I could sympathize with that unfortunate boy. I could picture myself in his position, but of course I no longer was Sleepy Chalmers. Now I was Wide-Awake Chalmers, an ambitious youth working hard for good money with prospects for even more because I was giving satisfaction. On my way home I was tired but much less so than after my day on the McIntyre grocery wagon, and there was happiness mixed with the fatigue.

Well, I knew I was dirty when I went in the front door, but I didn't really appreciate *how* dirty. Laura cried out, "Heavens above! What is this? Where in the world have you been and what happened to you? Never in my life!"

I started to hang my denim cap on the hat rack, then decided not to. "I guess I got kind of dirty," I said.

"Dirty! You look like a coal miner. You look worse than a coal miner. You look like a chimney sweep."

"That," I said, "is a kind of funny thing to say, as a matter of fact."

My mother, in obvious alarm over the exclamations, came from the kitchen. "Georgie!" she gasped.

"I guess I'll get my towel and go wash up," I said, "that is if the bathroom is free."

"Yes," said Laura. "By all means do. But I shudder to think what the bathroom will look like when you're through."

"Gosh," I said, "I'll clean it up. I always do, don't I?"

"Mostly," she admitted, "but I wouldn't say *always*."

[181]

After I washed and donned clean clothing and hung my sooty overalls, shirt and cap on my sleeping porch, I had to explain my day. I was glad that Ralph, who had just been promoted to vice-president-in-charge-of-mortgages, was working late and that I had only the women to contend with.

"Oh, George," my mother exclaimed, "I don't want my boy doing that kind of dirty work—cleaning chimneys, of all things."

"It's clean dirt," I declared, "and just on the outside, where it'll wash off. It's pretty hard work, but I don't mind that, and just because you get a little dirty, namby-pamby people are afraid of it, and it pays a lot of money. I happen to know Mr. Krueger took in forty-four dollars today and I'd like to know another trade, including banking, that pays as much. And Mr. Krueger is a very nice man to work for, even if maybe he don't stick out his little finger when he drinks a cup of tea if he ever drinks a cup of tea, and I'm very lucky to get a job working for him, and it's honest work and nobody needs to think they're going to talk me into quitting."

"Well," said Laura, "you're certainly not going to come home looking the way you did tonight. You can take some other clothes down to this man's shop or office and clean up before you come home."

"I can't do that."

"You've *got* to do it. Considering Ralph's position and the neighbors knowing you're my brother, I'm not going to have you coming in looking like a—like a, well, the way you looked this evening."

"There just isn't any place down there for me to clean up and change clothes. Mr. Krueger's only got a desk in the back of Lambert's Hardware Store and there's no boudoir in hardware stores, and what's the matter, I'd like to know, are you ashamed of having your brother doing honest work, even if it's a little dirty?"

Laura sighed. "Well, I don't know what to say. Mama, *you* tell him that he has no right to humiliate us this way."

My mother was looking very unhappy and before she could speak I said, "All right, Mama, you tell me. When my sister is so smart and educated that she's married to a bank vice-president, why is it that I'm so dumb I can't even go to high school and have to learn how to make a living doing work so dirty it makes lily-fingered people shudder? You tell me that."

"Oh, George," said my mother, "please don't talk like that. You're not dumb at all. If you had just learned to work as hard with your head as you do with your hands, there never would have been any trouble. But I know you could find a better job than sweeping chimneys."

"I'd like to know where. I guess you don't know how hard I tried to find a job."

"I know you've tried. But you must just remember, 'When at first you don't succeed, try, try again.'"

"Well, Mom, I tried and I tried and finally I got a good job and Mr. Krueger complimented me on my work and promised me raises in pay and if Laura doesn't want me here, for goodness sake, I don't have to stay here. Right now I'm making enough dough to live on and I'll get me a room someplace."

Laura said, "Oh, honey, it's not that we don't want you here. Please try to understand. Can't you realize that it's a reflection on Ralph for people to see you the way you were this evening and to know that you're Ralph's brother-in-law?"

"No, I can't realize it," I blurted. "I don't see why even a banker needs to be ashamed of a brother-in-law doing honest work. Abe Lincoln did hard, dirty work."

"Not sweeping chimneys, George," my mother said.

"He would have if there'd been chimneys to sweep instead of rails to split. And if I heard my Sunday-school lessons right, Jesus thought pretty well of a fisherman that must have smelled mighty strong of fish, and I mean Saint Peter."

Laura flared at that. "Mama," she said, "your darling boy is getting out of hand."

"Yes, George," my mother said huskily. She seemed on the point of tears. "What I'm afraid of, if you're going to be doing rough, dirty work with tough dirty men, is that they'll corrupt you. I just don't want my boy to be corrupted and sinful."

I thought she would be completely crushed if she dreamed how sinful I was already. I said, "I'm sorry, Mama."

"And," she went on, "I don't want you to speak again of going off to live by yourself at your age. You've *got* to stay here with me for a long time to come and if Laura and Ralph feel you must give up that dirty work, I don't see anything else for you to do."

"Look, Mama," said I, "I'm a working man now and it doesn't make any difference whether I'm fifteen going on sixteen or twenty-five going on twenty-six. I've got my rights. I say I'm going to keep my job with Mr. Krueger and I'm going to. If Laura and Ralph don't want me here, I'll just leave. But I'll do this to keep Laura from being ashamed: I'll get off the street-car a block down the line and come up the back alley and slip into my sleeping porch and take off my dirty clothes and then wash up."

"You, without a doubt," said Laura, "are the most stubborn silly goose I ever heard of, but, unless Ralph objects too strenuously, I guess I'll have to agree to that."

It was on my third day that I found out what Jake Krueger meant about a furnace grate job. It seemed impossible that he ever could have wedged enough of his broad-shouldered two hundred and forty pounds into that narrow ashpit door to work effectively. One grate bar could be removed from the top through the fire door. The other two were so warped and corroded that they couldn't be budged.

I crawled into the ash door with a ball peen hammer, cold chisel and fat candle. Jake hovered above anxiously with a flashlight which he turned occasionally into the fire door. "Now, for Christ's sake, George, take it easy," he said. "Whatever you do, don't bust one of them sockets that holds the grates."

In my cramped quarters I scarcely could do anything else but "take it easy." And when I gently tapped the bottom of one of the grates near its setting, rusted iron and encrusted cinders showered into my face. After repeated tapping, however, one of the grates broke loose from its moorings and Jake reached in a big gloved hand from above and pulled it from the furnace. "Good boy, George," he gasped, breathing as heavily as if he had been doing the work.

Because it was not bound by anything except its own twisted ends, the third grate came out more easily, and Jake, leaning in the fire door, smoothed the sockets by easy application of a rattail file and emery paper. Then he put in the new gray iron grates and we cleaned the furnace and pipe and Jake collected for the job while I carried two buckets of soot to the ashpit by the alley.

Jake was happy as we drove through the glorious summer morning toward a chimney-cleaning job. In his rumbling bass he sang a favorite ditty:

> Tom Swift was a wonderful fellow.
> No boy was so nimble and strong;
> He could turn ten somersaults backward,
> And stand on his head all day long.

He chuckled and said, "By God, boy, maybe you're a kind of a Tom Swift yourself. You did just fine on that grate job, and, fat as I am, I'd have had one hell of a time doing it myself."

I thanked him and was very happy myself. A knuckle had been barked on the job, but I didn't care. I sucked it and regarded the slight wound as a badge of valor. I had found my level and was appreciated and lauded. Could any lawyer or governor or artist or champion athlete ask for more? I gloried in my barked knuckle, I gloried in the dirt on my skin and clothing that marked me not as a stupid boy reduced to low, servile toil because of an inferior brain, but as a proud and successful young man not afraid to attack tasks that lesser mortals would shrink from. And, because of my indomitable courage, determination, and yes, guts, I would rise to heights far beyond the capacity of such sissies as Ralph Sterling. I was happy. I loved working with gruff, understanding, appreciative Jake Krueger. This job was down to earth. It occupied one's mind. It freed one from the curse of abstract thinking. The ubiquitous pustule of solipsism could swell and fester no more in the brain of a chimney sweep than in the bland consciousness of a Jersey cow. There were no horrors of unreality when one wrestled with the warped grates of a hot-air furnace. My job meant sanity. It meant life. Riding happily along with Jake Krueger, I looked westward to the jagged blue wall of the Rocky Mountains and I lost the terror that had overcome me on the cliff above Clear Creek, and I was proud and happy over that too.

And on this day of the first furnace grate, yet another fine benison was to come my way. Because of the attitude of Laura and my mother toward my job, I had been afraid to ask if my mother could put up a lunch for me, and each day Jake had stopped before a grocery where I could buy Bologna, cheese or sardines and crackers with apples or bananas.

After the first chimney job this day, however, when I suggested that he stop at a neighborhood grocery we were passing, Jake growled, "Naw, we ain't going to do that any more. It's a waste of time."

"Well, Jesus," I said, borrowing from Jake's vocabulary without thinking.

"Naw," he went on. "Funny thing. When the old woman bought me a shiny new dinner bucket for a birthday present couple months ago, she never did get around to throw away the old one what was perfectly good yet. So I tell her we have to waste time every day to stop at grocery stores so my new kid can buy something to eat and why don't she just put up another dinner in the old bucket for you so we can save the time we waste going to grocery stores and besides you're a good, polite kid what's willing to work hard and she says, 'Sure, it's no more trouble to put up two dinners than one,' so I've got a dinner bucket under the seat for you too."

"Mr. Krueger," I said, "that's surely wonderful of you and your wife and of course I'll pay you."

"Naw," he said, "you can think of it as a little raise in pay if you want to, but, hell, the Kruegers may not live very fancy, but we always have plenty to eat in the house, and more than we can eat, and probably what the old woman puts up for your dinner would get thrown away later on anyhow."

So, when we pulled into an alley for lunch, I found I had a sandwich with a thick, tender, succulent slice of roast beef, another sandwich of wieners smeared with mustard, a covered dish of cold sauerkraut, a banana, and a piece of apple pie wrapped in tissue paper. To my surprise, the dinner pail's coffee container was filled with milk. Jake chuckled at my exclamation. "Yeah," he said, "the old woman says milk is better for boys than coffee. But if you say you'd rather have coffee, I guess I can get her to give it to you."

"No," I said, "I like coffee all right, but if it's all the same I reckon I'd rather have milk.

Chapter 18

Things were going well with the Sterlings that summer. The twins were healthy, crawling all over the place, taking a few tentative steps before toppling, and Laura and my mother both insisted they could distinguish words in the ceaseless jabber. Now it was easy to tell Milly from Benny. Not only was the girl more aggressive, but she wore a small ribbon bow in her dark hair. Even I had to admit they were cute.

In the second house from the Sterlings toward the streetcar line was a family named Upjohn who belonged to our church. Mrs. Upjohn, who was ten or fifteen years older than Laura, was a proud, circumspect woman given to much talk about her old Alabama family and her daddy's plantation and the horde of "nigra" servants. Her husband, whom she always referred to as "the Major," was an officer in the Colorado National Guard and was a civil engineer by profession.

Laura was irked by Mrs. Upjohn's superior airs, and when the Upjohns bought a Ford automobile that spring, the Sterlings were virtually forced to do something to maintain status. They bought a Buick touring car. So, from then on, when Mrs. Upjohn referred to "the car," Laura could respond happily by speaking of "the Buick."

No doubt this annoyed the proud Mrs. Upjohn, and I supplied her with ammunition for a sly counterpunch. One day early in September I came home bubbling with elation because Jake had raised my pay to twelve dollars a week, and I had decided to say nothing about it to Laura. I slipped up the alley, through the back gate and into my sleeping porch. For a moment I stood there, feeling my new riches and wondering if I couldn't move elsewhere now. Winter was coming, and living on a sleeping porch, I had discovered, was no bargain in below-zero weather.

As I stood there Laura's voice spoke outside the curtain, "George—may I come in?"

"Sure," I said, "come on in."

Her lips were tight and her eyes narrowed and I wondered *what now*. "Sit down," I said, motioning to the chair while I moved toward the cot.

"No," she said, "don't you sit on the counterpane in your filthy overalls. You sit on the chair."

When we were seated she took a deep breath and said, "George, we went through all this a long time ago, but I was weak and let you have your way. Now I've got to insist that you find some way of cleaning up before coming home."

"All right," I said, "I told you then that there's no place at Lambert's to clean up and things haven't changed since then. There's no use of you telling me that I've got to quit my job because I'm not going to do it. If you don't want me coming here like this, I'll just move to another place."

"You're not old enough to go off by yourself."

"I'm sixteen and plenty able to take care of myself. George Washington was away from home and a surveyor when he was sixteen."

"You're not George Washington."

"I'm George Chalmers, though."

"That's just the trouble."

"Nuts. And, if you want to know the truth, I was just thinking of getting another place to live when you came in. This sleeping porch is no fun in the winter."

"It's good for you. Sleeping in the fresh Colorado air makes you hardy and well."

"Okay," I said, "after I go you can try sleeping out here when it's down to zero and see how hardy and healthy it makes you. I'd like to know what brought this thing up again, anyhow. Did some of your fine-feathered friends see me sneaking in the back way or something?"

Laura was reluctant to confess the details of her humiliation, but it finally came out that she had met the proud Mrs. Upjohn at a church meeting that afternoon and Mrs. Upjohn had said, "Oh, Mrs. Sterling, I was shopping the other day and the Major had the car and when I was coming home on the tramway I saw your brother. My goodness, but he does look like a hard-working young man, and I wondered what his profession is that he could get so extremely—well, grimy."

And Laura, caught off guard, had declared she had no idea

what I had been up to. She had laughed and said, "Well, Mrs. Upjohn, you know how these teen-age schoolboys are. They love to do things they think are manly, working on machinery and all, and the dirtier they can get the manlier they feel. George is devoted to our Buick and I suppose he may have been working on the engine."

Mrs. Upjohn had exclaimed, "Oh, are you having trouble already? We never have any trouble with *our* car."

"No, no," Laura had declared quickly. "No trouble at all, but George loves to tinker with machinery and I'm sure he knows more about our Buick than Mr. Sterling does."

So now that I had been called a schoolboy whose sootiness was attributed to my working on the Buick, which I was not allowed to touch, it would not be well for Mrs. Upjohn to see me dirty again after school started.

"All right," I said, "it's easy for me to protect your lie."

Laura looked at me pleadingly. "Please don't call it that," she urged. "It was just a white lie to keep that uppity woman in her place."

"Whatever," I said firmly, "I'm moving out just as soon as I can find a room."

"You can't do that, George. Mama would have a conniption fit."

"She'll get over it," I said. "She's just got to learn that kids do grow up."

My mother was not hysterical over my announcement, but she was vehement in her objections.

"I just won't stand for it," she declared. "As long as this is my home it's your home, too, and you're simply not old enough to go off by yourself. Not for a long time yet."

"I'm not figuring on leaving Denver. I'll be coming to see you all the time. There's just no use talking, Mom, I've made up my mind and I'm going to get myself a warm room where I can study in the winter."

"Study!" cried Laura. "Study what? You're a fine one to talk about studying."

"All right, all right. I can study things I'm interested in, but I can tell you it won't be algebra."

"Where do you think you're going to get this fine room?"

"I don't know. There are ads all the time for rooms to rent."

"Now, George," said my mother, "you just can't think of such a thing. What would you eat? Would you try to do your own cooking?"

"I don't know. Maybe. Pop taught me how to cook."

The worried wrinkles in my mother's forehead relaxed and she laughed. "Oh, my land," she said, "you'd get sick."

"Pop was a good cook," I asserted, "and I don't get sick easy."

"Oh, dear," Laura exclaimed, "I guess I can understand a boy's wanting to get away on his own, and in a couple of years he'd be old enough to get a room in the Y.M.C.A. where there'd be good, moral, Christian surroundings and then he might be making enough money so he could eat in their cafeteria. But he certainly couldn't ever go into the Y looking the way he does after work now."

"Is the Y.M.C.A. opposed to working people?" I asked.

"Of course not," said Laura. "Not to decent working people."

"Then," I said, "you figure that people who get dirty working, people like coal-wagon drivers and house painters and farmers, just aren't decent?"

"I didn't say that. Well, decent isn't the word, but there certainly are people in that class whom you wouldn't care to associate with."

"People that might end a sentence with a preposition?" I asked, dragging up one of the few things I had learned from Miss Zink but rarely remembered.

"George Chalmers," Laura snapped, "you're completely hopeless."

"I know, I know. I'm one of the class with whom you don't care to associate, and I'll see that you're not embarrassed by me much longer. But did it ever occur to you that there might be several layers of people in Denver who wouldn't care to associate with *you*? Maybe Mrs. Upjohn is one of them."

"All right, be insulting."

"Yes, George," my mother said, "mind your tongue. I'm sure the very best people would be honored to associate with a big bank's vice-president and his wife."

"Okay," I said, "but do they go to many high-society balls with people like Mr. Spence, where the men wear dress suits and the women low-cut—"

"I'll have you know," said Laura, severely, "that the Sterlings wouldn't be seen dead at one of these so-called high-society parties where they do nothing but swig cocktails and whisky and wine."

"Could you even go if you wanted to?"

Laura sniffed. "Of course we could. But Ralph and I wouldn't be seen dead at one."

The following Sunday I refused to go to church with my mother, who had been alternating with Laura in that pleasant duty while the other stayed home with small Benjamin and Millicent. Promising to go the next Sunday, I went downtown armed with the furnished-rooms-for-rent section of the paper.

Laura had given me an idea about the Y.M.C.A. If I could get in, it might be more pleasant than a room in some flat or private house, because I knew there'd be a gymnasium and other recreational facilities as well as possible congenial companionship. Knowing I wasn't going to return to school, I had made no effort to keep in touch with the few friends at Central.

So I went first to the Young Men's Christian Association and found there was indeed a room available. As reference, I gave Mr. Jowett and Ralph, feeling their names would carry more weight than Jake Krueger's. Because Laura had indicated the age minimum might be eighteen, I pushed my birth date back a couple of years, attested that I never had been convicted of a high crime nor misdemeanor, that I was a member of a Christian church, and that I was not a habitual user of alcohol or narcotics.

It was a small room, a very small room, but it seemed cozy and satisfactory. There was a steam radiator, a lavatory and mirror, a narrow single bed, a chest of drawers, a small table, a wooden chair, and, at the end near the door, a row of clothing hooks covered by a figured curtain. Above the bed was a colored picture of the boy Jesus in company with a group of pleasant-faced animals, both predatory and placid. The ceiling light was placed so it would be possible to read in bed by placing the pillow at the foot. Down the hall was the bathroom with two showers and two toilets. For the rent of a dollar and a half a week, I was to receive a change of bed linen and a bath towel and face towel. I was delighted with this snuggery, even though there was scarcely room to turn around in it. It was only a short walk to the big Public Library and I pictured my coming leisure hours, reading stacks of the kind of books I wanted to read, drawing pictures at the table or just resting, with no crying babies or Sterlings about to tell me what to do and how and when. My only regret about the room was lack of space to keep some groceries and absence of a gas ring or something on which I might make some coffee or heat some breakfast cereal.

My mother sighed when I made the announcement. "Well, George," she said, "I guess there's no stopping you. But you've got to make me one promise. If you don't promise me faithfully that you'll come back every Sunday morning and go to church with either Laura or me and have Sunday dinner with us, I simply won't be able to see you go."

So I promised. And she was comforted somewhat by Laura's assurance that I should come under good influences at the Y.M.C.A.

Residence at the Y did have a good influence on me. I lost some of the tension I lived under at the Sterlings', and also some of my stubbornness.

Of course there had been a washroom in the rear of Lambert's store all the time. Now I began to wash my hands and face at the end of the day to avoid possible criticism at the desk. And, after two or three days, I took to wearing decent clothing to work and changing to my overalls and jumper in the basement storage area.

Why had I refused to do this when Laura demanded it? I had followed most of the other suggestions and demands she and Ralph had made, with no open rebellion and only a minimum of argument. Perhaps I had reached an emotional point beyond which my ego could not move. It surely would have been more sensible and better strategy to have stood firm on returning to school. It could be that I thought of myself as a sort of martyr and that I enjoyed the role. It could very well be that I enjoyed parading my degradation. Surely I never attempted, very seriously at least, to analyze my acts and emotions in this regard at that time, but I suspect I resigned myself to being a stupid oaf as well as an unregenerate sinner and wanted an audience while I wallowed in self-pity. But I don't know. Anyhow, when Laura was annoyed at my coming home with dirty face and filthy clothing, I swore it was impossible to clean up at the hardware store. And when I moved to the Y.M.C.A. I washed and changed as a matter of course.

I was happy in the sense of freedom in my new lodgings. It was my very own room and I took down the picture of Jesus and the livestock and replaced it with my old Frederic Remington print of the Indian scout. I could read in bed and read as long as I pleased so long as I got up early enough in the morning to have breakfast in the cafeteria and meet Jake Krueger by eight o'clock. To insure myself against oversleeping, I bought a dollar alarm clock.

In the mornings I saw boys and girls of my age on their way to high school and I viewed them with a mixture of contempt and envy. They were still human larvae, and I was a man. But they were becoming educated to be what Laura would call respectable ladies and gentlemen while I was condemned to a life of manual toil. Or was I? Couldn't I educate myself by reading? Perhaps there also were night classes somewhere that I could attend.

One evening the desk clerk gave me a note to call a telephone number after six o'clock. I did and it was Bucky Saunders, the Central High School coach.

He said, "Well, George, I was worried about you and called your old address and they said you're living at the Y now."

"Yes, sir, that's right."

"Don't tell me," he said, "that you've betrayed me and enrolled in another school."

"No, sir. I had to quit school and go to work for a living."

"Oh, no. You can't do that after only a year of high school."

"Well, Mr. Saunders," I said, "there was nothing else to do. I'm sorry."

There was a pause. Then he asked, "What do you weigh now, George?"

"About a hundred and fifty, I guess."

"You've been growing. Think you're still growing?"

"I think so. I don't know why I'd quit for a while yet."

"How big was your father?"

"He was pretty big. About six one and two twenty or thirty when he died."

"What are you working at now?"

"Well, Mr. Saunders, I'm mostly a chimney sweep."

"You're joking."

"No, sir. It's a pretty good job, Mr. Saunders, and it pays

[193]

twelve dollars a week right now and I've got a promise of even more."

"George, don't you realize that if you quit school now you probably will be working at something like that all your life?"

"Well, it really isn't so bad and there's nothing else I can do. I can't make enough working afternoons to live on."

I heard him breathe heavily into the phone. Then he said, "George, old Central needs you—not only in track next spring, but if you weigh one fifty now we could use you at least as a backfield substitute this fall. Haven't you got any family who could help you out?"

"No, sir," I said, "I haven't."

"Hmm. Well, I'm going to see if I can't find a patriotic alumnus who might help out with a good-paying afternoon job or something. How were your grades?"

"Pretty terrible, I'm afraid. I failed in algebra and got an E in English, but did fairly well in zoology and art."

"Oh, dear," said Bucky Saunders. "That makes it difficult, but I'll see what I can do. If I have any luck I'll let you know. In the meantime, don't take in no wooden nickels."

"The same to you, Mr. Saunders," I said. "I hope your football team wins every game and I wish I could help out."

"Look, George," he said, "you take care of yourself and keep in shape. While you're at the Y you can work out in the gym. You're a natural athlete and I think something will turn up, if not now, later. You're only fifteen, aren't you?"

"Gosh, no," I said. "I'm sixteen."

He laughed. "Well, I hope to see you one of these days."

I was so pleased at Bucky Saunders' interest that instead of eating at the cafeteria, I went down Seventeenth Street to the Silver Grill and spent thirty-five cents for a steak dinner.

While I was expending a good deal of physical energy on my job, it still seemed to be good advice to work out in the gymnasium. I had my high-school gym suit and I bought a new pair of white rubber-soled shoes to replace the soot-stained ones I now left under Jake Krueger's desk each evening.

Middle-aged men were common at night in the gymnasuim, going through the monotonous routine of calisthenics led by a muscular young man named Stanley Koviak or throwing heavy medicine balls against one another's bulging bellies. But they took up only a small portion of the big gymnasium. In one corner were the wrestling mats upon which thick-necked young men struggled and grunted. In the other corner were the light and heavy punching bags and usually a couple of young fellows sparring with big boxing gloves. This corner interested me more than the wrestlers and I soon became fairly proficient with the light punching bag.

My first experience with boxing gloves came with a lithe, milky-skinned boy called Spike Donovan. He was quite slim and about my height, but I learned later that he had come second in the welterweight division at the Denver Athletic Club's tournament the previous year.

When he asked if I'd care to put on the gloves for a workout, I quickly agreed, thinking it would be a good thing to learn to box. This first lesson turned out to be more than I had bargained for, but that largely was my fault. Donovan danced gracefully around me, moving in and out, jabbing my face lightly with his left hand, hooking and crossing with punches that jarred but didn't really hurt while he easily avoided or blocked my efforts to retaliate. A half-dozen or so spectators were laughing at the exhibition and Donovan himself was grinning. It actually was not a sardonic grin, but it still was a grin and it annoyed me. His making a monkey of me was enough without grinning about it. I redoubled my efforts and when Donovan became careless and dropped his left after a jab, I shot in a fast, hard right to his jaw. It was the first clean blow I had landed, but it was a good one and Donovan sprawled full length on the shiny floor. He bounded to his feet instantly and said with a scowl, "Oh, you want it that way, do you?"

He sped up his two-handed attack, bewildering me with feints and footwork. I saw blood spatter on his white gym shirt, and the blood was from my nose. The gloves were large and comparatively soft, but they seemed to have the impact of a hundred-pound sack of sugar. My left eye caught a solid right cross and began to swell immediately. My nose was streaming. And I couldn't hit any part of Donovan but elbow and forearms.

Through my dizziness I heard a gruff voice say, "All right, boys, that's enough." And Stanley Koviak stepped between us.

"He tried to pull a funny one on me," said Donovan.

"I know," said Koviak. "I saw it. But this is enough."

He turned to me. "You better go shower. Let cold water run

on the back of your neck and it'll stop that nose bleed, I think. And you can hold a cold towel on the eye."

Koviak came into the shower room later and my eye was completely closed. "Well," he said, "I guess you learned a lesson. You don't know a thing, but that one punch you threw was a beaut. I never saw a better. And I'll bet Spike was never hit that hard before in his life."

My eye was paining and I held a towel on it. "He hit me a *lot* of beauts," I said.

"Naw," said Koviak. "Spike's a fancy dan and he took your punch pretty well, but he can't hit much."

My voice sounded odd because my nose had swollen closed. "Mister," I said, "if you'd caught one on your eye like this, you'd know he can hit plenty hard."

"No—you were tense. If you were loose and relaxed, that wouldn't have hurt you. But if you'd caught the one Spike caught on the chin, you'd be out yet. You want to learn how to box?"

"Yeah," I said, "I guess so—if I don't have to take a beating like this every time."

"Aw, that didn't hurt you any. Just remember, don't try to cold-cock a pretty good boxer the next time you're in a friendly sparring match. You flattened Spike and you had a lesson coming and he gave it to you. But you've got more what we call potential than Spike ever had. You're a natural puncher and he isn't. If you want to learn how to handle yourself, I'll see that you learn. I'll even give you some lessons myself to begin with."

"Thanks a lot," I said. "That'd be very kind of you."

"Not at all. Matter of fact, I'd like to see the Y have a guy with a punch for a change. And, don't tell anybody, but I'm glad you let that one go at Spike so I could see what you can do. What do you weigh?"

"About a hundred and fifty."

"Yeah, you're a middleweight, and you'll be a big one before you learn anything. Put another cold towel on that eye before you go to bed."

Jake was amused at my appearance the next morning. "What's the other guy look like?" he asked.

"I don't know," I said. "Maybe he's got a little spot on his chin." I told him about the encounter with Donovan and Jake said, "Hey, you don't mean *Spike* Donovan?"

"Yeah," I said, "that's what they call him."

"Say," exclaimed Jake, "I saw him in the last D.A.C. tournament and he was really good. If you floored him, you did more than anybody else did. In the finals it was a draw after the three rounds, and Spike just run out of steam in the fourth and they give it to a boy name of Spider Smith."

This was on a Saturday and the next morning my eye was partly closed and very black. My nose also was still swollen and red.

For a special reason I did not want to go to church in that condition. It was my mother's turn to go with Ralph, so I phoned from the booth in the lobby and said, "Look, Mom, it's a beautiful day and how'd you like to skip church and go on a train ride to the far-famed Georgetown Loop?"

"Well, George, I don't believe so, thank you. But what is that?"

"Haven't you heard about the far-famed Georgetown Loop? Well, look, Mom, you take a train, a little narrow-gauge train, and it takes you way up Clear Creek Canyon to the mining town of Idaho Springs, and I'm pretty sure Pop was there, and then on to another mining town of Georgetown way up in the mountains and then the train makes a circle over a very high bridge, and, well, I guess it just comes back again."

"Oh, I don't know, George. Isn't it terribly expensive?"

"No, Mom, it just costs two and a half apiece and I've got the money and I'd like to go myself and have you go with me."

She sighed into the telephone. "I'll tell you, George," she said. "You come on home right away and we'll talk it over."

So I went out with a small folder of the trip in my pocket, and the appearance of my eye and nose naturally caused exclamations. When I said that I had put on boxing gloves in the Y gym with a young man who turned out to be a good boxer, Laura said, "Serves you right."

"How do you mean, it serves me *right?*" I asked.

She raised her voice. "Anyone who demeans himself by putting on boxing gloves and trying to batter the face of another human being certainly deserves it when his own face is battered black and blue."

I said, "If I'd known how to box, I wouldn't have got a black eye, and I've got an opportunity now to learn self-defense and

I'm going to take advantage of it even if I do get socked once in a while."

"If you want to be a thug," said Laura, "I suppose that's your privilege."

The night before I had bought a paperback book on boxing full of pictures of such prominent citizens as James J. Corbett, Robert Fitzsimmons, James J. Jeffries, Battling Nelson and Stanely Ketchel, in professional poses, and I quoted from the foreword now "Any American citizen worthy of the name wishes to verse himself in the manly art of self-defense so he will be able to protect not only himself but his loved ones in times of emergency."

Ralph sniffed and shook his head.

"All right," I said. "Just suppose you were attacked by a hoodlum. What would you do?"

"Decent men," he said, "don't go places where they might be attacked by hoodlums. If I were confronted by a robber with a gun, I certainly wouldn't get myself shot by trying to resist with an uppercut."

I grinned at this and Ralph turned his back.

Laura said, "I'm certainly surprised that the Young Men's Christian Association would countenance fist fighting, let alone provide the equipment. I think I'll look into that."

"This," I said, "isn't the Y. *W.* C. A. you know. And it isn't fist fighting, but boxing."

"From the looks of you, the net results are the same," she said, "and you certainly can't go to *our* church looking like a prizefighter after a fight."

"I know that," I said. "I wouldn't want to go to church looking this way and so I'm going to take Mom on the far-famed Georgetown Loop today." I brought out the folder and gave it to my mother. "There's a picture of it, Mom."

"Your mother's got too much self-respect to go out in public with anyone looking as you do," Laura said.

My mother was looking at the folder and frowning. "Good gracious," she said, "does that train go over such a high spindly thing as that? Why, George, I'd be simply scared to death. I wouldn't think of it."

"All right, Mom," I said, "I know what you mean. We'll go another time, after my eye gets well."

"Oh no, no, George, it isn't that," she declared. "I'd be glad to go out with my boy no matter how he looks, but I just couldn't stand anything like that. You can go if you want to, but I'd rather you wouldn't. I'd worry every minute you were gone and if you go I want you to promise to telephone when you get back."

"No," I said, "I won't go, but we'll go together some nice day when I don't look this way. I'll go on back home and read a book now."

"Now, George, don't you want to stay to dinner?" Laura asked.

"No," I said, "it would take your appetites to look at me at the table."

So I went back to the Y, lay on my bed giggling at Mark Twain's *A Connecticut Yankee in King Arthur's Court* until dinnertime, and then had breaded veal cutlets in the cafeteria. While dreamily munching my dinner, I thought about a girl— the most gorgeous, ethereal, sprightly, graceful, sweet-faced creature this side of heaven. Of all people, as Laura most certainly would have said, she was the daughter of Major and Mrs. Upjohn, and her name was Marcella. From the moment I first saw her sitting with her mother and father, going to church was a joy for me. I could sit and look at her in a spiritual rapture, quite oblivious to the oratorical nuances of the Reverend Mr. Hamilton. She, however, seemed quite intent on the sermons and never, never looked my way although I had read that if one gazed closely at another person it inevitably attracted his or her attention. Not that I actually wished to attract her attention. It was enough that a chimney sweep could look at and worship a princess.

Two weeks before my black-eye Sunday, however, I had actually met this lovely elf and talked with her and now I was desperately if hopelessly in love. Well, perhaps not *quite* hopelessly. To a sixteen-year-old boy, even a chimney sweep who has proved himself incapable of assimilating a high-school education, nothing seems completely hopeless. This was the particular reason why I did not want to go to church that Sunday. If Marcella did look my way and saw my battered face, she might never look at me again.

The meeting had occurred when my mother, Ralph and I were filing from church after services. Had it been Laura's day at church she probably would have avoided reaching the door at the same time as the Upjohns, but we found ourselves to-gether in the sunshine on the stoop and the imperious Mrs. Up-john spoke pleasantly. I was introduced to Marcella and Mrs. Upjohn fell into conversation with my mother while the Major talked with Ralph.

I felt grateful to God for giving us this beautiful autumn Sunday. Had it been stormy, Ralph would have brought the Buick from its little brick garage he had built next to the alley, and no doubt the Major would have taken wife and daughter to church in their Ford. But now we were to walk the three blocks home and it would be unnatural not to walk together.

Marcella looked at me and I saw that it was true what I seemed to have known intuitively all along. Her eyes were Lit-tle Egypt's eyes—dark lashed, preternaturally wise blue-gray eyes that looked into my soul and gave me the glorious message that God, in his mercy, had forgiven me for murdering my pre-ordained bride with my sins and had sent her back to me in slightly different form.

We walked slowly together, behind Major and Mrs. Upjohn and behind Ralph and my mother. I was in a tongue-tied trans-port of weightlessness, but Marcella seemed quite at ease. While she was small, her dark hair coming only slightly above my shoulder, she seemed quite mature and poised and I sus-pected she was a year or so older than I.

"What is your business, Mr. Chalmers?" she asked.

"Well," I said, "I haven't any real business just now. I'm—well, I'm just studying to be an artist." The decision to study art came, of course, in that instant, and I didn't know whether I could find an art school or whether I should take one of the advertised correspondence courses or whether I should study painting, magazine illustrating or perhaps newspaper cartoon-ing, but I knew definitely that I should take up some form of art.

"How interesting," she said, and her voice was beautifully low and musical and touched just a bit with her mother's mag-nolia accent. "When you're starving romantically in a garret, perhaps I'll bring you a bowl of hot soup."

I found my tongue. "If I could count on that," I said, "I'd be willing to starve in a garret."

"Now that's really gallant." She looked up at me and the

usual sober expression of her beautifully formed mouth turned up slightly at the corners. I caught a faint whiff of intoxicating perfume, obviously triple-distilled scent from the most precious flowers of Elysium.

"Of course," I said, "all artists don't starve to death in garrets. Some of them make a great deal of money."

"But the good ones like Rembrandt starve and have to sell their best paintings for pennies to buy bread for their crying children."

"That was a long time ago," I said. "Now good artists like N. C. Wyeth and Howard Pyle and Maxfield Parrish get rich."

"They do, really?" I thought she seemed interested in that, but just then I caught sight of my right hand with its ingrained soot that no amount of scrubbing with mechanic's soap could eliminate, the blackened and split fingernails, and a healing scab on the thumb. I started to put my hands in my pockets to hide them, then realized that one didn't put his hands in his pockets when walking down a street with a fine lady. So I doubled my fists to hide as much of the hands as possible.

"Do you go to school?" I asked.

"Oh, yes. I'm at Miss Ridley's."

"Miss Ridley's?"

She looked at me, grinning widely, and her teeth (naturally) were perfect and her short nose wrinkled and those mystically wise eyes twinkled.

"I love that," she said. "You plainly never heard of Miss Ridley, and she thinks she's as famous as Jane Addams or Madam Tetrazzini."

"I guess I'm just ignorant."

"No, she's just not as important as she thinks she is. Anyhow, she operates a pretty good school for girls. At least, I'm sure it's better than the Denver public high schools, and we have cultural subjects as well as equitation and things like that."

"Equitation?"

She laughed. "Horsemanship. Haven't you ever ridden horseback?"

"Oh sure," I said. "I used to have my own cayuse on my uncle's ranch. But we never called it anything fancy like equitation. We just called it forkin' a bronk."

Again she laughed and I felt we were getting along

splendidly. My chest was full to bursting with several delicious constellations of blue-white stars that overflowed and ran down the insides of my arms to tingle in my doubled fists.

"Well," she said, "believe me, 'equitation' is Miss Ridley's word, not mine."

Then we were at the steps before the Upjohn terrace and Marcella was saying, "Reverend Hamilton delivered a wonderful sermon today, didn't you think?"

"Oh, yes," I said, not remembering a word the man had said. "Yes, indeed."

Then she put out her little white-gloved hand and I had to put out my scabbed and grimy paw to take it while she said, "So nice talking with you."

"I hope," I said, "that maybe I'll have a chance to talk with you again soon."

"Thank you," she said, and danced up the cement steps after her parents. I floated on with my mother and Ralph, and Laura had Benny and Milly in their high chairs, feeding some sort of gruel into one hungry maw and then the other.

So, as I sat in the Y.M.C.A. cafeteria with my black eye and dreamily ate my slightly desiccated breaded veal chops and vegetables, it was easy to dismiss the considerable array of obstacles that frowned between the exquisite Marcella and a grubby young chimney sweep. Obstacles were made only to overcome. Obstacles were made only to test the mettle and determination of a man so only the worthy could succeed to nirvana.

I did not think of Mr. Claude McCarthy and the sermon he preached to me in the train washroom, but the substance of the discourse was in my mind: I was George Chalmers the unvanquished, perhaps soot stained, but still a white knight and a determined eventual conqueror.

The quick decision I had made while walking with Marcella stood the test of sober examination. The praise of the lovely and perspicacious Miss Mignon Maloney proved that I had real artistic talent, and the wise man devoted his best energies to developing his best talent. I would also work toward improving myself in English composition. But art should come first.

Cursory inquiries into opportunities for studying art at night in Denver were probably made to the wrong people for I got no satisfactory answers. So, in answer to a magazine advertisement, I made application to a Chicago correspondence school of applied art. Now, I was convinced, I was on my way with time in my favor. Wonders could be accomplished in the four and a half years before I would be twenty-one years old.

Chapter 19

GENERALLY speaking, that winter was a happy one. I was giving complete satisfaction to Jake Krueger and making progress in my extraprofessional activities. Well, I was making no progress with Miss Marcella Upjohn, but I realized I must be content with maintaining *status quo* in that department for some time to come, and *status quo* meant that she showed she still was aware of my existence by giving me a pleasant if dignified nod if we came near each other after church on Sundays. This did not happen often on Laura's day to attend services.

My mentor at the correspondence school declared I was developing extraordinarily well in my course in illustration, both in pen-and-ink and wash drawings, although my composition remained weak and my figures too stiff. I seemed to have a knack for exaggerating the features of public figures and drawing recognizable caricatures of them, and this brought praise. At that time it never occurred to me to doubt the complete sincerity of this praise, but it's possible that some of it was designed to lure me into enrolling in subsequent courses.

Two or three evenings a week I worked out in the gymnasium, mostly boxing with Stanley Koviak or with other young men. Mr. Koviak ("Stan" now to me) was enthusiastic about the rapid improvement I was making, especially in footwork and use of my left hand. "You're faster on your feet right now than Spike," he said, "but of course a lot of yours is waste motion. And you're too tight all the time. A good punch would tear your head off. Stay loose, boy, stay loose." Twice when I threw a quick right that connected solidly, Stan grabbed my arms and shook me. "Look, kid," he growled, "lay off those haymakers on me or I'm going to murder you, and don't think I can't do it." I apologized, declaring I hadn't meant the punch to be a haymaker, and having no doubt at all that he could give me a much worse beating than Spike Donovan had in much less time. My only injury that winter in the gymnasium was a dislocated right thumb which troubled me greatly in my furnace work and made it necessary for me to hold pencil, pen or brush between my first two fingers for more than a week.

Meanwhile I read, I read in bed until midnight—magazines, books that I had heard about and books that I picked at random while prowling the open stacks at the Public Library. I purchased a desk dictionary and took it to bed with me so I could refer to it when I encountered an unfamiliar word, which was quite often, and I accumulated the sort of vocabulary that self-educated persons believe will be accepted as the hallmark of education. I became able to throw such an asinine phrase as "Your pristine unsophistication is matched only by your colossal megalomania" at the brash night clerk at the Y and to believe him completely crushed.

I read the American Winston Churchill, I read Jack London, I read the Bryant translation of the *Odyssey* and *Iliad*, I read *The Virginian*, I read *The Autobiography of Benjamin Franklin*. I thought the fatuous philosophy in Harold Bell Wright's *Their Yesterdays* more profound than that of Kant's *Critique of Pure Reason*, because either my dictionary didn't know the meaning of words or Herr Kant didn't. I read history, biography and romantic nonsense indiscriminately. And I had a wonderful time.

Traveling from job to job with Jake in cold weather was the worst part of the winter. Because I had grown so much in shoulders and chest, I couldn't get into my old overcoat. I bought a fairly good new coat, but I naturally couldn't wear that on the job. So even with a dollar sweater coat under my jumper, I froze on that wagon seat. Jake, who wore a gigantic coat of spotted horsehide, worried about me and finally made me wrap up like a cocoon in an old blanket during zero weather.

As a matter of fact, Jake had taken to treating me much like a son, and invited me home to dinner at least once a week. His wife, Lena, was almost as well-nourished as Jake but extremely neat. She boasted, "I'll bet there isn't a woman on Capitol Hill has as many new corsets in a year as I do."

No doubt she was right. It mattered not how stiff the stays in the rolled corset on our chimney-cleaning sack, they wore out after a few weeks and Mrs. Krueger bought a new corset, donating her old one to the business. She was a gray-haired, jolly woman who must have been quite pretty before putting on so much weight.

Their daughter Gretchen, however, looked more like her father. Gretchen, who was about Laura's age, also was a light-hearted, merry young woman despite the necessity of living her life in a wheel chair. She had been crippled years before by polio or what they then called infantile paralysis, and, while she was deft with her hands, one could see that her thighs, beneath her dress, were shrunken to the size of baseball bats.

Gretchen was wonderfully skilled in handling her wheel chair and could whip around their West Denver cottage faster than a normal woman would ordinarily walk, dusting and polishing woodwork, and other household chores. Her busy, clever fingers were never still, sewing, knitting or crocheting. She crocheted miles of doilies, mats and even beautiful bedspreads which found a ready market at good prices.

Fate seemed especially cruel to heap paralysis upon a girl already absurdly homely in the face. Yet Fate could have hunted a long time before finding another girl of the temperament and strength to accept outrageous misfortune so gracefully.

I liked all the Kruegers and I enjoyed my visits to their home very much. Often after a gigantic dinner we had what we called a musical, with Lena Krueger playing the old upright piano and all of us singing such songs as "In the Shade of the Old Apple Tree," "Schnitzelbank," "Just Break the News to Mother," and "I've Been Workin' on the Railroad." Sometimes Jake would practically drown out the rest of us with his resounding bass, but that was all part of the fun. Always he brought out some bottled beer to improve our voices.

The first time this happened, I was on the point of declaring myself a prohibitionist who never touched the stuff. Then I thought, These Kruegers may be a little crude, but they're just the nicest people on earth. They drink beer. Am I going to insult them by making out that I'm better than they are? A little beer isn't going to hurt me. And, after all, would I rather be like the Kruegers or like Ralph Sterling?

"Oh thank you, Jake," I said, and accepted the tall, frothy glass. The first sip was shockingly bitter and I steeled myself against making a face. I had assumed that beer was at least as good as Coca-Cola or people wouldn't drink it, but this was much worse than Rocky Mountain tea. Well, I had innocently taken on an ordeal and I should have to master it. It was foolish to sip medicine, so I took a good gulp. That definitely was the better way to consume beer—hold your breath and gulp it.

I was standing by the piano while we sang "Wait 'til the sun shines, Nellie," and Gretchen, with a blissful smile on her heavy face, was keeping time with her glass and singing a clear contralto and Lena Krueger was singing soprano and throwing in piano cadenzas and Jake was sprawled hugely in his armchair, boom-boom-booming happily, and my voice had changed long enough ago so that I had pretty good control of a baritone, when the doorbell rang.

Jake put down his glass, heaved himself up and answered the door. "We heard you, we heard you," a man's voice called, "and here we are."

It was a gangling plumber named Carl Francis and his tiny wife Minnie, from across the street. Carl Francis had a mandolin and a tenor voice. After greetings and introductions and glasses of beer for the newcomers, Carl Francis tuned up his mandolin and we went into "The Good Old Summertime," he contributing not only the pleasant tinkle of his mandolin but a true if nasal tenor. Mostly, Mrs. Francis just sat and smiled, breaking forth only now and then with a very small soprano, off key but too faint to matter much. She brought a sack of Bull Durham tobacco and a book of brown papers from her dress pocket and rolled a neat cigarette and lit it from a box of safety matches. She was the first woman I had ever seen smoke anything except a corncob pipe and she astonished me. Then she rolled another cigarette, put it in her husband's mouth, and lit it. Carl Francis may have missed a couple of beats while this was happening, but then went right on singing, with the smoking cigarette dangling from his lower lip.

Gretchen spoke up from her wheel chair, "How about me, Mrs. Francis?"

"Why, of course, honey," said Mrs. Francis, and deftly rolled and licked another brown cigarette, gave it to Gretchen and then lit it.

I looked at Jake and he raised his bushy eyebrows at Gretchen but said nothing. Gretchen drew on the cigarette, coughed slightly and said, "Oh, Mrs. Francis, that's so good. I wish you'd learn me to roll 'em."

"Any time, honey," said Mrs. Francis. "It's easy as pie."

"The Good Old Summertime" had rounded out its season and Jake said gruffly, "When you go learning to roll cigarettes do it outdoors so you don't spill tobacco all over the carpet."

"Why, Papa," said Gretchen, "I never knew you to think about the carpet before. You never run the carpet sweeper."

Jake noted that I finally had gulped down the last of my beer, and growled, "Help yourself to the suds off the dining table, George."

"No, thank you," I said. I was quite happy, but a little giddy from my first glass of beer.

Jake laughed. "Whoever heard of anybody drinking just one glass of beer? That's good beer, boy, go help yourself."

"No, thanks." I wasn't going to be cajoled into drinking any more of that nasty stuff and I stood firm in spite of Carl Francis' observation that a bird can't fly on one wing. It was only after the third or fourth musical that the bitterness of beer seemed to assume a refreshing, wholesome nature and I began to enjoy not only one glass but two, and on rare occasions three. I also liked what it did to me.

As that winter rolled into the brief Colorado spring, I was too self-centered to see any significance even in those world or national affairs which I noticed at all.

I was vaguely aware of grumbling about President Taft. Ralph felt the President was interfering with the personal liberties our forefathers fought for when he forced the dissolution of the Standard Oil and tobacco trusts, as well as giving his support to the graduated income-tax amendment to the Constitution. "The man's getting even more socialistic than Teddy Roosevelt," Ralph declared. On the other hand, the Denver *Journal* felt Taft was betraying his sponsor and the nation at large by not carrying on Roosevelt's conservation program. Personally I was more interested in speculating on the chance of Connie Mack's Athletics winning another pennant and World Series.

The newspapers worked up some excitement over Germany's sending a cruiser, the *Panther,* into the harbor of the French-held south Moroccan port of Agadir and making some demands. It seemed that the French had been moving into quite a bit of North Africa in an attempt to civilize the savages there and the Germans felt it was no more than right for them to assume part of the burden. So the excitable French got excited and began to mobilize their national guard or whatever they called it and the yellow newspapers began to yelp gleefully about the Triple Entente and the Triple Alliance and the chance of a war involving all of Europe, which, on the face of it, was ridiculous nonsense in the twentieth century. Even I, who didn't pay much attention to international affairs, knew that. And sure enough, Great Britain, a member of the Triple Entente with France and Russia, stepped in and calmed the excitable French and gave the Kaiser French Togoland so the Germans would have some Africans to civilize too.

In spite of all the headlines, I was a good deal more interested in what big "white hope" could be dug up to dethrone sarcastic Jack Johnson who had knocked out poor old Jim Jeffries in fifteen rounds. It seemed doubtful that I myself was going to grow large enough because here I was nearly seventeen and lacked almost an inch of six feet and weighed only a hundred and fifty-five on the Y gym scales. I had seen movies of the Jeffries-Johnson fight and knew I'd have to learn a great deal before I could compete with that black tiger even if I grew a couple of inches and gained forty pounds of muscle.

Well, there was an uncommon amount of nonsense being published and one had to use judgment in deciding what to believe. Wild predictions about what flying machines might do in the future didn't seem quite so crazy now that an aeronaut named Glenn Curtiss had won several thousand dollars by flying from Albany, New York, to New York City without stopping, and that was well over a hundred miles. But a recent Sunday supplement published a fantastic story about the power that could be released by splitting an atom. There was an illustration of the big German liner *Kaiser Wilhelm der Grosse* at sea, and the alleged scientist who wrote the article declared there was enough latent power in a single bean to propel this giant ship across the Atlantic. All one had to do was to split the bean's atoms to release the power. That was a fine thing to write. But if the author couldn't prove his case, no one could prove him a liar either. The very word "atom" meant the very smallest particle possible. It meant "indivisible." And it would take some doing with quite a cold chisel to split an unsplittable object that must exist only in theory inasmuch as it was so small it couldn't be seen with the strongest microscope. Obviously there was nothing a scientist loved as much as pulling the public's leg. Astronomers would write about looking at stars that were so far away from the earth that they could have died hundreds of years ago and yet their light was just reaching us, and that for all we know or can ever know these stars or suns have or had satellites such as the Earth, Mars, Venus and all. Well! Then these astronomers would go on and explain that light travels at about seven hundred million miles an hour or six trillion miles a year, and you take it from there for a whirl around Orion if you like arithmetic when it invades the realm of metaphysics.

All of this made me think about God. If our omnipotent God, who marked the fall of a lousy sparrow on this earth, still had to watch over the affairs of possible creatures on millions and billions of planets scattered over a universe trillions and quintillions of miles in extent, the extravagance of the concept pitched me to the edge of that lonely, horrible cliff of unreality from which I must either flee in panic or die.

How could astronomers write such things? How could they be brave enough even to think of such things? Didn't they realize the utter impossibility of their statements and the significance of the impossibility? I wondered if I were unique in my awareness of the terrible unreality of life and the world and the universe. It seemed most unlikely. I hardly could think of my brain as a superior instrument of ratiocination when I flunked elementary algebra. But I never had been able to speak to anyone of this dreadful matter; I wouldn't have known *how* to. Often I had wondered about my father. When he said I had the "hypos" on that awful night when I was a child at Christmastime, had he really understood what was wrong with me? I just didn't know.

There was no getting away from the fact that I was *I* and that nothing existed for me except through my senses or memory. Perhaps a hint of the truth lay in memory. There was no more substance to memory of my father than to memory of a dream of a strange woman. However, if all substance was an illusion, why all the intricate complications? There didn't seem to be any answer to that except that it didn't cost any more to make an illusion complicated than to make it simple.

It didn't occur to me that I was too self-centered for my own mental health, but I did sense that I was trying to beat a granite mountain to pebbles with a tack hammer.

What about the great brains of the past, the thinkers, the philosophers, the profound novelists? Had none of them considered the illusion of substance?

There was that old poet Wordsworth who was considered so great, and he actually preferred illusion to reality. I desperately wanted the world *more* with me, late and soon. I wanted no part of any mythical Proteus rising from the sea, nor of any fishtailed, horn-blowing hallucinatory character called Triton. The world was unreal enough to begin with and needed no invented grotesqueries. Great God! I'd rather be a chimney sweep for the moment, secure in sooty reality as I balanced on a real roof letting a real gunny sack and corset down a real chimney, than to be standing on his pleasant lea with William Wordsworth, contemplating the sea baring its imaginary bosom to the imagined lechery of an unreal moon.

Except in the unlikely event that I was unique in my thoughts and terrors, I thought again that this most important subject of existence must have been discussed at length by the great philosophers, and this was why I had tackled Immanuel Kant. But, as far as I was concerned, his *Critique* was written in algebra and the result was that X equals zero. Then I tried Nietzsche. Then I tried Spinoza. And X still equaled zero.

I was puzzled by some of the novelists. Such authors as Robert W. Chambers, Zane Grey and Mark Twain obviously wrote for no other purpose than to entertain their readers and to make money. But the celebrated Harold Bell Wright chose abstract themes such as honor and integrity and wrote about a gifted portrait painter who could have gained fame and fortune by making his sitters appear beautiful and noble, but had the courage to reveal their ugly souls in portraits. It seemed to me that Mr. Wright must be erudite enough and wise enough then to unravel the mysteries that troubled my poor adolescent brain. Did he lack the courage of his artist? Was the truth, as he must know it, too awful to be written clearly and simply? Was he, unlike his artist, afraid of losing his fame and fortune? Then there was Jack London, possibly even more renowned than Harold Bell Wright, and Mr. London reveled in tales of courage. His brutal Sea Wolf pontificated about Nietzsche and Kant and other philosophers, but if the Sea Wolf or his author learned any more about the reason or non-reason of existence from these abstruse texts than I did, they did not choose to mention it. The monstrous result of all of the Sea Wolf's serious reading and thinking was adoption of the theory of superman: the strong and cruel deserve the spoils. This mighty man thought so hard to reach this conclusion that his brain stripped its gears and he went blind and came to a bad end. The moral to this long novel was that even the strong-est man cannot afford to be an individualist. Happiness lies in dedication to the Socialist party, which the Sea Wolf despised. At least I gathered that the dramatic Mr. London's purpose was to advance this moral. But, despite Mr. London's exalting courage, he either never had the courage to write what I wanted to know or he didn't know the answers himself.

Of course I sometimes thought the Rev. Mr. Reynolds back home and the Rev. Mr. Hamilton in Denver hinted at the dis-quieting mystery and their answer apparently was to take ref-uge in Jesus. This, somehow, seemed to be avoiding the question altogether and taking an easy way out. I already was a baptized Christian and would have insisted that I did indeed believe in Jesus as the Son of God and Saviour of the world. My trouble was that I had periods when I didn't believe in the world or the universe or anything else except the inescapable and unhappy fact of my own lonely consciousness and Jesus either couldn't or wouldn't extinguish that consciousness or bring reality to a quivering, nebulous cosmos of which He, necessarily, was a part.

Why didn't I read the Bible when I was troubled? Well, I did. There was a Bible in my room, rubberstamped inside the cover, STOLEN FROM THE YOUNG MEN'S CHRISTIAN ASSOCIATION, DENVER, COLO. and I read a good deal of it, particularly from the Gospels, but, like Mr. Wordsworth, much of it seemed to be concerned with the world being too much with us, late and soon, rather than its being too little with us, yesterday, now and tomorrow.

Matter was substantial enough, however, while working with

Jake Krueger. That spring he took a contract to put in a new hot-air furnace at a sprawling tuberculosis sanatorium. Tearing out the old heating plant and putting up the gigantic new furnace was a hard job for the two of us, but I had a greater ordeal installing the new sheet-iron heating pipes. The basement was comparatively small for the size of the building and most of the asbestos-covered pipes ran under the first floor incredible distances in the dark, dusty, cobwebby space no more than two feet between the joists and the dry earth.

Jake demonstrated to me how the new pipes must be firmly joined and sealed with strips of asbestos. So I had to hunch my way under the floor on my back, sliding a box of supplies with me, pulling down the rusted old pipes, putting up the new and securing them with wire nailed to the floor joists. Ten feet from the basement it was as dark as a tunnel and I had to work with the light of a plumber's candle augmented now and then by a small flashlight. Every move I made brought up clouds of choking dust and my imagination charged the dust with tubercle bacilli that had been lying there for years waiting patiently for a foolish invader.

There was no room to work, but the job really required two men or boys—one to hold the pipe up while the other sealed the joints and nailed up the supporting wire. Jake was of little assistance. He couldn't have wedged his big body into the narrow space, let alone work. So I wriggled my way back and forth, struggling and coughing and cursing, for by this time, despite my religious upbringing, I had acquired most of Jake's vocabulary if not his basso-profundo fervor. Once, a sanatorium official came to the basement to protest to Jake. It seemed that I had been working directly under a sitting room where a group of tuberculous women was assembled and my monologue concerning the stubborn pipes and dust and lack of working space had offended them. Although I knew my mother would be horrified if she knew, I was not very ashamed of myself. Jake thought it was very funny. He said to the official, "You tell the poor old biddies that when they hear some good cussing they know they're getting a good job."

I spent the best part of three days under the floor and came out with red-rimmed eyes, a raw throat, cut and bruised hands and a lame back. Jake said, "George, my boy, you done just fine. You were wonderful. Without you I couldn't ever took that job in the first place and don't you think for one minute I don't appreciate it. From now on including this week I'm raising your pay five whole bucks a week and if you know another kid your age in Denver making seventeen bucks a week I'd like to know what he's doing."

Here was material success. Already I had a savings account, but not in Ralph's bank. Now there was a temptation to go into somewhat grander quarters than my tiny room at the Y, but I resisted the temptation in favor of saving more money toward the foundation of my fortune. Yet there was no reason why I shouldn't spend a little money now and then for pleasure.

The evening paper carried an ad for a Shakespearean repertory with E. H. Sothern and Julia Marlowe. I never had seen any sort of play in my life. My mother didn't believe that stage plays were quite moral, but I resolved to go the following night. Then, with quickening pulse, I had an even more exciting idea. Why not combine my first playgoing with my first real date with a girl?

I grinned at my homely face in the mirror, got a drink of water to bolster my nerve and went downstairs to the phone booth, looked up a number, dropped in my nickel and called it.

Major Upjohn answered. "May I please speak to Miss Marcella?" I asked.

"Well—uh—certainly. Just a moment."

Then came that soft, beautiful voice. "Hel-lo."

"Miss Upjohn," I said, "this is George Chalmers."

"Who?"

My heart sank. "You know," I stammered, "I—I belong to your church. Well, I've met you. Well, we walked home from church together once."

"Oh? Oh, yes. You're Mrs. Sterling's brother, aren't you?"

"That's right. Well, Miss Upjohn, the reason I'm calling is that I saw in the paper that tomorrow night the Broadway theater is having a play called *The Merchant of Venice* that's supposed to be very good with a couple of very famous actors named E. H. Sothern and Julia Marlowe and, well, the play's by Shakespeare, you know, and I just wondered if you'd care to go with me?"

I heard a quick intake of breath. Then, "Oh, I'm so sorry, Mr. Sterling—"

"Chalmers," I interrupted.

"I'm so sorry, but I have another engagement. But thank you very much for asking me."

"Well, I'm sorry too." I was inundated by chill disappointment and felt sure she would have turned me down whether she had a previous engagement or not. I said, "I hope you have a pleasant evening."

"Thank you," she said. "I hope you enjoy Sothern and Marlowe. They're very good."

I thanked her, wandered aimlessly out on the street for a few minutes and then went to my room to work on my correspondence-school drawing lesson although at the moment this seemed without much purpose.

The next evening I went to the Broadway alone, sat in the balcony and was transported into a fascinating realm of unreality more real than life. To me the experience was actually seismic; it shook me to my toes. No book, no movie, no music I had ever heard yet, no sermon, no lecture, nothing had moved me as did the marvelous Julia Marlowe as the scarlet-robed Portia and the equally marvelous E. H. Sothern as the cringing, crafty Shylock.

A new and unexpectedly wonderful door opened for me. It was not just the theater. It was bewilderingly wider in scope than just one art form. To say that I, who thought he wanted to be an artist, had learned something would be an exaggeration. But at least I began to suspect.

Chapter 20

MY NEXT door neighbor at the Y was a tall, cadaverous young man named Don Fitch, a second-year student at the University of Colorado medical school in Denver.

I first got acquainted with "Doc" in the gym where we had boxed and where I had noted his gaunt body. I had visited his room, which was a replica of mine, but I didn't realize that he was resolutely starving himself toward a medical degree until

I met him on the street one warm evening and suggested that we have a soft drink in a nearby drugstore.

"No, thank you, George," he said in his cowboy drawl, "I don't need a soft drink, but I could use a pack of Gilette blades."

I bought him the razor blades which his blue-black jaw did need and I insisted on his accompanying me to Barney's lunch counter for a dinner of corned beef and cabbage with boiled potatoes, apple pie and coffee. I knew by the way he ate that he was very hungry.

"Much obliged, George," he said as we strolled back toward the Y. "I'll try to return the favor next month when I get a check from home—unless I have to buy a new book or something. Getting this medical degree is going to be a tight squeak for me, but I'll get it or die trying. I stayed out one year and worked on a road gang and one thing or another, but what I saved out of that is gone now and my dad sends me what he can, which isn't much. There are five kids younger than me. Well, one sister is married, but three are still in school."

"Well," I said, "it just seems to me that a medical degree won't do you much good if you wear yourself down and get T.B. getting it."

He laughed. "I shan't get any T.B.," he said. "The Fitches are all tough constitutionally. I may not have as much muscle as you and I'm not much of an athlete, but I'm very strong and healthy. I'll bet you've been sick two or three times as often as I."

"I don't know," I said. "I had measles when I was four years old and a concussion of the brain when I was maybe six, but that's all." I thought about my illness that Ralph called "mountain sickness," but I had my own diagnosis of that and didn't feel like mentioning it.

"You've had colds, haven't you?"

"Oh sure. Everybody has colds, but I don't call that being sick."

"Hmm. It's not being well. What about that concussion? How'd that happen?"

"Horse ran away with my mother and smashed the buggy. Guess I landed on my head."

"Skull fracture?"

"Don't think so. Never heard of it."

"Have an X ray?"

"Don't think so. Don't believe they had X rays then, not our Dr. Davenport anyhow."

When we got back to the Y, I said, "Come on to my room, Doc, and I'll draw your portrait."

He chuckled derisively at that, but accompanied me into my cell and sat on the bed while I worked at the table, blocking out with a pencil his bony, high-cheeked, strong-jawed face.

"You know, George, I gathered from something Stan said that you may be thinking about professional boxing."

"No," I said, "nothing like that."

"You're pretty good with the gloves."

"Just good enough for a pro to murder me. But Stan thinks if I improve a bit I might do all right in the middleweight class at the D.A.C. amateur tourney next year if not this year."

The overhead light threw wonderful shadows on his bony face. "Well, George," he drawled, "I'll give you some free medical advice. Don't ever get into the ring, professional or amateur, without having a head X ray first. For all you or anybody knows, that concussion you got as a kid might have left a blood clot. One good punch might kill you or leave you crippled or nuts."

"Oh what're you giving me? That happened ten years or more ago."

"That doesn't make any difference. I'm just telling you to get an X ray before you go slugging it out in the ring with anybody. Of course I know that free advice isn't often worth what you pay for it."

He shifted irritably on the bed and I said, "What's the matter, you got fleas or something? How am I going to make your picture if you keep changing positions all the time? For heaven's sake, move back the way you were."

He laughed but obeyed me. "How old are you, George?"

I remembered that I had added two years when I registered at the Y and said, "Well, I'm nearly nineteen."

Don Fitch raised his heavy black eyebrows at me and I knew what he was thinking and resented it. To repay him I elongated his jaw and emphasized his stubborn underlip while inking in the drawing with a two-ninety pen. By this time my penwork was pretty fair even though it may have lacked the casual ease of a seasoned professional. It was a good likeness, not exaggerated quite enough to make it a caricature, and my subject exclaimed about it.

"Why, that's wonderful, boy!" he said. "I had no idea you were such an artist. You've got to do something with that talent. Of course you make me look like a mug, but I guess that's what I am at heart."

I thought about Harold Bell Wright's honest portrait painter and was pleased.

Don Fitch shook his head, grinning, and said, "Well, I'll be damned. Look, George, inscribe that to me and sign it, will you? This will be worth something when you're a famous artist."

I took the cardboard and wrote on the bottom with India ink:

TO:
Ol' Doc Fitch, that son of a bitch,
He couldn't cure a monkey with seven-year itch.

I signed it "Chal," which abbreviation I had decided would be a good signature for a cartoonist, and handed it back to Fitch.

He frowned and said, "Now, why in hell did you have to do that? I was going to send your picture to Dad and he'd have got a kick out of it. This isn't funny. It's puerile. It's childish. A little while ago you said you're nineteen years old. I doubted it because you've never had to shave, but I didn't say anything."

"I *have* shaved," I declared indignantly. "I shaved this morning." This was the truth. Recently I had bought a Durham-Duplex safety razor and had scraped the light fuzz from my face two or three times.

Fitch paid no attention. "Nobody except a half-wit or a kid under the age of puberty would write a thing like that."

"Then I reckon that fixes me as a half-wit," I said. "If you don't like poetry, give me the picture and I'll cut off the bottom."

With my pocket knife I sliced off a strip of the cardboard containing the objectionable verse and Fitch ordered, "Now write something sensible on it like 'To my friend Don Fitch,' and sign it with your real name."

I followed his instructions and he nodded his head. "Thanks

a lot," he said, waving the picture to dry the ink. "Now I've got to go and burn some midnight kilowatts. Good night."

I said good night feeling chastened. Then I thought he was mighty bossy toward me, considering my buying him razor blades and a dinner and then drawing a good picture of him which he liked. He was also insulting to me about the verse, but, after all, I supposed the silly verse was insulting to him so I had no right to feel hurt. I could learn a lot from Don Fitch. He had a bachelor's degree from the University at Boulder and now was well along toward his M.D. His friendship was worth cultivating.

The next time I was invited to Krueger's to dinner I took my material along and drew a pen-and-ink portrait of Jake, again emphasizing features but avoiding actual caricature. Jake howled with delight at the result while Lena and Gretchen proclaimed the picture "perfectly wonderful." Lena declared the portrait with the characteristic stub cigar in the corner of he mouth better than any photograph could be and said she would get it framed immediately and hang it on the living-room wall.

This had been done on my next visit, when Gretchen posed for me in her wheel chair. Mr. Harold Bell Wright was at least an accessory to my incredible stupidity as I used the same method on poor crippled Gretchen as I had employed on Don Fitch and her father, but my slight emphasis of the heavy face, small eyes, wide nose, shapeless mouth, thick neck and shoulders certainly was not revealing her long-suffering, cheerful spirit. I was monstrously cruel, not from malice but from sheer obtuse lack of understanding.

When I was finishing the shading Jake came and looked over my shoulder. I heard him breathe an ambiguous *"Mmm"* but he didn't say anything. Jake was no fool and I don't know why he didn't keep me from handing the picture to Gretchen. Perhaps he didn't know how. Gretchen would have demanded the right to see it. So I was allowed to pass the unflattering portrait blithely over to the young woman.

At first glance Gretchen smiled and then giggled. She stared at it and began to laugh. "So that's the way that, that . . . beautiful bitch . . . Gretchen K-K-Krueger . . . looks to you." Her hysterical laughter turned to sobs and tears rolled down her fat, pale cheeks. Suddenly she ripped the drawing in two, hurled it to the floor, whirled her wheel chair around and sped from the living room. A door slammed and I looked help-lessly at Jake.

Jake shook his head at me and spoke softly, "I know she ain't —well, she kind of takes after her daddy. But, George, couldn't you have made her look a little better, if you tried?"

Lena Krueger had gone after her daughter and all I could say was, "I'm sorry, Jake. I'm awful sorry, but it just didn't come out very well. I haven't had much experience drawing ladies."

"I guess not," he said, "but they're funny that way. All of 'em. I don't know nothing about art, but I think if you can't draw a lady to look kind of pretty, you better not draw her."

I was gathering up my material and said I thought he prob-ably was quite right and asked him to thank both Lena and Gretchen for the elegant dinner and went out to catch a street-car for uptown.

Several weeks passed before I was invited to the Kruegers' for dinner again and in the meantime I told Don Fitch about the experience.

He looked grim. "George," he said, "you're young and you're ignorant, but you're talented and I can't understand how you could have been so goddamn vicious as to caricature a homely, crippled girl."

"I don't either," I said, "except that it wasn't really a cari-cature, just kind of, and I had no idea she would take it so hard."

"You poor, stupid oaf. The trouble with you, or *one* of the troubles with you, is that you have no sense of empathy."

"I've got sympathy for her," I declared. "Hell, I feel sorry for her."

"I didn't say sympathy. I said *empathy,* and that means the ability to put yourself in other people's shoes. Kipling once wrote a story about an ape that had too much ego in its cosmos. That's you, George—too much ego in your cosmos."

I groaned and dropped back on my bed while Fitch leaned back in the chair with hands locked behind his head.

"Doc," I said, "I just can't understand why you'd say that about a chimney sweep living in this lousy little room in the Y.M.C.A. I'm not egotistical. What in hell have I got to be con-ceited about? You've just got me wrong."

"I didn't say you're conceited. You might even hate yourself a little after something like this with the crippled girl. But you're definitely egocentric."

"Well . . ."

"I mean that you can't think of anything except in its relation to George Chalmers. You feel that you're the center of the universe and everything circles around you. Isn't that right?"

Fitch laughed as I took a deep breath. I said, "I suppose you're right to some extent, but hell's bells, how can anybody be any other way? I can't see anything except through my own eyes, but I don't think I'm particularly selfish."

"You're not penurious. You've insisted on buying a couple of dinners for a poor medical student without much hope of a return. That could be pure selfless altruism. Then, couldn't it be that you got your money's worth in the personal satisfaction of filling the gut of a college graduate?" He laughed again. "Oh, I know I sound like an ungrateful dog, but I'm grateful all right, and let's forget that angle for a moment. We're having an objective discussion of the psyche of a fairly nice kid called George Chalmers in the hope that it may help him to realize a potential."

"Oh, nuts," I said. "You sound like a Methodist preacher sixty years old."

"I'm twenty-four," he said, "and my years count double in what I've studied and read and thought."

I snorted. "Now we see who's the conceited one."

"Okay, lad. I'll admit I don't underrate myself. But I was an A student my last three years at Boulder, in spite of working, and I'm top of my medical class. My business right now is reading and analyzing and remembering and the record shows I'm damn good at my business. So, my young friend, when I tell you I can read you like a book you'd be smart to listen. When I get my degree you'll pay cash for my advice. Now you get it free unless you want to buy me a platter of pork and beans sometime."

"Well," I said, "just the other day you said that free advice generally isn't worth what you pay for it."

"Okay, kid. You got me there and I'll shut up."

"No, go ahead, I'm listening. The way I look at it, if you go to a lawyer or a doctor or somebody and pay him for advice, it's silly not to take it, but if somebody comes to you and gives you advice free, well, then you can make up your own mind whether to take it or leave it."

"All right, I'm not making my diagnosis entirely on your treatment of the crippled girl. You have revealed a good deal about yourself before this, and your mean and tactless caricature just confirms my conclusions. You didn't want to hurt that girl's feelings, did you?"

"Of course not."

"And you were really surprised at her reactions?"

"I sure was. Well, gosh, she's always seemed to have a sense of humor, and she thought the picture I drew of Jake was funny and so did her mother and Jake himself laughed his head off at it."

"And you didn't see any difference in caricaturing—really making fun of—a rough, tough, middle-aged homely man and doing the same thing to a crippled homely girl?"

"Well, I didn't think—"

"That's just it. You didn't think. You didn't think about anything but George Chalmers. Here was a chance for George Chalmers to display his talent for making someone look ridiculous and that was all that mattered. It never occurred to you to consider how it might wound your subject."

"Gosh," I said, "she must be close to thirty and she ought to know by now that she's no beauty. If she doesn't, it's time she was finding it out."

"Great God!" Fitch exclaimed. "You just don't know *any-thing* about people, do you? You're a self-centered bastard and you're going to be a self-centered bastard all your life unless you wake up."

"Look, Fitch," I said, "you've got no license to be calling me any bastard."

"All right, get up and bust me one on the jaw. You can do it."

"I don't want to bust you on the jaw, but—"

"If you did, that would be just more proof that I'm telling you the truth, and you know it would."

"Well, in the first place you wouldn't have known about Gretchen if I hadn't told you and I wouldn't have told you except I was sorry and ashamed of myself and had learned a lesson about women—at least ugly crippled women—that I thought would interest you."

"And it did, it did. It was revealing—not about the girl but about you. In the same line, when you drew the good but funny picture of me, why were you impelled to write the silly, insulting verse on it? What had I done to warrant that? The answer is that I'd left myself open for you to exhibit what you thought was cleverness."

"Oh, hell," I said.

"All right, George," he said. "I'm talking to you like a Dutch uncle and it would be easier not to and just laugh it off. If I thought you were really as stupid as you sometimes seem, I wouldn't bother. But I don't believe you're essentially mean or really stupid either. I think perhaps all you need is to get next to yourself, and, in this case, getting next to yourself is getting next to other people. Think about other people. Try to put yourself in the other guy's shoes."

"Now look, Doc," I said, "there are some things you don't understand about that picture of Gretchen Krueger. An artist can be a dishonest flatterer and make everyone look beautiful or noble and probably he'll get rich and famous painting portraits, or he can be brave and honest: he can be true to himself and his talent and reveal people as they really are and that is explained very well in a fine book by Harold Bell Wright."

"Oh horse crap."

"Well, it's a fact. And the difference is between what they call a meretricious artist and having integrity."

Fitch was laughing at me. "I guess I make a mistake," he said. "I guess you're dumber than I thought and I'm wasting my time on you. If you not only read Harold Bell Wright but take him seriously, I might as well go to my room and review the horrors of parturition." But, with a grin spread across his thin face, he merely rocked back and forth precariously on the back legs of the chair.

"What's wrong with Mr. Wright?" I demanded. "Every book he writes leads the best-seller list. You can't even get one of his old books from the library without waiting weeks for it."

"Well," he said, "I suppose that's one of the things wrong with him. Then, you just used the word 'meretricious,' and I'd say the word could have been invented just to fit Mister Wright."

"Oh, now!" I exclaimed. "I think he's one of the most sincere modern authors I know."

Fitch was shaking his head sadly. "He's a sentimental hack who probably has done more toward corrupting American literary taste than Cyrus Townsend Brady and Laura Jean Libbey and Ella Wheeler Wilcox combined, and we don't have to go further than you for a horrible example. In other words, he stinks."

"That's just your opinion," I said.

"And the opinion of every other discriminating person who ever got past the sixth grade."

"There must be a lot of millions of people who never got out of the sixth grade, if you're right, which you aren't. My sister and her husband like Harold Bell Wright and they both went to college."

"What college?"

"Well, it was the normal school back home."

Fitch grinned.

"Well, I suppose you think the University of Colorado is better than Harvard or Yale or Oxford."

"I didn't say a word."

"All right," I said, "since you're so damn high and mighty, what do you think I should be reading instead of Harold Bell Wright? *The Hoosier Schoolmaster,* maybe?"

He ignored my sarcasm and said calmly, "Perhaps it'd be a good thing for you to start with Mark Twain."

I laughed. "That's just about what I thought. I've read a lot of Mark Twain and I admit he's very funny at times and he wrote some exciting books for boys. But he doesn't have any real substance or philosophy like Harold Bell Wright."

"Oh, God," Fitch groaned. "You better go read him again. Did you ever read *Life on the Mississippi?*"

"No, missed that one."

"Well, read it. Read Dostoevsky's *Crime and Punishment.* Read *The Scarlet Letter.* Read *Vanity Fair.* Read any of Conrad."

"What Conrad is that?"

He stared at me. "Joseph Conrad is just one of the greatest living authors, is all. And you never heard of him?"

"Well, I may have heard of him. What did he write?"

"He's written a lot. He's a Pole, but he writes in English—beautiful English—and somebody once said that to Conrad the English language is a pipe organ and he's a virtuoso."

"Maybe I wouldn't understand it. There's some pipe-organ music that's just a lot of racket to me."

"Read it slowly and carefully. You're not a complete dolt. Notice how he gets his effects by always using just the right word in the right place. Every word and every sentence does to the reader just what Conrad wants it to do."

"All right," I said, "wait until I get a pencil and paper and tell me some of his books."

I got a pencil and pad from my table, thinking that I could learn something from Fitch despite his being an intellectual snob. I thought, All right, maybe Harold Bell Wright couldn't belong to the intellectual union because maybe he hasn't gone to college or maybe only to a normal school or something, but if I, together with millions of other people, got entertainment and some spiritual uplift from his books, what the hell was wrong with that?

Fitch rattled off the names of *Lord Jim, Nostromo, The Nigger of the Narcissus, The End of the Tether* and then said, "The thing for you to do is to get a book called *Youth* from the library first. *Youth* is a great short story that can't help fascinating you. Read it slowly. Then in that volume there's a story called *Heart of Darkness,* and some call it a novelette and some say it's the greatest short story ever written. I don't know about that, but I also don't know anything that's in competition personally unless it's Kipling's *The Man Who Would Be King.* Read that too. And at least the first half of Kipling's *Kim.* But, back to Conrad, you'll never be quite the same after you've read *Heart of Darkness.* Don't gulp it down, but taste every sentence, and I doubt if you'll ever be able to read another page of Harold Bell Wright without gagging."

"Well," I said, "I don't know. But I'll read it."

"That's about enough now. But what of Shakespeare have you read?"

"Not much, but I saw E. H. Sothern and Julia Marlowe in *The Merchant of Venice.* It was wonderful."

"Good. I wish I could have seen it. But *read* Shakespeare— *Hamlet, Macbeth,* any of the tragedies. George, in a way I envy you, with most of the world's great literature ahead of you. Of course I've really got a lot of it ahead of me, too, which is something to live for. I've never read *War and Peace,* which they call one of the great novels of all time. Oh, there are hundreds of books I want to read, but I can't spare the time now. Sometimes I think I'd much rather be an author or literary critic than a doctor, but I'm committed definitely to medicine now."

"Why?"

He let the front legs of his chair down with a bang and shrugged his shoulders. Very seriously, he said, "Because, George, I have something that we talked about earlier and I've had it all my life. That's empathy. I can't help identifying myself with the sick and unfortunate and having a strong urge to help them. Ever since I was a young kid I've wanted to be a doctor—and this may sound like a lot of crap to you—but that wasn't because doctors usually make good money and usually have the nicest houses in town, but because I thought helping the sick and injured would give greater satisfaction than anything else in life. My dad encouraged me in that idea and it was something like a priest's vocation."

He grinned wryly and shook his head. "Now in medical school they tell us that a physician must be objective and look at his patients only as medical cases. They say if a doctor allows himself to feel really sympathetic for each sufferer, his emotions are involved and the strain will be too much for any human being to stand. In other words you've got to develop a good old sympathetic bedside manner while keeping strictly hardboiled inside. I don't like that much and I don't know whether I can do it. I've wondered whether I have the right temperament to be a doctor. When I see a suffering child or any person or any animal, as far as that's concerned, my heart goes out to them. I don't know whether I can get over it and I don't know that I want to."

"Well, Doc," I said, "I think that would make you a wonderful doctor."

"I don't know. Maybe a good doctor needs to be a cold-blooded bastard like you."

"Look," I said, "I've told you before. Don't be calling me any bastard. And you couldn't be more wrong when you say I'm cold blooded."

"Do you love people?"

"Love people? How in hell can anybody just love people in general?"

He raised his eyebrows. "Human beings are the most marvelous animals God ever created."

"I reckon that could be argued."

"What other animal builds hospitals to take care of the sick? What other animal shows charity? What other animal will go to war to free an oppressed people without hope of reward as we did to free Cuba?"

"All right," I said, "I'll admit that God made Man in His own image, and you'd be an atheist or something if you didn't say you loved God, so I guess you've got to say you love people made in God's image, but that's using the word in a pretty big general way and maybe automatic."

"Okay, George, do you really love any particular person?"

"Sure, I do. I'm in love with a very beautiful, high-class girl, but I'll never get anywhere with her until I get to be a successful artist or something else than a chimney sweep."

"I didn't say *in* love. That's just a sexual urge."

"Sex has nothing at all to do with this girl," I declared warmly. "If I ever marry her, sex might eventually enter the picture. But my feeling for her is cool and pure and wonderful and practically religious."

Fitch scoffed, "Puppy love! And what in hell would you know about sex?"

"You might be surprised that I know a lot more than you do, Buster. Maybe you have studied about sex a lot in medicine books and know exactly where babies come from, but I wouldn't be surprised if you aren't a virgin."

He laughed. "Meaning you're not, of course."

"Of course not."

"Oh get a shovel. Tell me, do you really love your mother?"

"What a question to ask a guy. Of course I do. For heaven's sake."

"Do you do anything to show it? Do you ever tell her you love her?"

"Well, after all," I said. "My family never has been much for talking about that."

"Do you ever do anything to show your mother you love her?"

"Well, I go out to see her practically every Sunday and I go to church with her every other Sunday when my sister doesn't go and I eat the Sunday dinner she usually cooks."

"That's one for the record," said Fitch. "The boy shows he

loves his mother by consenting to eat the spareribs and sweet potatoes she bakes. Do you ever take her a present? Ever take her a box of candy or some flowers or a book?"

"She doesn't expect me to bring her anything. She doesn't read books much, and if I ever took her a present when it wasn't her birthday or something, she'd scold me for spending the money."

"Sure she would. And be just tickled to death. Next Sunday why don't you try her out? Get a box of candy or some flowers and make her happy. You won't have a mother forever, you know. I lost mine when I was twelve years old."

"Well," I said, "that might be a good idea at that. I just never thought of such a thing before."

"Exactly what I mean, George. Exactly. It's easy to be kind to one's mother if the guy just thinks about it and that will be good practice toward being kind to other people and not thinking exclusively about yourself. All right, we've established that you probably love your mother but haven't been doing much about it. Now how about this sister of yours? Do you love your sister?"

I pondered that. "Maybe," I said finally. "I used to love Laura before she was married and before we came out to Denver and I lived with them for a while. But I never liked her husband very well and she's all for her husband. I don't hate my sister, but I guess I don't love her very much any more."

"How about her babies? Your niece and nephew?"

"For heaven's sake," I said, "what's the idea of all this cross-examination? You think you're a prosecuting attorney or something?"

"Not at all. I'm just your doctor trying to diagnose your case. I'm just trying to find out why you are capable of doing cruel things without thinking and perhaps cure you of being a self-centered stinker and turn you into a kind, tactful human being. You don't really want to be a stinker, do you?"

"I haven't admitted that I am. My God!"

"Realizing what's wrong with you is the first stage of getting cured. When a patient comes to a doctor's office with tuberculosis, he doesn't have to admit he's got the disease. The doctor can make tests and tell. Then the patient has to accept the evidence that he's a lunger and follow the doctor's instructions before he has a chance of being cured. What you did to the crippled girl is as good evidence of stinkeritis as a hemorrhage is of TB."

"That," I said, "was just once and I was sorry about it and ashamed, and I don't know why I ever was silly enough to tell you about it. I'm sorry about that too."

"I'm not. It was a lucky thing for you that you told somebody capable of putting you straight—if you want to be put straight. One really mean act can be as significant as one hemorrhage, especially when the mean act was toward these people you admit have been especially kind to you—what's their names?"

"Krueger," I said.

"Have you ever done anything at all to show you appreciate that kindness?"

"Well, hell, I always thank them and I work real hard for Jake."

"If they ever invite you out to dinner again, why don't you take some flowers to Mrs. Krueger? Not to the girl, but just in a general way to both the mother and the girl. Give 'em to the mother."

"That would be kind of silly. They have flowers growing in their yard."

"They won't have big pink roses and women are nuts about big pink roses. You can get a bunch of 'em for a buck."

"Look," I said, "if I went over there carrying a bunch of roses for the Krueger women Jake would sure enough give me the hoo-raw."

"Let him. It might set a good example for him, make him kinder to his women."

"Jake is kind enough to them. Right now his wife Lena brags that she has more new corsets than any woman on Capitol Hill." I had to explain that to Don Fitch and he thought it very funny.

"Well, George," he said, "the whole purpose of this discourse is to try to get you to think more about other people and less about yourself. That really is the basis of Christianity, but apparently you never learned it in Sunday school and church. Everybody has faults. Learn to make allowances for them. If you're going to be any kind of artist, you've got to learn about people and what makes them operate the way they do. When you learn to make allowances for whatever faults you think your sister has, you'll get over whatever hostility you feel toward her now. The same way with your brother-in-law. He must have his good points. Not many people are really thorough-going bastards."

"Well . . ."

"Isn't he kind to your sister and the babies?"

"Of course."

"And how about your mother? What does she think of him?"

"Oh, she thinks he's wonderful."

"I think I get the picture," said Fitch. "Now that you're not living with them any more, suppose you make a point of always speaking to him pleasantly and respectfully, and I expect his attitude toward you might change."

"I doubt it. He thinks I'm too stupid to learn anything and that I'm a disgraceful dirty chimney sweep and he's ashamed to have me around."

"Hmm. Is he a big, husky man?"

"Lord, no. He's a little sissy shrimp."

Fitch nodded. "Sure. And when you see him you've got a chip on your shoulder. You get on a mean expression and you look like a tough young thug to him. All right, I'll tell you what to do, boy. The next time you go out there, don't try to be too familiar with your brother-in-law, but smile in a friendly way and speak to him pleasantly. Take that chip off your shoulder and quit being on the defensive. Isn't that worth trying?"

"Well," I said, "I suppose it's worth trying except that I don't care much about being friendly toward the son of a bitch."

"Inasmuch as your mother lives with them, wouldn't it make her a lot happier if you were on better terms with her son-in-law?"

"Maybe."

"And you claim you love your mother?"

"I get what you mean, Doc, and I thank you for your tough lecture and suggestions. I guess you're right."

"All right, George, and there's another thought to remember. Kindness is really a very contagious but pleasant disease. If you make a real effort to be tactful and kind to people around you, you'll be surprised how fast the disease spreads."

"Okay, Reverend Doctor, I reckon it's worth trying."

[229]

Fitch chuckled. "Wonderful. Now I'll tell you a nice way to start off your kindness program. It would be a very kind act if you could lend me two bucks until I get my dad's check."

Chapter 21

So I TRIED to follow Don Fitch's advice about thinking more of other people and being pleasant and kind and smiling. This was rather difficult and not wholly successful. I don't believe that I went around habitually with a surly expression on my face, but I still was not a natural grinner and it took an effort to smile pleasantly at all our customers, especially those who regarded Jake and me as dirty, low characters who probably would steal at the slightest opportunity. I tried to make allowances for them. I tried to put myself in their place. Jake and I did look pretty disreputable by midday.

Ralph Sterling's response to my polite pleasantries was not notable. I tried to make allowances for that too. After all, a bank vice-president-in-charge-of-mortgages must be inured to faked geniality. My change in attitude must have puzzled him. What special considerations could I be looking for? I couldn't be working for an extension of a nonexistent loan. I couldn't be looking for a loan because I owned no collateral. But my actions must have seemed suspicious and Ralph was wary.

I took my mother little presents almost every week—some candy, a bunch of violets or a magazine—and she hugged and kissed me for them. This made me feel good. And, as if to prove Doc Fitch's declaration that kindness was contagious, Laura responded by buying our mother a beautiful changeable silk Sunday dress. But that may have been competition instead of contagion.

The distaff Kruegers finally forgave me and I took a two-pound box of chocolates with me when I went out to dinner, and after a few uneasy minutes everything seemed as jolly as ever. I was a little surprised to see my portrait of Jake still on the living-room wall, but, naturally, no mention was made of my art studies. Although candy and beer are not usually regarded as compatible companions, we consumed the whole two pounds after dinner.

It was soon after this that I walked home from church again with the Upjohns. But this time, to my regret, we got paired off differently. Major Upjohn, in a hail-fellow manner, began talking with me on the church stoop, which resulted in Mrs. Upjohn pairing off with my mother and Ralph with Marcella.

I thought the Major, as Marcella's father, was deserving of my best Doc Fitch brand pleasant smile and he responded by slapping me on the arm and saying, "Well, you've grown into a tall, sturdy fellow since you've been here. You ought to enlist in my battalion."

"Thank you, sir," I said, "but at present I don't see how I could find time for military training."

We fell into step behind the others and the Major declared, "Nothing better in the world than some military training for a young fellow. Nothing. It builds you up spiritually and mentally as well as physically. It teaches you the discipline so necessary in competing with modern conditions. It gives you pride in belonging to a great patriotic organization which is practically America's first line of defense because the Regular Army is completely inadequate and filled with men who are essentially loafers and not inspired by a sense of duty to our flag and Constitution."

"Well," I said, "I don't know much about the National Guard, but I imagine that is all true."

"True as the Gospel, young man. All of America's wars have been won by civilian soldiers—after adequate training, of course. As I look at it, every able-bodied young man in America owes it to his God and to the land that gave him birth and freedom and opportunity to devote a little of his time to military training in the National Guard."

Ralph and Marcella were chatting along ahead of us, naturally and easily. I wondered what they were talking about and I was jealous. Still, it wasn't a bad idea at all to get on friendly terms with her father.

"Moreover," went on Major Upjohn, "a young man owes it to himself to get the military training that may save his life later on. Also, when war comes, you, for example, probably would be a corporal or perhaps a sergeant when the units are filled with recruits."

A corporal or sergeant didn't seem to me high enough in the military hierarchy to be worth bothering with, but I didn't mention that. I said, "There certainly isn't going to be any war with the United States in it, is there?"

He looked up at me sternly. "I hate to say this, young man, but war is inevitable, and perhaps sooner than even I think."

"For goodness sake," I said. "Who with?"

"You surely have read and heard a good deal about the Yellow Peril?"

"Well, sir," I said, "I know somebody important said that China is a sleeping giant and that if the hundreds of millions of Chinese ever wake up, it might be bad for the rest of the world, but I guess it'll be quite a while before that happens and even then they might have enough trouble at home so they wouldn't be declaring war on the United States. Of course I heard about that Boxer war, but I never did understand just what that was about and it didn't seem to amount to much."

"I gather you didn't hear Captain Richmond Pearson Hobson lecture at the Consistory the other night."

"No, sir, I didn't. Who is Captain Hobson?"

Major Upjohn shook his head. "You should have—you should have. Captain Hobson was one of our greatest heroes in the war with Spain. He sank the *Merrimac* at the harbor entrance to Santiago, under very heavy fire from the forts, and it was a miracle that he escaped with his life."

This puzzled me. I didn't want to contradict Major Upjohn, but I decided that either it was a woeful slip of the tongue or that he was shockingly mixed up on his history, for a military man. I was positive in my own mind that the *Merrimac* was in a quite different war, a Confederate ironclad, as a matter of fact, that fought a celebrated duel with the federal ironclad *Monitor*. I decided that anything else Major Upjohn said should be regarded with suspicion even though he did happen to be the father of the entrancing Marcella.

"Richmond Pearson Hobson," Major Upjohn went on, "is probably our foremost expert on international military affairs and a very eloquent speaker. He rightly views the expansion of Japan with alarm. He has analyzed the Jap history and character, and, as far as I'm concerned, proves that Japan is preparing to attack the United States and soon."

"Why ever would they want to do that?" I asked. "Didn't

Teddy Roosevelt send our Great White Fleet over there to show 'em we could blow their little old island out of the water if they ever got funny with us?"

The Major laughed. "Yes, he did. And that's one of the reasons America must draft Roosevelt to be President again when he gets back from Africa. But in the meantime Japan has been building up her Navy at a furious rate and training a remarkable Army. Those little yellow men make great soldiers, as they proved in the war with Russia. They can live on a handful of rice a day and shoot a rifle just as well or better than a six-foot Russian."

"But, Major Upjohn," I said, "I still don't understand why they would want to attack us. We never did anything to them."

"There are three reasons," he said solemnly. "One is that they are Buddhists and hate Christians. Another is that they hate the United States because we exclude them from American citizenship and have shut the gate on their immigration, which they take as an insult. But the principal reason is that their islands can't support their great and growing population, so they need new territory. They took Formosa away from China in 1895, they grabbed territory from Russia in that war, and now they have taken Korea. Next will be the Philippines, if they can do it, and then Hawaii and finally California."

I didn't understand exactly what we were doing with the Philippines, which seemed to be just a source of trouble, or with Hawaii either, but I didn't want to expose my ignorance any further and said nothing.

When we reached the Upjohn steps, my mother and Ralph went on home while Mrs. Upjohn and the beautiful Marcella went into the house. Mr. Upjohn and I stood on the sidewalk and I said, "If the Japanese want more territory, I'd think it would be closer and easier to move into China."

"Well, of course they already have taken over Port Arthur and part of Manchuria and what we can eventually expect, unless we nip it in the bud, is the Japanese directing the hordes of China in the destruction of Christianity and the white race."

"But," I objected, "if they just want territory, it would seem that there's all the territory in China they could possibly use."

Major Upjohn shook his head. "You should have heard Captain Hobson. The Yellow Race will never be satisfied until it conquers the world. Emperor William of Germany is one of the few really intelligent, farsighted monarchs Europe has seen in modern times, and he was one of the first to recognize and name the Yellow Peril to Christendom. Among his many accomplishments, the Kaiser is a talented artist and he painted a remarkable picture entitled, 'Nations of Europe, Defend Your Faith,' in which Germania, with drawn, glittering sword, was pointing out the danger to Britannia, La Belle France, Italia and the others. This great painting has had its effect, especially in Germany, where they are building up a magnificent modern military machine. But if the Europeans are in danger, how much more so are we with our Philippine Islands a relative stone's throw from Japan? We *must* build up our military strength. We owe it not only to our forefathers who fought and died to preserve our glorious land, but to God, who has blessed us with liberty, and to Jesus whose love assures the faithful of salvation. War against the Mongolian unbelievers would be as holy as that of Charlemagne against the infidels and of the Crusaders seeking the Holy Grail. You can see that, can't you?"

"I suppose so," I said, "especially if Japan really attacked the United States."

"The way to prevent them attacking us is to be so strong they'd realize it would be suicide to try. And the way for us to be strong is to build up our Navy and Army—especially the National Guard. I know you must be a Christian because you're a member of our church. And I'd hate to think you're not a patriotic American."

"Oh, I'm patriotic all right," I said. "My goodness. If America had to go to war, I guess I'd be one of the first to enlist, but I just don't see how I could—well, I've got so much to do now with my studies and work and everything, I don't see how I'd have time for the National Guard until later. And in case of war you'd have a lot of recruits, wouldn't you, and you'd have to go to training camp for a while so the recruits could learn before you'd be ready for battle? Isn't that so, sir?"

He nodded. "To some extent, yes. But our boys who have been drilling one night a week and going to summer encampment would have the edge on the recruits and a good share of them will become noncommissioned officers."

"Well," I said, "I don't believe I'd mind being a private soldier for a while if there was a war and I'm not sure I'd make a very good officer, and I doubt that it would scare Japan very badly if they heard George Chalmers had joined the Colorado National Guard."

He laughed and slapped me on the shoulder. "Perhaps not, George," he said, and I sensed that this was the first he had known my name although realizing that I had some connection with the Sterlings. "But," he went on, "the National Guard has other duties and other responsibilities besides fighting and winning wars against the foreign enemies of Christ and America. There's a growing wave of Socialism and anarchy among the working classes, mostly foreign-born, ignorant men, frequently led into labor unions and strikes against the public good by shrewd and evil organizers, more often than not foreign born themselves and often disbelievers in Christianity. These enemies of state and nation would deny the right of an American employer to hire whom he chooses and to fire whom he chooses and to run his own business as he chooses."

"Yes, I know," I said, although from what I had read about conditions in mine towns and steel mills I thought there were things that could be said on both sides.

"If a man doesn't like his job," Major Upjohn continued, "he has a perfect right to quit it when he pleases. To refuse him that privilege when he hasn't signed a contract to work a definite period would be slavery. But, on the other hand, when working men organize a union and strike, it's anarchy for them to use violence or any other means to attempt to prevent other men from taking their jobs. That sort of thing has been happening all too often. And when it happens that local law-enforcement officers are unable to maintain order, it's the duty of the state's governor to call out the National Guard, and it's the duty of the National Guard to restore order, using whatever force is necessary."

"You mean," I asked, "that you would shoot the strikers?"

"If the strikers held a picket line to keep strikebreakers from entering the plant or mine, the officers would order them to disperse, and if the lawbreakers didn't comply, the troops naturally would drive them away—using bayonets or even bullets if necessary. Otherwise, you'd have a state of insurrection against the United States."

"Well," I said, "it would be pretty bad for American troops to shoot down Americans."

"Most of them aren't American," he said. "Especially these troublemakers in Colorado. They're Mexicans and Italians and such. But, even so, when policemen get into a gun battle with bandits, it doesn't make any difference whether the bandits are Americans or spiggoties. And in the Civil War, Americans shot other Americans to save the Union."

"That was pretty bad too."

"Yes, but the Union was saved and slavery was abolished. My father was a troop commander in the famous Illinois Black Horse Cavalry and I guess the military is in my blood." He chuckled. "Mrs. Upjohn's father and uncles were rebels, so we don't talk much about the war at our house although one of my proudest possessions is a brace of beautiful pistols presented to my father by his men. I'd like to have you see them sometime."

"I'd like to very much," I said. After all, Major Upjohn was the gorgeous Marcella's father.

"Why not come in right now?"

"Fine."

So I was led into the house which was home to that beautiful creature—into the living room where probably every chair had been pressed by her dainty bottom, where the rugs on the floor must have rejoiced hundreds of times at the touch of her tiny feet, where the walls must have been permeated by the lilt of her voice—and Major Upjohn, apparently oblivious to his sacred environment, opened a cabinet under a bookcase and brought out a large case of highly polished dark wood and placed it on the table. Ceremoniously, he took out a key ring and selected a small key with which he unlocked the case and lifted the lid. Resting on slightly faded purple plush were two silver-plated, ivory-handled Colt revolvers, one pointing right and one pointing left, in recesses made to fit them. In their own recesses were a small, silver powder flask, bullet mold and round percussion-cap container. Every inch of metal on the revolvers was covered with elaborate floriated engraving.

"My!" I exclaimed, and I was taken back to my first visit to old pard Calvin Campbell's room and his prized horse pistol without a firing pin. "Will these shoot?" I asked.

Major Upjohn laughed. "Will they shoot? No more accurate hand gun was ever made than these old cap-and-ball Colts. Of course there was the difficulty of molding your bullets and loading and capping each chamber, but they'll lay lead exactly where you hold it. Well, here's the interesting thing." He pointed to a silver plate screwed to the inside of the lid and I leaned forward and read:

PRESENTED TO CAPTAIN JOSHUA UPJOHN BY THE OFFICERS AND MEN OF H TROOP WITH RESPECT AND AFFECTION. MAY 28, 1865.

"That's wonderful," I said. "May I pick up one of the guns?"

"Certainly, but take it by the butt. Finger marks tarnish the silver."

I reached down for an ivory handle and then said, "They're not loaded, are they?"

"No, no. I never load them unless I want to try them out, and there's some difficulty in getting the percussion caps and fine-grain black powder."

"Well," I said, remembering old pard Cal Campbell again, "a lot of people have been shot with unloaded guns."

"That's quite true, but you don't have to worry about these." He took one of the revolvers from the case and twirled the cylinder. "See—to be loaded a brass cap has to be fitted over these nipples."

I took the gun from him and it was well-balanced and fitted nicely into my hand. When I raised it close to my face to sight it, Major Upjohn exclaimed, "No, no. At arm's length. Here."

He took the pistol and stood erect, with left hand resting on his hip, cocked the gun as he raised it and then brought it down slowly, even with his right shoulder, and pulled the trigger. With the sharp click he said solemnly, "Bull's-eye."

As he handed the revolver back to me there came the roar of a heavy gasoline engine outside and a long, red roadster pulled up in front of the house.

Major Upjohn called out, "Oh, honey-bun, Courtney's here."

Marcella's voice seemed a little shrill as she replied from upstairs, "Tell him I'll be right down."

A tall man in checkered jacket and cap came with a bouncing stride toward the house and Major Upjohn went to the front door. "Well, Courtney, my boy," said the Major, "come in, come in."

"Thank you, Major." The voice was a not unpleasant high tenor. "Most happy to do so."

"The girl says she'll be right down."

The man had removed his cap and his head was bald back almost to its summit. His round blue eyes opened even wider as he saw me standing with the revolver in my hand.

"Gracious!" His voice was a falsetto, and perhaps he was exhibiting a mock consternation. I didn't know.

"Mr. MacGregor," said the Major, "meet my young friend George Chalmers who's interested in my father's Colts."

I transferred the revolver to my left hand and shook hands with Courtney MacGregor. His hand was soft but strong and I looked at him and thought, Why, this man's middle aged; they shouldn't allow the precious Marcella to have a date with a man who must be past thirty years old. He smiled pleasantly, showing even white teeth which might have been false.

"My goodness," he said, "I didn't know quite what I was getting into here, finding a young character flourishing a horse pistol."

"I wasn't really flourishing it," I said, in embarrassment and jealousy.

Major Upjohn laughed. "How's your roaring demon performing, Courtney?"

"Best car in the world," MacGregor asserted.

I looked out the window. "What is it," I asked, "a Winton?"

"No, sir," said MacGregor. "It's an American Underslung. It hugs the road like a badger and takes off like a gazelle."

"Do you really think it's better than a Locomobile?" the Major asked. "Why don't we all sit down? Marcella will get here when she gets here."

We sat in chairs, I with the silver revolver in my lap.

MacGregor grinned widely. "To answer your question, I'll say this: if any Locomobile man wants to put up say five hundred on the side, I'll be happy to take him on. Oh I know the Locomobile won the international Vanderbilt two or three years ago, but that was a special model and there's been a lot of development since then."

I asked, "Are you an automobile racer, Mr. MacGregor?"

Both he and Major Upjohn laughed and MacGregor said, "You can call me that, if you know anyone who wants to bet against my Underslung."

Marcella came tripping down the stairs, dressed in gray tweeds, with a filmy scarf about her dark hair. We all stood up.

"Hello, Court," she called. "I went to church this morning and prayed, and see, we have a beautiful day."

"Thank you, my dear," MacGregor said, bowing.

Then she saw me, smiled slightly and said, "How do you do?" Turning to her father, she said, "Well, Daddy, are you going to sell those old muskets to Mr. Chalmers? Goody."

The Major spoke sternly. "My girl, for a military man's daughter to call a beautiful cap-and-ball revolver a musket is most ridiculous. And while young Mr. Chalmers may become a very wealthy man, he'll never in the world have enough money to buy these guns. Never. And to make sure that neither you nor your rebel mother ever sell these Yankee guns, I'm going to write a codicil to my will, leaving this brace to a historical museum in Illinois. That I will."

Marcella shocked me slightly by giggling. "Daddy, I think you're real mean," she said. "Mama and I might need the money."

Marcella stood on her toes and kissed him on the cheek. "So long, Daddy," she said.

"Good-bye," said the Major. "Have a good time and get home early."

"We will," said Marcella.

MacGregor and I murmured at each other and shook hands again. I was tempted to clamp down on his hand, but didn't.

Marcella called a good-bye to her mother upstairs and Mrs. Upjohn repeated the Major's admonition about returning early, and I heard Marcella laughing merrily as they left the house and wondered drearily if she was laughing at something MacGregor had said about me. Then I thought, There I go again, self-centered and thinking only about myself. It was more than likely they were laughing about the Major and his Civil War revolvers or about what they were going to do or any number of things. Neither of them would consider me important enough to talk about—a wondrous creature like Marcella and a mature man rich enough and important enough to own a big, red American Underslung roadster hardly would waste time talking about a teen-age chimney sweep, even if they didn't know he was a chimney sweep. But there I went *again,* self-centered and depreciating. I wouldn't be a chimney sweep all my life. Or would I?

MacGregor had cranked the big car into roaring life and I

glanced out the window to see him clamber into the seat beside Marcella, push levers and dash away, with Marcella's filmy scarf fluttering behind her head, and leaving a cloud of dust from the gravel street.

I was standing in the middle of the room, still holding the silver-plated revolver and Major Upjohn took it from my hand.

"My," I said, "I certainly don't blame you for being proud of these guns. Did your father use them in battle?"

"No, no. Didn't you notice the date of presentation? These were given my father as a tribute by the officers and men who fought under his command. They were the ones who knew his true worth."

The Major took a white handkerchief from his hip pocket and carefully wiped off the revolver before replacing it in its purple-plush nest.

"Well, Major," I said, "it was very kind of you to show me the beautiful guns. Thank you ever so much."

"You're welcome. Glad to show them to someone who appreciates them."

"Well, I suppose my Sunday dinner must be about ready," I said.

The Major was closing the case and locking it. "Now you think over what I told you about the National Guard."

"Yes, sir. I'll think it over all right," I promised and left the hallowed precinct of the lovely Marcella, who even then was being whirled away to goodness knew where in a roaring red monster beside a balding man old enough to be her uncle if not her father.

"Well!" Laura exclaimed when I went into the kitchen to get a drink of water. "Didn't Mrs. Upjohn invite you to dinner?"

"I didn't see Mrs. Upjohn in the house," I said. "Major Upjohn just invited me in to show me some beautiful pistols the Civil War soldiers gave his father."

"That must have been *very* interesting," she said, sarcastically. "I wonder why he did that?"

"Well, he also invited me to join his National Guard regiment."

"Oh, that was it. Of course you agreed—but you're not old enough yet and I can assure you Mama won't let you."

"No, I don't think I want to join it."

"I'm surprised. But I hope you got to talk to Mama's darling little carbon copy. I've a feeling you're a little sweet on her."

"Well, you're wrong as usual," I blurted, forgetting about the new, kind, polite George Chalmers. "Sure, she was there and she went away in a great big, red American Underslung that makes your Buick look like a tin lizzie, with a bald-headed old man named MacGregor."

Laura laughed and called to Ralph who was engaged with the Sunday papers in the living room. "Ralph, did you hear that?"

"No, what?"

"Little Marcella Upjohn is out again with Courtney Mac-Gregor."

"It's none of my business," asserted Ralph. But he came out into the kitchen, shaking his head.

"After all," said Laura, "he's a pretty notorious playboy, isn't he? And he's been married and divorced. And Marcella was just graduated from Miss Ridley's school."

Ralph rattled the financial section of the Denver *Post*. "That playboy stuff probably is exaggerated," he said. "Anyhow, he's not letting his outside activities interfere with business. His brokerage firm is doing well and his financial standing is very good."

"He looks pretty old to me," I offered.

"Oh, he's not old," Ralph said, without looking at me. "Court's in his early thirties and he's regarded as one of the brightest young businessmen in the city. He's prominent socially and well-liked. I'd say there are at least a dozen girls and young women have their caps set for him. Little Marcella probably would be very lucky to get him."

"But," Laura objected, "he's been divorced, and I don't know what in the world the Upjohns are thinking of to allow that child to—"

"You're pretty old-fashioned, Laura," said Ralph. "People's ideas of divorce have changed. And the Upjohns are probably thinking it would be wonderful to have Court for a son-in-law. Besides establishing the girl with social prominence and money, it'd help the madam socially too."

"Perhaps," said Laura, "until there's another divorce. Besides, I doubt that he has any intentions of marrying that child anyhow. I'd say it's probably just another dalliance on his part with a young girl he may think is pretty."

"Oh," he said, "she's pretty, all right." I tried to remember back to when Ralph had said something before which I agreed with. "Of course," he went on, "I have no idea what Mac-Gregor's intentions are, but I think he'll get plenty of encouragement from the Major and the madam."

"Well," said Laura, "it's none of my business and I don't care much more for the girl than for her mother and it might serve the girl right to be married to a man like that, but the mother is such a fool that she probably will be too eager and scare the man away."

My Sunday dinner was, as they say, ashes in my mouth, and after dinner I played a while on the living room floor with Benny and Milly. I tried to build castles for them with their elaborate set of blocks, but before I could get far one or the other would gleefully knock them down. I thought sadly that this was quite symbolical and went back to my Y.M.C.A. cell to work on my correspondence-school lesson and to finish reading Kipling's *The Light That Failed,* which was about another artist suffering from hopeless love, and sad enough to match my mood.

Feeling forlorn, I went out and knocked at Doc Fitch's door, but there was no answer. So I went downstairs and strolled down Seventeenth Street, trying not to think about Marcella and Courtney MacGregor and what they might be doing, trying to think about Kipling's romantic novel instead of about my self-centered self, but I still was thoroughly identified with the unfortunate Dick Heldar, and the author's description of black-haired, gray-eyed Maisie fitted Marcella—and also the lost child Little Egypt. Was there more than coincidence to this? Had the genius of Mr. Kipling divined that beautiful girls with dark hair and light eyes were a symbol of sorrow?

I crossed Curtis Street and looked to the right at the electric glow of the Isis Theater. No, I didn't want to go to a movie. But at Lawrence Street I stopped at the famous Silver Dollar saloon. I never had had a drink in a saloon, but now I would stride in recklessly and have a glass of beer. Inside the swinging doors the floor was paved with white disks, obviously silver dollars worn smooth by thousands of male shoes. Inset in the dark, polished bar were more and unworn silver dollars, glittering along with the mirrored pyramids of glassware to the rear.

"What's your favor, young man?" asked a wax-mustachioed bartender.

I had come in for a glass of beer, but heard my voice saying, "Whisky."

"Rye or bourbon?"

"Bourbon," I said, feeling that sounded more elegant.

Deftly and swiftly, he produced a quart bottle, a small glass of water and a whisky glass. I poured amber bourbon carefully into the shot glass, lifted the glass and sniffed. It smelled awful. I sipped it and it tasted worse. So I gulped about half of the shot and it scorched my mouth and burned on down my gullet. Hurriedly, I swallowed some water. Then I looked down the bar at the dozen or so men lined up, some of them in conversation and others staring unhappily into the mirror. What in hell, I asked myself, am I doing here? And why did I ask for this nauseating stuff instead of beer?

I tossed off what whisky was left in the shot glass and almost gagged before I could get a drink of water. Then I waited a minute to see what effect the horrible stuff would have on me and when it didn't seem to have any effect at all, I poured myself another drink. That I took as medicine, quickly, desperately, and my unsophisticated stomach retched in rebellion. Only the pure, cold water saved me.

Now I began to feel pleasantly lightheaded and more reckless. I looked at the bottle of bourbon, but didn't believe I could swallow any more of that stuff. I wondered if they didn't make any intoxicating liquor more appetizing to the taste. Then in the mirror I caught sight of a painting on the rear wall and turned to look at it more closely.

She was rather plump, this pink-and-white naked girl on the lounge, and her expression was pensive and her dark hair hung in waves about her smooth shoulders. Her large eyes were definitely a shadowed blue.

I tried to view the picture with professional objectivity and told myself that it was a fine piece of drawing with excellent foreshortening. But by then the bourbon was working and I thought that the picture was a great advertisement for Market Street. A guy could come in here, have a few wallops of liquor, look at that picture and he'd head for the redlight district as fast as he could go. Well, if there was a gal like that down there instead of those awful perfumed whores, it might be worth while. Brother! Perhaps in the fine parlor houses they did have them. But, from what I had heard, you could pick up a destroying venereal disease just as easily in a fine parlor house as in a low crib. About one more slug of that nasty bourbon, though, and I'd be willing to take a risk.

Resolutely I turned my back on the provocative nude and put a silver dollar down on the bar. "That'll do," I said to the bartender.

"Thirty cents," he said, and gave me my change.

Outside, I looked down Seventeenth Street, then took a deep breath and turned the other way. I could feel the whisky singing in my blood, but I felt no happier. In a drugstore I bought a dime's worth of chocolate peanut cluster and a *Saturday Evening Post*, thinking that one drink of whisky cost that much and it wasn't worth it.

Chapter 22

ON SUMMER Saturday evenings I frequently went to City Park for the band concerts. It was a big brass band and good and it played not only the traditional brass-band marches but operatic overtures and semiclassical numbers— programs tailored to the taste of the multitude.

One balmy Saturday evening a handbag slid off the lap of a woman sitting next to me and she thanked me graciously when I picked it up. We exchanged appreciative comments after each number, and then, at the intermission, we watched together the electric fountain throwing its varied and multicolored plumes of water in the lake. She was a rather slim woman, neatly dressed in a blue suit, and, I estimated, about thirty-five years old. She was an ash blonde, and while not really pretty, was far from unattractive. As we stood watching the electric fountain she surprised me by taking my arm. This was curiously exciting, and during the second half of the concert we sat closer together, her arm frequently pressing mine.

At the close of the concert I anticipated an invitation and was not disappointed. Wouldn't I like to come to her apartment for some scrambled eggs and coffee? I'd be delighted.

Her name was Helga Johnson. She had come to Colorado from Wisconsin three years before with her ailing husband, a carpenter. But the climate had failed to work its magic on John and he had lived only a year. Since then she had lived alone in a terrace apartment, supporting herself as a receptionist in an osteopath's office. I must understand that she definitely was not in the habit of picking up strange young men, but I looked so kind and understanding, really like homefolks. I reminded her of her husband before he took ill.

I told her my name was George Hotchkiss and that I lived with my parents on Columbine Street, borrowing the name of an elderly couple whose flues Jake Krueger and I had cleaned that morning. I told her that I was a plumber, technically still an apprentice because I had not yet got my union card. Why did I lie to her? Perhaps I was developing deviousness. Surely, as we took the tramcar toward her apartment, I anticipated something more exciting than just scrambled eggs and coffee, but I feared getting too deeply involved. My love for the adorable Marcella was hopeless enough, perhaps, to warrant a possible liaison with a pleasant older woman, but still not completely hopeless, and it seemed wise to open an avenue of escape if I wished to escape.

So, as George Hotchkiss, apprentice plumber, I went to Helga Johnson's immaculate little apartment in a flat-roofed row of connected brick terraces, and there I ate scrambled eggs, toast and coffee, and there I spent the night.

Perhaps it was because of a native restraint on my part—an inability to abandon myself in wantonness—that Helga remarked, "Darling, you're terribly young, aren't you? Tell the truth. You're not even twenty-one, are you?"

"No," I said, "but I'm twenty."

"Oh, dear!" she exclaimed. "I'm a cradle-robber. But you certainly were no virgin."

"I certainly was not."

"But I'm a lot older than you. How old do you think I am?"

I thought that an extremely silly question to ask, but knew

what was expected of me. I thought she was at least thirty-five and probably older, judging from the fine wrinkles around her eyes and the slightly crepy skin at the base of her throat. "Well, you're not very old," I said. "Maybe twenty-five."

"I'm even older than that," she said sadly. "I'm twenty-eight."

You poor thing, I thought, you ought to know you can't stay young forever, so why don't you make the best of it? It didn't occur to me that she probably *was* making the best of it.

Pleading that I had to get home before my parents were awake, I left Helga in the gray dawn and ate breakfast at a lunch counter before going to the Y.M.C.A. for a shower and a brief nap, cut short by the alarm clock in time to change clothes and go to church with the Sterlings.

While I certainly felt remorse over my sin, there was none of the unspeakable disgust that racked me after my session with the crib-house woman. In fact, there was a sense of fulfillment in a daring if unlawful enterprise in company with a quite kind, affectionate and appreciative human being. When I kissed Helga good-bye, I promised that I would see her again soon, but I had no intention at all of doing so. This was a closed incident, I felt, a curious and rather exciting breakdown from rectitude and not to be repeated. However, I had written in my notebook the phone number of her osteopath's office and had declared I would call her within a few days. She had no telephone at home, and, to block any possible attempt on her part to call "George Hotchkiss," I had said my parents did not feel we could afford a phone.

At church Marcella was not with her father and mother and I felt sad and corrupt and jealous. I felt particularly sad in the thought that I meant so little to Marcella that she would be indifferent as to how I had spent the night, but still would be shocked. At least I *hoped* she would be shocked. During the Reverend Mr. Hamilton's sermon I fought a battle with drowsiness.

Convinced as I was that sleepy Sunday that I should never see Helga again, on Thursday I still watched my chance in the morning when Jake went to the toilet and used his phone to call the osteopath's office and was excited to hear Helga's faint Scandinavian accent with the rising inflection at the end of sentences. And I made a date to take her to dinner and a movie on Saturday evening.

Again at dawn of Sunday I vowed that this was definitely the last—that this must not become a habit or my life would be ruined. So I did not call her for a week. One week. Then I decided it would be mean to break off from such a nice, sensitive woman abruptly and I called her. Helga was disgruntled. "You could have phoned me at least?" I made a lame excuse about having to go somewhere with my parents Saturday night.

"There are no nights except Saturday? You are with other girls on all other nights except Saturday?"

"No, Helga," I declared, "but I have to get up early on other mornings and work hard, so I have to get sleep."

"You are a weak young man who will be sick unless he sleeps eight–nine hours?"

"No, but I have to study at night. I'm taking a correspondence-school course, so I have to study my lessons. I'll tell you about it when I see you. I've got to go now."

It began to strain my imagination to make conversation with Helga about my life as George Hotchkiss and the correspondence course in short-story writing I was taking because I wanted to become an author, trying to avoid the slightest contradiction which Helga's sharp brain would catch immediately.

"Why would you want to be a writer of novels and stories that are not true instead of being an honest plumber?" she asked.

"Well," I explained, "I'd just like to be an author and it would be much easier work than plumbing and pay a lot more money."

"You don't think union plumbers make enough money? Isn't it good to make good wages helping poor distressed people whose plumbing is out of whack instead of writing lies for silly people to read? If you like writing lies, maybe you like telling lies too? Maybe you tell me lies? Maybe you're married already and you lie to your wife and you lie to me and you only come to me for a change?"

"No, Helga," I said, "I'm not married and I'll have to be making an awful lot more money before I ever get married because I have to support my mother and father."

"But you will get your union card pretty soon?"

"Well, *fairly* soon."

"Next year?"

"Yeah. Well, probably late next year."

"So then you have a young girl who is too *decent* to go to bed with you until you're married and you will marry her then?"

"No," I said, "I haven't got any girl at all—except you."

"And I'm too old for you to ever marry? I'm just young enough to be your mistress?"

"I didn't say that, Helga."

"But you think it?"

"I'm not thinking about getting married at all until I've got a bank account and am making enough dough to support my parents and a wife, too, and that's a long time off."

"So, five years maybe? Then you come and say, 'Good-bye, Helga, nice knowing you'?"

I said, "Look, Helga, you know what my situation is, and if you aren't satisfied with it and if you want me to stop coming to see you, just tell me so."

"You are tired of me? You want to stop coming to me?"

"If I didn't want to come, I wouldn't be here, would I? The only thing, there's no use of hinting about getting married because I can't do it."

"You mean you don't want to and when you say you love me it's like the lies you want to write in silly love stories?"

"I don't plan to write love stories."

"You just like to play at making love?"

"Don't you?"

"W-e-l-l, maybe you don't believe I never was, well, intimate that way before with anybody except my husband?"

I said, "You've told me that before and I never questioned you." But I thought, if that's strictly true, it's strange that you had those rubbers on hand.

"You probably think I'm a bad girl and have gone to bed with a lot of men?"

"No, I haven't thought any such thing."

"Then, maybe it doesn't hurt your conscience any, but don't you think it worries me being sinful and immoral this way with you?"

"All right, Helga," I said, "then we'll quit."

"Would you still come to see me if we quit being bad?"

"Well"—I said—"sure."

So we weren't "bad" again until the next time I came to see her, which was in two weeks, and I continued living the double life as George Chalmers and George Hotchkiss except for a brief period when I led a triple life, becoming George Krueger also, and then dropping back to the relatively uncomplicated single life of plain George Chalmers.

With the Denver Athletic Club's amateur boxing tournament coming up, Stanley Koviak decided that I was ready to enter, although he was somewhat apprehensive because I had outgrown the middleweight division and at an inch over six feet and one hundred and seventy-two pounds would have to face the light heavyweights. "Some of those big guys can hit like hell," Stanley said, "and you're still not as loose as I'd like to see you. But you're fast on your feet and fast with your hands and you got a good left hook now to go with that Mary Ann right. With a little luck I think you can go through the light heavies. For one thing, they're generally clumsier than the middles."

Because of my mother, and secretly also because of Marcella Upjohn, I didn't care to enter the tournament under my own name, and Jake Krueger himself, in full confidence of my ability, suggested that I take Krueger as a *nom de guerre*.

I neglected my drawing lessons and my reading to train each evening in the gymnasium, sparring with Stanley or Spike Donovan, who was still a welterweight, or with anyone else who cared to put on the gloves. Mornings I ran down to Lambert's store to strengthen my legs. Considering the fact that amateur bouts were for only three two-minute rounds and an additional round in case of a draw, I thought I was in pretty good condition. I was confident, so confident that I didn't believe I ever should have to box a fourth round.

However, my confidence drained away sadly on the tournament's first night when I was scheduled to meet a highly regarded boy called Irish Danny Farley. I met Farley in the dressing room before we were called up and he towered over me at least two inches. He was black browed, pug nosed and tough. He sneered at me, "So you're my first victim, eh? Nothing I like better than licking Dutchmen."

I don't know whether I was actually afraid of him, but my mouth felt like the inside of a corroded old furnace firepot and my heart was pounding at a terrific rate and I could feel the muscles inside my thighs trembling. I wished he knew I wasn't really a Dutchman but a good, clean American boy named Chalmers.

Once in the ring I wished fervently I were *out* of the ring. Under my old robe I could feel the cold sweat trickling down my ribs. Across from me, Farley was grinning in conversation with his seconds, and the hazy crowd beyond sounded like a convention of ten thousand blackbirds, with the shrill cries of boys selling peanuts and soft drinks rising above the harsh rumble. Suddenly I was nauseated and very dizzy, and while I never had fainted in my life, I was afraid I should collapse if I got to my feet.

Stanley was speaking emphatically into my ear, his hand gesturing up and down. "This skinny guy's weak in the middle, George. Go right after his breadbasket."

I didn't tell him that *I* was weak all over. Instead I asked for the water bottle and rinsed out my parched mouth. To my surprise, my legs did not fold under me when we were called to the center of the ring for instructions from the pudgy little referee, but I didn't hear much that this official said until, "Now shake hands and come out a-fighting."

Stanley stripped the robe from me, lights dimmed over the crowd, the bell clanged and I was confronted by Irish Danny Farley, his white body corrugated with lean muscle, his black brows scowling. He danced around me and jabbed me a glancing blow on the chin with a left that seemed as long as a telephone pole. Suddenly I was all right and I moved after him, missing three left hooks in succession. I couldn't get inside that astonishingly long left jab, some of which I blocked, some of which I evaded, but which landed lightly too often for comfort. I knew he was scoring point after point and I was doing nothing but try to box him. Now Farley was grinning derisively at me and a bull voice rose above the roar of the crowd, "Kill 'im, Danny! Kill 'im."

He wasn't killing me. He wasn't even hurting me. He was doing nothing with his right hand except to stroke his nose with the thumb. But he definitely was winning and I hadn't landed a solid blow until we passed near my corner and I heard Stanley shout, "Crowd him, George! The body! The body!"

Obediently, I rushed in, taking the sharpest left jab yet on the forehead, feinting for the face with my right and landing a left hook to the body. I heard him gasp and I was on top of him as he lowered his guard. The right I threw was not willed but automatic, and I felt its impact on bone through my wrist into my elbow and knew it had everything in it from the right ankle up the calf and thigh and back and shoulder. I stumbled over him as he went down and almost fell myself. He had rolled over and risen to hands and knees by the count of eight. But at ten he relaxed and went back down on his side.

I helped him to his feet and he shook his head violently and stared at me. "What happened?" he asked.

"You just got careless and left an opening," I said.

By that time his handlers had him, and he started to cry. "I was winning easy," he said, "I was winning easy."

"Sure, Danny," soothed a burly man in a red sweater, "it was just an accident. It'll be different next year."

Stanley wrapped my robe around me and gave me a hug. "My boy George," he gloated. "The Y.M.C.A. is just a bunch of soft sissies, eh? My boy George." He led me to the dressing room and then said, "Why didn't you go after his body sooner, like I told you?"

"I don't know," I said. "It didn't seem that I could get past that long left. I never saw a left like it."

"All you had to do was take one and get inside. The round was practically over when you got him, and it was that hook to the body did it. If the bell had of rung, he might have recovered and begun to work you over with his right. Don't never box a guy who's a better boxer than you. Fight him. Now you listen to me next time or you'll get licked. You got the punch and I got the brains, so you listen to me."

I won my second and third bouts by first-round knockouts, and the sports writers were calling me One-Round Krueger when I reached the semifinals against a crudely clever southpaw named Tony Peruzzi who got off the floor twice to drop me with a roundhouse left after a confusing shift just before the bell ended the first round.

"The guy won't stay down," I complained to Stanley in the corner.

"You will," he said grimly, "if you blunder into another like that. He'll try that again right away. Watch for it when he starts the shift and murder him with a right cross."

That strategy was successful, but my one-round record was gone. However, after I had showered and dressed, I was approached by a smiling little round man with a gray derby and black cigar, who said, "Congratulations, Krueger. With proper management and training you can go places, high places. I'm Abe Boston and I'm willing to give you a contract right now."

"Contract?" I asked.

"You want to turn pro, don't you?"

"No," I said, "I don't think I do. I haven't even won this tournament yet. And I don't think I want to be any professional prizefighter."

"Why get your brains knocked out for nothing when you can get rich and famous in a few years?"

Stanley Koviak cut in there. "George hasn't even shown that he's got any brains to be knocked out," he said. "All he's shown so far is a pretty good punch."

"That's what I'm interested in. You know who I am, don't you?"

I said, "Well, you said your name is Boston."

"I know who you are, all right," said Stanley.

"I've been manager of some top-notch boys—Spider Randolph, Tommy Cuscaden, Kid Gonzales—but I'm looking for a big boy with a wallop, that can be brought up. This Krueger is rangy enough now so he can grow into a bona-fide heavy. I'm aiming high—Li'l Arthuh, eventually—but first we bowl over some ham-and-eggers and then wade through those big fat elephants they call white hopes."

Stanley asked pointedly, "Where's Kid Gonzales now?"

Boston shrugged his shoulders. "Well, sure, that's why I want a strong, big boy. It's the frail little guys that go punchy."

"It's the big guys that take the hardest punches," Stanley said. "And I'm looking after Krueger. He's not turning pro unless I decide he's got a chance, and that's that."

Boston ignored him and handed me his card. "Think it over, boy," he said, "and come to my office and see me sometime. Maybe I'd even stake you to a living while you're training."

"Nothing doing, Boston," said Stanley. "This is *my* boy, so go on and peddle your papers."

My opponent in the finals would have seemed ludicrous if it hadn't been for the fact that he also had fought his way through the tournament. His name was Luther Coy, and while he must have been much younger, he looked to be forty. He was about five feet seven inches tall and appeared to be at least twenty pounds overweight with a roll of fat showing above his trunks. His arms were short and massive, but with no show of muscle.

"Watch this guy," Stanley told me in the ring. "He's got a killing left hook, but he can't be in any sort of condition. Box him. Keep away from him and wear him down. I'll be satisfied if we decision this old fellow."

Coy bowed politely to me when we were introduced in the ring and smiled slightly, and when we came out at the bell he was in a deep crouch with his thick, right forearm high. He advanced, slapping his left foot on the canvas, and I danced around him, feinting and jabbing but catching nothing but gloves, forearms or the top of his head. This was ridiculous. I had no target at all.

Suddenly Coy darted out of his shuffle, blocking my left lead, and slammed a combination into my body. One left hook on my chest had tremendous power and worried me, but at the end of the exchange I caught him with a right cross high on the head that sent him backward a couple of steps. To follow this advantage, I dashed forward, letting go with a right hand that should win me the light-heavyweight championship of the D.A.C. tournament. But it never landed. The left hook that sent me flat on my back felt as if I had been hit on the jaw by a fully swung baseball bat. I sat up immediately and through bleary eyes saw Luther Coy dancing in a corner with the roll of fat jiggling above his black trunks. The referee was standing over me, swinging his arm up and down—"two—three—four," and there was Doc Fitch's drawling voice, "X ray . . . old blood clot . . . one good punch . . . crippled or nuts." I shook my head and I was dizzy. The arm was going up and down—"six—seven—eight." I made no effort to get up from my sitting position until after the count of ten when people were in the ring and a voice bellowed, "Hi-ya, Pappy Coy!" And another yelled, "It's One-Round Krueger, all right."

Then I was on my feet and Stanley was leading me to my corner, saying bitterly, "I think you could have got up all right. I think you're just plain yellow."

"Stanley," I said, "you just don't understand. I should have got an X ray. A doctor told me that I probably got a blood clot in the brain from an old concussion and should get an X ray. But I didn't."

"Nuts," said Stanley. "You weren't anywhere near knocked out. I guess what they say about the Y.M.C.A. boys is true. They got no guts. The first time they get clipped they quit. I thought maybe you were tough and different, but I'm disgusted. You had the title on a silver platter, with a fat old man old enough to be your father. Why didn't you do what I told you and box him? Why'd you rush in that way like a fool and get tagged?"

"I thought I had him."

"Nuts. If you can't lick a little old fat man, you won't think about turning pro anyhow."

I said, "Well, I'll get an X ray and see if I've got a blood clot."

"Blood clot, my royal patootie. Get an X ray of your back and see how wide the yellow streak is."

"Well," I said, "if you won't believe me, there isn't much else I can say except that this Coy may be little and old and fat, but you got no idea how hard he can hit. I'm not sure he didn't break my jaw."

"Nuts again. If you had kept loose and boxed him instead of rushing in tight and tense, you'd have won the fight easy."

"Look, Stan," I said, "I'll get an X ray, and if I haven't got any blood clot, I'll enter again next year. Will you be in my corner if I do?"

Stanley Koviak looked down at the floor. "Maybe," he said.

During the tournament I had neither seen nor called Helga, so it was not a complete surprise when she seemed a little cool when I did telephone her at the osteopath's office. I asked if I was to see her that Saturday evening.

"Well," she said without a show of enthusiasm, "I guess so."

She answered my knock without smiling and bowed. "Good evening, Mr. Krueger," she said.

I grinned and when I started to kiss her she evaded me. I said, "How did you know about that?"

"How did I know? Well, I saw your pictures in the *Post*. Who else could they be?"

"Gosh," I said, "I didn't suppose you would read the sporting pages and I didn't think you would like me if you knew I was fighting and I didn't suppose anybody would recognize me from newspaper pictures unless they knew I was in the tournament."

"You didn't think I would like fighters? Well, I don't. But you think I like liars better?"

"What do you mean, liars?"

We were standing face to face just inside her front door and her green eyes were like arctic ice. "I mean why did you lie to me in the first place? Why didn't you tell me your name is George Krueger?"

"Because my name is *not* George Krueger. I just took that name to fight under because my mother doesn't like boxing and she wouldn't want people to know I was in the tournament."

"What is your real name then, or are you afraid to tell that?"

"You know my name."

"If your real name isn't George Krueger, how can I know? Do you ever tell me anything but lies? First you tell me your name is George Hotchkiss, which it is not, so how can I tell?"

"Who said I wasn't George Hotchkiss?"

"I did. And if you are not George Krueger, why should I care if your name is Jesse James or Henry B. Walthall? You lie all the time. Let me tell you, young man, should I? When I see pictures of One-Round Krueger in the paper, and it's surely my George Hotchkiss, why wouldn't I wonder? And you do not call. You say you live on Columbine Street with your mama and papa and they do not have a telephone. So why wouldn't I look in the city directory and see just one Hotchkiss living on Columbine Street? So why wouldn't I then look in the phone book and see this same Hotchkiss living on Columbine Street? So haven't you lied to me about not having a phone? So if you're not George Krueger fighting in a prizefight, but are really George Hotchkiss at home on Columbine Street studying your lesson on how to be an author instead of a plumber, and you lied to me so I wouldn't phone your home, wouldn't I be mad? Wouldn't I? Who do you think I am, an old whore or something?"

"My God, Helga," I said, "listen—"

"Haven't I listened to you too much already?" she interrupted. "Now isn't it the time for you to listen to me? So listen. At nine o'clock in the evening, when you are perhaps at home studying your lesson on how to become an author unless you are fighting another man with boxing gloves, I go to the drugstore phone booth and put in a nickel and call the number of Mr. Wallace Hotchkiss on Columbine Street, and when a man answers I ask if I can speak to George? And the man says, 'I'm sorry, you must have the wrong number, there's no George here.' And I ask doesn't George Hotchkiss live there? And he says, 'My name's Wallace Hotchkiss, but I don't know any George Hotchkiss.' And I say, 'You haven't got a son named George Hotchkiss?' And he says, 'Not that I ever heard of,' and laughs and then says, 'I have a son named James Barton Hotchkiss, but he's in San Francisco. I don't believe I ever heard of a George Hotchkiss in my life.' So I say, 'Thank you, sir, I'm sorry to have bothered you.' And he says, 'Lady, if someone told you his name is George Hotchkiss and that he lives here, I hope you didn't buy anything he has to sell or lend him any money.' So now, Mr. George non-Hotchkiss and Mr. George non-Krueger, I don't care whether you say your real name is George Washington, which it isn't because George Washington wasn't any liar. And isn't the only reason you lied to me about your name was because you were ashamed to be coming to see an old woman like me? Isn't it?"

"No, Helga," I protested, "it wasn't that at all."

"And now aren't you trying to think up another lie? Aren't you? Well, I can tell you right now that I am ashamed of thinking one time I was in love with a sneaking little liar so I just say good-bye to bad rubbish. Shoo!"

There didn't seem to be anything more for me to say so I bowed politely and said, "Good-bye, Mrs. Johnson." And I walked all the way back to the Y.M.C.A., feeling very miserable indeed.

Chapter 23

FORTUNATELY Jake did not feel I had disgraced the honest name of Krueger. He had attended every bout, cheering me on, and he declared my first round "knockout" in the finals was "just one of them accidents that can happen to anybody."

To Doc Fitch, however, I confessed that I could have risen after the knockdown and why I did not do it.

He grunted. "Well," he drawled, "I've heard about people getting some sense beaten into them, but this is about the first case I ever knew about. Of course it came a little late. If you'd had any sense, you never would have entered the tournament, especially without getting an X ray first. Of course the X ray probably would show you're all right, and if you'd got it you'd probably have bounced up and licked this Coy and won the title and then turned professional pugilist and really got your brain addled. Now maybe you'll forget this nonsense and become an artist."

"How?" I asked.

"I don't know, but you ought to be able to find out. Maybe save up your money and go to New York. You want to draw illustrations for magazines, don't you?"

"Sure. I guess so."

"Well, New York is where the magazines are."

"I don't know," I said. "I don't think I'd like living in a place like New York, and besides, I think I want to enter the tournament next year and redeem myself."

"Good *night!*" said Doc and got up and left my room.

I didn't know how to explain to Fitch the exquisite reality I found in boxing. Confronted by an opponent even in the gymnasium, I must concentrate on a reality that was the complete antithesis to the unhappy apathy of wonder. A boxer might be an egoist and probably was an egotist, but never a solipsist while working at his trade. It was far better, even, than cleaning chimneys or repairing furnaces as a means of escape from the eternal "why." It was not, as the uninitiated hold, just two brutes trying to beat each other to death. Well, not *entirely* that. In boxing, I did not want to injure my opponent seriously and I did not particularly enjoy being struck on the nose, but it was the quintessence of competition where you suffered physically for your mistakes and triumphed through your skill, ingenuity, animal strength and agility. To me, boxing seemed to be the most exciting competition that could be devised, supplanting the awful, imponderable fears of the unknowable with the insignificant fears of the flesh. The insignificant fears of the flesh, through familiarity, could be conquered, bringing new strength through the victory, a strength that could allow me to repel the horrors that hovered malignly at all times in the shadows of my being. In short, boxing was real. And reality was mental health.

As to art, my ambitions and ideas were extremely vague. To the best of my knowledge, the great contemporary artists of America were such magazine illustrators and decorators as A. B. Frost, Frederic Remington, N. C. Wyeth, Harvey T. Dunn, F. R. Gruger, Henry Raleigh, Franklin Booth, Maxfield Parrish, J. C. Leyendecker, James Montgomery Flagg and Charles Dana Gibson. The revolutionary Armory Show was yet to come in New York. I never had heard of John Sloan or Robert Henri or George Bellows. Cézanne, Renoir, Gauguin, Degas and Van Gogh were not even names to me. And I should have been even more scornful than were the Paris galleries of the work being done by a Spaniard named Pablo Picasso and a Frenchman named Georges Braque if I had seen it. Of course I knew about such old masters as Michelangelo, Leonardo, Rembrandt, Vermeer, Hals and Titian, from magazine prints, and I thought they were all right if you liked that sort of thing. It was a matter of personal taste, of course, but I really preferred the paintings of Western scenes and Indians and cowboys by Paul Gregg and Clarence Ellsworth, reproduced in color each week on the covers of the Denver *Post* and *Rocky Mountain News* Sunday magazines.

I, together with practically everyone else, was ignorant of a great many things developing in fertile brains all over the world, which would eventually transform the world materially and in thought. In laboratories, universities, parliaments, palaces, hovels, blacksmith shops, newspaper offices, studios, army barracks, back bedrooms, high schools, ship forecastles, a few pulpits, farmhouses, sidewalk cafés, wilderness outposts, everywhere, ideas were churning and developing in human brains, being discussed with other humans, discarded or elaborated, and these ideas, through Fate or genius or both, would profoundly affect me personally and every other person on earth as well as billions yet unborn.

The Renaissance and the Industrial Revolution were almost minor social unheavals compared with the seething unrest and spirit of innovation that, step by step, seemed to involve every facet of human activity and thought the world over. Quite oblivious to the mighty forces at work, I went blandly on with my chimney sweeping, reading, drawing; wondering who ever could whip Jack Johnson; wondering if the New York Giants could win the National League pennant again; horrified when the unsinkable *Titanic* struck an iceberg and took more than fifteen hundred to the bottom of the Atlantic; interested, but, as a prenatal Democrat, pleased when Theodore Roosevelt bolted the Republican national convention and formed his own party; clinging with increased confidence to my sense of reality; still mooning somewhat over the delectable Marcella Upjohn, with a two-column picture of her beautiful face clipped from a society page in my dresser drawer, the announcement of her engagement to Courtney MacGregor cut away. In that connection, Laura told me in *strictest* confidence one Sunday that Major Upjohn had taken out a second mortgage on their house, with Ralph, to finance a swank wedding for Marcella, but—and Laura found this very funny—the Reverend Mr. Hamilton would not marry a divorced man and they'd have to get a Unitarian minister or a justice of the peace or someone like that. In those circumstances, it seemed to me, there was a faint possibility that Marcella might see the light and call the whole thing off.

Laura, however, was either misinformed or the Reverend Mr. Hamilton changed his mind because Marcella Upjohn became the bride of Courtney MacGregor in our church with the Reverend Mr. Hamilton officiating. Laura pretended annoyance at receiving an invitation, but I suspected she would have been more annoyed if she had *not* received one. The annoyance seemed to center on the necessity of buying a gift; and if the Sterlings gave anything at all it would have to be something fairly expensive just to preserve the Sterling status.

Naturally, I was not invited, but I read all about the wedding and the reception and the happy couple departing for Europe on their honeymoon, in all of the society sections. I did *not* save any clippings.

Speaking of the Sterling status, it had been increased mightily. Ralph's Uncle Benjamin died, and, after several weeks on tenterhooks for Laura and Ralph, the board of directors elected Ralph president of the bank. So, at the time of the Upjohn-MacGregor wedding my sister and brother-in-law were poring excitedly over plans for the home they were to build on Montview Boulevard. It was to be on a large corner lot, a house worthy of any bank president.

To me, a more important change than Ralph Sterling's good fortune was announced one noon when Jake Krueger and I were parked in an alley, eating the lunches Lena Krueger had put up for us. Jake had had little to say and was looking off into space as he took a huge bite of sandwich. He chewed away sadly and then said, "George, I'm raising your pay to twenty dollars a week including this week."

"Wonderful," I said. "Thank you, Jake."

"I'm doing this now to be sure that you get proper pay, on account you're going to have to work a little harder for a while."

"How do you mean?"

"Well, George, the old woman and Gretchen and I are going to move to California. Lena's brother Adolf has got what they call an orange and lemon ranch near a place called Pasadena, and he's doing fine and the place next to him is for sale at a good price and it's an easy life out there where they don't have any winter and it probably would be good for Gretchen, and I'm getting a little old for this here business any more so I'm having Adolf buy that orange orchard for me and we're moving out."

"Gosh," I said and tried to puzzle out the implications. "Look, Jake," I finally stammered, "I don't know quite what to say. I guess that might be a good thing for you, but what about me? You don't expect me to run this business all by myself and then send you all the money except twenty dollars a week, do you?"

"No, George. No, no. As a matter of fact, I've sold the business to Carl Francis. You know him."

I gasped and then said, "Well, sure I know him. He's a plumber, but he doesn't know this business does he?"

"No, not *all* about it. But he's a smart guy and it won't take him long to learn. That's what I mean about you going to have to work harder for a while. You'll have to kind of learn him the business."

"Hell's bells, Jake, I don't think much of that deal. With you it was all right, but I don't think much of doing practically all the work and teaching him the business for even twenty dollars a week when he'll be averaging maybe forty dollars a day."

"That's not all clear profit, you know," said Jake mildly.

"Enough of it's profit. What I can't see, Jake, if you wanted to sell out, why in hell didn't you tell me and give me a chance to buy the business?"

"To tell the truth," he said, "I never even thought of such a thing. I never even considered you had the money, for one thing."

"It sure enough wouldn't take much money," I asserted. "All you've got is Teddy, and he's getting pretty old, and this wagon and the stuff in it."

Jake shook his head. "That stuff isn't important," he said. "I've been in this business here a long time and the valuable part of the business is what they call goodwill and all my regular customers."

"What," I demanded, "did Carl Francis pay you for all the goodwill and Teddy and the wagon?"

"Fifteen hundred dollars, and don't tell me you could have raised that much money."

"Maybe not," I admitted, "but I could have paid you about two hundred and fifty and paid the rest out of the profits."

"Well, I'm sorry," said Jake, "but I really wanted the cash so I could get this orange ranch running, and besides, you're not of age and it'd be against the law for you to make a business deal like that. You'd have to have a legal guardian."

"My mother's my legal guardian and she could have signed with me. Jake, you've been fine with me all along and I do appreciate it, but I sure enough think you've let me down now. You know what I think? Well, I think what you're selling along with that goodwill and Teddy and the wagon is *me*."

"Now, George."

"Yes, now George. You're selling me to Carl Francis like a slave, and you can't do it, because Abe Lincoln freed the slaves a long time ago. You can't do it because, by God, I ain't for sale."

Jake shook his head and put a half-eaten sandwich back in his dinner pail. "George," he said, "you've took my appetite. You really have. Do you mean you're going to leave me in the lurch and quit your job? You know I've always tried to treat you right, don't you?"

[261]

"Sure," I said, "I know and I thank you for it. But you also know I always worked as hard as I could for you and on a lot of jobs did practically all the work. The thing that gets me is that you probably told Carl Francis that I went with the business and never asked me whether I'd want to work for him."

"I told him nobody ever had a better helper than you, but I sure didn't promise him anything about how long you'd work for him."

"As near as I can make out," I said, "he's going to be *my* helper but take most of the loot. And if I was going to hire a helper myself, I know I could find somebody better than a man who must be forty years old."

"Now look, kid," he said, "please don't get on your high horse. You're very young and you wouldn't know how to run a business."

"For heaven's sake, I know how to add and subtract and how to answer a phone and I can tell you something you do that I wouldn't do if I were running the business. I wouldn't be paying retail prices to Lambert for furnace parts. I'd get 'em from a wholesaler the same as he does."

For the first time during the conversation Jake grinned. "That's one of the things, and you don't know what you're talking about. Part of the deal with Lambert for my desk space and having somebody answer the phone for me is that I buy my furnace parts from him and he gives me a cut rate, not retail, and I can always make up the difference by what I charge the customer. See?"

"Okay," I said. "Then maybe I'll buy me a horse and wagon, or better, a second-hand Ford and go into competition with Francis, advertising speedy service and reduced rates. And I'd buy wholesale."

"You wouldn't do that to me, George."

"It wouldn't be doing it to *you*. It'd be competing with Francis and there's no law against it."

Jake shut up his dinner pail, but I continued eating my lunch. He turned on the wagon seat and looked at me closely. "George," he said finally, "as an old friend do me a favor, will you?"

"Probably," I said, "but it all depends."

"You've been doing all right, haven't you?"

"Sure. Up to now."

"If there's another kid your age in Denver making twenty bucks a week, I'll bet he's working for his father. I didn't have to keep raising your pay. You look around and you'll find that any boy your age even doing mean, rough work like this is doing pretty good if he gets twelve dollars a week."

"That may be so, I don't know."

"All right, George, I've been favoring you and I want to ask a favor in return. Promise me that you'll work for Carl at least until he learns the ropes."

"Well," I said, "if you put it like that, and out of friendship to you and Mrs. Krueger and Gretchen, I'll promise. How long do you think that will take?"

"Oh, I don't know exactly. I'd say three or four weeks."

"All right. But I'm going to ask him for a day off now and then."

"You're not going to try to start a business of your own?"

"Well, I could, but I don't think I will. As a matter of fact, Jake, I've been wanting to get into art work one way or the other for a long time. I probably would have tried to get an artist job before this, but I didn't want to let you down."

"Do they have jobs where artists just draw pictures?"

"Of course. On newspapers, magazines, in advertising offices."

"Would they pay an artist twenty dollars a week?"

"Maybe not right to start, but some artists back East get rich, and I'd guess that Paul Gregg on the *Post* and Clarence Ellsworth on the *News* make twice that or even more."

"Hmm. I wouldn't think you'd like sitting down at a table drawing pictures all day."

"I like to draw pictures," I said. I held up my scratched and scabbed hands. "And besides, it'd be a lot easier on your hands."

Jake chuckled. "If that's what you want," he said. "Then maybe you could go to one of those gals in the barbershops and get your fingernails fixed up real pretty. But now we got a job of work waiting for us."

He got down from the wagon and took the oat bag off Teddy's nose. Then he looked up at me and said, "If that's what you want."

Jake had intended to stay on the job with Carl Francis a few days, but Francis was tied up with his plumbing work until the Krueger's furniture was shipped West, and they had only two or three evenings together going over the books.

Carl and Minnie Francis, as well as Mr. and Mrs. Chester Lambert, were at the Union Station to see the Kruegers off. The Kruegers were taking a night train and traveling in style, not only in a Pullman, but, because of Gretchen, in a drawing room. There was confusion and excitement and some worry about the wheel chair, but the Pullman conductor and porter took charge of that and Jake carried his daughter into the car— a real task even for a man of his strength. They all promised to write to all of us and we all promised to write to them and there were shrill wishes of good luck and some kissing and the Kruegers were gone.

I said to my new employer, "Well, Mr. Francis, I'll see you in the morning."

"Sure, George," he said. "But don't mister me. Call me Carl."

Carl was a little late but jolly about it the next morning. We set off on the first chimney-cleaning job with me on the right driving old Teddy, and as soon as we reached a residential district Carl's tenor voice broke into the old ditty. "Oh, you don't know Nellie like I do, said the sassy little bird on Nellie's hat."

When we reached our customer's house, I dropped the hitching weight, and, as Carl showed no inclination to take the initiative, I went to the back door to be admitted and inspect possible flue stops and the basement. On my return, Carl was leaning against the wagon, smoking a Bull Durham cigarette.

"Well," I said, "it's okay to go to work." I lifted out a ladder and placed it against the eaves on one side of the house. Then I took the weighted and corseted burlap bag and rope from the wagon and carefully explained to Carl the method of operation.

"You want to take it easy," I said. "Let it down slowly and bring it up slowly, and if the corset doesn't reach both sides of a big flue, it takes a little longer. You've got to get the sack oscillating so it catches one side and then the other."

"You got to have the sack what?"

"Oscillating—swinging from one side to the other, and that's kind of tricky until you get used to it."

"I see."

I noted that he was wearing heavy work shoes instead of

sneakers, and said, "Look, Carl, you want to watch your step up there. You should wear rubber-soled shoes so you won't slip."

He guffawed. "Whatever makes you think *I'm* going up there?"

"Well," I said, "I thought you wanted to learn the business."

"I'll learn it from the ground. That's *your* job going up on roofs."

"Suppose sometime I'm not here?"

"Then I'll get another kid. I haven't lost anything up on anybody's roof."

"Okay," I said, "but I'd think you'd want to learn how it's done so you could tell somebody else."

"Don't you worry about me. It don't take any college graduate to let a loaded sack down a chimney."

"Have it your own way. You're the boss."

I went up the ladder and cleaned the two chimneys. Then I came down, knocked the soot off the sack and corset into the street, and stowed them and the rope away in the wagon. Then I got the bucket and fire shovel and brushes and broom, put them into the washtub, and Carl, who was rolling another cigarette, said, "What you going to do now?"

I said, "Well, you can't just let the soot stay clogging up the bottoms of the chimneys. I'm going into the basement and clean it out."

He followed me down and stood to one side to avoid flying soot while I shoveled out the two flues and cleaned the furnace smoke pipe and put the pipe back and swept up the cement floor. He didn't offer to help, even when I was putting the pipe back, and I was growing more and more annoyed.

When I had finished he said, "So that's all there is to it."

"Yep," I said, "all but carrying out the soot and dumping it in the ashpit. Easy job for a boss who doesn't want to get his hands dirty."

"Easy job for anybody," he asserted. "Can't understand why Jake would be paying you twenty bucks a week for just that. You must have known where the body was buried."

"Jake worked himself, and he knew it isn't easy as maybe it looks, especially when you're repairing old furnaces. Now,

[265]

maybe while I'm carrying out the soot you'll want to go collect from the lady. It'll be eight dollars for the two chimneys. Or, if you want, I'll do that too."

"No, thank you," Carl said, "I'll do the collecting."

Because we had started late and I had no help, we did only one more job, a one-chimney cottage, before noon. Carl had brought no dinner pails, not for himself and not for me, and when I had finished the second house he looked at his watch and said, "Well, I'm ready for grub. There's a hash house back there on Cherokee. Better turn around and we'll see what they got to eat."

"Well," I said, "that's all right for you, but I'm pretty dirty. They might not even let me in."

He looked at me and chuckled. "You *are* pretty filthy at that. What you usually do at noon?"

"Mrs. Krueger," I said, "always put up two fine lunches in dinner pails, one for Jake and one for me."

Carl whistled. "You mean old Jake paid you twenty dollars a week *plus* lunch every day? How simple can a man get?"

"Look," I said. "I promised Jake I would stay with you at least as long as it took you to learn the business. But if you're not satisfied with me, that doesn't keep you from firing me any time you want."

"Steady there, boy, steady. I'm not about to fire you. And maybe they got a can in that Cherokee joint where you can scrape a little of the crap off your hands and face."

There was indeed a foul washroom in the little restaurant where I managed to clean up enough to be acceptable as a counter customer. Carl was half through a platter of liver and onions by the time I got back and I ordered pork and beans which took no preparing.

Each day I grew more dissatisfied with the situation. The most that Carl Francis ever offered to help was to hold a flashlight in a furnace fire door while I, in the ash hole, struggled with warped grates. Although I had promised Jake Krueger that I would stay with Carl until he learned the business, Carl was making no attempt to learn. The situation seemed hopeless. I didn't see how he ever could operate with an inexperienced helper. But should my promise hold me more than two or three weeks? I decided that at the end of three weeks I should quit and try to get a job as a newspaper artist.

Carl, however, relieved me of the necessity of waiting even that long. At the end of the week he spoke solemnly, "George, this ain't working out exactly the way Jake said. I haven't taken in as much money this week as he said he did and as his books tried to make out."

"We haven't done as many jobs," I said stiffly. "After all, Jake worked himself. He knew just what to do on every job and he did it."

"Well," said Carl, "I'm not accusing you of really loafing on me, but the fact is we ain't took in more than two-thirds what we should, and it's ridiculous paying a kid like you any twenty bucks a week for what you do."

"Okay," I said, "fire me."

"No, I ain't going to fire you. I'm paying you twenty bucks this week like I agreed, but next week it's going to be fifteen, take it or leave it, because it's goddamn nonsense paying a kid like you any twenty dollars a week for the kind of work you do and I can hire all the helpers I want for ten or twelve dollars a week and you ought to know it."

"Go ahead and hire 'em," I said. "The agreement was that I get twenty dollars a week. If you don't want to pay it, that relieves me of the promise I made Jake. Good luck to you and, mister, you're going to need it."

"You mean you're quitting?"

"I'm certainly not taking any five dollars a week cut in pay. As far as I'm concerned, it's twenty or nothing."

"Look, boy, why don't you try to use your head? You ought to know you can't get fifteen dollars a week any other place for anything you can do. Think about it over Sunday and you can come to work Monday with no hard feelings. More than that, I can't advertise for a new helper before Monday. You go out and look for a job Monday and when you find out the situation, come to Lambert's Tuesday morning and I'll give you first choice over the other kids at fifteen instead of the ten I'm going to offer."

"That's very kind of you, Carl," I said, "but don't hold your breath until I show up."

Monday I made up a portfolio of pen-and-ink caricatures of public figures from the worlds of politics, sports and the movies, as well as cartoons. I didn't know exactly how to apply for a job as newspaper artist, but decided to call on my local heroes, Paul Gregg and Clarence Ellsworth, and ask their advice. Because Ellsworth was on the smaller newspaper, the *Rocky Mountain News,* I thought he might be less imperious over his lordly status, and I telephoned him, expressing my long admiration for his work and asking for an audience.

He seemed hesitant. "Well," he said, "if you want to see me, sure. I'm busy right now. Why don't you come around four thirty?"

The telephone operator directed me through the noisy local room to the art department in the rear, and I found Clarence Ellsworth to be a small, shy young man obviously embarrassed by my adulation. But he grinned at some of my drawings and said, "Well, you've really got something there, but have you had any newspaper experience? Can you make layouts?"

"Layouts?"

"Sure. Layouts of photographs. That's the biggest part of a newspaper artist's work. Look . . ."

He took me to another artist's desk where a young man was assembling four photographic prints on a large piece of white cardboard. "Oley Hansen here will cut the pictures to make the sort of layout he thinks is best and paste the pictures down with rubber cement in size for half reduction to fit column measure and maybe draw a little border and sometimes a little decoration or sketch. It isn't hard to learn."

"What do you mean, Michelangelo, it isn't hard to learn?" Hansen blurted.

"Well, it really isn't," Ellsworth insisted, "but it's something all newspaper artists have to do except perhaps the big, famous cartoonists in New York and Chicago."

"How can I go about learning?" I asked.

Ellsworth shook his head and smiled at me in a kindly way. "I really don't know, unless you can get a newspaper job. I like your drawings and you've got a fine professional touch with the caricatures, but there certainly isn't any opening now on the *News.* Of course Mr. Chapman does all the hiring, but there isn't much use seeing him now."

The artist Hansen had pasted down his photographs on the cardboard and was flattening them with a rubber roller. "What about the *Journal?*" he asked. "Steinberg just went to Chicago."

Ellsworth nodded. "That's an idea," he said. "Why don't

you go see Joe Crowder on the *Journal* and tell him I said you're his cartoonist?"

"Wonderful," I said. "You're very kind, Mr. Ellsworth."

"Wait a minute," he said, "I'll phone Joe. He's city editor and does the hiring for the art department too. Tough guy and some people don't like him, but he knows his business."

Ellsworth lifted the phone, asked for outside and called a number.

Hansen observed, "Joe Crowder knows his business because he's been trying to hire Clarence. But Clarence wouldn't leave the old homestead for any money. He was raised here."

"Hello, Joe." Ellsworth was standing and I noticed that the seat of his blue serge trousers was shiny. "Fine, Joe . . . how are you? . . . No, not yet . . . Well, you know how it is. Look, Joe . . ." He glanced down at my drawings on his desk. "I'm sending a young man named Chalmers over to see you. With Steiny gone he may be what you're looking for. He's got something . . . No, no experience, but . . . Well, you look at his stuff . . . I don't know . . . Well you look at 'em . . . Okay, he'll be right over. Bye."

Ellsworth grinned at me. "You beat it right over to the *Journal* and see Joe. There's an outside chance that he might give you a try."

I thanked my little hero and Hansen, went to the *Journal,* and was directed to the city desk where one burly, black-mustached young man in a green eyeshade was jabbing viciously at typewritten pages with a heavy black pencil and across from him a small, middle-aged man with a round hat on the back of his head growled into a telephone.

The burly man looked up at me and said, "Yeah?"

"Mr. Crowder?" I asked.

He pointed across the desk. "Anything I can do for you?"

"Well," I said, "I wanted to see Mr. Crowder."

He returned to his editing and Mr. Crowder said into the telephone, "Goddamn it, Tommy, you know better than that. Now you get on the ball."

He slammed up the receiver and looked up. "Mr. Crowder," I said, "Clarence Ellsworth suggested—"

"Okay, let's see what you got."

I opened my portfolio on his desk while he lit a cigarette, and he squinted through the smoke at the top drawings. Lately

I had developed a style of strong contrasts, crosshatching heavily, sometimes using a sable brush on emphasized lines or shadows. I knew this was faking to some extent, but I thought it
effective.

Mr. Crowder's face was impassive, but he breathed an ambiguous "hmm" as he turned over the first two pictures. Then
he came to a caricature drawn from a photograph of handsome
F. G. Bonfils, publisher of the Denver *Post,* and he laughed.

"Look at this one, Smitty," he said to the burly young man.

The young man leaned over the desk, laughed with his boss
and said, "Wonderful. He's revealed Bon's noble soul."

A slight, pink-haired man with rimless nose glasses was attracted to the desk and chuckled at the caricature. Then he exclaimed, "Hey!" at the next one, which was a full-length drawing of champion Jack Johnson in a fighting pose with exaggerated loose-jointed, muscular build, gigantic feet and toothy
grin.

"I want that," he said. "Are you selling these or—"

"Well," I said, "I guess I'm trying to sell myself."

He looked at me closely and shook a handful of galley
proofs at me.

"Don't I know you?" he asked. "Your name is—"

"George Chalmers."

"No—that wasn't it. I've got it, weren't you in the D.A.C.
boxing tournament? Or you've got a double."

I wasn't too comfortable over this but I said, "Well, as a matter of fact, I was, but I didn't use my own name."

"What was it you used?"

"Krueger," I said, "George Krueger. Well, as a matter of
fact, I didn't want my mother to know I was fighting so—"

"I remember you. I remember you well. Light-heavy and
going like a house afire until old Pappy Coy got to you in the
finals—the way he's got to so many promising kids."

He took hold of my arm. "You know, I picked you after your
first bout with Danny Farley and I bet on you. I said, 'There's
a lad who's going places.' And here you turn out to be an artist.
If we'd known that we could have made something of it. I hope
you're not discouraged because—"

"Goddamn it, Red," Mr. Crowder interrupted, "this fellow
is here looking for a job and you may have time to waste but I
haven't."

"Go ahead and hire him. We need somebody like this."

"On the sports-department budget?" Mr. Crowder asked sarcastically.

"You know I've got no budget to hire artists, but look at this." He held up a lantern-jawed Woodrow Wilson in a gleaming silk hat.

"And," said the city editor, "I've got no budget to hire pugilist bodyguards for skinny sporting editors."

The city editor looked at Woodrow Wilson and several others and then asked, "How are you on layouts?"

"I'm sorry," I said, "I haven't had much experience with layouts, but I know I can learn quickly."

"How much pay would you expect?"

"Well, sir," I said, "I've been making twenty a week, but—"

"Better stick to your job then. All I can give you is twelve dollars to start."

I took a deep breath. "I guess," I said, "that I could get along on that—for a while."

Joe Crowder closed my portfolio and handed it to me. "Okay. Come to work at one P.M. tomorrow." He pushed a heavy pencil at me. "Write your real name and address here. Red, you've got nothing else to do. Take this young fellow back to the art department and introduce him. This, Mr. Chalmers, is Red Haig, the famous sporting editor."

"Sports editor," said Haig.

Joe Crowder was back in his swivel chair, bent over a stack of copy. "I prefer sporting editor for you," he said.

Red Haig shook hands with me and I told him I had read his column for years and was honored to be working with him.

"We'll get along fine," he said. "And now that you're on the staff, I'd like to have that picture of Jack Johnson."

"Sure," I said, starting to open the portfolio.

"Come on in the sports department first," he urged, and ushered me through a door to introduce me to a teen-age youth named Charley Christian and a middle-aged giant called Tiny Webb.

"Mr. Chalmers is our new artist," he said, "but he fights under the name of Krueger. You remember him, Tiny, at the D.A.C."

"Oh sure, sure," said Webb. "I remember him."

I produced the Jack Johnson picture, which they admired

and which Haig stuck on the wall with a thumbtack. "I'll be using that one of these days," he said, "when something comes up about Johnson."

"How'd you like to take on that fellow?" Webb asked.

"Not me," I said. "I'm an amateur—and I didn't come out so well at that."

"Sit down for a moment," said Haig.

I sat down, but was wondering about meeting the art department.

Haig sprawled before his desk, took off his glasses and polished them with a white handkerchief. "You couldn't have done better," he insisted, "until you ran into that sneaky left hook of Pappy Coy's. You should have been warned about that."

"Well, I was," I said. "Stanley Koviak warned me, but I guess I was too cockey."

"Will you try it again?" Webb asked.

"Maybe."

"Ever think about turning pro?" Haig asked.

"Not much," I said. "Man named Boston made me an offer just before I met Coy."

"Oh, boy," said Haig, leaning back in his swivel chair. "He would, and he's bad medicine."

"That's what Stan Koviak told me."

"Has Koviak got any contract with you—any signed contract?"

"No," I said. "We're just friends and he's taught me what little I know."

Haig grinned. "Well, if you put on some weight so you're a real heavy, I might be interested in you myself. I surely liked the way you moved and the authority you've got in your dukes. The way you move in reminded me a lot of a skinny-legged black Irish kid up in Cripple Creek and Victor. He didn't know much and was right-hand crazy, but he was a tiger and I thought he could go to the top if he had the right training and learned to use his left. Kind of a tramp kid and I haven't heard anything about him in a long time. Probably turned honest and got a job."

"Yeah," said Tiny Webb. "I knew him well. He had a lot of possibilities but never learned anything as far as I know. Somebody overmatched him with Fireman Jim Flynn and the kid was kayoed in the first round. Probably took the heart out of him."

"What the hell was that kid's name?" Haig asked.

"Dempsey," said Webb. "There were two of them up there —brothers. They were from down Manassa way. Jack was the oldest and biggest and he was fighting all around the Western Slope, then the kid brother Bill tried it, and when Jack quit fighting Bill took over the name Jack to take advantage of his brother's reputation. They called Bill Little Jack for a while. I think he might have gone places if he'd got the training and the right managing. Kind of skinny, but he might have grown into a heavyweight if somebody fed him regularly. He had a killing right hand, and like you say, fought like a tiger."

Haig nodded at me. "This boy's much like that, and he's got a fair left hook already. But there's a pretty good chance he's got a glass jaw, too, remembering how Pappy Coy cut him down."

The sports editor looked at me and laughed in a friendly fashion. I could have told him that I didn't have a glass jaw and that I really had quit cold, but I decided that wasn't necessary.

"Yeah," said Webb, "considering that one-round knockout by Jim Flynn, a glass jaw may have been what kept young Dempsey from getting anywhere. Flynn never was a killing puncher."

Then Haig took me to the art department and introduced me to portly, snuff-chewing Jerry Carruthers, the soft-spoken, kindly head of the department, and dark, impassive Timmy Rogers, part Cherokee and addicted to occasional bouts with firewater, who were to be my friends and associates for a long time to come. The other member of the *Journal* art department, Miss Dorothy Sumner, worked days and had gone home.

Chapter 24

UNDER the patient tutelage of Jerry Carruthers, I soon learned to make passable photo layouts and became an accredited professional newspaper *artist*. My mother was delighted. Laura was astonished. Ralph had no comment except that I was trying to advance the cause of Socialism by working for the morning *Journal*. As a matter of fact, the *Journal* was Democratic in politics and had supported Woodrow Wilson whose platform was far less socialistic than that of Theodore Roosevelt's Bull Moose party.

As far as I know, Ralph never protested the frequency of my Sunday visits to the Sterling home. But he was remarkably adept at looking through me, talking through me, and ignoring my conversational contributions at dinner. I don't even know whether my mother and Laura noticed his attitude. I had come to take it for granted.

In the *Journal* editorial department, I was accepted as a member of the human race almost immediately. Newspaper people are notoriously democratic. Even the venerable and erudite Isaac Warner, chief of the editorial page, who analyzed politics, economics, druid mysticism, lessons-to-be-learned-from-the-ancient-Greeks-and-early-Romans, astronomy, the curse of internal-combustion engines, Henry David Thoreau, Thomas Jefferson, the psychology of crime and the wonders of the Rocky Mountain West, in beautiful English for our readers, deigned to sit in the same booth with me at dinner, with no show of arrogance or superiority, and even to laugh at some of my jokes.

My first success came, however, with the sports department. Red Haig would take me to the professional fights held every week or two in the Stockyards Stadium where I made caricature sketches of the action. These brought me compliments not only from the sports staff but from Jerry Carruthers, City Editor Joe Crowder and various reporters. It also spread the word around the local room that I knew very well what I was drawing and how, and it caused our pert, green-eyed girl artist Dorothy Sumner to attach the appellation "Thug" to me. The name caught on and presently I heard myself referred to as Thug Chalmers right and left. I was unhappy about that because I knew it would hurt my mother deeply if she ever heard the term or knew that I had a local reputation as a fighter. But there was nothing I could do except ignore it.

In those days photographers were not allowed in courtrooms during trials, so, because of my success with action sketches at the Stockyards Stadium, Joe Crowder sent me to the old West Side Court to make character sketches at a murder trial where all principals were prominent socially. In a smart uptown barroom a supposed gentleman had made an uncomplimentary remark about a beautiful social leader with whom he had once been friendly. Not taking into account the fact that five cocktails might be talking instead of the supposed gentleman, the lady's current lover promptly knocked him down. So the gentleman-turned-cad, on the floor, drew his revolver and fired at his assailant, killing, as Fate would have it, the lady's husband who was sitting quietly and moodily at a table at the far end of the room.

The *Journal's* appeal was not primarily to the upper classes and it was not highly impressed with what it called Denver's "washtub aristocracy." Finding humor in a murder trial probably is in questionable taste, but I started writing short, ironical pieces to go with my daily courtroom sketches. If I was prompted by jealousy because the former Marcella Upjohn as Mrs. Courtney MacGregor now was a member of the set represented by the principals in court, I was not conscious of it. However, my sketches, both written and drawn (after editing by Roy Smith) attracted attention and brought an offer from the Denver *Post* which I declined even before using the offer to blackjack a raise in pay from Joe Crowder.

It was after this that I felt real success had come to me, and life was practically ecstatic. I had friends, fascinating young men whose cynical knowledge of the world was bewildering to me, but they treated me as an equal. In the old Press Club in the Denham building I became friends with supposedly bitter rivals on opposition newspapers. I played pool with them, learned to drink hard liquor with them, lost money playing poker with them, and listened in some awe to their discussions of various sons of bitches in high positions in the worlds of government, business, the arts, sports and religion.

There were girls too. Not in the Press Club, which was strictly stag and limited in membership to working members of editorial departments and alumni, but there were girls whom I met on our staff as well as in other editorial and business offices.

It was all slightly Bohemian and wonderful, and, from being something of a loner, I became practically gregarious. I worked from 1 P.M. until about 11 P.M. ordinarily, but there are things to do at midnight and after if you don't need much sleep. Because the *Journal* had no Sunday issue, most of us had Saturday night off and Saturday night is traditionally Saturday night. If I dozed slightly sometimes during one of the Reverend Mr. Hamilton's Sunday morning sermons, I didn't seem to have missed much when the Sterlings and my mother discussed it at dinner.

Despite this moderate amount of dissipation, however, I worked hard and drew cartoons aimed at the editorial page on my own time in my room every now and then. Ike Warner used perhaps one-third of those I submitted, and in the course of my first year, two of these were reproduced in *Literary Digest*. I displayed these proudly at the Sterlings' and even Ralph seemed impressed.

I heard from Doc Fitch. He had finally got his medical degree and a commission in the Navy to serve his internship. He wrote me from Brazil that the sea was a cruel mistress—that the mere rattle of an anchor chain made him seasick.

The pattern of my Saturday nights changed after I wrote a piece and drew sketches about a Weber and Fields comedy called "Hanky-Panky" and the manager of the Broadway Theater phoned me and enthusiastically told me I could have a pair of complimentary tickets to any play I cared to attend. "Just phone me in advance," he said, "in case there may be a sellout." Discovering that I was equally welcome at the Tabor Grand and the Denham, I became a habitual Saturday night playgoer, basking in the ultrareality of Thespian make-believe.

I took my mother first, but unfortunately the play turned out to be a Cosmo Hamilton bedroom comedy, and after the first act she turned to me and said gravely, "George, we'd better go."

"Why, Mama," I said, "it's all right. It's just good, clean fun."

"It's not clean," she retorted, "and it's not fun and I'm ashamed to be seen here." So we went home.

I took Dorothy Sumner to *The Roundup* with Maclyn Arbuckle. It was exciting and deafening, with an attack by Indians in brown union suits and a rescue by the U. S. Army, blasting away not only with Civil War Springfields but with a real Gatling gun. Mr. Arbuckle, the fat, heroic and wistful sheriff, lost the girl to the handsome young juvenile and was alone on the darkened stage in the final scene. He was sitting silently and sadly before an electric campfire, leaning against his saddle. Presently he drew out a sack of tobacco and rolled a cigarette with one hand. Applause. He snapped a match with his thumbnail, lit the cigarette, and continued to stare moodily into the electric campfire. Then he sighed and said, "Oh, hell, nobody loves a fat man." Curtain to the wildest applause and laughter.

Outside, Dorothy said, "Well, Thug, I can't thank you enough for bringing me. I will always remember *The Roundup* and associate it with you."

"Well," I said, "I surely enjoyed your company. But, look, I wish—well, why do you always call me Thug?"

She took my arm and laughed. "Because, my dear," she said, "you *are* a thug, you know. But rather a sweet thug."

I don't know how much dislike for the nickname had to do with my not being in shape for the next D.A.C. boxing tournament. Working nights, I couldn't train with Stanley Koviak at the Y, and I had done practically no boxing for months when the time came to register.

Red Haig was disappointed. "Why in hell didn't you tell me?" he asked. "I'd have got you into the Eighteenth Street gym where you could have worked out mornings with pros and really learned something."

"It's too late now," I said. "Maybe next year."

The sports editor encouraged me in my writing as well as my boxing, however, and I frequently turned out short illustrated features for him. I had learned to operate a typewriter by the hunt-and-peck system, and because I didn't mind working after 11 P.M. or before I was officially at work at 1 P.M. and wasn't particularly discouraged at rejections, my name was appearing more and more in the *Journal*.

Haig argued several times that I should allow him to build me up as a sports personality by signing my writing and drawing "Thug Krueger," but I was adamant in my determination to keep these careers far apart.

"Does your mother read the sports pages?" he asked.

"No, but other people do and they'd identify me and she'd hear about it."

"All right, but so many people know about it already I'm surprised she doesn't know. I'd guess she already knows but doesn't say anything about it."

"You don't know my mother and sister," I said.

Haig and other members of the editorial department helped me with my writing and education, especially Ike Warner, chief of the editorial page.

Haig: "Never use a passive verb in sports when you can find an active one. Be colloquial. Don't try to use big, uncommon words. Take this 'pristine,' how many sports fans will know what that means? Use 'fresh' or even 'virgin.'"

Roy Smith, assistant city editor: "Quit writing 'different than.' A thing is different *from* something else. And stop trying to write long sentences. Long sentences have no place in a newspaper, and besides, you're inclined to get all tangled up in them."

City editor Joe Crowder: "Did you ever hear of redundancy? 'A new and novel experiment,' eh? Why not old and ancient? And what do you mean, 'preventative'? There ain't no such word as preventative. The word is preventive."

Political analyst Thornton Taylor: "Read Brand Whitlock's *The Thirteenth District.*"

Isaac Warner, A.B. Amherst, M.A. Harvard, to whom I had confessed (perhaps unnecessarily) my lack of schooling: "Read, boy. Read good things. You've got a flair for the comic, so read Stephen Leacock. Ask me now and then and I'll recommend books you can get at the library. Ever read Benvenuto Cellini's *Autobiography*? It's fascinating. Read *Leaves of Grass.* Read Saint-Simon, and, yes, Lafcadio Hearn. Write simply and be careful of your figures of speech. Unless a metaphor or simile is natural and sharp and apt, don't use it. A labored figure of speech is an abomination; worse than a bad pun. But live, sharp metaphors and similes often make the difference between vivid and dull writing."

So time went on and the Sterlings moved into their new stone house which seemed a mansion to me with its two bathrooms upstairs and a toilet downstairs, and Laura now had a full-time maid as well as our mother to help her. As nearly as I could tell, my mother was as delighted as were Laura and Ralph. The twins now were large enough to be taken to church, and they lived too far to walk, so I usually met them at church, still keeping the promise I made my mother.

There were occasions when Laura whispered to me tactfully, "Honey, we're having some of Ralph's business associates to dinner and I know you wouldn't be interested in them. Of course you can come if you wish, but. . . ." There were other occasions when I had other ideas and I'd telephone Laura on Saturday that I couldn't make it to dinner but would try to see them at church.

Being a newspaperman, I was more conscious of news— local, national and international. I knew that China now was supposed to be a republic under Sun Yat-sen and people wondered if the sleeping giant really was awakening. At least they were cutting off their pigtails. Rebellions continued to rack Mexico. War was chronic in the Balkans.

Although it had been sponsored by Woodrow Wilson, Ralph graciously approved the Federal Reserve Act.

A coal-mine strike in southern Colorado persisted and when violence occurred after the operators evicted strikers from company-owned houses, the National Guard was sent down to maintain order. Some battles were fought in which Major (now Lieutenant Colonel) Upjohn distinguished himself, and the shotguns, twenty-twos and deer rifles of the miners were no match for the Krag-Jörgensens and machine guns of the National Guard. To put a stop to what appeared to be insurrection, the state troops made an all-out attack on the shanty town in which the strikers and their families had taken refuge, burning the huts and tents and killing women and children as well as miners. This attack came to be known as the Ludlow massacre, but it was defended as necessary by certain law-abiding citizens such as my brother-in-law. There was, however, great indignation in other quarters, such as among most working newspapermen, and I congratulated myself on not being a member of Colonel Upjohn's militia.

In the city of Sarajevo, which I had never heard of, in the province of Bosnia, which I had never heard of, in the kingdom of Serbia, a scrawny kid named Gavrillo Prinzip became a Page-One sensation in the newspapers of the world by displaying much better than ordinary pistol shooting in killing the Archduke Franz Ferdinand and the Archduchess of Austria as they rode by in an open car. Whether a maniac or a patriot, young Gavrillo didn't live long enough to gloat over his marksmanship nor to realize the magnitude of an act which was to affect the life expectancy of millions in lands he had never heard of and profoundly to change the lives of countless millions of others, including mine.

There was a mild threat of war when Austria-Hungary made demands on Serbia. The threats became more acute when Russia, which didn't care to see Austria gain any more influence in the Balkans, warned Vienna to take it easy.

Suddenly the newspapers were talking about the Triple Alliance and the Triple Entente again and it seemed that the impossible might be possible after all. Germany, Austria-Hungary and Italy; France, Britain and Russia. It couldn't happen, but it did. And that magnificent war machine that Emperor William was building up, according to Colonel Upjohn, to thwart the Yellow Peril, was marching inexorably through Belgium, scarcely pausing while reducing the supposedly impregnable fortresses of Liège.

There was the gallant French taxicab army. There was the incredible slaughter of Russians fighting with clubs and stones, for lack of firearms, at Tannenberg. There was the valor of the British at Ypres. There were the stories of German frightfulness in Belgium and France, stories of women's breasts being nailed to barn doors, which seemed an extraordinary thing to do with women's breasts, even for Huns, and pictures of small boys and girls, each with one hand gone. It seemed that German officers delighted in sabering off the hands of children.

Jake Krueger was a German and I couldn't imagine his doing anything like that. But of course Jake really had been born in America, although of German parents.

Americans were among the twelve hundred lost when the *Lusitania* was torpedoed, and pressure was building for the

United States to enter and win the Great War for Civilization. I didn't like the idea. I read graphic stories of the horrors of trench warfare and I didn't believe I could stand it. I felt certain that I should go insane with terror if subjected to that sort of thing—groveling in the mud and probably being shot as a coward.

A new wave of indignation swept America over the execution of British nurse Edith Cavell as a spy, and Theodore Roosevelt loudly denounced President Wilson as a lily-livered poltroon, especially after Wilson's remark that the United States was "too proud to fight."

Well, I also was under some prodding to fight, from Red Haig and others, and when asked if I was too proud to enter the D.A.C. tournament, I perhaps lacked the moral courage to declare that a fact. Or perhaps I really wanted to see if I could win the light-heavyweight title.

First, however, I took Don Fitch's advice and went to a physician, asking for an X ray of my skull.

This Dr. Nichols, recommended by Red Haig, asked if I had been having dizzy spells or many headaches, and he seemed amused when I admitted I sometimes had a headache when suffering from a cold and that I was dizzy once when on a mountain cliff. When I told him I was about six years old at the time I was knocked unconscious in the buggy wreck, he laughed and slapped me on the shoulder. "Forget it," he said, "or you'll be a hypochondriac the first thing you know."

When I started training at the Eighteenth Street gymnasium, I found myself several pounds overweight. There was little opportunity for road work, but in spite of the fact that I was sitting down a great deal these days, I didn't believe my legs needed much strengthening for three two-minute rounds. I skipped rope in the gym and did a lot of dancing around while shadowboxing. I boxed with professionals who were glad to get the service of a free sparring partner. I got down to one hundred and seventy-two pounds.

From the professionals I learned a good deal, but at times the experience was quite discouraging. This was particularly true with a good-natured middleweight named Hymie Thrall who was to go on and win a national reputation, losing to the world's champion only by a narrow fifteen-round decision. I probably boxed a total of twenty-five rounds with Hymie, with the big gloves, and he was as elusive as a whiff of smoke. His footwork was a thing of beauty. His forearms seemed to have eyes of their own, always in the way of the trickiest sort of body punching or quick shifts. He would urge me to give him the works, but although I was much taller and outweighed him fifteen pounds, he was comparatively gentle with me. Because of Hymie, I was not overcharged with confidence when the tournament started.

However, the extreme difference between a good amateur and an average professional was very evident when the bouts began. My old nemesis, Luther (Pappy) Coy, had retired on his laurels and I had a moderately easy time reaching the finals except that Irish Danny Farley had improved and gave me a black eye in the semifinals before succumbing to a right cross in the second round.

The sports writers, particularly Red Haig, paid me more attention than I wished, Haig predicting a bright future for me as a professional. I protested that and I also protested his coy sentence that the public would be surprised at the true identity of the tiger fighting under the name "Thug Krueger." That, I feared, would cause some other paper to investigate and publish my real name so my mother and the Sterlings would learn that I not only was fighting but going under the name of Thug.

"Why do you have to call me Thug all the time anyhow?" I demanded. "You referred to me as a tiger. Why don't you call me Tiger Krueger or something?"

Haig seemed to enjoy this. "Because, my boy," he said, "there are always lots of tigers but there's only one Thug."

My final opponent was a squat, dark, tough youngster called Angel Angelo who had the protective instincts of a snapping turtle. Boxing from a low crouch, he would hurl himself forward, slamming away viciously at the body. Some of those body punches hurt and tired me and made me realize that I was not in as good condition as I had been two years before. My gloves and forearms were not educated to act instinctively in blocking body blows as were Hymie Thrall's, and I did not need Stanley Koviak's warning after the second round that Angelo was piling up points on me.

In the third round Angelo began to vary his attack and

caught me a nasty left on the nose. My eyes watered and my nose immediately streamed what old timers used to call the claret. Angelo obviously was now trying for a knockout and straightened from his shell. I caught him just a little high with a right on the jaw and he went down, lay quietly through the count of three, pulled himself to his knees and rose at eight to go completely in his shell. In a few seconds the bell rang and we both wobbled to our corners.

This knockdown saved me. They called it a draw, which meant that we must fight a fourth round to decide the match and the light-heavyweight title.

In my exhaustion and nausea from the body punching, I didn't believe I ever could go another round. My gloves weighed ten pounds apiece. My legs quivered from weariness. The championship seemed the least important thing in the world. But they put ice on the back of my neck, sponged my bloody nose, gave me whiffs of smelling salts, slapped me on the back and as the bell rang yelled into my ear, "You've got him now, Thug. Go cut him down."

So I did, after one minute of the fourth round, and received great acclaim and a gold watch suitably engraved to prove that someone named George Krueger was light-heavyweight champion of the Denver Athletic Club's amateur-boxing tournament for one year. Of course someone might think George Chalmers bought Krueger's watch in a pawnshop. But life was exciting and I was living in a real world.

In the bigger fight German submarines were stepping up their campaign against merchant shipping carrying American munitions to the Allies, sinking without warning even vessels flying the United States flag. President Wilson wrote notes of warning and Teddy Roosevelt's scorn was boundless. We *must* enter the war and save the Allies (now including Italy, former treaty ally of the Central Powers) but particularly La Belle France. Hadn't the gallant Lafayette and de Rochambeau rescued the embattled colonies in our Revolution? There were enthusiastic mass meetings and parades in the interest of preparedness, but little actual preparing was done. Someone, probably directed by the Kaiser himself, threw a bomb into the midst of such a parade in San Francisco, killing ten and wounding forty. In the resulting hysteria, two men with the quite un-Teutonic names of Mooney and Billings were convicted of the crime, although the evidence was fairly ambiguous.

But not everyone in America wished to rush into the European holocaust. Despite the coast-to-coast fulminations of Theodore Roosevelt in the interest of Charles Evans Hughes, Woodrow Wilson was re-elected by a narrow margin, largely on the slogan, "He kept us out of war." But of course women, who usually take obligations more seriously than men, were not yet allowed to vote. Because organizations of women seemed especially and even fiercely conscious of our debt to Lafayette, it could be that their vote would have turned the balance and elected Judge Hughes.

In the long run, however, it would have made no difference, as far as the war was concerned. On a bright Friday in April, one month and two days after his second inaugural, President Wilson went before Congress, asking for and getting a declaration of war against Germany. This was no surprise to anyone. The United States had broken off diplomatic relations with Germany two months earlier after the submarines started unrestricted warfare and American merchant ships were armed.

I had had plenty of time to think over the situation, and while my abhorrence of trench warfare was practically a phobia, I thought I knew what I had to do. Newsboys were screaming extras on the streets when I went toward the office shortly after noon. Groups of men and women were standing on the street, talking excitedly and reading the brief announcements set in big type under the six-inch headlines.

The excitement was even higher in our editorial office, with privileged outsiders standing behind the telegraph editor, reading bulletins over his shoulder as they were delivered by the wire-service boy.

I went to my desk and got out a cartoon I had prepared on my own initiative several days before. It showed an angry Uncle Sam with bare, muscular forearms, stripping off a pair of boxing gloves. I took it to the city desk, but had to wait a couple of minutes to get to Joe Crowder.

"What you got, Thug?" he asked finally.

I put the cartoon on his desk. He frowned and read the caption aloud, " 'Taking off the gloves.' Oh, I get it. Bare knuckles now, eh?"

"Yep," I said, "playing for keeps now. Well, Joe, this may be the last thing I draw for you for a while."

He looked up at me questioningly.

"I'm going to go join the Army tomorrow."

"No!"

"Yep."

"Well—why all the rush? Can't you at least give us a couple of weeks to get somebody to take your place?"

I laughed. "You can't get anyone to take *my* place—especially not for the lousy twenty-five a week you're paying me."

Crowder frowned, got up from his chair and led me to the middle of the room where he lowered his voice. "Listen, George," he said, "this war's going to last a while. It can wait for you. We might be able to raise your pay to thirty a week if you'd stay around for a few months."

"Thanks," I said, "but in my pocket I've got a watch that says I'm a fighter. They just rang the bell and I can't very well sit in my corner until they prod me out with broomsticks. You can give me that thirty—or thirty-five—when I come back."

He scowled at me. "By God, Thug," he said, "you're all right. I wish I were twenty years younger and didn't have a family. You going to join the Colorado Guard?"

I shook my head. "We're up against something more than coal miners and women and children now," I said, "and I shan't join any tin-soldier militia. I'll go join the Regular Army."

He grinned and said, "I've got something you'll enjoy." Back at the city desk he handed me a sheet of a symposium about the declaration of war being gathered from prominent Denver citizens and he pointed to a quotation from Lieutenant Colonel Upjohn: "When the Colorado National Guard gets through with him, Kaiser Bill will wish he'd never been born."

I said, "I'm still going to join the Regular Army, if I can pass muster."

He put out his small, cigarette-stained hand and we shook. "Good luck and God bless you," he said and took the telephone Roy Smith was holding out to him.

I did not, however, feel as brave as I may have sounded to Joe Crowder. I didn't feel brave at all. Fighting for one's country was a thing any decent young citizen did when his country went to war, but wars seemed to have changed. There might be something thrilling and even glorious in a cavalry charge, but everything I had read about trench warfare in France was horrible and disgusting.

In my mind was the thought that if I applied early I might get into a combat department that didn't huddle for months in muddy trenches with the corpses of both comrades and enemy dangling in the barbed wire of no man's land. From what I had read there was something stupendous and thrilling, even if monstrous and awful, in the picture of British and French aviators in dogfights with German aviators thousands of feet in the sky, shooting one another down in flames, and I wasn't sure I wouldn't be paralyzed by fear even to ride in a flying machine. But I decided that they probably taught you by easy stages and if other young men could learn this fearsome trade perhaps I could. If so, I could beat the trenches. If not, it would be a reasonably quick and clean death.

In my pleasant, active, gregarious newspaper life plus the boxing, I had left the terror of unreality pretty much behind me. But I frequently was conscious that the specter still stood in the shadows. And there was a conviction, not thought out in so many words, that this ancient horror inevitably would join the trench horror in enveloping me worse than Laocoön. Of course there was no logic in this. But was there logic in any of it?

Saturday morning I went to the Army recruiting office upstairs on lower Seventeenth Street. Half-a-dozen young men were ahead of me, most of them shabby, most of them self-conscious and nervous, but all of them, certainly, were inspired either by a sense of patriotism or of adventure. In the outer office a young man in uniform, probably a sergeant, sat at a desk, interviewing the applicants and sending them either to an inner office or back down the stairs. The sturdy fellow just ahead of me brought a paper from the pocket of his threadbare jacket and unfolded it on the desk.

"Look," he said, tapping the paper with a thick forefinger. "I'd like to get back in the Sixteenth."

The man in uniform nodded. "Sure, Sergeant," he said, "I don't think you'll have a bit of trouble with that. But it's been more than two years. You'll have to re-enlist as a private."

"I know. But with a war on it won't take me long."

"I'm sure of that, Sergeant. Go on in and sign up with the lieutenant, and good luck."

The soldier looked up at me and I said, "I'd like to enlist to be an aviator."

He shook his head. "We're not taking any enlistments in air service now."

"Oh? Well, do you think you'll be taking enlistments for fliers a little later, if I waited?"

"Are you an aviator now?"

"No, but I'd like to learn."

Again he shook his head. "They'll be filling up that department of the signal corps with qualified men from other branches. If you want to fly, the best thing is to join a line outfit, make a good record, and then ask for a transfer."

"What's a line outfit?"

"Infantry, artillery, cavalry."

"Are we going to use cavalry in this war?"

"Maybe some day, after we break the Hindenburg line. Probably use cavalry to chase the krauts back to Berlin, but mostly now they'll just patrol the Mexican border. If you want any action you'd better take the infantry."

"What about the artillery?"

"Sure, if you like loud noises. The light field artillery will see plenty of action."

"And you say I could transfer from that to aviation later on?"

"I couldn't promise that, but there'd be a chance. You had any experience with horses? Can you ride?"

"Sure," I said, "I think I'll take the light field artillery." At least, I thought, the field artillery is back of the trenches.

He took my name and address and sent me to the inner room where I was told to strip naked and was given a physical examination by three Army surgeons, was interviewed by a calm, neatly uniformed officer, and then filled out a blank concerned with such statistics as birthplace, nearest of kin, education and occupation, and signed it with my full name. Then I assumed I was in the Army and was worrying whether I should be given opportunity to go tell my mother good-bye.

The officer told me to join a dozen or so others lolling and smoking on benches across the big room, and a pimply youngster asked me if I knew where they were going to send us.

I said I hoped they'd give us a chance to go home first before sending us anywhere. He didn't believe they would. "I couldn't go home to Greeley nohow," he said, "and I got no other place to go."

After signing up two more men, the officer settled this for us.

Standing stiffly erect before us he barked, "All right, you men, line up there."

We formed a ragged, slouching line and he said, "Now you're free to go wherever you please, but be here at eight o'clock sharp Monday morning. Any of you who're from out of town or don't have any place to go can get meal tickets and bed tickets from the sergeant. Behave yourselves between then and now and don't get into any kind of trouble. Our country is in a serious war and you're taking on a very serious job. I'd advise you all to go to church tomorrow morning. And pray for our country and for yourselves. Monday morning wear old clothing and don't bring any unnecessary equipment. I'd advise nothing but toilet kits. If you are found acceptable at the recruit center, the Army will supply you with everything you need from now on. Remember now: any man who fails to be here at eight o'clock sharp Monday morning starts out his Army career with a black mark against him. You'll find out later that's not good. Dismissed."

I walked all the way back to the Y.M.C.A. in a solemn mood and told the clerk I would check out of the tiny room I had occupied so long on Monday morning. When I told him why, he looked at me in wide-eyed amazement and said, "Well, George, come to think of it, I guess I'd expect that of you." He may not have meant that as a compliment, but I took it as one.

With all of Saturday afternoon and evening ahead of me, I had nothing definite planned. I could go to the Press Club and probably find someone to shoot pool with and perhaps get up some sort of party for the evening, but I didn't feel in the mood for that. Finally I went to the phone booth and called Dorothy Sumner's home, where she lived with her widowed mother.

Dorothy answered and I said, "Hi, Dotty, this is George."

"Hi, Thug, what's on your so-called mind?"

"Dotty, could you have dinner with me this evening at the Navarre?"

"Well, Thug—this is pretty short notice. After all."

She had been tied up with some advertising-department work Friday afternoon and I had not seen her. I said, "Look, Dorothy, this is kind of special. Maybe you haven't heard, but we've gone to war with Germany."

"Silly. What's that got to do with it?"

"I've just now joined the United States Regular Army and I'm going to France to fight the Germans and this will be the last time I'll get to see you."

"You're kidding."

"Kidding? I'm a fighter, remember? And Uncle Sam needs some fighters to whip the Huns. So now he's got one."

"George!" I felt a pleasant warmness at her calling me George instead of Thug. "George, are you telling me the truth?"

I laughed. "Why would I lie?"

"Oh, I don't know. Listen, Thug, I'm flattered that you'd ask me at such a time, but I really have a date for tonight."

"I'm sorry," I said, "is it an important date?"

"All dates are important. But if this is really the last chance I'll have to see you, I'll cancel it. He'll understand—I hope."

"Well, if this is your Number One guy—"

"There's no Number One guy. Can you call for me about six? No, better make it six thirty."

"I'll be there. And thank you."

Then I phoned Laura and told her I'd be out fairly early Sunday morning. I gave no explanation.

Dorothy Sumner was not an especially pretty girl. Perhaps her light brown hair could be called mousy. But she kept it neat. Her figure was trim but feminine. Her green eyes were not feminine but wide set and shrewd. When she looked at me I got the impression that she could see how much gravel was in my gizzard down to the last pebble. I was not in love with Dorothy. Sometimes I didn't even like her, especially when her sharp wit wounded me. But I had respect for her intelligence, and when she showed enthusiasm over something I had drawn or written, I was made even happier than by praise from Ike Warner. Her sense of humor often coincided with mine and her unaffected laugh might not have been approved by Miss Ridley's School. She kidded with the boys, but didn't flirt. There's a difference. When I took her home after our first date, I moved toward giving her a good-night kiss on her front porch. "Down, boy, down!" she said. "Leave us keep this association on a strictly platonic basis. Okay?"

"Sure," I said, "if you want it that way." I didn't want to kiss her much anyhow. But I did enjoy her company—most of the time.

Our dinner at the Navarre was very pleasant. On the way down on the tramcar we covered the subject of my enlistment and the war and then ignored it entirely. In our deep-cushioned booth we had cocktails, a marvelous planked steak for two with salad, followed by *petit fours* and black coffee.

As I carved the steak I suddenly thought of my father and how he would have enjoyed this meal. I also wondered what he would think of my joining the Army. I didn't know. He might have warned me against acting impulsively and urged me to think it over for a few weeks. But wouldn't I do the same thing no matter how long I thought it over?

Dorothy was telling about a curious mixup in the advertising department over some fashion drawings she had made for one department store but which appeared in the advertisement of another store. This reminded her of something that had happened when she was a student at the Art Institute in Chicago.

I asked, "Did you go to Chicago to study fashion drawing?"

She laughed. "No, I was going to be a portrait painter. I still am someday, but right now I need a steady job to keep Mama and me. I ain't bad," said she modestly, "really."

She looked at me intently and said, "You know, Thug, I'd love to do your portrait one of these days. For a young man your face is so . . ."

"Ugly," I said.

"No, not ugly at all, but rugged and, well, thuglike." She laughed lightly and then suddenly her eyes filled with tears.

"Well!" I exclaimed.

Hurriedly, she drew a small handkerchief from her purse, wiped her eyes, and forced a smile. "I'm all right—it's all right," she declared. "I just never should take two cocktails. One's my limit. Shall we go now?"

"All right, where shall we go? Would you like to see a movie?"

"No, no movie. Are you feeling strong?"

"That depends. You want a piano moved or something?"

"No, it's spring tonight, and it may snow tomorrow. Would you like to walk me home?"

"Sure," I said. So we strolled the two miles to her mother's cottage, discussing office characters and everything apart from the war until we reached her front porch. There she suddenly threw her arms around my neck, kissed me and cried, "Oh, Thug, darling, please, please take care of yourself, promise me."

Completely astonished, I said, "Why, honey, of course I will. Why wouldn't I?"

"But wars are such dangerous things."

"Of course. But I shan't be in the trenches. I'm in the artillery where we lie back of the front-line trenches and lay down barrages on the enemy."

"Still that's dangerous. Will you write to me?"

"Of course, if you'll write to me."

"Oh, I will, I will. And I'll pray for you too."

I kissed her again and she responded warmly. Then she pulled away from me and whispered, "Good night, Thug, darling, good night," and fled into the house.

With very conflicting emotions, I caught a streetcar back to the Y.

Sunday morning early I packed my old suitcase and a new cheap straw one with my meager possessions including the books I had acquired and went to the Sterlings'. The colored maid opened the door for me. Ralph, not yet dressed for church, stared at me questioningly, wondering I suppose if I expected to move back with them.

" 'Morning, Ralph." I spoke cheerfully. "I was just wondering whether I could leave some things in my mother's closet or the attic or basement or some place?"

At his puzzled, "Well . . ." I put the suitcases down in the hall and said, "I'm going away for a while and . . ."

"Going away? Where?"

"France, I suppose. Ralph, I've just joined the Army."

"What was that?" Laura called from upstairs.

"I joined the Army yesterday, Laura, and I'm going away early tomorrow morning."

"Heavens above," she cried. "I'll be down in a minute."

Then I heard her speak to my mother and my mother's cry of dismay.

"For goodness sake," said Ralph. "Are you going with Colonel Upjohn's outfit?"

"Hell, no," I said. "Pardon the expression, but I wouldn't go into that tin-soldier army. We're in a serious war and I've joined the Regular Army."

Then my mother was downstairs in a wrapper, seizing me and beginning to cry. "Georgie, Georgie," she sobbed, "how *could* you do such a thing that way?"

"What do you mean, Mama, what way?"

"Well, just going and enlisting without talking it over with me?"

"I'm of age, Mama, and it's a thing I have to do and you'd have just tried to talk me out of it and felt very bad when you couldn't. After all, your father went to the Civil War because he was a good American, and I hope I'm a good American."

Finally she dried her tears, said she supposed she must be brave and went back upstairs to finish dressing.

We drove to church in their new Cadillac, all of us fairly quiet except the twins. The Reverend Mr. Hamilton preached an emotional sermon about the war and gave an even more emotional prayer in which I joined fervently.

At the church door, following services, Ralph took my arm and surprised me by directing me to the pastor and saying, "Reverend, you'll be interested to know that George here has already joined the colors and is leaving tomorrow morning."

The Reverend Mr. Hamilton never before had addressed me by name, but now he clutched me by both arms and exclaimed, "George, George, I'm proud of you. I just wish I had known before the sermon. You're the first of my flock—except Colonel Upjohn, of course. God bless you, boy, and you can be sure you'll have all of our prayers."

"Thank you, sir," I said. "I shall need them."

I spent the afternoon with the Sterlings, playing with the twins and trying to keep the conversation away from the war and my departure. Laura urged me to spend my last night in their spare room, but I declined. My toilet articles were still at the Y, I had to check out, and must get up very early in the morning.

Late in the afternoon I went to my mother's room and changed from my Sunday suit to an old pair of trousers and an equally old turtle-neck sweater. Downstairs, Ralph genially poked me on the shoulder and said, "My goodness, you look like a prizefighter." I wondered if he knew, but decided he didn't.

Ralph was to drive me down to the Y, but the women decided against going. Then my mother shed more tears which were joined in by Laura and the twins, and I—close to tears myself—said, "Well, for pity sake, there's nothing sure about my getting killed, you know. Grandpa Mosby came back all right, didn't he?"

In front of the Y Ralph put out his hand. "Good luck, old boy," he said, "we're all proud of you." Suddenly, to my own astonishment, I felt fond of my brother-in-law.

Monday morning a motley group including me was waiting on Seventeenth Street before the sergeant arrived to open the recruiting-office door. By ten o'clock at least forty recruits were aboard a grimy railroad coach near the Union Station and excited voices speculated on our destination. "They're going to take us to the Mexican Border for training," one declared. "Oh for Christ's sake," another asserted, "why go out of our way? We're going back east near where the steamboats go to France." Actually, we rode this car just ten miles to the recruit center at Fort Logan, Colorado.

Chapter 25

FEW Americans these days have any interest in the First World War. For that small minority of scholars, war buffs and nostalgic oldsters who are still interested, public-library shelves still hold hundreds of volumes on the subject, perhaps even including my own *Hurry Up and Wait* (profusely illustrated by the author; Lothrop-Lee, 1918). But this first book of mine, despite its astonishingly large sale and despite the ridiculous motion picture produced under the same name, has been out of print for years.

So at this time there is no reason for me to describe my own undistinguished military career in great detail. I believe I spent about ten days at the recruit center at Fort Logan. It was long enough for me to be revolted at the puerile vulgarities of a recruit barracks room and to recover from the revulsion. It was enough to be uniformed in ill-fitting olive drab, to be vaccinated and inoculated after passing a much more severe physical examination than I had in Denver—an examination which dismissed several of the recruits. It was enough to learn that most important item of all military regulations, the right-hand salute, as well as the elements of close-order drill. It was enough for me to serve my first session of kitchen police, which turned out to be from 5:30 A.M. to 8:30 P.M., a stint which reduced the weaker recruits to actual exhaustion and left me caring for nothing but my barracks-room cot. There were the usual experiences with tough old Army sergeants with their hackneyed sarcasms. Then we hurried up and waited. Then we were issued our colored hat cords, and the infantry-blue hat cords went to Texas and the cavalry-yellow hat cords went to Arizona and we with the artillery-red hat cords were shipped to Fort Sill, Oklahoma, where we hurried up and waited. I don't know where those in the engineers and signal corps and medical corps and quartermaster corps went.

Mid-April seemed to be late spring in Fort Sill where we drilled and exercised horses, counted off and put down "dry" barrages with three-inch fieldpieces. Our regiment, or at least Battery D, filled to wartime strength, was composed of about 70 percent old career soldiers, 10 percent of men who enlisted during the excitement a year before, after Pancho Villa raided Columbus, New Mexico, and 20 percent of us recruits. The old-timers naturally lorded it over us newcomers to some extent, but we probably learned faster than would have been possible in a new organization.

I found it all interesting and often amusing. The griping about discipline usually came from boys who needed discipline for their own good. The griping about the monotony of the chow usually came from boys who were better fed than ever before and who were gaining weight.

There were some pretty rough boys among the recruits and

as soon as we were definitely members of the battery they began the curious development of a pecking order. I tried to keep strictly out of it. I was content to be regarded as a good-natured, earnest slob among us second-class citizens and to keep out of trouble.

When a quarrel started in the barracks or outside, old sergeants delighted in stepping up and ordering, "None of that here. Stop it now or let's go down to the stables and settle it." So, unless one or both backed down, there'd be a parade to the stables where, with a sergeant to referee, the disagreement would be adjusted with bare knuckles.

A rangy, hook-nosed Wyoming cowboy named Godfrey had been climbing up the pecking order by merit of two victories at the stables. I had seen one of these bouts while on stable police and Godfrey had rushed upon his opponent, swinging viciously and relentlessly with both hands, overwhelming the boy in less than a minute. But Godfrey was a complete sucker for anyone who could keep calm and who knew even the rudiments of boxing.

About a week after his second victory, Godfrey approached me outside the mess hall, scowled and said, "You think you're tough, don't you, Chalmers?"

"Not particularly," I said, "but tough enough."

"You want to know what I think of you?"

"No," I said, "I don't give a damn what you think of me."

He raised his voice, attracting several soldiers including an old sergeant named O'Toole. "Ha!" Godfrey shouted, shaking a finger at me, "I seen you sitting on your bunk drawing pitchers and you think you're a goddamn artist and all artists is fruits and I think you're a goddamn fruit."

I tried to be calm. "Listen, Godfrey," I said, "do yourself a favor and shut your mouth. I don't want to hurt you, but . . ."

"Down to the stables," Sergeant O'Toole commanded, "unless you want to back down. You want to back down, Chalmers?"

"Look, Sergeant," I said, "I don't want to fight this clown."

"You afraid of him?"

I laughed. "I'm just afraid I might kill him," I said.

"Down to the stables," he ordered again. The group grew as we walked toward the stables, and I became very angry at being forced into this. Among other things, there always was a possibility of breaking a hand in a bare-knuckle fight, and this was all so unnecessary and childish. I heard bets being offered on Godfrey, with no takers, and odds were raised and raised again until one congenital gambler risked fifty cents on me against two dollars.

By the time we had stripped to the waist, I was ready to give this fool everything I had regardless of consequences. He made a furious rush at me, as I expected, and I easily stepped inside his flailing right and felt his beaked nose crunch under a short left hook. He scrambled up from the dirt and this time my right cross caught him on the cheek. It was a stiff one, and I heard someone exclaim "Jesus!" as Godfrey's shoulders raised dust. This time he was slower getting up and I had time to suck my stinging knuckles. I thought it would have been wiser to go for his body and soften him, but I didn't want to waste the time.

Godfrey was game all right, but in his next rush I waited for the opening I knew must come and the straight right landed on his jaw. That was it. They took him to the hospital.

That evening the battery clerk summoned me to the orderly room. Sergeant O'Toole was slumped in a corner chair. At his desk Captain Jenkins gave a perfunctory return of my snappy salute.

"Sir," I said, "Private Chalmers reporting."

He looked at me with narrowed eyes. His lean face was sallow, probably from malaria in the Philippines. "Private Chalmers," he said grimly, "I have a report that you are responsible for Private Godfrey's being in the hospital with a fractured cheek bone and a fractured jaw."

"I didn't realize it was that serious, sir. I'm sorry."

"Do you realize you could be court-martialed for committing mayhem on a soldier of the United States Army?"

"No, sir, I didn't realize that. I'm sorry, but I didn't want to fight him."

"You could have refused, couldn't you?"

"I suppose so, sir. But the captain wouldn't want a soldier who would back down from a fight when it was really forced on him, would he? I tried to warn this man, sir."

"Sergeant O'Toole has told me about it. How many times did you hit Private Godfrey?"

"Three, I think, sir."

"And how many times did he hit you?"

"Just glancing blows on the arms."

"Are you a fighter?"

"Not a professional, sir. I've boxed as an amateur."

His grim face broke into a grin. "All right, Private Chalmers," he said, "when we need fighting done, I'll remember you're in the battery. Dismissed."

So I saluted, did a smart about-face, and left the orderly room. I was bothered no more by young men ambitious to improve their standing in the battery pecking order. The story of my encounter with Godfrey spread and one evening after chow I was approached by a pleasant, middle-aged man in a Knights of Columbus uniform. He introduced himself as Eddie Fitzpatrick and asked if I would be kind enough to spar three two-minute rounds with a man from headquarters company at the K. C. hut Sunday afternoon.

"I'll *spar* with big gloves," I said, "but I want it understood that there's to be no slugging. I'm not going to get sucked into any more fights."

He agreed, and I sparred three fairly fast rounds with a rather clever middleweight named Molino. After the show, which consisted of another boxing exhibition, some gymnasts and a male quartet, Mr. Fitzpatrick cornered me. "I'm interested in you, Chalmers," he said. "I've trained some pretty good boys in Chicago and elsewhere and I wish you'd get in touch with me after the war. From what I hear, you've got a killing punch, and from what I saw today, I'm sure you could be built into a top heavyweight. I think I might be able to carry you even to the championship."

I laughed. "Against that giant Jess Willard who killed Bull Young with one punch? No, thank you, Mr. Fitzpatrick. I've got a good job waiting for me after the war. I enjoy sparring with a good man like Molino, but I don't expect to ever go in the ring again, even as an amateur."

"Can you make a million bucks on that good job? The guy who takes that big slob Willard has got a minimum of a million dollars in his poke."

"I don't particularly need a million dollars," I said, "and I don't need to get my brains any more addled than they are already. Willard may be a slob, but he knocked out Jack Johnson, didn't he?"

"Maybe. And maybe not. Li'l Arthuh was all through any-how." He took a card from his pocket. "Anyhow, Chalmers, put my card in your wallet and think it over. And when the war's over, drop me a line."

"From what I hear," I said, "the war isn't very nearly over."

"It won't last long once you Yanks get over there."

I thought he was more confident than I and I thanked him for his interest and he thanked me for sparring with Molino and I put his card away in my wallet, pleased but doubtful that he'd ever hear from me.

We drilled with our sidearms, thirty-eight-caliber Colt revolvers which we wore high on our right hips with the butts forward, not at all like the Western heroes of the movies. We each fired several hundred rounds at target, which was decidedly more fun than the interminable drilling with the three-inch guns and horse exercise.

Then came the big day when we actually went on the artillery range and blasted holes in the Oklahoma hills, changing by the numbers every few rounds, with the squad corporal firing first, shifting next to the No. 1 cannoneer, then the No. 2, until supposedly every man was acquainted with every job. We had three days of this exciting fireworks. Then there was the even more exciting announcement. We were moving out. Where? That was the big, top secret. And we hurried up to pack and then waited for transportation.

After some days we marched to the railroad and climbed aboard tourist sleepers with rattan seats while the regimental band blared "The Stars and Stripes Forever."

The tourist sleepers indicated we were going a long way, which we did—clear to Camp Mills, Long Island. There we had further physical examinations and hurried up and waited in the sultry June heat for a ship to take us overseas. We had left our artillery and horses back at Fort Sill, but Battery D, especially the young recruits, was quite ready to take on the Kaiser's best with our thirty-eights.

Then early one morning we were wearing full packs and marching briskly through the streets of lower Manhattan, to the cheers of gawking New Yorkers on the sidewalks, unable to get a comfortable gawk at the tall buildings ourselves because we were held strictly at attention, and presently the gigantic ring-streaked and striped camouflaged bulk of the liner *Aqui-*

tania loomed before us and we were herded up gangplanks, each given a red, numbered card, ordered to hang onto the cards, driven down narrow iron stairs into holds dimly lit by purple electric bulbs, and directed to find the bunks designated by the numbers on our red cards. The bunks were four tiers high. They were about two feet wide. The aisles between the rows were about two feet across. There was about two feet between bunks up and down—narrow quarters for a man and his pack.

The noise inside the hold was deafening. Probably there was plenty of noise outside, too, but I couldn't hear it. I didn't even hear the whistle, if indeed they blew it, but after a long time I was conscious of movement, an ever so slight rising and sinking of this whole roaring, purple-lit inferno. Finally we were allowed on deck to line up with our mess kits for dinner, and we were out of sight of land, with the early afternoon sun blazing on an expanse of blue water almost as smooth as City Park Lake in Denver. It was my first sight of the ocean and I was disappointed. It was too calm and the horizon didn't seem as far away as it does on the high plains of eastern Colorado.

It was calm and sunny all the way across, with little seasickness among the soldiers. Except for the nights in the close, fetid, noisy hold, it was a pleasant voyage as we zigged and zagged our way across the blue, bronze and purple North Atlantic. Once I spoke to a British sailor, saying, "I'm surprised that we're going it alone. I thought ships like this would be convoyed by warships to take care of submarines."

"No, Yank," he said, "the old Acky is too bluidy fahst for the bluidy U-bowts to catch."

I said, "Well, isn't the *Aquitania* a sister ship of the *Lusitania?*"

He said, "I know, but the old Lucy wasn't cammyflajed like us and was probably dallying to save fuel because who'd think the Boche would be such bluidy bahstids to sink her without warning? Don't worry, Yank, they'll never get the old Acky, not half."

I hoped he was right. From the main deck it was as far down to the opalescent swirl and froth of the ocean as down from the roof of any building in Denver except the Daniels and Fisher tower.

The recruits and one-year men did a great deal of griping

about the "limey" chow, which seemed to feature oatmeal gruel for breakfast and strong mutton stew for dinner, with sweetened tea instead of coffee. The old-timers who had served in the Philippines and Canal Zone and Guam mostly took it in their stride.

In England we were issued British steel helmets and American gas masks. During our few days of "rest camp" we hurried up to formations and then waited. We did close-order drill. We griped. One evening a Zeppelin came over, almost filling the sky with its dark bulk. Before they could be halted by officers, twenty or more of Battery D opened a futile fire on the monster with their thirty-eights.

In the gathering darkness I heard one man yell, "By God, I think I hit it. I saw some feathers come down."

"Balls," said another. "That was just the Huns flushing their toilet. They always wait till they get over England for that."

Crossing the channel was as rough as the transatlantic voyage was smooth. The little ship was a shambles, and I felt a little squeamish myself.

On the cobblestones of France I thought, Well, this is the last country a lot of us will ever see. But I didn't realize just how true this would be proved in the next sixteen months.

We stood at ease in the dark waterfront street, but still we stood and waited with our packs on our backs, and La Belle France was starlight on the black shapes of buildings and the stench of sewage. We were called to attention and then at ease several times and then we marched some blocks to a row of those famous or infamous tiny boxcars labeled HOMMES QUARANTE, CHEVAUX HUIT, counted off in forties and squeezed into the cubicles. The obvious conclusion was that if these cars were designed to hold forty men, the French couldn't be more than half the size of standard Americans. Not more than half of the artillerymen could sit at a time, let alone lie down. It took four and a half boxcars even to carry Battery D, and as I was to learn later, two trains for the regiment and its supplies.

At last there was a neck-snapping jar as a locomotive coupled up with our train, considerable screaming back and forth by French voices, answering Anglo-Saxon not-so-funny witticisms from the boxcars, and finally we went rattling and jerking and banging down from northern France, with a peanut-wagon whistle shrilling up in front. If disgust sold for a dime a pound, there was a billion-dollar cargo aboard our train.

By early morning we were in the Paris railroad yards, shunting this way and that way, and at last we were allowed out of the cars to stretch our aching muscles and we were approached by a chattering company of French women in blue-cotton uniforms, bearing huge pots of hot chocolate, hard rolls, pastry and (we didn't appreciate the uniqueness) real American doughnuts. We were apparently the first American soldiers they ever had seen, and some of them shed tears and they kept crying *"Vive l'Amérique!"* and the artillerymen forgot their peevishness and yelled, "Hurray for France!" while wolfing their rolls, doughnuts and chocolate, and many of the women insisted on kissing us, the young and pretty meeting no resistance at all and no violent resistance even for the middle-aged and mustached.

Then back to the misery of the boxcars, rattling south, halting, banging, shunting, backing, cursing, eating corned beef and hardtack from emergency rations, trading positions, relieving ourselves out the open doors into the French countryside, and in a state of exhaustion reaching the terra incognita of our destination in the middle of the night.

We pitched our pup tents in the middle of a field and slept gratefully on the silent, stable ground until wakened at dawn by the arrival of the regiment's second contingent.

Here we established a camp and did foot drill to kill time and keep in condition while the war raged an undetermined number of kilometers away. A limited, well-behaved few were granted passes each evening, after lectures by Captain Jenkins on their responsibilities to the reputation of the United States and the dangers of venereal disease, to trudge into one of the two villages within a soldier's walking distance to get a relief from slum, beans and canned salmon (goldfish) with *jambon et oeufs* and French fries and wine, and later possible dalliance with Jeanne or Marie or Yvonne.

The French were supposed to supply us with their marvelous *soixante-quinze* with which we vibrant, fresh Yankees were to put the quietus on the Hun. But apparently the French felt they could put better use to their seventy-fives than to turn them over to amateurs for practice.

After a fortnight, however, someone sent us a hundred

horses and that gave us something to do besides foot drill and policing up. We could put up picket lines, curry horses, do stable police, horse drill and horse exercise.

In another two weeks great news flashed over the camp. The guns had come. Indeed, they had come—three of them, enough for one battery. Headquarters cherished them and loaned one gun at a time to each battery, together with a one-armed French lieutenant who thought he spoke English. On the third day Battery D got its chance for two days and we admired its newness, commented on its quaint appearance with the recoil cylinder on top of the barrel, and most of us got an opportunity to work its mechanism. Captain Jenkins understood enough of the lieutenant's lecture to explain that operation of a seventy-five was quite different from our old three-inchers. With the French gun, the corporal or gunner only aimed the piece. The Number One cannoneer, sitting in the right-hand bucket seat, fired on command and operated the breech, all with his right hand to avoid the possibility of getting his left hand in the way of the recoiling barrel or opening the breech at the time of firing and probably blowing off the head of the cannoneer sitting on the trail into the next *département*. Then our beautiful seventy-five went to Battery G.

We got more horses. We got three more guns. And summer waned.

It was a dull but anxious period. We enlisted men got little news except what seeped down from regimental headquarters, and that, more often than not, was unconfirmed rumor. There had been uprisings in Russia, we heard, and if Russia surrendered that would throw the whole eastern front German Army against us. And there we were with six unfired guns for the regiment and no ammunition whatever.

I put in my spare time keeping up my diary, making countless sketches and writing letters to my mother, Dorothy Sumner and other friends. Dorothy's letters were cheerful and witty and a delight to read. Dorothy was not at all what I considered my type of girl, but I felt a growing affection for her and now was amused rather than annoyed at her persistence in addressing me as "Dearest Thug."

In driblets we received more seventy-fives until we had enough to arm more than half the regiment. Then we got more horses, poor beasts mostly, compared to those we had at Fort

Sill. Perhaps half had come from the United States and the rest didn't understand English—even the most profane and obscene English. Some of the men insisted that they must be captured German animals because even French horses couldn't be that ornery. But at that stage in the war I doubted that the French had had opportunity to capture many German artillery horses.

At last we got a consignment of ammunition, but the colonel couldn't get permission to practice with it in that peaceful region. So, late in October when we finally got the exciting order to move to the *front,* not one of our seventy-fives had even been fired.

Our front was a quiet sector in the Vosges, a *very* quiet sector which both the French and the Germans had been using, by tacit agreement, as a sort of rest sector for a couple of years.

But our Colonel Stuart apparently was as restive as any of us. Here it was November and we had been in France since the first of July, supposedly to win a war. What the hell!

We deployed our twenty-four guns on a rolling terrain flanked on both sides by silent French artillery.

Ahead of us were American infantry units in trenches for the first time. Beyond them, supposedly, was the hated Hun.

The sky was low and gray, but an earlier slight drizzle had ceased. Only a few of the scattered giant oaks in the vicinity showed the effects of war. The others still retained about half of their red-brown leaves and these were bright from the recent rain.

Tall, slim Lieutenant Sparling seemed tense and he paced back and forth behind Battery D. We had been ordered to prepare for action, but I, at least, took it for granted it was just a drill. At the moment, however, I was Number One cannoneer, sitting in the right-hand bucket seat of Number One gun, and I did not know that a dozen or so high-X shells were stacked to the right of the trail. Corporal Dann was in the gunner's seat. Captain Jenkins was with other officers and his battery commander's telescope on a knoll to the left rear. First Sergeant Matthews was with the captain to operate the telegraph buzzer, and back of Battery D was Sergeant Powell wearing earphones on the other end of the wires running down the knoll from Matthews.

I could hear the buzzer faintly, but, although I had learned the continental code, the message was not distinguishable. Sergeant Powell said to Lieutenant Sparling, "Aiming point, church spire, southwest, all guns," and the lieutenant shouted the command with a surprising quaver in his voice. After all, we had done this hundreds of times in dry runs. Corporal Dann deftly turned his sight to the rear, squinted through it and fixed it. "Target, three—nine—five—oh mils." Dann rapidly spun the crank, swinging the barrel horizontally. "Range, one —one—zero—zero." Dann cranked the barrel upward, peering at the gauge, and then locked it.

Lieutenant Sparling called to each gunner in turn, "Ready?" Each gunner responded, "Ready, sir."

"Load!" And to my surprise the Number Two cannoneer shoved a long, brass-cylindered projectile into our open breach, and I automatically slammed shut the breechblock. Immediately a gun blasted way down to the left at Battery A. Then another and another, followed by *whang-whang*-WHANG of Battery B and *bang-boom-blooey* of Battery C. My right hand was gripping the shiny handle and as Lieutenant Sparling called out I pushed down sharply. I must have blinked, for in that instant our gun barrel was sliding smoothly back from recoil position. Because we were protected by our gun's steel shield, the blast from Number Two gun was much more pronounced than our own. The firing rippled on down our line and I thought it was just possible that I was the tenth American ever to fire a shot at a German army. As I yanked open the breechblock and saw the expended shell sail out to be caught by the cannoneer sitting on the trail, there seemed to be some distinction in that possibility.

Tendrils of gray smoke were still oozing from the breech when Number Two slid another shell into the gun. On orders, Corporal Dann reduced the range by fifty yards, and again we fired. Then the gun crews were shifted and I became Number Eight cannoneer while Number Two took my place to fire two shots. Then another shift while Corporal Dann retained his position as gunner. In this manner all members of the regular gun crews got in their two shots, and then we were moved out to make way for members of gunless batteries.

If there had been any doubt that a German army actually was hidden behind the ridge ahead of us, it was dispelled by the time our fifth volley was fired. Shells and shrapnel began raining down from the clouds well to our rear. By the time we were relieved, the Germans had reduced their range and the high-explosive shells threw up black geysers of dirt, with a terrific roar. I wondered whether our shells made that much noise and doubted it; I thought the Germans were using bigger stuff on us.

Now, I had worried a good deal on how I should react to being under fire and I know it is customary for war veterans to declare that anyone who says he wasn't scared to death is a downright liar. Well, this really was desultory fire, but on our way back Lieutenant Sparling and all of us dropped flat when a shell ripped down too close for comfort and I frankly was excited and elated because here I was actually under enemy fire and not at all terrified. Our guns were still banging away behind us, so I had engaged in what certainly could be called a battle. This would be something to tell my grandchildren, if any.

I was amused at the wide-eyed expressions of a couple of teen-age recruits, and when another shell came down—perhaps seventy yards ahead of us—I didn't even bother to drop. That is, I didn't drop for a split second after the explosion. Then I dropped, because something—either a shell fragment or a stone—struck a violent blow high on my right shin just above the canvas legging. I sat up immediately, and, in agony, grasped my leg with both hands.

The others were scrambling up, and Lieutenant Sparling called, "What's the matter, Chalmers? Are you hit?"

"Yes," I said, "but . . ."

He came over and I got to my feet to hop around painfully. "Well," he said, "your leg can't be broken. Let's get out of range and then we'll look at it."

By the time I had hobbled the best part of a mile back to our quarters, the pain had subsided greatly. I took off my legging, let down my breeches, and pulled up the government-issue balbriggan drawers. The leg was swollen and inflamed. The lieutenant laughed. "You're lucky, Chalmers," he said, "if a piece of shell did that, it must have hit you with the flat side."

I asked, "Don't I get credit for a wound by enemy fire?"

He shook his head. "Skin isn't even broken. Be a stout fella, Chalmers. That isn't enough even to relieve you from duty."

The next morning brought another intermittent drizzle and

I was ordered out for horse exercise, in fatigue dungarees. My leg was very sore and I was glad I didn't have to wear leggings.

To spare saddles and blankets from the weather, we were to ride bareback, each with a lead horse on a halter, and I was unlucky enough or stupid enough to draw a recalcitrant lead horse and a perverted French mount. When we were maneuvering into a column, my lead horse pulled back on the halter shank with a jerk and I turned slightly to urge him on. As I did so my mount nuzzled the tail of the horse in front and that indignant beast cut loose with both hoofs. One hoof caught my swerving steed in the shoulder. The other got me on the right leg a couple of inches below the bruise. That hurt. For a moment I wondered if my leg was broken, and was about to slide off the horse. Then I remembered that old "stout fella, my lad" routine of Lieutenant Sparling and decided I must not make a show of injuries two days in succession. I could move my foot up and down, which I believed proved the leg wasn't broken, and went on, riding some miles at horse exercise. Before we returned to the picket line, however, I could feel that the drawer leg was wet with blood.

After securing my horses to the line, I hobbled away and old-time Stable Sergeant Leo Kowalski called to me, "What's the matter there, boy?"

I tried to grin. "Horse got me in the leg."

"Bad?"

"Well," I said, "leg's not broken, but . . ." I looked down and there was a bloodstained hole in the dungarees. "Well, the calk cut through my pants, and it's bleeding."

"Come on over here and let's look at it."

I limped to the stable sergeant's quarters, sat on a canvas stool and pulled up the pant leg. The balbriggan was red clear down to the ankle.

The stable sergeant took out an efficient-looking pocketknife, slit the drawers up the side to the knee and peeled back the cloth to expose the wound.

"Hmm," he breathed, "he really smacked you. You just let your horse crowd up too close, didn't you?"

"I guess so. The worst of it is that yesterday I got hit by a piece of German shell just above there." I pointed to the bruise.

"I see. But that don't amount to anything. Well, I can fix this up for you all right. You don't want to go to the infirmary with a thing like that, do you?"

"No," I said, "if you've got some disinfectant."

"I got everything. I'm practically a veterinarian, taking care of horses."

With some gauze he swabbed out the hole with alcohol. That was *not* pleasant. He disinfected his knife blade with alcohol and cut away a loose shred of skin. Then he discovered a white toothpick of bone in the wound and picked that out with tweezers.

"Now," he said, picking up a large bottle of iodine, "hang onto that stool and don't be surprised if you wet your pants on account this is really going to hurt. But I'll guarantee that spot will heal right up with no trouble at all."

He drenched the wound again and again with iodine and he was quite correct about the pain, although my sphincters preserved my honor. His guarantee of healing was not very good, however, although he put a quite professional gauze bandage on my leg.

On the third day my leg was badly swollen and throbbed unmercifully. I gave up that morning and went to the regimental infirmary on sick call. The captain surgeon was not at all sympathetic.

"Why didn't you come here immediately with a thing like that?" he demanded.

"Well, sir," I said, "I didn't want to bother you and the stable sergeant fixed it up."

"I'll say he fixed it up. If you haven't got enough brains to realize this was serious, the stable sergeant certainly should. What's his name?"

"Sir, I don't want to get him into trouble. He was very kind and thought he was doing the right thing."

"*What's his name?*"

"Sergeant Leo Kowalski, sir. He's been in the Army more than twenty years and is a very good stable sergeant. I hope the captain won't make trouble for him."

"Lie down on that bench and bare your belly."

"Yes, sir. But what—"

"Don't you know that horse manure is the prime carrier of tetanus?"

"No, sir."

"Without a doubt in the world tetanus toxin was forced into your bloodstream by that horseshoe and you should have had an antitetanus shot immediately. Now, after three days, I'm going to give you a massive slug in an attempt to save your life, but I wouldn't bet on its working."

By then I was on the leather surgical couch, with my shirt and undershirt pulled up. A medical-corps sergeant swabbed my belly with alcohol and another handed the captain a huge hypodermic syringe with a three-inch needle. It took perhaps a minute for the captain to force the whole load under the skin and I didn't like it.

"Another thing," he said, "is the fact that every cubic inch of French soil is full of everything from gangrene to gonococcus."

"But, sir," I said, "Sergeant Kowalski really did disinfect this with alcohol first and then iodine."

"Disinfect, my royal ass. The thing is infected right now. If you don't die of lockjaw, it's a ten-to-one chance that you'll lose this leg. I'll do what I can, but the chances are it's too late. And then do you know what will happen? Because you neglected to come to the infirmary when you should, you'll get a blue ticket."

Now he was probing into the wound with a scalpel. "A blue ticket?" I asked.

"A surgeon's certificate of disability. A discharge without honor, meaning no compensation and no pay from the time of the accident until discharge."

"A dishonorable discharge, sir?"

"No, that's a yellow ticket following a court-martial. A blue ticket isn't quite that bad."

"But look, sir," I said, sitting up and pointing to the purple bruise above the wound. "The day before the horse kicked me, I got hit right there by a piece of a German shell. That was in action with the enemy and that's what made this other so bad."

He looked at the bruise and shook his head. "Did you report to the infirmary with that?"

"No, sir, the lieutenant said the skin wasn't broken."

"Quite right. And that had nothing at all to do with this."

He probed deeply into the wound and swabbed it out carefully. Then he covered it with a gauze pad and bandaged it thickly.

"That," he said, "is all I can do now. I'm marking you 'quarters,' so you keep off that leg all you can and be back here on sick call tomorrow morning."

"I'll be back all right, sir," I said, thoroughly worried.

That night I slept little from pain, worry and a fever from the hypodermic injection. The next morning I was really ill, with a huge welt across my abdomen that prevented my either stooping or straightening with comfort, and I was still feverish. When the captain unwrapped the wound it showed no improvement. If anything, the swollen section was more discolored. I spent the day on my canvas cot, rousing myself from a doze only to go to chow and the latrine, and I wasn't much interested in chow. I developed a petulant theory that the hypodermic caused not only my illness but the throbbing pain of my leg.

The following morning the captain took one look at the leg and said, "That settles it. You've got to go back to the base hospital where they can dig deeper into that thing and keep you in bed so they can drain it. Sergeant Skinner, take Private Chalmers down to Battery D to get his gear and bring him back so we can load him into the ambulance this afternoon."

"Sir," I said, "do you know what I think? I think that big shot in the belly not only made me sick but made my leg worse."

"Chalmers," he said, "try not to be a *complete* idiot. It may count against my own record, but I'm not going to report to the hospital about your delay in coming to the infirmary. That'll protect you against eventualities."

I thanked him and asked, "Sir, do you think—"

"I don't think, Chalmers. I just wish you luck."

It was a long, long, bumpy, painful ride back to the hospital in the Ford ambulance and my companion was a sick, fearful boy from Battery F who coughed, moaned and wept all the way. When I asked what was wrong with him, he said they wouldn't tell him but he knew he was dying. I suspected he was telling the truth.

At the hospital, medical corpsmen looked at my tag and carried me to a ward on a stretcher. It took a little argument with the officious fellows for me to retain my sketches, journal, writing and drawing material, along with my toilet articles. I was given a pair of purple-striped pajamas (the first pajamas I had worn since April sixth), a cotton robe and a towel, and was ordered into a vacant bed. As I hobbled around, some men in nearby beds greeted me with "Hi, buddy"; others stared at me with incurious eyes. One emaciated fellow in a robe strolled up and asked what was wrong with me.

"Well," I said, "a chunk of German shell caught me in the leg."

He opened his mouth incredulously. "For Christ's *sake!*" he said. "You been in *action?*"

"Sure," I said and crawled between the deliciously smooth, cool white sheets.

"How'd we come out?"

I was very tired and sick and I shook my head. "We just shelled each other," I said. "I don't know." Then I heard him going down the aisle, saying, "Hey, this new guy's been in action and was hit by a German shell."

They didn't allow me to rest long in my new beautiful bed. I was just dozing off when a couple of medical corpsmen came in with a rolling stretcher and wheeled me to the surgery.

A sallow-faced woman nurse impassively unrolled my bandage and clucked her tongue. Then a surgeon with graying hair beneath his white cap came to peer closely into the wound while he tortured me by squeezing the leg.

"Well, son," he said, "we've got to dig into that thing pretty deeply to get the infection out so we'll give you a general anesthetic."

"Right now?"

He nodded.

"Couldn't we wait until tomorrow?" I asked. "I'm pretty tired and sick now."

He smiled. "No," he said, "this needs immediate attention. If we waited until tomorrow there's a possibility you wouldn't *be* here."

"I'll admit I don't feel very well," I said, "but I don't believe I'm that feeble."

"A microscopic bug of septic poisoning can knock off the strongest man in a matter of hours," he declared. "And you've got a colony of them working on you."

They stripped me of my purple-striped pajamas and helped me into a Johnny shirt that tied in the back. A medical corpsman shaved my leg, being gentle around the suppurating sore which now had spread to an area almost as large as a baseball.

Then I was wheeled into the operating room, a nose cone was put over my face and I was told to breathe deeply. I drew in the pungent vapor and immediately felt pleasantly dizzy. After a few breaths I began to rise delightfully from the operating table and a man's voice said, "Now, count, Chalmers," and I began to count. I did not get far with my counting.

I awoke to pain and nausea and a kind-faced woman nurse taking my pulse.

I said, "Well, I guess it'd be a good idea to go to work on my leg right away at that. I think it's gone clear down into my foot."

She smiled sympathetically and I asked for a drink of water.

"You'd better not for a little while," she said.

The pain in my foot was excruciating and I said, "Whew! It feels as if every one of my toes are crushed."

She said, "I know. I'll take care of that right away." She departed around a gray screen, and I saw that I was back in my bed, but shielded from the rest of the ward. So they had finished treatment of my injury already.

Then she was back with a small hypodermic syringe and gently gave me a shot in the arm.

"It's all over, isn't it?" I asked.

"Yes, it's all over."

"I hope they got all that infection dug out."

"I'm sure they did."

"But I can't understand why my foot and toes hurt so terrifically." A beautiful drowsy numbness was stealing over me, and she said, "Well, boy, they don't actually. You might call it a harmonic response."

I didn't quite understand that, and, inasmuch as the pain had diminished greatly, I drifted into a delicious sleep.

That night, however, my toes were throbbing dreadfully again and when I complained to the rather stern middle-aged nurse she said, "When you grow older, if you also become wiser, you'll learn that the most severe pains we suffer in this life are fictitious. We fall in love with a shadow and suffer when we discover the shadow has no substance."

"I know what you mean," I said, and she gave me another wonderful shot of morphine.

I did not, however, know exactly what she meant, not thinking very clearly at the time. It was left for the operating surgeon to break the news to me the next morning. To save my life, he said, they had been forced to amputate my leg below the knee. The seeming pain in my foot and toes was from severed nerve ends that thought they still ran to the appendages.

He took my hand and said, "I'm truly sorry, Chalmers, but it was a real emergency. We were able to save a good enough stump so you'll be able to use one of these marvelous artificial limbs they're making now, and you'll be able to walk with scarcely a limp."

My thoughts were racing in curious fashion. Now I might as well take that card of the Knights of Columbus secretary Eddie Fitzpatrick from my wallet and tear it up. I'd never box again. The right leg is the anchor in boxing and what you might call the fulcrum for a right-hand punch. I would never run another race. I could never go on another roof to clean a chimney. Somehow I didn't feel too bad about any of these. As a matter of fact, there was a strange sense of relief about the boxing.

I said, "Well, sir, I believe I'd just as soon have a peg leg and make no bones about it."

"Oh, no," he asserted, "not in this day and age. And the government will provide you with the very latest and best-model artificial leg made. Have you any trade or business in civilian life?"

"I'm a newspaper artist and writer."

"Wonderful. Your misfortune won't interfere at all with that. And, of course, the war's over for you. You'll be hospitalized until that leg is completely healed and you're fitted with an artificial leg, but you'll be sent back to the States as soon as you're able to travel."

"Well," I said, "I surely haven't been any bargain to the government. They've fed and clothed and trained me since last April seventh. I pumped a total of two shells in the general direction of the Germans, and now they've got the expense of keeping me in hospitals and getting me a wooden leg."

[312]

"You've done your bit," said the doctor, "don't worry about that. You gave your good right leg to your country."

"There's another thing, sir," I said. "If they gave me a good old peg leg, I could go home and parade it and tell stories about the heroism of our boys in the Great War and sell Liberty Bonds."

He grinned, slapped me on the shoulder, and went on his rounds.

When the pain from the amputation began to abate, they tapered off on those pleasant shots in the arm and I came out of the narcotic haze and took an interest in the surgical ward where I lived—the appendectomies, herniotomes, mastoiditis cases, practically everything except war wounds. I sketched the patients, the ambulatory ones who came to my bed to talk or play pitch or checkers. Because it was assumed that the Germans shot off my leg, I was a celebrity in the ward and I did not feel it was necessary to explain that a French or American horse deserved a little credit for my disability. There always was a chance that a doctor or nurse might unveil me as a fraud, but they apparently felt sorry enough for me to let the deception stand. And, after all, perhaps that bruise from the shell *did* contribute to the infection.

From keeping up my diary, I began experimenting to see if I could possibly write a short, humorous book about the Army and the war from the viewpoint of a private soldier. I wrote in the first person and I made the narrator just a little more stupid than I. That, I had noticed from reading many humorous first-person accounts of adventures, was the time-honored secret of success. But because this was a private's observations, I felt at liberty to poke fun at some officers and noncoms. I did *not,* however, belittle the essential nobility of Americans and their purpose in the war or the gallantry of our Allies. I thought I had a good idea and I wrote a little on it or drew illustrations for it every day. At first this work was just a means of keeping myself entertained, and if I had any thought at all of publication, it was to turn the material over to Joe Crowder when I got home, for a possible series in the *Journal.*

Days in the hospital were not at all unpleasant. But after lights out, those late November and early December nights were interminable. There still was enough pain to keep me from sleeping well and I longed for the privilege to have a light so I could read even the old pulp-paper magazines which constituted our library.

Hour after hour I lay and thought, reviewing my completely unimportant and comparatively uneventful life from childhood on, and realizing what a jungle of terrors, anxieties, forebodings, remorse, misapprehensions and menacing shadows I had traversed, cringing, fleeing or turning against with the overcompensation of a cornered mouse baring its teeth at a tomcat. And, as I examined myself, I discovered that I no longer was frightened by life.

In the dusky ward with the dim light at the far end over the night nurse's desk and surrounded by the snores and moans and mutters and stenches of my fellow patients, I even dared to move boldly into Mr. Henley's "horror of the shade," and discovered that I could view it now with calm and dispassionate interest. Then I knew I had left childhood and adolescence and solipsism behind me.

True, the intricacies of the universe were still beyond belief; so were the intricacies of my own digestive apparatus and circulatory and nervous systems, which, so I had read, were practically identical to those of a dog or ape or bear or any mammal. I was a consciousness existing curiously in a complicated organism of flesh and bone, and, as far as I was concerned, the rain pattering outside on the French countryside and the sounds and sights and smells within this Army hospital ward existed only in my consciousness, just as the rest of the world I had known existed only in my memory. But why get excited about it? The pain in my nonexistent toes was an interesting phenomenon. Life, real or not, was a *fascinating* phenomenon.

Apparently I had been very close to death. Had I died, what would have happened to my consciousness? Would it have continued, as I had been taught to believe, as the core of George Vincent Chalmers in the everlasting bliss of Paradise or in the everlasting torments of hell to pay for my earthly sins? Or, as so many pagans seemed to believe, would my consciousness be transferred to a new-born child by reincarnation? Or if my death meant extinction of my consciousness, would the universe, as it registered on my consciousness as so unbelievably intricate, simply evaporate?

[314]

Far from growing hysterical with horror at contemplation of this question, I now found myself only entertained. I no longer was afraid of life, and I told myself I was not afraid of death either, no matter what lay beyond the grave. Despite the shoutings of emotional ecclesiastics, I believed the traditional picture of hell ridiculous in this well-ordered universe. If there was life after death in any form, it would be a most interesting experience. If death meant extinction, well, I'd never know it.

As a matter of fact, my consciousness, my ego, the "I" called George, Sleepy, Thug Krueger and Private Chalmers, seemed curiously apart from the crippled body lying in the hospital bed. During my happiest hours, meaning when I was completely engrossed in matters that led me furthest from introspection, body and consciousness were one. I supposed some individuals went through life with consciousness an unquestioning prisoner of the flesh, and perhaps they were the happy ones, with thought and emotion directed entirely by bodily appetites, pains, comforts, discomforts and those fears generated by primitive superstitions which could be gloriously dispelled by amulets and incantations—if they worked.

It seemed that I had moved to a higher level from the pride I felt in my physical strength and agility. It wasn't that I now felt contempt for my maimed body, not at all. I would cherish what was left of my body and care for it as one might care for a good work horse. My body was the host to my consciousness, but I should be a considerate guest instead of a parasitic liver fluke. Asceticism and flagellation of the body seemed as silly as narcissism or over-indulgence of the appetites.

Suddenly I was very happy and I wondered if I had reached a condition which might be called a State of Grace or Nirvana. From my long association with most of the fears in the catalogue, I felt sure that fear, generically, was the greatest curse of the human race. Now, I was confident, I was purged of all fear for the rest of my life.

I remembered an evening when Laura gave a party for members of the Christian Endeavor Society and I was permitted to stay up past my bedtime to see a shadowgraph show they produced. A couple of bed sheets had been basted together and hung across the living room, with producers, their props and the big lamp behind.

Being under school age, I was a little bored with some of the shadowed tableaux, no matter how much delighted giggling they brought from the adolescent audience, and I was dozing on the floor when an excited voice announced, "Flee for your lives! There's a tiger loose in the house!"

Sure enough, on the screen was a gigantic black tiger, crouched to spring from left to right. I was paralyzed with fright. But a heroic youth (possibly Ralph Sterling), much smaller than the tiger, rushed to the scene armed with a spear and the voice announced that he would save us from the beast or die.

The tiger leaped and his great shadow blended with that of the little man and they both disappeared while the tiger obviously devoured the hero.

I screamed in terror and it took some effort on the part of my mother and others to quiet me down. It was explained that the tiger was only our tomcat Yancey whose shadow was huge because he was close to the lamp, and the young man was smaller because he was close to the sheet, and that Yancey didn't really leap at the man but at a string pulled in front of him.

Still, I had seen the horrible shadow tiger with my own eyes and I suspected that a shadow tiger could be even more dangerous than a real, striped tiger. A shadow tiger could blend in with other shadows and leap out when you least expected it. A real tiger could be put behind the bars of a circus cage where all he could do was pace unhappily back and forth.

A shadow, I was firmly convinced, was a mysterious, slinking thing of unknown power and nothing to be fooled with, even by big boys and girls who belonged to the Christian Endeavor. If you played with matches, you very likely would burn the house down. If you created a shadow tiger, how could you know he wouldn't slither away from you and join the other shadows at the turn of the stairs?

For a long time—years, as a matter of fact—I was wary of shadows. Dark shadows formed a mystic jungle that might contain not only shadow tigers but other malign forces. Shadows also hid the comfortable and familiar things about me that constituted such a large part of reality before the awful night of solipsism.

As I looked back, it seemed that my long season of terror

was largely a flight from shadows and that it all began with the black tiger on the sheet. And now the flight was at an end. Now I was a man, unafraid of either shadow or substance, of life or of death. And, relaxed in my comfortable hospital bed, I was very happy.

Naturally, the loss of my leg was a blow. But in the long run it might prove a blessing. Now I should get out of the war early, with only a minor handicap. Suppose it had been my right arm or my eyes or I had been paralyzed?

Perhaps this was a strictly unreal world, but life in it could be very sweet. Unreal or not, God had made it beautiful and had given us the power to view the beauty and to love it. Practically my whole life lay before me and I resolved to make the most of the joy of living.

I had been proud of my physical strength and agility. Now I was a cripple, but what of it? I no longer felt the need to prove something. I had a small gift for drawing and perhaps for writing also, which had brought me some local respect and distinction. Why shouldn't I, if I worked hard, improve those talents and go further? And now there'd be no danger of my ever succumbing to the blandishments of a manager or promoter and turning professional fighter on the promise of riches. Perhaps I could make all the money I'd need for a comfortable life, with my other talents.

When I was a boy and under the yoke of solipsism, I used to wonder why God hadn't made me more intelligent when he had seen fit to endow me with the awful responsibility of universal consciousness. I still had no illusions about my intelligence and I felt that I had no responsibilities to God and man except to try to be a decent human being and to do the best I could with what I had. There was a strong impression that I was on earth as an observer instead of a participant or a leader in mighty affairs. Whether I was competent for such a mission was God's problem, not mine.

In the meantime, there was my book. I surely had no idea that this was an important project, but I did think I might turn out a diverting tour de force to give civilians a picture of their wartime Army and incidentally make a little money. That it would prove a bonanza never occurred to me.

So far I hadn't been able to write home about my amputaion. I knew the news would distress my mother greatly and it seemed just as well to put off the truth as long as possible. I had written that I had hurt my leg, to explain the hospital address, but had been casual and terse about it.

There was an Army hospital at Aurora, just east of Denver, and perhaps they'd send me there for convalescence. It would be wonderful if they did that before Christmas and I could get someone to buy me some French toys for the Sterling twins. Thought of that little girl and boy gave me a warm feeling and made me grin to myself.

I wondered how Dorothy Sumner would react to my being a cripple. From some quarters, I knew, I must expect to be smothered by maudlin sympathy. But not from Dorothy. She would be considerate but tactful. If a one-legged man couldn't take long walks with her any more, there were many other things to do.

Perhaps, and I chuckled to myself at the thought, perhaps she'd like to go with me on the far-famed Georgetown Loop.

MIZPAH